MURDER
OF A NOVELIST

DEATH IN LORD
BYRON'S ROOM

Sally Wood

MURDER
OF A NOVELIST

DEATH IN LORD
BYRON'S ROOM

Sally Wood

COACHWHIP PUBLICATIONS
Greenville, Ohio

Murder of a Novelist / Death in Lord Byron's Room
© 2021 Coachwhip Publications
Murder of a Novelist © Sally Wood Estate, published
   with permission.
Portraits of Sally Wood and Lawrence Kohn © Sally
   Wood Estate
Introduction © Curtis Evans
Cover elements: Flower © Naddiya; Mountain © Julia Art

Sally Wood (1897-1985)
Murder of a Novelist first published 1941
Death in Lord Byron's Room first published 1948

CoachwhipBooks.com

ISBN 1-61646-512-3
ISBN-13 978-1-61646-512-4

INTRODUCTION
Curtis Evans

Classic mystery writing is said to be the quintessence of escape fiction, where one can retreat from a harried, all too imperfect life and inhabit, for a brief time, a world where baffling problems are always solved by the end of the story and there is usually, as a happy amatory bonus, an impending marriage (or two) on the horizon. The pair of detective novels written by American author Sally Wood, *Murder of a Novelist* (1941) and *Death in Lord Byron's Room* (1948), conform to the classic mystery paradigm in some ways, although notably both novels are lacking in tidy happily-ever-after matrimony for their determinedly single amateur series sleuth, Ann Thorne, a confirmed New England "spinster" despite being intensely desired by men whom she encounters, even well into her middle age. This latter point distinguishes Ann from other so-called "spinster sleuths" of her day, such as the Misses Marple and Silver, those snoopers extraordinaire created respectively by British detective novelists Agatha Christie and Patricia Wentworth, and the regiment of implacably nosy unattached aunts enlisted in the cause of crime fighting by a myriad of American mystery writers, in that none of these ladies ever really emerge from their amazing adventures as genuinely sexual beings. Reading Sally Wood's two detective novels, both of which are included in this volume, I was powerfully struck by the unique appeal of Ann Thorne. In contrast with the Miss Marple of the *Agatha*

Christie's Marple television series (2004-2013), a romantic
past did not have to be invented for Ann Thorne, because
such a past was integral to the character as Sally Wood had
conceived her.

Murder of a Novelist introduces Ann Thorne and her
pretty seventeen-year-old niece, Nancy Thorne, who also
appears with Ann in the later novel. When the story begins, Ann, an ambassador's daughter and onetime debu-
tante of transatlantic reputation, is at her solitary breakfast table in her gorgeously decorated home in Middlebury,
Connecticut (a real place, then populated by about 2200
souls), her faithful maid Hannah in attendance, reading
over the dullish accomplishments of her various sister
alumna in the latest issue of her college magazine. "I can't
go to reunion," she thinks to herself wryly. "I'd be too
much of a disappointment to them." Yet when a corpse
is found among the chrysanthemums in her garden and
the dead man turns out to be one of her neighbors, famed
novelist and utter bounder Anthony Bayne, with whom
young Nancy had been ingenuously flirting, Ann with her
sophisticated "continental mind" triumphantly arises to
the sleuthing occasion, solving the case for her less astute
friend, county sheriff Ezra Gates, who falls under Ann's
spell like other men of his age: "She sounded intimate and
warm, full of sad trust that was not quite reciprocated. In
fact she had shed the old maid. There suddenly appeared
the legendary charm that always conquered just because it
didn't try. She was again the clear-eyed girl who had astonished Europeans, straight as an arrow yet not obvious and
never, never naïve."

The man who attracts Ann, however, is yet another
novelist, who had recently arrived in Middlebury for a
fateful visit: the Hemingway-esque man's man Adam Carthage, with whom Ann shares a past, as they say, from the
previous world war, when she, like other daring women
of the day, was a young ambulance driver in France. Adam,
whom, it transpires, is himself still smitten with Ann,

becomes Ezra's prime suspect in Bayne's death. As she resourcefully restores order to her carefully cultivated New England garden by investigating and elucidating Anthony Bayne's violent murder, will Ann reach some sort of rapprochement with Adam?

In its sensitive balancing of detective and human interest and its insistence on the centrality to the narrative of the emotional experiences of the lead character and sleuth, *Murder of a Novelist* is a strikingly modern detective story, one which attracts readers not only to the problem but the people. These same qualities are found in *Death in Lord Byron's Room*, wherein Ann, along with her winsome niece Nancy, is plunged yet again into the depths of a dark mystery. The novel opens with Ann—now, like the author, nearing the age of fifty—sitting before her hearth fire in her gracious home in Middlebury thinking, "I've retired to the chimney corner . . . like an old Cinderella. Nothing, thank, God, will get me out of here." How wrong she turns out to be! On account of her old prominent European social connections and the very inherent deceptiveness of her sex in such a role, Ann is tasked by the U. S. government, not long after the end of World War Two, with infiltrating a sinister fascist cabal operating in Switzerland that is threatening the postwar security of Europe—and the world! As one character explains: "These fascist parties that spring up in France, they have caches of the latest weapons, handsome uniforms, their own newspapers. They are waiting till the Communist threat gets very bad. . . . Then they will say democracy doesn't work. They will seize control, join with the Nazis who are still strong in Germany and . . . we will have a fascist Europe."

Naturally Ann takes with her Nancy, now a Red Cross worker grieving over the death of her wartime boyfriend. Once arrived in a delightfully scenic but decidedly deadly Switzerland, Ann and Nancy encounter in the polyglot country many mysterious and frequently handsome men—Swiss, French, German, English and American—and a gangling young Englishwoman named Diana, who becomes a sort of satellite of the American pair. But in this land of multiple heritages, of double identities and double crosses, where hearts have as many holes as the cheese, which men can these women trust?

This suspenseful, highly enjoyable spy tale, reminiscent of the espionage fiction of Francis Beeding and Manning Coles in that it is light without being lightweight, boasts a strong setting in the towns and cities along the shores of Lake Geneva which doomed English Romantic poet Lord Byron once haunted (particularly pleasing is a bravura suspense set piece on a Lake Geneva paddleboat), as well as a most appealing set of heroines in our trio of female adventurers. The fear of a fascist revival in Europe may seem overwrought to readers today (or not), yet that fear was real indeed in the postwar years, as the author indicates when she makes reference to the notorious Nazi leader Martin Boorman, former Secretary to the Fuehrer and a staunch advocate, during his monstrous tenure, of mass deportations, murders of Jews, thefts of art treasures and implementation of forced labor. Up until Boorman's remains were discovered in Berlin in 1973 and he was officially declared deceased, he was thought to have made it out of Hitler's bunker and escaped somewhere abroad, where doubtlessly he was up to no good. (In fact he had been killed on the same day of his bunker breakout.)

Ann meets yet another man from her past (and the previous one from *Murder of a Novelist* is briefly referenced), while Nancy carries on her own interesting affairs of the heart. As in *Murder of a Novelist* there is a clever mystery plot underneath it all (Sally Wood was a tremendous fan of premier mystery plotter Agatha Christie), but there is plenteous action too, as femme force exhilaratingly proves more than a match for brute fascism:

> Ann unlocked her dressing-case and drew out
> the pearl-handled revolver.

"You might slip this in."

Diana's eyes were like saucers.

"Oh, I say!"

"It's only a toy," said Nancy, putting it in her purse. "I hope it doesn't drop out when I buy my ticket."

But she applied her lipstick with a new interest, wiping it all off twice.

Miss Ann was watching from the window. The stout craft, with paddle wheels at the side like Mississippi steamboats, was warping into the dock.

"Ready, girls," she said.

****

The devisor of these two original and entertaining crime novels, published seven years apart, was Sally Calkins Wood (1897-1985), a descendant of a socially prominent progressive family in Rochester, New York. Both her father, Hiram Remsen Wood, and her maternal grandfather, Horace McGuire, were noted attorneys, the latter serving as Deputy Attorney General of New York between 1905 and 1907. As a young man in Rochester, McGuire had been a typesetter on abolitionist Frederick Douglass' newspaper the *North Star* and he witnessed a meeting between Douglass and militant antislavery leader John Brown, whose acts of righteous violence did much to hasten the onset of the American Civil War.

Sally graduated with honors from Wellesley College in 1918, at the height of American involvement in another conflagration, World War One. Having written the prize play her senior year at Wellesley and been awarded the Masefield prize for best poem in her graduating class, she had dreams of a post-college literary career. Desiring in the cause of humanity to put her education to practical use, however, Sally not long after her graduation enlisted in the army nurses training camp at Camp Devens, Massachusetts, against the wishes of her own parents, who were concerned about her weak heart, a product of her childhood bout with scarlet fever. Ironically, Camp Devens itself became the site of a devastating humanitarian crisis when an outbreak of Spanish Flu struck the site in August. "This epidemic started about four weeks ago and has developed so rapidly that the camp is demoralized and all ordinary work is held up till it has passed," confided a doctor, who dramatically added:

> We have been averaging about 100 deaths per day, and [are] still keeping it up. . . . We have lost an outrageous number of nurses and doctors, and the little town of Ayer is a sight. It takes special trains to carry away the dead. For several days there were no coffins and the bodies piled up something fierce. We used to go down to the morgue . . . and look at the boys laid out in long rows. It beats any sight they had in France after a battle.

Fortunately Sally survived the pandemic and made it to Europe in the aftermath of the conflict, caring for war orphans as part of her work with the International Red Cross in Geneva, Switzerland, which had become the temporary home to nearly seventy thousand displaced persons. A confirmed Francophile, Sally also spent much time in France, as did her brother Remsen Vanderhoof Wood, an Amherst College graduate and aspiring painter who later dabbled in avant garde film, co-producing *Lot in Sodom* (1933), and helped to develop the optical devices known as diffraction gratings. After her return to Rochester, she found employment as a public health nurse and composed a series of articles stressing the need for "intelligent and cultured girls" to take on public health work. In 1923, when she was twenty-six years old, Sally married Hilmar

Sally Wood in her nurse's uniform

Stephen Rauschenbusch, a graduate of Amherst College, volunteer ambulance driver in France during the war and son of theologian and Baptist minister Walter Rauschenbusch, a leader in the Social Gospel movement and professor at Rochester Theological Seminary. Young Hilmar Rauschenbusch, who would later go by the comparatively anglicized cognomen Stephen Raushenbush, was, like his father and his new bride, a progressive and he had been employed for the last several years with New York's Bureau of Industrial Research. At the time of his marriage Stephen was engaged in compiling mining industry data for the Federal Coal Commission, an entity which had been enacted the previous year; after honeymooning with Sally for a month in the Poconos, he published his findings later that year in his first book, *The Anthracite Question*, which advocated increasing the wages of coal miners. "The service given by the men who work with their hands and touch death with their gloves not only calls out the best that any men have in courage and perseverance," Stephen ringingly declared, "but also merits a high place in the regard and consideration of a country which in the past has admired hard work, perseverance and courage for their own sakes."

The next year Sally and Stephen moved to Greenwich Village, where Sally met and became close lifelong friends with Caroline Gordon, future novelist and wife of Southern Agrarian poet and essayist Allen Tate. (Not long before her death, Sally published *The Southern Mandarins*, a volume of Caroline's letters to her.) In 1928 Stephen published his first novel, *Men Atwhiles Are Sober*, about Lathrop Baker, a man "who loves passionately but not wisely." The same could be said, it seems, about Stephen, whom Sally later divulged had beaten her with such terrific violence during their marriage that he caused her to miscarry the couple's child. Afterward she was unable to bear children. The couple parted before 1930.

Stephen Raushenbush, the technocrat who so idealized men who worked hard with their hands, went on to enjoy a lauded career as a public intellectual, working with congressional committees and authoring more books of a progressive liberal bent such as *Red Neck* (1936), a labor novel he co-authored with socialist activist McAlister Coleman; *War Madness* (1937), a scathing indictment of the munitions industry co-authored with his second wife; and *The March of Fascism* (1939). When he died at the venerable age of ninety-five in 1991, the *New York Times* singled out for especial praise his service in London during the Second World War, when he helped devise the allied plan of attack against German U-boats in the Battle of the Atlantic. Stephen's second and third marriages are mentioned in the article, but there is nary a whisper of a word about Sally Wood. (Indeed, his second marriage is erroneously referred to as his first marriage.)

Sally remarried as well, more durably than her husband. In 1935, when she was nearly forty years old, she wed, to the umbrage of even her progressive family, Dr. Lawrence Kohn, a kindly Jewish assistant professor of medicine at the University of Rochester School of Medicine. The couple remained married for over four decades, until Lawrence's death in 1977. Not long after their marriage, Sally and Lawrence adopted a young boy from Oswego, Edwin "Ted" Bayer Kohn, whose mother had tragically died when he was two, leaving his depressed father to drink himself to death five years later. Sally's intense longing to have a child of her own later found poignant expression in *Murder of a Novelist*, in the maternal feelings of Ann for young Gregory "Gubby" Lawrence, whose mother has died, leaving him to be raised, in a manner of speaking, by a distracted father. Sally's granddaughter, Sally Kohn, shared with me warm memories of her grandmother, recalling that although she disliked television on principle she allowed her grandchildren to watch the

Dr. Lawrence Kohn,
photo from his Identity Card,
American Expeditionary Forces,
as a 1st Lieutenant in the
Medical Department

Sixties American comedy series *Get Smart* after she investigated for herself and heard some of the characters speaking in French. (Perhaps it did not hurt either that the series was a spoof of spy fiction like Sally Wood's second novel.) It is also easy to discern something of Ann's attitude to her first husband in her scathing portrayal of the titular novelist and exploiter of women, Anthony Bayne, who might be said have paid with his life, in Sally's eyes, for Stephen Raushenbush's unacknowledged sins.

Indeed, one can see both of Sally Wood's detective novels as an extended exercise in wish fulfillment, where Sally Wood through her heroine Ann Thorne got to live a more exciting and highly colored life than she did in the real world (and where her own life tragedy was averted). In her own life, for example, Sally never actually made it "over there" during the Great War, in contrast with Ann, who was even awarded the Croix de Guerre by Marshall Foch himself. Detractors may dismiss Ann Thorne as a "Mary Sue," albeit likely without acknowledging that the king of male Mary Sues is hard-boiled icon Raymond Chandler's Philip Marlowe; yet I will guarantee you that they would not dare to say such a thing in the face of Ann, whose mastery is both feminine and formidable.

Sally Wood and her granddaughter, Sally Kohn

MURDER
OF A NOVELIST

To Caroline Gordon

1

A college magazine lay by the solitary breakfast plate and it was opened to "Class Notes." Miss Ann read first that someone's daughter had recovered from the measles, somebody else's son was chairman of a Prom. She turned a page to "Publications" and read after two familiar names, "Some Aspects of the Formation of Concepts" and "Action Now Foils Next Year's Plant Pests." She raised one eyebrow and smiled gently to herself. "No," she said. "I can't go to reunion. I'd be too much of a disappointment to them."

Hannah clumped in with bacon and scrambled eggs and the paper. "That Pieter's late again," she said, giving the fire a poke.

"So am I, Hannah." Miss Ann smiled serenely. "Have you never reflected that one of the advantages of being an old maid is that you can enjoy your breakfast?"

Hannah gave her a glance in which respect and annoyance made their usual mixture. It was not for her to say that her employer should have taken the Englishman. (She could never have got used to saying "My lady," not when they both were born right here in Middlebury.) Nor that she should have taken this or that rich or famous one. Those were the great days when Hannah was maid to the Ambassador's daughter and had nothing to do but look after her clothes. She could always have done lots more. In Washington Miss Ann had chided her the winter she came out and said a butler always ran the White House anyway.

She and her explanations! Being a motherless child she'd
never had to make them to anyone but Hannah. And there
were many things about which none were offered.

Yet they had been content at home these last few years;
anyway Ann Thorne had. Looks hadn't changed an inch,
Hannah thought loyally, overlooking the gray streaks in
her hair, the little wrinkles round the eyes and mouth, the
rough gardener's hands lighting a cigarette.

Miss Ann was looking at the fire through a haze of
smoke, then at the window which framed a square of
bright grass dappled with shadows of fruit trees. A small
boy wandered toward her like Alice in Wonderland over
the chessboard. One sock was up, one down, his shirttail
had come out of his shorts, his hair had not been combed.
"That housekeeper *must* get up earlier. I will speak to his
father about it." She leaned back. I have even got a family,
she thought, amused.

She heard his feet clump to the door.

"Go wash your hands, Gubby," she said without turning round.

The sounds retreated to the bathroom very briefly; then
he was standing by her breathing hard. "Can I have some
warm milk?"

She put her finger to the bell. "A saucepan of the usual, Hannah, please. . . . What kind of an animal is it this
time?"

"The cat. . . . I've *almost* found her. Not the kittens, of
course. I know she's in the barn. . . . And perhaps? If they
should be there? . . . I thought if I could have some warm
milk . . ."

"Quite right. . . . I think perhaps also. It's certainly
time. . . . How about tying that shoelace?"

"Busted."

He fished around in his pocket, brought out three marbles, a medicine dropper, a Yale lock, a very dirty handkerchief, and finally part of the lace.

"Come here, Gubby."

He climbed on her lap. For two people so businesslike with each other, so impersonal, neither seemed to mind the position. Even after the lace was tied he remained, Ann smoking quietly out of the side of her mouth.

Light fingers tapped on the front door across the square hall from the dining room. Without time for an answer the door opened. In stepped a young girl with her soft curls rumpled almost as much as Gubby's mop. Her socks were turned down over oxfords as blunt as his. The likeness stopped there. She was exquisitely clean and a brand-new shade of lipstick made a Valentine of her pretty mouth.

"Good morning, Nan." Miss Ann looked at her curiously. "So early? . . . Would you like breakfast?"

"No thanks, Aunt Ann," She sank down on a footstool by the fire.

Peering again, her aunt observed what might pass for a wrinkle on that fresh brow. I must remember she's grown up, she thought. But, Lord, was I as young as that at seventeen? No, never, not when I was born. . . . Gubby has never been either. . . . But then—she raised one eyebrow shielded by his head—we're not in the grip of passion.

"How was the date?" she asked.

"There wasn't any. He didn't come."

"Dear me." Ann's voice was lightly caustic. "Bourgeois mortality caught up with him?"

"Don't joke, Ann. I don't know what's the matter. Something is."

And more will be till you get over this, thought Ann.

She disliked her neighbor, Tony Bayne, and his lush, motherly wife, "the cabbage rose" Nan's father always called her. But Ann had spent too many years in the diplomatic service to show it. Nan's mother was a fool; tried to repress the girl. She had been quietly doing the opposite, rubbing her nose in it. She will learn to tell the odor of skunk after a while, thought Ann. The thing that worried her most was Nan's taking him for a serious writer. She will learn about men but never about style, Ann thought.

The sunlight shone more brightly through the window. From behind the border at the end of the lawn came the stout figure of her gardener, Pieter Puyster. How like an elephant he walked, lumbering with a roll from side to side. He headed toward the kitchen door, then his back came in sight going around the house. I must really get at those chrysanthemums, she thought. Pieter has brought the stakes. But it was all so peaceful this morning. Gubby, for one thing, sat unusually still.

She took a last puff at her cigarette just as Hannah came in.

"Excuse me, ma'am." Hannah stood firmly, her feet braced apart. "Pete says that there's a dead man in the garden."

Miss Ann ground out the cigarette. "Ridiculous. . . . Gubby, go in the kitchen now and get the milk."

They were all motionless, like an old-fashioned movie that has broken down. He slid from her lap.

"All right." He turned to look at her. "You think children don't know anything. . . . They do."

"I'm far from thinking that." She returned his severe glance with interest, "And what's more you know it."

His feet dragged out. He shut the door much harder than he needed to.

"Who is it, Hannah?"

"Well, ma'am. . . ."

"Go on. What ails you? Gubby can't hear."

Hannah was looking, strangely enough, not at her mistress but at Nancy Thorne. "It's that Mr. Bayne next door."

Nan started up with a gasp but Ann was on her feet first.

"Rubbish," she said. "You listen to the radio too much, Hannah. It's addled your wits. . . . Stay here," she snapped as they moved to go with her.

She turned with one hand on the French door and she was never more herself than at that moment. "Hannah, give Miss Nan some coffee."

It was a long way down across the little lawn. The thing she was looking at got bigger and bigger, a huddled body crushing her young plants. The handsome empty face lay with one cheek in the fresh dirt; dark blood was matted in his hair. How many had lain like this in the war! At the end of a trip, there they would be in her ambulance no matter how fast. . . . She bent to close the eyes. She always did that first. Noticing that the skin was warm she felt for the pulse. Nothing. She laid her hand inside the thick sports shirt against the heart. Nothing again. She started to straighten the head, then stopped. What struck her was not death; it was the peace surrounding it, the quiet, the chrysanthemum bed. It was all false and wrong. She got up slowly.

At the house—she was walking toward it—things would be worse. The calm she had made for herself was shattered. Evil had found its way. . . . She raised her chin and stepped into the dining room.

"It's really he, my dear, and he's really dead."

Before Nancy had time to answer, even to clutch the back of her chair, Hannah came with the coffee.

"It hasn't dripped," her mistress said severely. "Did Pieter see anyone else down there?"

"No Ma'am."

"What did he say, exactly?"

"He said, 'Can't tie chrysanthemums. Man down there, dead. Mr. Bayne!'"

"Then he is in the classic role of having discovered the body. . . . It suits him."

"You want me to go get Mrs. Bayne?" Hannah said.

"God forbid. I want you to call the sheriff."

"The sheriff!" Nancy cried. She was now really out of her chair, stiff as a bowstring, her white knuckles tight at her sides.

Her aunt looked at her sharply. She decided, no, she won't have hysterics. Blood will tell. Though Louella's training hasn't fitted her for one thing in this life.

"Child," she said patiently, "I don't think he fell down. Nothing to trip over. And he always struck me as quite healthy. A pack of nonsense the way his wife fussed about him. Hannah, telephone Ezra Gates."

The sheriff of the county lived in Middlebury, an arrangement to which the Thorne family was no stranger. A New York gang three years before had tried to use the village as a hide-out. Miss Ann had persuaded her brother to use his influence not only in Hartford but in Washington. A shrewd and honest man had been put on the ticket and elected in a landslide.

"What shall I say?" A hint of pleasure showed in Hannah's voice.

"Nothing. You know the operator listens in. Just say I'd like to see him right away."

When she was out of the room, Miss Ann said quickly, "Take a roll and some jam and eat it. Here's a plate."

"Why?" Nancy drew back aghast. "You can't imagine I'm hungry."

"What I'm imagining is what you know about this."

"Nothing. I swear it. Absolutely nothing."

"Then have the grace not to look as if you did. Nor act it. Eat."

A faint pink came to Nancy's cheeks as she obediently took sips of her coffee, broke off bits of roll, at first small ones and then regular-sized pieces with plenty of jam. Her aunt remembered with a pang how the appetite of youth survives everything, even heartbreak. Hunger was one of her vividest memories of the war. She would never forget that half loaf of bread behind Givenchy; it was her habit to think of it suddenly at elegant dinners.

A small car purred up her drive and ground to a stop. Hannah must have been watching too, for she opened the door before the tall officer had time to ring.

He took off his hat slowly. "Morning, Hannah. . . . Didn't waste time."

She gestured toward the dining room and he strolled in, his gait very easy and deliberate. One hardly noticed it was really fast, his legs were so long.

The difference between Miss Ann and the other ladies in Middlebury was that she did not rise and she never fluttered.

"Good morning, Ezra." Her back was quite straight. "Won't you sit down?"

He eased himself into a chair by the wall.

"My niece and I were having breakfast," said Miss Ann. Without turning her head she was aware that Nancy's plate and cup made a satisfactory picture, her face looked only suitably distraught. "I was going to tie up my chrysanthemums," she said. An edge of disapproval crept into her voice. "Pieter went with the stakes to the lower garden. Then he came back and said there was a man there dead. It's Mr. Bayne. I looked at him. It was too late to call a doctor."

Ezra clicked with his tongue on the roof of his mouth. "That's bad," he said. "A young fellow, too. . . . His wife is going to take it hard."

"So I thought," said Miss Ann. "I wanted your help. . . . We haven't told her yet."

Ezra hoisted himself with apparent slowness but he was at the French door instantly.

"I'll come with you." She came. "He's right in the chrysanthemum bed," she said with some bitterness.

As they reached the middle of the bright lawn well out of earshot of the house she said, "It's all soft dirt. There was nothing to fall on. But there's a kind of dent in his head. . . . I don't know whether it was deep enough. . . . I couldn't find what made it. It seems absurd, Ezra, but I suppose it's murder."

2

Ezra parted the hedge between Miss Thorne's garden and the Baynes'. He had phoned the state troopers. They had a homicide squad with a photographer, Sam Calkins, whom he knew well. Ezra had left his deputy to guard the body till they came. Silently as an Indian's his head thrust through the leaves. It had been a temptation to spend a lot of time looking for footprints, trying to figure out broken twigs, but he had to choose. He chose trying the people first.

The gray cottage lay as still as its late owner. Past eight o'clock, Ezra thought, funny they ain't missed him. He threaded his way through the sprawling, erratically tended vegetables, some as flourishing as any in the town, others gone to seed through carelessness, he noted, full of weeds. He sloped up to the back door. "Howdy, Mabel."

She was just tying on her apron, pushing her hair out of her eyes.

"Not a very early riser, be you?"

"Not when I'm washing dishes until after ten o'clock."

He clucked sympathetically. Mabel was not highly thought of in the village. She was neither neat nor industrious, he knew, by his wife's standards, but he intended to be unaware of that. He wanted her confidence.

"Miz Bayne cooked one of her fancy dinners," she grumbled. "Used every dish in the place."

"You must have had a lot of company."

"No, just one." She slapped the coffee percolator on the stove. "But is he important! . . . They were beside themselves when they heard he'd come. Didn't expect it. To them he's like the President would be to us."

"Speak for yourself, Mabel," Ezra murmured. "Who is this man?"

"He's an author. They all are." She sliced oranges viciously through the middle. "Did you see that picture, *Spring Flight?* It's from a book of his. But they won't hear it mentioned. Say it insults the book. It was a dandy picture too. The stars were Clark Gable and, let's see. . . ."

Ezra said quickly, "Folks up yet?"

She gave him a look. "Won't be for hours . . . not authors. Mr. Bayne stays in his bathrobe until noon. Except when it's hot and he lays out on the ground in his shorts. . . . You want to see him?"

"I want to see Mrs. Bayne."

"I'll tell her when I take this in." She pointed to three trays and said in an indescribable tone, "They eat in bed."

Ezra's eye wandered over the arrangements. "Must be a lot of trouble for you. . . . Can't they make one tray do— for a married couple?"

"Can't even make one room do. Mr. Bayne has to sleep by hisself. So if he gets an idea in the night he can get up and write it down. That's what *she* says. But I think he likes to go out now and then. Room's on the ground floor. Land knows it's the only chance he gets. You want a cup of coffee? . . . Sometimes I'm sorry for him," she went on. "Others I think he's just an alley cat."

"I'll wait in the sitting room," Ezra said. Much as he wanted to hear more he knew she'd be furious afterward thinking he had pumped her. He had learned anyway that people in the house might possibly not know about the body lying in Miss Thorne's chrysanthemums.

He crossed the kitchen in two strides and opened the door. A man was kneeling by the fireplace putting on a log.

"Hello." He looked up. "Have you got a match?"

Ezra passed him his box. The man lighted it neatly. He'd built it well and it blazed up at once.

He rose, dusting off his hands. He was middle-aged, Ezra saw, with a lined, rather ugly face, clean-shaven, lit by very pleasant eyes. Ezra noted his figure carefully, no extra weight at the belt, what looked like a fair amount of muscle under quite ordinary clothes, gray flannel pants and a dark sweater. He even had a necktie on. Middlebury's idea of literary life had been furnished by Mr. Anthony Bayne. Could this man be a writer?

Mabel appeared in the doorway. By the way her jaw dropped Ezra saw that he was.

"I'm afraid my host and hostess aren't up yet," the man said. "Won't you sit down?" He pointed an armchair flanked by dirty glasses and overflowing stale ash trays. He hesitated a moment and then dumped the contents of the latter in the fire.

"Thanks," Ezra said. Different ideas were shifting through his mind. First, he don't know a thing about it, danged if he does, and then—but it ain't natural to be so natural, not before breakfast anyway.

The man made a motion to hold out his hand. "The name is Carthage," he said.

Ezra grasped it. So it's *that* guy. This idea drove the others out. That's where I've seen him, on the cover of *Time.* I've read a couple of his stories even, Hetty's first year in college. How can I ever find out anything from him?

"Have a cigarette?" said Adam Carthage.

Ezra shook his head. His wavering eye came to rest finally. Its gimlet quality returned. "Your first visit here?"

"Yes"

"Known the Baynes long?"

Mr. Carthage smiled. He's figuring I'm small town, Ezra thought, but he doesn't mind.

"No, not very. . . . As a matter of fact I didn't know they lived here until day before yesterday. I jumped at the chance to come up. . . . Are you from the paper? If so you can say I've always wanted to see Middlebury."

"Why?"

"It was bound to be an unusual place on account of the people who live here. . . . People come here because it's . . . I suppose peaceful is the right word."

"I'm not from the paper. I'm the sheriff."

A door burst open. Mrs. Bayne stood there clutching a thin negligee together as if she'd just slipped it on. But her hair was tidy and her face powdered.

"I *thought* I heard voices," she cried. "But I thought it was a dream. . . . Couldn't you sleep, Adam? . . . And no brrreakfast!" She rolled the *r* tragically. "Mabel! Coffee, *please,* right away!" Her rich soprano sounded artificial in the small room; it was pitched for the theater.

Ezra got up, uncoiling himself to his full height. "No hurry, Mabel," he remarked. "I want to ask these folks a few questions."

"Oh, Mr. Gates! But you can wait. Come back in an hour," she pleaded deeply, ending in a trill. "Then I shall be *very* charming."

"When did you last see your husband?" he said sternly.

"Last night, of course. What a strrrange question!" Her hand tightened on the door jamb.

"What time last night?"

"I don't rrreally see why I have to tell you." She shrugged her shoulders. "But if you *care,* I went to bed early. . . . Tony was talking with Mr. Carthage by the fire."

"What's happened?" Adam Carthage asked quickly.

"A . . . a sort of accident," Ezra said. "Get ready for a shock, Mrs. Bayne. . . . I'm afraid I must tell you. Your husband was hurt." Her hand flew to her mouth. All her face changed. She looked ten years older. Adam Carthage was leaning on the mantel as before. "I'm afraid I can't spare you. . . . He's dead." She drew in her breath as a thirsty man gulps water. "We think it's murder."

He waited for the shriek but it didn't come. She expelled the air in a long shuddering sigh and collapsed in a limp satin pile in the doorway.

"Mabel," Ezra said. Mabel was there. She knelt by her mistress but, before she touched her, turned round and looked up avidly. "I heard them," she said. "Last night I heard the two of them, Mr. Bayne and this man. They were quarreling something terrible."

Adam Carthage stepped forward. "What's the next thing to do?" he said quietly. "Get a doctor?"

Ezra surveyed the aimless fussing of Mabel for a minute. "No . . . not yet. But she'll catch a cold there. Hasn't got hardly anything on. Let's put her to bed."

He was not surprised at the ease with which Mr. Carthage lifted his end of the load. The man was an athlete, all right. An idea struck Ezra as he pulled the blanket up to Mrs. Bayne's chin. "I'll have to ask you to stay here." He looked down the bed. She was breathing all right. "And don't use the phone. I'll be right back."

He was out of the kitchen door before they could turn to look after him and through the vegetable garden to Miss Thorne's trees. There were Sam Calkins and the deputy sheriff at the right distance on the grass, and Sam was taking photographs of the body. He was a good guy, Sam, all business. Wait till the other monkeys got there.

"You, Jake," said Ezra. "Cut around to the front door of the Baynes' and set just inside. Don't let anyone in or out and don't do any talking. See if you can keep that Mabel from shooting her mouth off." Jake scratched his head. "And if I find the mark of one of your big feet anywhere it shouldn't be, you can go back to raising potatoes."

Jake went, trying to tiptoe in his number twelves.

"And, Sam, I know it's your routine to phone the doctor and have him look at the body as it lies. I'd take it as a favor if you'd ask him afterwards to come over and see Mrs. Bayne. You don't need to hurry. Point is I don't want a pill pusher there too soon."

His long strides took him up the lawn and into the dining room. Miss Ann was sitting in the same place where
he'd found her but in different company. Her sister-in-law,
Mrs. Charles Francis Thorne, was walking back and forth,
giving one of her speeches, it looked like. She appeared
on every platform in Middlebury from the Congregational
Sunday School to the park bandstand on the Fourth of
July. She was always giving diplomas and receiving bou-
quets. He was a little astonished—he thought these two
didn't see each other much—but he couldn't wait.

"Excuse me, ladies." He stood on one foot. "If you
could spare the time, Miss Ann, I'd like to have you come
over to Bayne's. . . . It wouldn't take long, Mrs. Thorne."
Like everyone in Middlebury he was a little afraid of Mrs.
Charles Francis.

"Certainly," said the lady, inclining her head graciously.
"I understand there's been a sad accident. . . . If I can be
of help, Mr. Gates, you have only to call on me."

"Yes, ma'am, I will." She made a forward motion; he
said hastily, "At some later time."

"Well, then, good-by." Her tone was cold. "I was just
going, Ann, as you know."

When she had seen her sister-in-law to the door Miss
Ann turned toward him. "What can I do for the law now?"

"Go along with me over there." He gave a shrug in the
direction of the garden. "I'm not used to that kind of folks.
You are." He scratched his head. It was a relief to be frank
with one person. "Danged if I can tell if they're lying or
not. Mrs. Bayne, now, if she was born in Middlebury and
looked like that I'd say she was no better than she should
be. Yet there's some thinks she don't care about one thing
but cooking. . . . As for *him* there"—he peered out of the
door—"I guess they haven't moved him yet. He had about
as much morals as a hound dog. But yet the Rotary Club
said it was a good thing when he moved here. Kind of
advertisement. Make Middlebury a second Westport. They
got him to write a piece about it." He twiddled his hat.

"And they's a guy visiting there that's the prize puzzle of the lot. Famous. Going to bring all the New York papers down here like a bat out of hell."

"I see," Miss Ann said. "What you want is moral support. You're a perfectly good judge of character, Ezra."

"I can tell a Chicago killer from a Tenth Avenue one."

"Oh, very well, I'll go. But first I'll have to tell Nancy." She made a wry face. "She was going to help me in the garden this morning."

As she went up the stairs, slowly for her but holding herself very straight, Ezra walked to the lavatory by the front door. The light had been left burning, unusual in this well-ordered house. The first thing he saw was a very dirty towel, big and thick, but a guest towel like the others. It was stained with earth and fairly fresh blood. He folded it and put it in his pocket.

When they met he asked her at once, "Who's been in your lavatory this morning?"

"That's not a subject I pay much attention to. . . . Why?"

"Blood on the towel."

"Oh." She took a few steps in silence. "That was my new weeding knife. I was trying it out this morning and it cut me."

Ezra didn't answer. He didn't need to look at her hands. If she'd used the towel she would have put it in the hamper directly under the towel rack. He knew his Middlebury. Even when wildly excited she wouldn't have left the lavatory like that, and she'd been perfectly calm when he came in.

He looked sidelong at the competent figure walking along so briskly. Miss Thorne nodded to Sam Calkins, walked round the body with composure and parted the trees. In spite of himself the sight reassured him. He sighed.

"We'll leave that . . . for the moment," he said with unmistakable meaning. "Now this visitor. His name is Adam Carthage."

She stopped. "It isn't possible!"

They were in the middle of the hedge and he was pushing back a branch for her. It scratched his face. She didn't help. She didn't appear to see.

"Well, it's so," he said sharply. "Book of his was made into a movie, too. Mabel saw it."

"So did everyone else. It was a pity. No one knew that better than the author, but I suppose he couldn't help it."

"Why should he? Must have made a lot of dough."

"He's not that kind," she said severely. "He didn't like it—Hollywood vulgarizes everything. Adam Carthage won the Pulitzer prize with that book. He's pretty sure to win the Nobel prize next time it goes to an American. . . . Does that mean anything to you?"

"Yes'm, it does. That's what I kind of thought. That's why I came to get you."

They were passing the vegetable garden. She said, "I know Mr. Carthage."

"That so?" He was deeply pleased that his hunch about getting her had turned out so well. "Is he quiet like he acts? Maybe not, eh? Got a violent temper?"

"I haven't seen him for twenty years."

"A man can change a lot in that time."

"So I suppose."

He wished they weren't walking so fast; he would have liked to get a line on Carthage. But she was nearly round the house, flying ahead as if it had become a race. When they came to the vine-covered door, the leaves faintly yellow in the sun, Jake slowly getting to his feet from the settle, she stopped. For a moment Ezra thought she might dart away in quite another direction. She had that poised, frightened, and yet collected look of the chased hare. It was only a moment.

She said, "Good morning, Jake," and went straight in, not even holding the screen door.

Ezra could see over her shoulder. Mr. Carthage was having his coffee at last, the saucer on the table among the dirty ash trays. Mabel, just like her, had left her charge and was in the kitchen. She had made everything all right by leaving the door open. The unconscious body of Mrs. Bayne lay on the bed, just twitching now and then. A cheerful breakfast, Ezra said to himself. Funny that Mr. Carthage sat there so quietly.

But he was getting to his feet, blinking as if it was hard to make them out in shadow against the sunlit doorway. Ezra saw his face change. For the first time that morning feeling showed in it. But not grief or horror.

"Ann?" he said like a question; then with a faint assurance, "Ann."

He was coming across the room.

Miss Thorne didn't move or speak. When he was quite near she held out her hands. He took them and said for the third time, "Ann." Ezra scratched his head. He didn't know what to do so he turned round and glared fiercely at the deputy.

Mrs. Bayne was beginning to moan; she let out a cry. Mabel was goggling in one doorway, Jake in another. The sheriff couldn't get into the room. Miss Thorne and Mr. Carthage were standing there perfectly still.

3

She let go his hands. "Unfortunately for you, Adam, your host has just been murdered." She stepped into the room. "I'm afraid that deserves attention."

"The same voice," he said. "Like dry white wine."

"Mr. Gates is a friend of mine," she went on. "Mr. Carthage, Mr. Gates. He's the sheriff. He has to ask you questions."

"Of course, certainly. Delighted, Mr. Gates." He started to hold out his hand but then hesitated and bowed.

"I still can't believe it. It isn't real to me at all . . . any more than you are." His eyes returned to Miss Thorne.

She looked at Ezra. "We used to know each other in the war, the old war that seems so long ago. What do you want to ask him?"

She went swiftly to Mrs. Bayne's bed, gave a considering look at the closed eyes, felt her pulse, and returned.

"You, Jake," said Ezra. "Get out your pad and pencil and take all this down."

They sat on the edge of chairs, Jake near the door beside a little table.

"First of all," Ezra said. "How long have you known Mr. Bayne?"

"Only about three days."

"That's not long."

"Oh, I knew his work, of course. . . . That is, I admired his first book."

"Why did you come here, then?"

"We all met in New York, at a party. We got talking about places to write."

"And the Baynes asked you here?"

"Yes. . . . It was an impulse on their part, I think. Certainly on mine." His eyes just flickered but he shut his jaws and looked steadily ahead.

"And the very night you arrive Mr. Bayne was murdered."

The visitor started. "It sounds queer, like that. But actually there's no connection."

"Had Mr. Bayne any enemies?"

"I didn't know him well enough to know."

"And yet you knew him well enough to quarrel with him!" Ezra leaned forward, fixing the other's rather blank face.

"I don't understand. We never even talked of anything personal."

"What did Mabel hear?"

Perplexity covered Adam like a fog. Then his eyes lighted. "Of course!" He sighed with relief. "We were discussing poetry."

"Oh yeah?" Ezra was heavy with sarcasm. "Poetry!"

"Yes. He said Baudelaire and Rimbaud were the equal of English poets. They're just a lot of prettified sounds."

Mabel's head popped through the door. "He called Mr. Bayne—excuse me—a Goddamn fool!"

"And so he was. There's no such thing as lyric poetry in French. . . . Of course I'm sorry the poor fellow's dead."

Mabel went on, "Mr. Bayne said he wouldn't take that from anyone and he went out and slammed the door."

Miss Ann nodded, "It's authentic, Ezra."

"Could they get that worked up?"

"Oh, easily. . . . And yet it doesn't strike me as a cause for murder."

They heard the scuffle of heavy feet outside. Mrs. Bayne gave a cry; then she began to sob, shaking the bed. Ezra

disappeared in the kitchen where he seemed to be helping Sam Calkins and the doctor. There was a door to the
late master's bedroom from the kitchen; they would not
have to take his body past his wife. Adam and Jake moved
toward them instinctively. Two or three state troopers
came in.

"I'm going home," Miss Thorne said quickly.

She slipped out the front door and took the path
through the garden, breathing the morning air in long,
deep draughts. If I'd had the least idea! she kept thinking.
The thing that had carried her through, really, was just
an accident. She had seen Adam Carthage once since they
both were young, just once in the near darkness of a movie
theater. She was prepared for his looks, even his character;
she'd watched him closely. But he hadn't seen her at all.

What a ridiculous set of circumstances! she thought.
She wouldn't use another word. Appalling for Adam to
land in this mess! . . . Handles himself well, I must say.
Being a great man hasn't spoiled him. She pushed through
the trees and looked at her trampled flower bed, bending
over to see which stalks were crushed. "I don't know when
I'll get around to tying those chrysanthemums!"

Her feet were carrying her to the tool shed, a little
lean-to built against the barn where gardening things were
kept. Just before going in she cast one glance at the path
to see if by chance the sheriff were following. "I'm a poor
liar," she said to herself. "And he knows it but that's no
reason for being utterly preposterous."

She found the new weeding knife, bent over with both
hands in position as if she were using it and cut a neat
gouge in her left hand. She laid the knife down as it was
and sucked the cut until the blood clotted. "Now I must
find that wretched child."

Gubby had heard her in the shed and was just coming
out of the barn doorway. He was dirtier than at breakfast
and his shoelace was untied again. "Oh *there* you are," he
said. "I've been looking all over."

"Have you?"

Gubby glanced toward the end of the garden. "*He* isn't there any more," he said. "I'm glad. He was a bad man."

She thought with dismay, He's seen far too much. How *could* the troopers let him? But I suppose they didn't even know. She said absently, "Why do you think that?"

"He threw a stone at Ethiopia. . . . She was going to have kittens, too." There was a pause. He added with a burst of fairness, "I don't suppose he knew that. Me and you had just noticed it."

She couldn't answer.

He said, "Never mind. Everything's all right now. . . . She's *had* them." His round face was turned up to hers, lit with the purest pleasure.

"That's what I was looking for you for," he explained.

She thrust her thoughts aside. "Let's go and see the kittens."

They went into the still bam—Nancy's horse had been kept there until recently—and up a rickety ladder to the loft. They lay on their stomachs in the dry prickly mow without speaking. They didn't need to any more. Most of Gregory's short life had been spent somewhere on her place, because the Lawrence garden, next door, grew every year more neglected and gloomy. The shrubs, that were meant to be trimmed, were almost trees and shut out the sun. Mrs. Lawrence had died at Gubby's birth and ever since, her husband had closed his mind to his child and his home. He fulfilled his duties—New England saw to that—but not a jot besides. All the small, secret paths Gubby made in the underbrush led to Miss Thorne's.

The cat was lying in the hay about ten feet in front of them. Under her flanks were little nuzzling movements.

"I think there are four," he whispered. "I'm going to name one Blackie, one Spot after my dog that died, and I don't know about the others. Would you like to name one?" he said reluctantly.

"No, I rely on you," she said. "Gubby, about that towel. . . . You left a pretty dirty towel when you washed up this morning."

"Oh, was it?"

"Yes. . . . Did you cut your hand?"

"I don't think so." He looked at them, scratching the dirt off to see better. "Just old ones."

"What had you been doing?"

"Well, there was one bad thing about this morning. You know my animal graveyard?"

"Of course."

"Someone took the best stone, the one I got for Spot—the one we brought all the way from the creek—and it was there beside that man. All bloody."

"So what did you do?"

"I washed it off with the hose and I put it back. . . . I *hate* people that take my gravestones."

"About what time was this, Gubby?"

"I don't know." He was chewing a piece of straw. It was very peaceful there on the hay with the sunlight coming in one long shaft from the diamond-shaped window.

"Was it before Pieter Puyster came?"

"Oh, much."

She heaved a long sigh and got up, picking the hay off her skirt. "I'll have to go down now and see to things."

It was hard getting down the ladder though she had scrambled up like a young girl. . . . There he'd sat on her lap after breakfast, so still for so long. . . . What chasms there were in a child's mind, what dark, unknown spaces!

The maddening thing was that he'd washed off any fingerprints there might have been. Only the body had been there, still limp and warm. *Anyone* could have felt for a minute like killing Tony Bayne. Anyone could have shied a rock. But who would have thought of it so quickly as a small boy?

4

Hannah was waiting for her in the dining room by the French window.

"You look all to pieces." She could be unexpectedly human in emergencies. "I'm going to get you a glass of sherry."

"Thanks. Make it brandy. We don't have a murder every day."

Hannah poured out the tiny glass and remained hovering. She even thought of a cigarette and lit it for Miss Ann. "I s'pose that woman took on."

"She was beginning to." The brandy disappeared. "I went to see the new kittens to calm my mind."

"Did they make you feel better?" Her usual tones returned to the New England voice.

"Not markedly. . . . Where's Nancy?"

"Up in your room," Hannah said. "Moping," and then sharply, "What have you done to your hand?"

"Didn't you notice it at breakfast?" Miss Ann said. "The new weeding knife. I'm not used to it yet; it slipped."

With the cigarette still in her fingers Miss Ann climbed the stairs.

"Nan," she said. "I've been a long time but a lot has happened."

The girl sprang to her feet. "What? Tell me! what?"

"Nothing that throws any light on the murder." She sat down. "Formalities. . . . And now maybe you'd better tell me *your* story."

43

"Poor Tony, poor, poor Tony!" Nancy cried. "Who *could* have done it? That awful wife? Do you think she could have been jealous of *me?* . . . Really there wasn't anything. This was going to be our first date!"

"She could have been jealous of ten or fifteen other women and undoubtedly was." Ann's voice might have produced a steel engraving.

"I don't see why you're so horrid about him," Nancy choked.

Her aunt decided that surgery was the thing.

"This isn't the first time," she said, making a clean cut with the knife, "that I've picked up the pieces after Tony Bayne. About a year ago Pieter came to me, Pieter Puyster. Do you remember that he has a daughter? She keeps house for him and does laundry work. She has about the same mentality as Pieter but she looks like a yellow tulip, a double tulip, to be exact. Of course, you're not to mention this under the circumstances. Mr. Bayne, it seems, was hanging around the house while Pieter was away. I had to speak to him about it. I had to tell him that that sort of thing just wouldn't do in Middlebury."

"Oh Middlebury!" Nancy cried. "What do people around here know? You ought to realize this wasn't an ordinary affair with a . . . a *businessman* where it's all dull and sordid. An artist *has* to have somebody who understands him . . . in order to write. You might remember Mary Shelley wasn't married, or that girl in *Spring in Savoy.*"

Miss Ann began to rock in the little chair. "How classical is modern life," she murmured. "*'Ronsard me célébrait du temps que j'étais belle.'*"

"I don't see why I expected you to understand," said the girl. "I suppose because you were the success of the century when you came out, and you've lived everywhere, but after all . . ." She stopped.

"I'm only an old maid," Miss Ann said lightly. "As such I have my poor frustrated sympathy with lovers. What I didn't like was the idea of your being described in rather revolting physical detail and very bad prose, nor," she added, "the experiences that would be likely to precede that result."

"Why do you have to talk about it *now?*" cried Nan.

"Because there isn't any other time, my dear." She had decided to lay it on with a trowel. "You haven't read Tony Bayne's books. I have. He had a basic contempt for women, more or less covered up with slush. That's what it usually means when a man has to have so many. He just couldn't stand them."

Nan's jaw had dropped. She said defensively, "That girl in the book I read was wonderful."

"Oh, *Madeleine Pigor,*" Miss Ann mused a moment. "That was his first book and the only good one. It's always been a puzzle to me. Sometimes a man is taken right out of himself, his own character. But it doesn't happen again. And now, where were you going to meet him last night?"

"In our own garden," Nancy said. "Back under the big oak. You know there's a bench there and it's awfully dark." Her voice became uncertain. "He said he'd enjoy it more if it were almost under mother's nose."

"I don't always see eye to eye with Louella," Miss Ann said. "But I must say I don't like that. No wonder he was murdered."

"I didn't like that part of it either," Nancy said in a small voice.

"What did you do when he didn't come?"

"Just sat there feeling awful. It was *very* lonely. Mother thought I was in bed."

"Have you any notes from him or did you write him any?"

"No."

"Thank God. The beginning of wisdom."

"I'd scarcely seen him before Saturday night. That was when we danced together the whole evening. *You* know. I told you about it."

"Your house isn't more than a long block away," her aunt said thoughtfully. "If you were listening the whole

time you might have heard someone going toward the
Baynes'. Try to think back."

Hannah stumped up the stairs.

"It's the police again," she said. "Don't expect me to
get through my ironing by noon with these interruptions."

"Would you like someone to help you?" Miss Ann said.

This was a remark that never failed to drive Hannah
into a frenzy. It reflected obscurely on her age which was
the same as her mistress', only Hannah minded and Miss
Ann did not. It also failed to take account of the worth-
lessness of young girls in the village, a subject about which
Hannah had

talked often enough to have convinced Miss Ann. But
there remained a doubt whether she had. She began to
sputter but swallowed it. Only a few words came out,
"Tracking up the whole place" and "I didn't know if you'd
want them in the parlor."

"Certainly." Miss Ann rose, smoothing her skirt. "A
sheriff is a very important person, as we're likely to find
out."

She descended the stairs with that dignified skimming
motion that isn't taught any more. At her heels Nancy
came bumpily as if she were posting to a trot.

In the hall Ezra was standing in his easy slouch. Jake
shifted from one foot to the other, looking down often at
his shoes. A strange young man was just taking the hat off
a well-shaped blond head.

Miss Ann was aware that Nancy was feeling in her pocket for the lipstick. There was a little smile on Miss Ann's
face as she greeted Ezra.

"I thought I'd ask if we could use your house," he said.
"Can't hear yourself think over there. I want to get a statement from this man. . . . Mr. Paul Augustine, Miss Thorne
. . . and Miss Nancy Thorne," he was forced to add. She
showed no sign of leaving.

"Can't the doctor do anything with her?" Miss Ann
said.

"Not yet. It's the autopsy she's objecting to now." He jerked one shoulder. "This is Mr. Bayne's agent, works for his publisher, Huntington Reed. He just turned up this morning from New York. At 2 a.m. to be exact. Not the best time to come under the circumstances. Will you be present at the interview? What I want is background."

"Yes, if you like." She started for the parlor.

Nancy's violet eyes were opened to their widest in the direction of the stranger and they were eyes that stopped the average man like a lifted pistol. This one was no exception. Turning her head Miss Ann took in the scene. A pleasant, somewhat too sensitive face, she noted; he'll be the type that suffers. Tony had been completely callous. No use letting the child fall from the frying pan into the fire.

"Nan," she said clearly. "You might begin trimming the hedge by the front door."

"I want to see your gardener," Ezra said.

"Nan, will you tell Hannah to keep an eye out for him?"

"Yes, Aunt Ann." It was her demurest voice.

The stranger pulled himself together with a jerk and entered the doorway. His eyes traveled from one side to the other. "What a charming room!"

"I've rather got away from New England," Miss Ann said.

"I should say you had." He looked at the glittering chandelier, the pale green walls, the Louis XV chairs covered in different shades of lilac.

"Are you by any chance a French queen," his eyes twinkled, "doing a turn as a milkmaid?"

"I was born right here in Middlebury," she said severely, "and so were my grandparents on both sides. Jake, use that table."

Ezra leaned forward in an antique bergère. It suited him for it was long in the base, comfortable, and rather shabby. Against the faded background of upholstery his face looked tough as leather and its lines were deeper than they had been in the morning.

"Tell me again," he said. "Why you got here at two o'clock in the morning instead of some decent hour?"

The stranger started. He'd been absorbed in the room, curious and amused by the contrast between the policemen and, Miss Ann saw, herself.

"I'd intended to be here sooner," he said. "But I broke my exhaust backing up to a filling station at Hood Corners. The man had nothing but some picture wire to fasten it up with. I suppose I should have stopped somewhere else—it made a racket like all hell and probably waked people up—but I was selfish about it. I was looking forward to the Inn here; it's a pleasant place. And Ellison's garage is good. I had to drive slowly, of course. I knew I could sleep on in the morning, as indeed I did."

Ezra leaned forward and fixed him with a stern eye. "How long had you known Anthony Bayne?"

"For quite a while." The stranger seemed astonished. "About ten years, I think. Why?"

"You been working for Huntington Reed all that time?"

"No, indeed. I knew Bayne long before, when we were both living in Greenwich Village." He talked easily, almost eagerly, as if he were among old friends, not at all like a man being questioned by the police. "As a matter of fact, he got me my present job."

"He was not in the habit of doing good turns for people," Ezra growled. "How did that happen?"

"Oh, I was doing advertising then. I thought I might be a writer. All advertising men do. So I showed some stuff to Bayne. He said it was no good." He flinched mechanically, as if from habit. "And so it proved."

The *artiste manqué*, Miss Ann thought. One has to get over the disappointments of youth, but he's the type that never does; that explains it.

"It turned out to be lucky," he went on still easily and openly. One got to be this way with writers, she thought; they talked about their feelings more than other men. "Tony got me this job. He'd just made a big success and he was very lordly—throwing around patronage, you know, fixing up your career with a line written on a scrap of paper in a bar."

She interrupted him. "Did you *like* Anthony Bayne?"

"I can't say I did." He looked at her frankly. "But I didn't dislike him either. One had to know how to treat him. Believe me, Huntington Reed is going to miss Tony. One of the steadiest moneymakers on our list. I handled all his business; I'm the chief mourner."

"Didn't know there was one," Ezra said, "outside of his wife."

"She was no more unconscious this morning than I was," Miss Ann said.

"Yes'm," he said. "I noticed it. Now, Mr. Augustine, did he have any enemies that you know of?"

The rather pale brow was knit. "There wasn't any real harm in him," he said slowly. "Just not grown up, you know, and liking to show off. Except where women were concerned. That was different."

"Get down to cases," Ezra barked.

"I don't know any. Just the general gossip. . . . Oh, I used to know his first wife."

"What was she like?"

"A nice sort of girl. She supported him while he got his start. He couldn't stand the idea of it afterward. Hurt his pride. So he divorced her."

"Where is she now?"

"I don't know. Haven't seen her for years."

"And his present wife? How long have you known her?"

"Just since he married her. Oh, I heard her sing once before when she was Rosa Liederstraum. She's good, too. But she couldn't stand concert tours, hated the life."

"Was she happy with Mr. Bayne, do you think?" said Miss Ann.

He shrugged. "As happy as any woman could be. She mothered him all the time. So when he was unfaithful it was just the baby getting into mischief."

"Did you see them often?"

"Two or three times a year anyway . . . and much oftener when Tony had a book coming out. I liked going there," he said boyishly. "Rosa is a superb cook if you like garlic, and then she'd sing after dinner." He turned to Miss Ann. "She has one of those singing voices that sound awful in conversation, stagy and never anything to say, either. But if you hear her sing once! . . . It's her way of talking."

There was a light rap on the door. Jake lumbered to his feet and opened it. Nancy stood there, looking as if butter wouldn't melt in her mouth.

"Here's Pieter," she said, moving aside to show his vast bulk. "I found him myself."

Paul Augustine had risen instantly.

Pieter shuffled in, placid as always, his cheeks as pink as an advertisement for cleanser, his trousers baggy, the general effect such that you had to look twice to be sure he wasn't wearing wooden shoes.

"Then if you're through with me—" Mr. Augustine turned politely, "I'll clear out. I shall be staying at the Village Inn, waiting till Mrs. Bayne is well enough to let me have Tony's manuscripts. I'll have to phone Mr. Reed now," he said. "If you don't mind?"

"Go along," Ezra growled. His temper was getting noticeably shorter as ground was covered without anything coming to light.

Miss Ann, who sat near the window, noticed that Paul Augustine had not asked to use her phone. He was going out of the front door with Nan. That young lady carried no pruning shears or any other sign of toil. They were turning down the road to the village. Her aunt stifled what might have been a snort. From one unsuitable person to another, she thought. Well, it's all education. She ought to have approved but she didn't. Without any reason she just didn't like it. She didn't like it at all.

5

After they had all gone, Ann Thorne sat quietly smoking in her parlor. She was waiting for the room to have its usual effect on her. The mood it induced was light and gay but not forced, witty but not shallow. It was like chamber music by Mozart. Any feeling one brought there was reflected in the patient oval of the mirror, the worn flowers of the carpet. They said, Yes, we have seen this before, but it passed.

Today the light mood was slow. Instead of waiting she began to count the few facts she had learned. Chief among them was the dirty towel Gubby had left in the washroom. It's too bad not to tell Ezra, she thought, it makes it harder for him but I haven't the slightest intention of doing it, not if I'm had up for concealing evidence. She also made a note to ask Pieter if Mr. Bayne had been bothering Gretel again, not that one could imagine a person of Pieter's vast calm having anything even remotely to do with this.

There was a tinkle of the doorbell and Hannah's feet approached like the Stone Gods of the Mountains. It's nice always knowing where she is anyway, thought her mistress.

"Mrs. Charles Francis," Hannah announced with gloom.

Well, really, thought Miss Ann, there's enough on my mind without two visits from Louella in one morning.

"Come in," she called.

Mrs. Charles Francis appeared and sniffed. She was known for her dislike of tobacco, especially pipe smoke,

but had never been able to control her family on this subject.

"Do you mind if I open a window?" she asked, suiting
the deed to the word. "I came back because what with Ezra
Gates interrupting us—you *encourage* him, my dear, you
do really—I forgot what I meant to tell you this morning."

Miss Ann lit a cigarette.

"I know you're interested in little Gregory." The visitor lowered herself to a chair. Mrs. Charles Francis, her
husband said, acted as if sitting down in his sister's parlor
was like yielding to illicit love. She always referred to the
room earnestly as "such a *good* example of the period,"
exactly what period no one knew, though it was obviously
one that history did not whitewash for Louella.

"Of course, if his father married again," she went on,
"and not exactly the right person, it would be a *tragedy.*"

Her sister-in-law smiled. "Who is it you've seen him
with this time?"

"It's more than that, my dear. His *secretary,* of all things,
is staying at the Inn. She came up with him yesterday. I
ran into them and I had to meet her, to be introduced. She
evidently intends to go back and forth with him on the
train every day. The opportunities such women have; it's
outrageous! . . . You know he won't even go out to dinner
here."

"What kind of girl is she?"

"Quite mousy. No charm that I could see. No poise."

"Does she like animals?"

Mrs. Charles Francis lifted her hands. "How *like* you,
Ann! How could I possibly know?"

"I don't think it's reasonable to condemn Jonathan
Lawrence to a life of celibacy on account of his son." Miss
Ann was enjoying herself. A tilt with Louella, however
familiar all the thrusts and parries, was more fun than the
police. "Gubby could get along with almost anyone," she
said. "And if his father married again he'd stay at home
more, I presume. That's what the child needs."

"But when there are so many nice girls right here in Middlebury," Louella sighed, "and such a shortage of really nice men."

The other's mind traveled like lightning over the village and her family's place there.

"Nancy should be allowed to travel," she said abruptly. "Or at least have a season in Washington."

"Oh, Ann," Mrs. Charles Francis said. "We've been over that so many times! You cannot understand she's too young! She hasn't the least bit of judgment. Only Saturday"—she lowered her voice —"at the Country Club, she made a spectacle of herself with that dreadful person. And since then he's been *murdered*. I can't say I'm surprised. If this hadn't happened I should have been forced to take steps. I knew more about it than she thought this time."

All of a sudden Miss Ann wondered why Louella had come over so early that morning. Did she know something was going to be found in the garden? Did she know Nancy had had an engagement that night? Her sister-in-law ceased to amuse her. What steps had she planned to take? Did they involve a rock?

"I must get on with my gardening." She rose. "My plans were, to say the least, interrupted. Will you stay while I labor?"

"Thank you, no, I have a great deal to do." Mrs. Charles Francis took a stately leave.

Miss Ann put on her old straw hat with an elastic under her knot of hair, found her gardening gloves and two pairs of clippers, and hooked a large basket over her arm. Not the least of my troubles, she reflected, is that I shall have to have a cocktail at the Inn. Middle-aged women who go to bars alone are one of life's depressing spectacles. So much pleasanter to do one's drinking at home. But I must see this secretary, not on account of her designs on Jonathan, but because she came to town when she did. Too many people have just come to Middlebury. I daresay it will strike Ezra, too.

The smell of cut green branches in the sun restored her. Quick, vicious jerks on the clipper handles, a little harder than was necessary, gave her great satisfaction. She had done all one side of the path and was rubbing her forearms—they were beginning to feel it—before she looked up. People were passing to and fro on the road, more people than usual. Two men had stopped to look at her curiously. The rest seemed to be on their way to the Baynes'. A state trooper stood at the gate; they were not destined to get far but they were thickening, in a knot like swarming bees.

I had better keep them away from here, too, she thought. What a nuisance. Where's Pieter? Leaving her tools, she hurried off and met him coming out of the barn door.

"I want you to stay by the gate," she said. "And keep anybody we don't know from coming in."

"Sure," he said. "Bad for grass."

"And Pete," she said. "There may be reporters. Don't answer questions. There's no telling how they may twist things round and try to trip you up."

"I don't know nothing," he said. "True, too."

"Had Mr. Bayne been to see Gretel lately?"

"No, ma'am, not for a year anyway. Scared. Phaw!"

"I'm glad to hear it. Where's Gubby?"

"Don't know." He shook his head slowly from side to side. "Went somewhere. Mad at me."

She called in the barn a few times without getting an answer and then went, rather curiously, back down the garden toward the chrysanthemums. She wanted to see, now when no one was there, just how long a throw it was from the animal graveyard to the spot where Anthony Bayne's body had lain. One needn't assume that the rock was thrown all the way. The murderer could have snatched it up and carried it part of the distance. But if the crime was the result of an impulse the distance was not likely to be great. There was the chrysanthemum bed, a great crescent at the end of the lawn; behind it, nearly in the middle, the old prune tree, its thick overhanging boughs almost but not quite shading the plants; on the other side, the gap in the hedge through which one could get to the Baynes'. Anyone coming from there would have passed the animal graveyard on the right. It was just a collection of stones to the uninitiated, Spot's easily the biggest. She stood beside it and paced off the distance to the crumpled plants under the tree, twenty feet at most.

She was just bending over to see how many of the plants were broken and how many merely bowed over when there was a rustle overhead. Fear gripped her; she was frozen. She was trying to decide whether she dared to run for it.

Someone said, "It's me."

The little childish lonely voice gave her a sharp reaction. It was a minute, though, before she could speak.

"What are you doing"—her breath was ragged—"up there?"

"Thinking."

"Oh . . . about what?"

"Pieter . . . he's horrid."

"What has he done?"

"Asked me how many of the kittens we wanted drowned."

"He was just being funny," she said patiently. "Don't you understand Pieter's humor?"

"Funny! I'd like to drown *him.*"

A little cold air struck her. She made herself say lightly, "It would take a lot of water. Stop being silly and come down."

She walked back with him through their private path to his father's house. It was a tunnel through the bushes, really. Anyone older than eight had to stoop a good deal. Even at that, the back of the Lawrence place wasn't as dismal as the front. A double border of pines, already tall at the time of Mrs. Lawrence's death, lined the walk from the gate to the front door. These had become so thick their branches interlaced, their trunks were mossy. They shaded the downstairs windows so completely that the rooms

were like vaults. She took him to the kitchen door which
was slightly more cheery and explained handsomely to the
housekeeper, Mrs. Hodges, that it was her fault he was late
for lunch; she had forgotten to tell him the time.

The afternoon she spent alone. At five o'clock Paul
Augustine was grudgingly let in by Hannah.

Miss Ann surprised herself by being glad to see him.
To be sure, he'd be bad for Nancy, the too-sensitive type
with his flattering appreciation of everything. One always
found in the end—she'd spent years learning it—that a
young man like this appreciated himself most of all. Just
now his eyes were traveling over the details of her room,
understanding it as few did, and yet he had the sense not
to exclaim. That old-young look, too, how that would appeal to some women! I'm not maternal enough, thought
Miss Ann. I can see that he's over thirty-five in spite of
that blue-eyed candor that makes him look like a tired
boy. But he'd be just the dish for the Cabbage Rose.

He turned from inspecting the room to inspecting its
owner. "You seem to be the power behind the sheriff," he
said with a smile. "Couldn't you influence him to give
me Tony's manuscripts? Rosa won't even see me." His face
fell. He collected himself at once though. "It must be his
orders."

Made for the Cabbage Rose, Miss Ann was thinking.
She could take care of him just as she did of Tony but he'd
be more grateful—much more.

"Sit down, young man," she said. "You'll have to brush
your hair if you do that to it. . . . I haven't seen the sheriff."

"But you will? It's a matter of money," he said engag-
ingly. "The greatest human motive. If we can publish
something of Tony's quickly we can cash in on all this
publicity."

Why won't she see him? thought Miss Ann. Does she
worry about showing she's fond of him for fear she'll be
suspected of the murder?

"Will you drink tea?" she said. "Or will you have a whisky and soda?"

"Well, tea, for once. It's more of a novelty."

When he had been sitting in the Louis XV chair for some time and was on his third cup his left hand had ceased to beat a tattoo on the chair arm.

"It's old Huntington," he said apologetically. "He's done this to me. I have to call him up again tonight. But you must see what the situation is from his point of view. The book the late Tony was working on is pretty lush— and how this would launch it!"

"You're not the type," she said severely, "to be interested in that kind of game."

He gave her his most boyish smile. "Thank you. It's just that I'd rather have a job than not. . . . And I don't quite understand Rosa not asking for me. We're awfully good friends. On that ground alone I . . . I thought she'd want me round."

"She has one guest already." Her eyelids were half lowered as she put a plate back on the tray; she could see through the lashes.

"Has she? Who is it?"

"Adam Carthage."

He nearly dropped his cup. "What?" It was skating around on the saucer. "*That* wasn't in the papers."

"I expect it will be."

"How did they ever know him. It's unbelievable that he and Tony had anything in common. He must have heard her sing."

Hannah had plodded to the door. "Mr. Gates," she announced.

He loomed behind her. Augustine leapt up.

"You've been awfully good to me." He stuttered in his haste. A few minutes before he'd wanted to see the sheriff and now he couldn't wait to be gone. It was curious. "I'm going to try Mrs. Bayne again," he said over his shoulder. "You won't forget my message, will you?"

They both stood looking after him.

"Seems nervous," Ezra said. "That's a young man I want to keep an eye on. He knew Tony Bayne longer than anyone else."

"I like him," she said. "Do you think he's mixed up in it?"

He was taken aback. "Why?"

"He seems to be quite fond of Mrs. Bayne."

The sheriff half smiled, looking down his nose. "Well, now she's a fine lady and all that. But as a *motive* . . ." He shook his head.

"You may not be doing her justice. Remember she likes younger men and she can make them very comfortable. This one could do with a spot of comfort."

Influence of the movies, she thought. Americans think vampires must be thin. But there had been that one in Holland for whom her friend, the second secretary gave up his career . . . a hundred and seventy pounds if an ounce.

"Anyway," said Ezra, "Augustine wasn't here. He got into the Inn at 2 a.m. Had to crawl from Hood Corners where he broke his exhaust. We've checked that. It's correct. Hood Corners is all of forty-five miles away. He left New York at eleven. And Bayne was hit on the head between eleven and twelve last night although he didn't die until this morning."

"How dreadful!" She suddenly felt it to the full. "You mean he was lying there all night, alive? Could he have been saved if we'd found him?"

"I don't know. Here it is." He pulled a paper from his pocket.

She read, "Contusion and laceration of scalp, comminuted fracture of the inner table of the skull through the parietal bone, rupture of right middle meningeal artery, subdural hematoma, compression of brain."

She said, "What does it mean?"

"It wasn't much of a blow for a murder. But it was just hard enough to crack the inner side of the skull, right above the largest blood vessel of the brain's surface. That's what Dr. Winslow said. Bayne was probably unconscious from the start, from concussion, but he would have waked with nothing but a headache if it hadn't been for that broken artery. Blood poured out and made a clot the size of an orange, pushing the brain over, keeping him unconscious and killing him in five or six hours."

"Oh," she breathed. "And if he'd been found and taken to a doctor?"

"They don't know. If the doctor had guessed what it was and operated right away, they think he might have had a chance. But Doc Winslow wouldn't say. All he said was 'either a very unfortunate accident or a devilish clever blow.'"

She said, "And what kind of weapon?"

He hunched his shoulders. "Anything you could hit hard with. The good old chestnut, a blunt instrument."

"Could it have been something *thrown?*"

His eyes hardened and bored into hers. "Just why do you ask that?"

6

Miss Ann was still sitting in front of her fire though it was quite late. She had so often created in herself a state of composure after a state of the opposite that she had a formula. First one tried the letters of Mme. de Sévigné, this time opened at the trial of Fouquet. How truly the marquise expressed her sympathy for her unfortunate friend and at the same time managed to avoid criticizing his enemies too freely so that, had her letters been opened by the couriers of Louis XIV, no harm would have befallen herself or her daughter! Miss Ann admired that perfect balance for the thousandth time—but rather abstractedly. She could hear each end of burned wood fall in the fire with a plop and a hiss.

Hannah's steps had gone round the whole first floor like a watchman's as she locked all the doors and windows. She had stood looking at her mistress rather anxiously but managed to keep her thoughts to herself. She only said, "I'm going to leave my door open, ma'am, so if you want to call . . ." Her steps creaked slowly up the stairs.

Now and then a page did not hold the reader; she looked up to listen. Nothing, of course. The garden was as peaceful as it had been—no, she shivered, not last night. "The wrong book," she said firmly, and took down *Famous Cases of Circumstantial Evidence*. It usually calmed her mind to read of people who'd been honestly convicted, only to be proved innocent years after they'd been hanged. It reduced one's present troubles to a just proportion. A poor girl was being dragged to the gallows; she stopped. What was that? Just the leaves rustling? There wasn't any wind.

Then she heard something, a soft tap. She had a moment of weakness, wanting to call Hannah. "Nonsense," she said, "it's someone who wants to speak to me alone." She set her lips, rose and marched like a soldier to the dining room. One hand went to her throat, though, as she opened the door.

The face of Adam Carthage appeared in the gap.

"Thank you," he whispered. "I was hoping you'd let me in." He shut the door, with its drawn curtain, carefully behind him. "How well we know each other, after all!"

She did not reply. This time he had taken her by surprise. And yet perhaps not quite. . . .

"Damn the police," he said. "I've been trying to get away all day. It's made me feel like a boy again. Ann, surely you don't mind?"

"Let's not wake anybody up." She led him into the drawing room and closed the door. Thank God he couldn't hear her pounding heart, only the acid voice. "Receiving clandestine visitors is not a part of my routine."

"But you don't mind?"

She bent over, to gain time, and offered him the box of cigarettes. "I mind a great deal that my neighbor has been murdered in my garden."

"Yes, I want to talk about that. But seeing you again. . . . I've never been on a mountain since . . . I will never forget . . ."

"Nor will thousands of other people." She smiled slightly.

"I've wanted to know all these years what you thought of the book."

"I shuddered," said Miss Ann, "when I fell over the cliff."

"It was a bad ending, but not so bad in the book as in the movie. I hope you didn't see that."

"But, of course, I did."

"I tried so hard," he said, "to prevent it, but that was the time when Hollywood didn't know about understatement. They've learned since. Even for war pictures. There was a dreadful passage in *Death March,* in the book, where a mother sees a bomb fall on her baby. They've just made a movie and the director had sense enough to leave out that scene! The same man who ruined *Spring Flight!* . . . But my ending was bad in itself. I know that. It wasn't explained. No more was the reality. Ann, why . . . ?"

"Adam," she said, "we could spend the night talking about the past. It must have occurred to you that I don't want to or I should have made an opportunity in the last twenty years."

His face which had been eager in the lamplight turned weary. "It occurred to me . . . Yes."

"We are middle-aged," she said gently. "We have arranged our lives." His eyes dropped. "You have your children . . . and, I presume, a wife. I also have my little interests. Here we are in a blaze of publicity and danger. It's not the time."

"Why danger? I did think of the rest. That's why I came in this private manner."

"Adam, you're bound to be a suspect. So are others," she hesitated, "who are dear to me."

He looked astonished. "Why?"

"Ezra Gates doesn't know it but I've found the weapon. Now if you'll put your mind on this, I'll tell you about it."

"All right, Ann."

She told him about Spot's gravestone and the autopsy.

"Poor devil," he said. "That makes it a lot worse. Lying there bleeding. That rock must have been thrown with tremendous force to have cracked his skull. In professional baseball, when a man is hit in the head, he isn't killed. It would be a lot easier to hold a weapon in your hand like a bat or a crowbar. No wonder Ezra assumed . . . Ann, I don't think a woman could have thrown it. Certainly not your little boy."

She bowed her head. She said slowly, "From above? . . .
He spends a good deal of time in the tree."

He gave her a long look. "So that's it. A case for Saki,
Sredni Vashtar."

"I don't think he did it," she said. "Oh, I'm sure not,
especially now that we know it was done before midnight,
not in the morning. That lets my gardener out too, as well
as the editor boy. P. Puyster wouldn't be up in the middle
of the night any more than Gubby. He didn't like Tony
Bayne and he found the body, so for a moment I imagined
. . . but its being done before midnight changes all that.
Anyone who knows Pieter knows that he couldn't get angry enough to hit anything anyway, and as for being up at
midnight, impossible! But we must find the murderer. I
have to know in order to . . . see to things."

"Yes, dear." He smiled. "I wish you were 'seeing to' me
still."

She ignored him. "What about Rosa Bayne, Adam?"

"She's a strange woman. If it weren't too fantastic I
should say she's making a . . . sort of pass at me. Over
the dead body of her husband. It's pure Wagner. Crash of
chords and thunder in the wings. I don't like it."

"Do you have to stay there?"

"I mentioned the Inn, but it's full of reporters, she
says, and she says she's afraid. I was foolish enough to tell
her I had a revolver and she calls that protection."

"The sheriff won't let you leave town?"

"That's it. You know most of the time I think there's
some method in her madness. I don't think she likes me;
she wants something from me. She keeps trying to make
me look over her husband's manuscripts."

"And have you?"

"I tried just before I came." He shook his head. "At my
age there's more and more stuff that I just cannot read."

"As I remember you," she said, amused, "you could not
have read Tony Bayne at any age."

"How well you understand me, Ann! It's bilge, all except that first book. And he told me about another—not the one he's writing—just an idea that had possibilities. But it would have turned sour if he'd worked on it—a fellow like that. You understand me, yes—so much better than I understand you!"

She stayed impassive for the second time but it was harder. She hadn't remembered how those light eyes glinted in his dark face. "There's nothing, absolutely nothing suspicious that you've noticed?"

"No. Only the absence of regret. Nobody seems to mind at all about the poor devil. His wife passed for being so devoted to him and here she is appealing to me. Oh, there are plenty of tragic airs but she wears them like . . . oh, like a costume for Isolde. She even exercised her charms on that editor boy."

"That will bear watching."

"*She* was the one who was being friendly. He was keeping his mind on his work."

"Are you quite sure? Perhaps he was being careful. Adam, he's deeper than he looks. There's likely to be something between him and Rosa. But she's the one who had most motive for the murder if I'm a judge of Tony. . . . What happened?"

"He came over about six o'clock today and she was offering me a drink when he came to the door, so she had to see him. We stay in the front parlor, you know, because the body and the flowers are in the back part of the house." He shrugged. "There she was, all draped in black, being heavily alluring, not twenty feet away from poor old Tony. She put on a little extra for the editor. She explained afterward it was because she wouldn't give him the manuscripts—on the ground that *I* was going to read them!" He made a face.

"Thank you, Adam." She rose abruptly. "You've been a help. You've given me a picture." She stood with her hand against the door frame.

"And I," he said softly, standing before her, "have spent another evening of my life with Ann Thorne. Even though she hasn't been specially kind."

"Not unkind, though." She held out her hand. "I don't imagine that you exactly lack consideration."

"As if that mattered." He turned and walked to the French door without looking back. He had it open before she could reach it. "Good-by, Ann."

She stood in the doorway, looking after him. A broad band of light came out on the grass. In order not to attract attention she stepped outside and closed the door softly behind her as she watched him walk quickly and silently down the lawn. She would lose him for a moment under the shadow of the fruit trees as if he were a swimmer going part of the time under water. There was no moon visible but the whole sky was light. The moon must be there behind a thin screen of clouds because there was a gray illumination over the garden. Now he was on the edge of the dark pool under the plum tree.

There was a ping, a sudden crackle of twigs. She was running, running down the lawn, not even breathing so she could listen.

"Adam, Adam!" she was calling in a sort of panting whisper.

The bushes rustled. "Ann, get back! That was a shot!"

"I know it was," she snapped. "Do you take me for a fool?"

"Oh!" He laughed out loud. "That was how you used to talk!"

"Are you hurt?"

"No." His arm was round her shoulders. He said very clearly, "I've never been better in my life, never. . . . We didn't grow old, Ann, after all. We couldn't. We're just the same."

"Not so loud." She put her hand on his mouth.

He shook her. *"'But thy eternal summer shall not fade,'"* he kept on, almost shouting.

> *"'Nor lose possession of that fair thou owest;*
> *Nor shall Death brag thou wanderest in his shade*
> *When in eternal lines . . .'"*

"Adam Carthage!" she hissed. "Do you want to be killed going on about your own genius?"

"I can't help it, Ann—now that I know you haven't forgotten!

> *"'How can my Muse want subject to invent,*
> *While thou dost breathe that pour'st into my verse . . .'"*

She raised her voice too, in exasperation. "Your last six or seven books have been about quite different people. We'll both be killed unless we get out of here. And it won't be . . . *'too excellent, For every vulgar paper to rehearse.'*"

"All right, Ann. Since you can still cap . . . See that lane of shadow behind the grapevine?" She turned without taking her hand from his thumping heart. "Walk in that back to your house."

"What are you going to do?"

"Sneak away, too. But not till you get started. If you want me to go, hurry yourself."

"How shall I know you're safe?"

"I'll put on the light in the attic for a minute. You can see it, because I can see your window from there. You do the same. Go on!"

She bent double under the bushes till she reached the grapevine. One glance back showed her that Adam had deliberately stepped out into the full moonlight, brilliant now. Drawing the fire, she thought, the utter, blasted fool. It would make him worse to go back. But two can play that game. She trailed her hand along the grape leaves as she ran so that they made a path of sharp sound.

At the end of the arbor, looking back, she saw he had disappeared. She waited to make sure. He must be doing the same thing; he had understood. There was nothing

but silver grass and black, fearful shadows. In spite of
herself she had a bad second just before the door. When it
opened, the light inside would show her all too plainly—a
good target. But she must see that attic window quickly,
quickly. She slipped in.

It was the work of a moment to lock the door, turn out
the light, and fly up the stairs to her bedroom window.
The gable on the Baynes' roof made a point in the sky between the rounded treetops. She fixed her eye on it for one
of those interminable spaces of time that only afterward
one knows were five minutes. A light winked on, went out,
then on again. She pushed her lamp to the window and
lighted it twice also.

When it was out, the dark was very dark. She couldn't
help but listen for steps outside, for rustling. . . . Could it
have been one of the troopers who fired? In the terror of
the moment she hadn't thought of that. But no. He would
have challenged first. He would have spoken afterward.

"Now," she said. "I *must* find the murderer. This has
gone too far."

She became conscious of Hannah's gentle snore.

7

A little breeze ruffled the curtains of white dotted Swiss. It stirred the matching ruffles of the bed, an old four-poster with a canopy. Nancy Thorne looked at her room, all white even to the rugs, from an immense distance. In her hand was a copy of *Madeleine Pigor*—author, Anthony Bayne. "Poor mother," she murmured. "Couldn't keep me in the nursery, no matter how she tried. . . . She can't, even now."

She was rereading the book in order to argue with Aunt Ann. Did Tony really have a contempt for women . . . all women? He hadn't shown any to her. He had just stroked her hair and said "that wavy little mane" when all the boys her own age would have necked. Of course—one must say this much for her aunt—Nancy had known there would be more to it. She was a little afraid and that was fun when all her family, everyone she knew, even Aunt Ann, wanted her to be safe. She could always have stopped—right on the brink if need be—and drawn back.

Tony's hero, Ewald Pigor, was a painter in Greenwich Village. Easy to change a writer to a painter, she thought. He had married a cabaret girl in one of the joints. (This was an old-fashioned Greenwich Village, not visited by people from uptown.) She was a rather common girl with hardly any looks or talent but a great deal of vitality. Her chief virtue was that she wasn't a gold digger. (In that neighborhood there was little to be dug.) She had fallen in love with Ewald's popularity, his wildness, the fact that the

other painters thought him a great man. They compared
him to Leonardo; he was a good mechanic and dabbled in
science. Of course, she didn't understand a thing about his
pictures. But this wasn't a drawback, Nancy thought. Tony
hadn't failed to make a warm attractive creature of her.

Ewald Pigor had a long illness—this took up most of
the book—and became dependent on her. She took care of
him generously, really with all her heart, but now, when
she said the wrong things about his pictures it irritated
him; he thought she was doing it on purpose. When he
didn't get better he was afraid that she would be unfaithful to him. This fear increased and rode him until he put
all kinds of restrictions on her, even had her watched and
accused her, quite unjustly, of mercenary motives.

But no, thought Nancy, you don't have to think he despised her. It was all inside *him,* all those crazy ideas.

Little by little the pain that was in him he managed to
inflict on her. Although she was a simple girl who loved
him, the strain grew and grew. Finally he drove her to the
very thing he was trying to prevent.

But it was *not* her fault, thought Nancy. Tony made
that plain. She's much the better of the two, as I always
thought. Aunt Ann hasn't a leg to stand on. . . . I did really have a date with a genius and she was mean about it.
She must be simply full of inhibitions!

Nancy got up and listened. It was her plan to go to the
Inn, a thing strictly forbidden, alone. It seemed a likely
place to find Paul Augustine. He was old enough, thank
God, to know something about Life, not like the children
her own age who only thought of tennis scores.

Out on the street she was amazed by the late afternoon
shadows. The commuters' train must have come in while
she was reading and she hadn't even heard the whistle.

The Village Inn looked dignified and only just a little
quaint behind its guard of elms. An unusual number of
cars was parked by the curb. They looked far from expensive. Reporters, she thought, and assumed an expression

that would discourage being spoken to. She opened the
door marked *café* and her flowerlike face held more than a
hint of Mrs. Charles Francis. She was looking so straight
ahead she didn't hear her name.

A tall man with stooped shoulders had to get up and
stand in front of her. Then her jaw dropped.

"Why, Mr. Lawrence!"

"Miss Nancy." He smiled and she noted that he really
was good-looking in an old-fashioned, sad, romantic way.
"I was trying," he said, "to catch your eye to ask you to sit
with us but it was definitely hard—or are you waiting for
someone?"

"No, no!" She was a trifle too hasty. "I'm not. I'd love to!"

She let him steer her to a table where a girl was sitting—a girl or a woman, one could not tell. The figure
in the gray dress was slight, the face partly concealed by
the plainest of hats which was yet very graceful. When she
turned and looked up wistfully, Nancy saw with pleasure
that she would not have to endure a Child. Oh no, indeed.
The face had many lines. They shifted constantly in different patterns like clear water ruffled by every breeze.

Nancy saw now the underdressing was deliberate. It
was a background for this play of feeling. She was like
an actress they'd seen once in school who did only mono-
logues in a small room.

Nancy grasped the thin hand, held out so tentatively
over the table. No, she changed her mind. It's not art; it's
shyness. She's merely making the best of a fault. . . . Then
it came to her, rather late. The secretary, of course!

"I'm awf'ly glad to meet you," she said.

"Will you have a cocktail?" said Mr. Lawrence, bowing
a little in his distinguished way.

"No, thanks. Lemonade." She was a trifle embarrassed
but determined. Drinking had been her experiment of *last*
summer.

"I'm so glad to meet someone who belongs here." The
secretary, Miss Fern Ellyn (what a pretty name, thought

Nancy), turned to her a face all interest. "Mr. Lawrence
says the place is full of strangers."

She winced a little looking at the bar. It was draped
with bored young men, hats on the backs of their heads,
talking around the cigarettes that never left the middle of
their mouths.

"We're not like this usually," Nancy said. "Have you
ever been here before?"

"No," Miss Fern Ellyn said. "But I adore New England.
. . . Where I was born in Ohio everybody's grandparents
or great-grandparents came from here and talked about it
more and more as they got older and handed down their
silver spoons, you know, or little rocking chairs they'd
brought in covered wagons."

"Quite nice to hear, isn't it?" Mr. Lawrence said. He
smiled at Nancy as if they belonged together. "People take
cracks at New England as a rule."

Mr. Lawrence had never noticed her before. He wants
me to like the secretary, she thought quickly. Well, I do.
And not just because mother doesn't either. It must be
wonderful to have a job. Lucky the family didn't know;
they didn't even suspect. She had tried to get one herself
in June at the close of school and failed quite miserably.

"If you'd like anyone to show you things," she said
rather timidly, "please let me."

A surprised look of pure gratitude melted the lines.
What a face to watch!

"I can't imagine anything I'd like better," the secretary
said.

Nancy's eyes traveled past the other's head to the smoke
at the bar. We might be on a desert island, she reflected,
for all the reporters care. I needn't have been so forbidding; all I did was freeze Mr. Lawrence.

But now there was a stir among them. One of the men
had to move his feet to let someone pass. Nancy couldn't
believe her eyes. Aunt Ann! She was thanking the man who
moved his feet, and he got up. "How to Enter a Bar" by

Miss Ann Thorne, thought Nancy. Getting more of a hand than I did and Spinster written all over her.

Yes, with that spare figure and the ramrod way she held herself Aunt Ann could never have had children . . . to muss her up. Nor yet a husband. He might have wanted to move the furniture in the parlor! Yet she was being feminine with the reporters, a faint trusting smile, a frank upward glance at the tall one who'd got up. If you've once been very beautiful, thought Nancy, you always act that way and so it doesn't matter if you aren't any longer.

Her aunt saw them at once but not before Mr. Lawrence had seized an extra chair and pulled out cigarettes. He made quick introductions and she took Miss Ellyn's hand in her much browner, stronger one.

"You have a delightful boss, Miss Ellyn," she said. "He's the only young man who remembers what cigarettes I like and never offers me any others."

Miss Ellyn's face mirrored agreement and—why, it was relief. She's actually pleased at being treated like a human being, Nancy thought.

She knew her aunt wouldn't say anything in front of the others about her being in a bar. She dared to say, "I didn't know you were such buddies with reporters, Ann."

"Oh," said her aunt. "I had to deal with the press often at one time. . . . Jonathan, what do you think of the murder?"

"I try not to," he said. "And I try to get home early. If I could think of any place away from here to send Gregory I'd do it like a shot."

"I do so hope to get a glimpse of him!" said Miss Fern Ellyn wistfully.

"Really? He's probably in bed now. . . . Ann, if I should have to be away would you keep the brat overnight? Mrs. Hodges is very deaf. She's not much protection."

"I'd love to. And the dog and the crow with the broken wing? . . . Do you think he'd leave the goldfish with Mrs. Hodges?"

"He sounds delightful," Miss Ellyn said with longing. "I used to have a menagerie, too."

Miss Ann turned toward her. "I hope you're enjoying Middlebury . . . even though you haven't much time."

"Oh, *yes*. I'm hunting around for old things really . . . to furnish a New York apartment. . . . It makes a sort of half vacation. Mr. Lawrence"—she gave him her wide gaze—"is good enough to let me off early."

Nancy had been watching her aunt's tall reporter. He made for their table. Ah-hah, Ann, she was thinking, you deal with them, do you? To her surprise he spoke not to her aunt but to Miss Ellyn.

"How do you do," he bowed. "I've been trying to see under the hat . . . but you *are* the one. . . . You remember, don't you?"

She shrank back. "No, oh no," she gasped. "I don't know you."

"It was at Webster Hall," he said. "Some years ago, but we spent the whole evening together. Let me see . . . you were with . . ."

"Oh, *don't!*" she whispered. "You are trying to take advantage . . . I don't know you at all." Her face was all crumpled together like a child's who is going to cry.

Miss Ann looked first at her and then at the reporter. "After all, it's the lady's choice," she remarked. "Now *I* should have said I remembered perfectly even if I'd never seen you before." She gave him a little twinkling nod.

He stepped back for a moment, puzzled.

"Come, my dear," Aunt Ann said quickly. "Let's go to my house."

They were all on their feet. She had set them in motion but the reporter stepped forward, blocking their way. He might have held them but his eyes, above their heads, suddenly veered away toward the door at the back that opened into the lobby of the Inn. His interest slid from them like a dropping meteor and he slid after it with just one excla-

mation that satisfied Nancy fully about the vocabulary of
the press.

Craning her neck she saw that a rather ugly, middle-
aged man in tweeds had caused the excitement, and it was
excitement. All the reporters streamed toward him, shoving chairs, leaping over tables.

"Who *is* it?" she said.

Her aunt's lips quivered; it wasn't quite a smile. "It's
Mr. Adam Carthage and he won't get away in a hurry."

She whisked them out of the door.

Miss Ellyn took a deep tremulous breath. "The *air* is so
good out here. How can I ever thank you?"

Ann patted her. "Nonsense. . . . I didn't want to be
questioned either."

They approached her high white gate and Mr. Lawrence
took off his hat. "Fern," he said. "Now that you're in good
hands I'd better be going." The little wrinkles round his
eyes gathered half sadly. "I play hookey from home only
too often."

"Oh . . . must you?"

"I'd better." He seemed to relent. "Look here, if you
want to see that brat I'll wash him and bring him around."

Her eyes followed him with their thanks. Nancy took
her arm and steered her toward the door past the too-
clipped hedge which drew sniffs from its owner. They were
let in with her key.

"How lovely!" said Miss Ellyn in the hall.

"But not native. The garden, now, is early American.
I'd better let you wander round it while Nancy and I find
you some heirlooms."

"Oh . . . you're too kind."

"Not at all. The pink hollyhocks are from the House of
Seven Gables. . . . Then there is sweet William and bleeding heart and so on. You must come in June to see my old
roses—I have the Queen of the Prairies and the Baltimore
Belle."

The secretary stood in the French door. "It's like something I've dreamed of," she said in an awe-stricken voice.

Nancy felt her arm touched by her aunt. "Now, my dear. We'll have to look in the attic." She followed her upstairs where they could not hear the screen door opening or the noise of Hannah's egg beater in the kitchen.

When they came down, the house was absolutely still. They laid the loot on a table in the parlor and went to the French door. Two people were strolling at the end of the garden and, looking up, they hastened their steps—Miss Ellyn and Paul Augustine.

As they came through the late shadows Aunt Ann said, "I see you've introduced yourselves. . . . Good."

The sunlight touched Paul Augustine's bare head. "I got here before you did," he said. "Hannah let me wait in the garden."

"And didn't tell me," Aunt Ann smiled. "Because she was making mayonnaise—a habit of hers when I have several callers. . . . Well, Miss Ellyn, we've dug out some of the past for you." She opened the door.

Nancy watched Paul Augustine. He didn't move and so she walked out to him.

He murmured, "I was hoping you'd come."

Her aunt gave them a look and then vanished after the visitor.

Nancy glanced at the light hair now silvery in the sun that left dark shadows on the face beneath. How different blond men are, she thought, from dark ones. . . . I believe they're more subtle.

"You're the one grace of this ill-gotten village," he said. "Let's forget about it for a moment, shall we?"

"I'd like to," she said. "But you don't know how hard it is. You don't live here."

He laughed. "When you get older you're going to be like your aunt. Why didn't I meet you ten years ago?"

"Because I was playing with my dollies . . . or really, with a dump truck."

"That's Thorne." This time he didn't laugh but smiled gently. "What did the other one play with? Fire, I think. . . . I wish you were anywhere else but here with me, of course. Your aunt could come and yes, Mr. Adam Carthage, we'd let him in." He steered her toward the grape arbor where there was a bench.

"I suppose you can't understand," he went on, "but it's really painful to enjoy people as much as I do you. . . . I haven't cared about anyone in so long, not anyone at all, even myself. . . . I don't know whether it can last."

There was a clatter in the leaves behind them. A crow flew out with two or three ungainly swoops and flopped to the ground. A small, anxious face poked under the vines. "Have you seen Jimmy?"

"I believe we have." Paul Augustine picked up the crow and tried to smooth its harsh black feathers. "Here, son."

Children . . . ugh, thought Nancy. Why can't they leave you alone?

"Thanks." Gubby took his pet, perching him on one finger like a falcon.

Paul Augustine remained standing though she made room for him on the bench. "I'd better go," he said. "I've talked too much already." A minute frown crossed his face.

Nan felt helpless. Just as it was getting interesting! Why didn't the child leave? She said, "Gubby, Aunt Ann wants to see you. She has a visitor in there who wants to see you."

Gubby turned but just like a snail, dragging his feet over the grass.

Paul Augustine chuckled. "He'd rather stay with you. . . . Well, so would I but I mustn't."

She saw by his eyes that her white dress made a picture against the grape leaves. She hoped not a Greuze. Old people always compared her to a Greuze—the exact opposite of her ideal!

Paul's eyes had the right look. He murmured, "Not now, anyway . . . not till I can arrange . . . How about dinner tomorrow? At the Village Inn?"

"I think I could," she said. "I'll have to ask Mother."

"I'll count on it then." He walked quickly away toward the house.

When she arrived a few minutes later there was no one there but Gubby talking with Aunt Ann.

"And did you like Miss Ellyn?" she was saying.

"Huh?" He was petting the crow who glared up with a beady yellow eye.

"Now, Gubby, you heard me."

"I wish she'd go away. Mrs. Hodges says she came here to see Daddy."

"She's taking her vacation here."

"I wish she'd go." he said. "Mrs. Hodges said she came here to marry Daddy. That other man didn't know who she was, did he? the man that caught Jimmy? . . . He thought she was Mrs. Bayne."

"No, Gubby. He knows Mrs. Bayne quite well."

"He called *her* Mrs. Bayne."

"People often misspeak," Aunt Ann said patiently.

"But he thought she *was* Mrs. Bayne."

Nancy sighed. Why did Ann bother so interminably?

Her aunt said in a different tone, "What exactly did he say, Gubby?"

What little mimics children were. Gubby was producing a funny, grown-up voice, "I hope you aren't minding this . . . too much, Mrs. Bayne?"

"Your father's waiting for you, dear," Aunt Ann said. "Run along. . . . I suppose you were in the tree?"

"Uh-huh. . . . Come on, Jimmy. We're going home and get a *nice* supper." The screen door banged.

Nancy flung herself on the love seat in the corner. "Why do you let him say all that stuff," she said wearily, "about Miss Ellyn? She's so sensitive and she wants him to like her. I think she's really in love with his father."

"I think so too," Miss Ann said softly. She sat down opposite her niece. "Or she wouldn't go into such danger."

Nan's brow wrinkled.

"You must learn to observe." Her aunt reached for a cigarette. "Now was it your impression that she knew the reporter?"

"I didn't think. I just thought he was bothering her."

"Yes, but she was afraid. Why was she so afraid?"

The lovely forehead was now definitely knit. "I don't know, I did notice she seems fonder of Mr. Lawrence than he does of her. Oh, I do hope she gets him and comes here to stay! You feel she'd always understand. . . . That face!"

"It was particularly good with the child," Miss Ann said like a connoisseur. "*'Une figure de petite fille souvent battue.'*"*

"You could tell her anything," Nancy went on. "She would know, somehow. What a relief from my crowd." She remembered Tony's book, *Madeleine Pigor,* and what her aunt had said about him as a writer; she would lead up to the argument.

"Why, I could even tell her about me and Tony!"

"I shouldn't if I were you," Miss Ann said.

"Why not?"

"She might not be as sympathetic as you think."

"What right have you to say that?"

"Children are wonderful sources of information. Didn't you hear Gubby? He told it quite plainly. . . . She was Tony Bayne's first wife."

* She was quoting Cocteau's description of Mistinguette.

8

The Sheriff walked from the Bayne cottage through the back path to Miss Thorne's, a way that was familiar even in his dreams. As he came over the smooth lawn, looking straight ahead, he saw the French door of the dining room and behind it people having dinner. A week ago he would have felt confused, would have slowed down. Now he just didn't mind at all. He still admired Miss Ann; he knew she could help him more than anyone. She wasn't doing it. She had told him this cock-and-bull story about Carthage being shot at in her garden.

The funny thing about it was how in the world he got there, if he did. Jake, under what amounted to a third degree, admitted that he'd spent a while in the kitchen with Mabel. Long enough for Carthage to get out and get back? That was what the man claimed. Why didn't Jake hear the shot? Not even the moss-covered alibi about a car back-firing. Jake merely said he didn't know there was a revolver in the case and so hadn't listened for one! If it hadn't meant the troopers would find out the defects in his staff he would have fired Jake then and there. Instead he put the fear of God in him. You had to say this much for the flat-foot—in spite of being a Thorne, Miss Ann might have been lying. He intended to put pressure on her.

"Excuse me, ma'am." He looked at her and took off his hat, for the first time that day. "I'd like to see you a few minutes."

Young Nancy Thorne was having dinner with her, seemed to eat all her meals over here.

"Certainly, Ezra. . . . Will you have coffee . . . dessert?"

"No, ma'am," he snapped. "I found the revolver."

She rang the bell. (Nancy's eyes were like saucers.) "Hannah, bring coffee for Mr. Gates and me to the drawing room. . . . Sorry to have to leave you, Nan."

Although her voice was as composed as ever, Ezra noticed that there was a piece of pie on her plate not even touched, and Hannah's pies were famous.

He followed her across the hall. He thought: the way she walks it's too bad the sergeant can't get her to drill Company H.

She asked him to close the door and sat down.

"The revolver that was fired in your garden belongs to Adam Carthage."

"But that's impossible!"

"It's a Service Colt, recently fired. He can't explain it. He admits that he loaded it shortly after the murder was discovered. *He* says with some idea of protecting Mrs. Bayne. One cartridge is gone, that's all. No fingerprints."

"What possible reason could he have had for firing it himself?"

He shrugged. "I can think of one."

"Well, I can't. Somebody must have stolen it to throw suspicion on him."

"With Jake guarding the house?"

"Was he guarding his room?"

"Oh, I can think of fancy explanations too. But the plain one is that he fired it himself . . . to draw the scent *away* from Adam Carthage."

"That's absurd."

"It is unless he did the murder."

"That's more absurd. What motive did he have?"

"I don't know yet but it's funny he came here so suddenly, not knowing them any better than that." Ezra had been doing some research. Carthage had studied medicine, to begin with, at the start of the First World War. He had been in Paris taking some course or other and he'd joined up with the French. Later transferred to the A.E.F. and all along saw plenty of trouble. His books, Ezra gathered, didn't pull any punches. When they weren't full of fighting it was only for a moment on account of a girl or because somebody was fishing. They were gloomy, too. The hero usually got his or you could see he would. Plenty of deaths and diseases, and what happened to the mind was just as violent as what happened to the body. A tough hombre.

Miss Ann's lips were tight shut. She looked like a neat box that had been locked and the key thrown away.

Ezra was going on. "They had a quarrel, Carthage and Bayne. That stuff about poetry might go down with me. It wouldn't with a jury. You know the citizens around here. Figure it out yourself."

Her face looked pinched but she said evenly, "Aren't you forgetting that this case will be tried in the newspapers? Adam Carthage is a national figure . . . oh, more than that. People who make headlines would swear that it would be natural for him to quarrel about poetry."

"It wouldn't matter," Ezra said sternly. "As long as they weren't there that night. He has no more right than a W.P.A. worker to murder. . . . And the guy they're trying in the newspapers right now is *me.*"

Miss Ann sighed deeply.

"I'm going to arrest your Mr. Carthage as a material witness."

"I know what you're doing, Ezra. You're threatening me. . . . I'm not trying to obstruct justice, though you think I am. I hate to see people hounded unless there's a real likelihood of their guilt. . . . All right." She let fall her hands. "I'll tell you something I picked up. But will you handle it . . . with gloves?"

Ezra sat back in his chair. "I am the judge of how I handle things."

"Then I'll just have to trust you." She sighed again. "There is a woman here who was once involved with Anthony Bayne. She's more or less concealing her identity. Not, I think, for criminal reasons. She is in love. She thinks if she reveals her past it might scare off the man she hopes to marry."

"Huh! You might say it plainer. To make sure Bayne doesn't tell she murders him, eh?"

Hannah knocked ostentatiously and brought in the tray. She went out again closing the door very firmly to make plain that she didn't want to hear, not *she*.

Ezra knew he was jumpy. He didn't usually accuse first one and then another. Maybe, by God, it was the right idea!

Miss Ann said, "Cream and sugar, Ezra? She couldn't have concealed it by murdering him. It's all on record at the courthouse or wherever they keep such things. She was his first wife."

"What was there to hide about that?"

She handed him the cup and said, "I'm going to make a phone call. Then I'll tell you."

Ezra frowned. He looked disapprovingly at the tiny cup and drank the steaming contents at one swallow.

She sailed back. "I told her that it was better for her to be frank."

He said, "Better for you, too."

From now on he was going to rush them.

She smiled. "You see the man she's in love with is conventional. He has a small boy. If he knew she was divorced and had spent years in Tony Bayne's—well, in his corner of Bohemia—he might not think her the right person to bring up his child. Of course, she'd have to tell him in the end but not till she was sure of him."

He clenched a fist. "The Ellyn woman! I'd made a note to interview her."

"Please do it gently. I don't think she's guilty but she may know something."

"Guilty, hell!" He clapped on his hat. "You don't think anybody's guilty but I do. I've got so I suspect my best friends."

"I noticed it," she said pointedly.

He strode out.

Gates, you're slipping, he thought, pulling up at the Inn. Letting her warn the woman. You've got to watch out for Ann Thorne. Not but what she can get information. And hand it out or not just as she takes the notion.

He stamped in at the main entrance, his boots making an angry ring on the old painted floor. A busy murmur came from the café side. Otherwise the place seemed deserted. There was no one behind the counter where an inkwell used by John Adams held a quill for guests. His hand was almost on the bell when footsteps sounded from the parlor.

The tall distinguished figure of Jonathan Lawrence appeared, a very pale, very quiet lady beside him. In spite of himself Ezra slowed up. He feared neither God nor man but he respected some people. The town hall where he had his office was Lawrence Hall, and had been for a hundred years. The blood hadn't run thin either. This Lawrence handled shipping interests on Wall Street.

His hat came off a second time. "Excuse me, sir. I'd like to see this lady. Miss Ellyn, isn't it?"

"Our sheriff, Ezra Gates," said Mr. Lawrence. "You don't mind if I stay. It's just routine, I presume."

Ezra got ready to object; the lady saved him.

"Oh, no, it isn't necessary, Jonathan. . . . I don't mind." Her lips were trembling; she bit them. She added desperately, "It's long past Gubby's bedtime. Really, you ought to take him home."

"That's so." He looked around. "Where is the child?"

"Up in my room, I think. Looking at picture books."

He said, "Well, I suppose you're right. I hate to leave, though, now. Somehow, all this . . . It hasn't been a very good vacation."

She managed a blinding smile. "Oh, yes, it has. Gubby can take the books home. They're a present."

His footsteps retreated. She sat down and folded her hands.

"Go ahead, Mr. Gates. I'll answer your questions. It's only that . . . if you don't have to make public? . . ."

He fixed her with eyes of steel. If he had been impressed with her brave front he didn't show it.

"You were once married to Anthony Bayne?"

"Yes."

"Why didn't you come out and say so?"

"What would have been the use?" Her hands twisted together. "We had no longer any connection. My employer, Mr. Lawrence, didn't know it. Why should he? I always used my maiden name for work."

"Why shouldn't he? . . . A divorce is nothing to be ashamed of."

"It depends on the person you're divorced from. You see, Mr. Bayne had written some very embarrassing things about me. That is, about a woman anyone could see was his wife."

Ezra was still smarting. They'd all hidden so much.

"That might be an excuse for ordinary times. Not when there's been a murder."

"But, you see, Mr. Lawrence is the kind of man who would mind *particularly*. He would simply hate it. . . . It was enough for Tony to make me miserable when we lived together. That he should keep on ruining my life forever—no, no! That was too much!"

"And so you killed him!" Ezra shot out.

"I did no such thing!"

She drew herself up. They heard a man's tread and a child's patter. She sank down again but pulled herself together when they came to the door. She even rose and smiled.

"Oh, you forgot the picture books!" Her hands went to her heart.

"Gregory seemed to think he shouldn't take them." His father hesitated. "I think he was afraid of depriving *you.*"

"But, dear, I got them for a present."

Gubby squirmed.

"Didn't you understand?" she said sweetly but too urgently with a sort of tragic pressure.

"Don't want them," he muttered.

His father looked down. "We'll take it up another time," he said sternly. "Our manners need to be improved. Good night, Fern, good night, Mr. Gates."

She waved to them with an attempt at cheerfulness that would not have deceived anyone who'd been looking. But they were too intent on what they were going to say outside. The front door closed.

Ezra said, "You can't make me believe it was an accident your being here two days ago."

She drew in her breath. "I'll tell you absolutely everything. I did come in the hope of seeing Tony but I didn't manage to. I never even had a glimpse of him."

"Did you try?"

"Yes."

"When?"

She whispered, "The night he was killed."

This is the way, thought Ezra. Rush them and you get some place.

"I walked to his house," she went on, "about ten-thirty and hung about in the road. I didn't want to go in for fear of making talk. His wife . . . I heard voices that seemed to be arguing on and on. They just wouldn't finish so I came back."

"Whose voices?"

"Tony's and another man's. I didn't hear what was said. It's quite a way from the road."

Ezra had taken out his notebook and was writing. "You don't have to sign this," he said grimly, "unless you want to. You can see a lawyer. You're bound to be charged."

"But why?" Her hands pressed her heart. Her eyes and mouth were round and hurt like a child's. A wonderful actress, Ezra thought.

"I didn't *have* to tell you this," she cried. "But Miss Thorne said to be frank. You would never have found out!"

"Why? Didn't anyone see you?"

"N . . . no."

"Does that mean yes or no?"

"I said no."

"Now just why did you want to see Anthony Bayne?" He held his pen poised.

"Oh," she gasped. "Must we go into that? I told you he wrote awful things about me! He was going to do it again. We met in New York accidentally and he taunted me. I was going to beg him . . . to pray . . ."

"You're making a strong case against yourself," Ezra said half reluctantly. "Now don't go saying I forced you to sign this. But if you're just being frank . . ." He held out the notebook.

Her face was twisted in positive torture. Ezra waited.

"I've lost everything," she breathed. "I've lost everything anyway, being dragged in. And I've done nothing at all! Why should I tell any more? What does it matter?" She signed her name without reading the notes, gave him one stricken look, and went out of the door. He could hear her footsteps going up the stairs, light but halting, curiously uneven.

"She's as guilty as hell," he said, his eyes glued to her in spite of himself. "At least she *might* be. It will be something for the papers."

But he felt unhinged, as if he'd watched a very good performance in a theater.

He shook himself and rang the bell at the desk. The awed proprietor was shown the deputy who had been waiting at the door. He got two men to watch the other entrances. "I expect to make an arrest in the morning," Ezra said with more confidence than he felt.

He went to his office and called the New York police to look up newspaper reports of the Bayne divorce. Then he set out for Miss Thorne's.

Only the pierced iron lantern was winking at her doorstep, shedding sparks of light like fireflies on the grass. Hannah answered the bell slowly, pushing electric buttons as she came.

"Out for the evening," she said with satisfaction.

Ezra stood a minute. "I'll wait for her."

He opened the door without, as Hannah said to herself, a by-your-leave. He strode ahead of her into the parlor. She followed very slowly and turned on one lamp, allowing herself to bend over and look at his boots.

He went to the bookshelves. Among the B's there was only one Bayne, *Madeleine Pigor*. Glancing through it impatiently he found nothing to get his teeth on. It seemed to be about a guy who was sick all the time. He started to walk back and forth, thinking, I haven't got a case. I could arrest her, yes, but it wouldn't stick. It would keep the reporters quiet for a day or two. "Sheriff Appears Baffled." Hell. She could have done it, but there's not a scrap of evidence.

How late Miss Thorne was staying. Nobody stayed out late in Middlebury as a rule. He brought himself up sharp by the mantel. Those state troopers had picked up nothing on the spot, nothing. There ought to be *something*. He hadn't had time to look. Feeling the powerful torch in his pocket he went rapidly to the French door.

The torch worked better than sunlight. It lit the under side of leaves and showed up small depressions in the ground as if they were a topographical map. The troopers had kept the place clear; he had to hand them that. The flat place in the dirt where the body had lain was as well preserved as a plaster model. The broken branches had withered; the bent ones, he supposed, sprung up again. What a thick mat of leaves on the chrysanthemums! He squatted down and poked in the torch sideways, going

over each plant. He made a study of the leaves like a jew-
eler looking for flaws in emeralds. . . .

So great was his concentration he seemed to *will* into
being that tiny object, a minute disk. It stuck between a
leaf stem and the plant. His big fingers dislodged it carefully, a small gray button—too small for a man.

The fingers shook; it almost dropped. Go slow, Gates,
he said. Now go slow. Don't go and be a Goddamn fool.
You've got to wait till you hear from New York. Too bad
you didn't have a witness to finding this. Mark the place
right away. He thrust in a stake. You don't *know* that this
came from her dress. But if it did you've got the start of
a case!

9

At this same time Miss Ann was sitting in the library of the Charles Francis Thornes' considering the subject of Family Life. Louella stood by the fireplace—the state of her feelings such that she had to stand; Charles leaned back gracefully in his great-grandfather's chair, half turned toward his desk to symbolize his detachment; Nancy crouched on an ottoman halfway between, her coltish arms and legs gathered together for a spring. Louella raised her chin as if she were going to call the meeting to order, then dropped it again and took little short steps back and forth like a plunging horse. Her family was a meeting that never came to order; she knew that.

Amid all the electric waves that shot from one to another Miss Ann felt imploring messages from Nancy, but she was deaf to them, lost in abstraction like her brother. She was wondering why Louella was that way—a subject he had given up years ago. He just didn't care. But after accepting her sister-in-law all this time Miss Ann was suddenly thinking about her. One couldn't take anything for granted now. The whole familiar life of Middlebury had become strange, even dangerous.

Nan broke the silence. "I never promised to go to the Girl Scout meeting! . . . They have them all the time and I hardly ever get a chance to meet an Interesting Man."

Her mother sighed, "You don't seem to understand that the younger girls have their eyes on you. If you stay away for purely frivolous reasons they will too. You have a certain obligation just because you are a Thorne."

Miss Ann and her brother gritted their teeth silently.

Nan muttered, "A lot of good it's ever done me."

"And has it done you so much good," her mother rapped
out, "to make these social . . . experiments? Augustine! It
has a German sound. Nobody knows him. . . . The last one
you picked out managed to get himself murdered! And no
wonder, from all the lurid details in the papers. I should
think you might tend quietly to your own business for a
while."

Nancy took this with unexpected calm. She turned to
her father. "That's the trouble. I have no business of my
own to attend to!"

She kept her eyes on him longingly. He could stand up
for her so easily if he'd take the trouble, but he never did
. . . never. Sympathy hovered in his expressive eyes. He
looked like Robert Louis Stevenson even to the mustache
and the brown corduroy jacket. He could be a perfect companion! But for years now she'd seen that he never contradicted her mother even when she was most outrageous. . . .
Ann was eyeing him, too.

He waved his long fingers. "I think you'd better go to
bed, Nan dear. And leave your problems in our hands." He
smiled delightfully but without conviction.

She smiled back but she clenched her fists. "All right.
I've certainly been getting nowhere fast. Good night, parents, good night, Ann." She whirled out.

Louella plumped herself down on a chair, but even with
the drop she remained perpendicular from the waist up
like one of the toys which always right themselves.

Miss Ann said mildly, "What have you against the
young man?"

"There's nothing against him that I know of . . . though
there's nothing *for* him. I simply don't want Nancy to be
made conspicuous."

"Is it conspicuous to walk down the street and have dinner in a respectable hotel? Now if it were the bar you objected to . . ."

"Oh, *that* was quite all right. She was with Jonathan Lawrence."

Miss Ann pricked up her ears. So there was where the wind lay.

"With Jonathan and his paramour," her brother added dryly.

"Not at all. It's not that," she said quickly. "I was with them. It's my habit to observe."

"You can't tell me she's any better than she should be," cried Louella, "coming out on the train with him every day!"

"A train is hardly the place for indiscretion. At least a parlor car!"

"Ann's continental mind," said Charles. But he controlled the slightest of smiles and turned his chair further round in order to detach himself completely.

"I don't understand, Louella," his sister said, frowning, "why you think Jonathan Lawrence has a mistress—which offends you—and at the same time think he's the best possible companion for your daughter!"

"Of course, it's not right," Louella admitted. "But he's been in a very sad situation since his wife died—refusing any consolation as he has, refusing to see his old friends here in town. . . . And that woman threw herself at him! One can't expect such a man not to be pursued—so much charm, so successful in business *and* a Lawrence!"

Miss Ann felt a warmth in the voice, even a hint of wistfulness that astonished her.

"If he should take an interest in Nancy," she went on. "Of *course,* I'd be delighted. There could be *nothing* that would be more suitable."

"But he's twice her age! He's nearer to our generation than he is to hers!"

"Just what the child needs," she said vindictively. "She's never had anyone to control her." Her eyes traveled to her husband's indifferent, remote brown velveteen back; a glimmer almost of hate showed in them for a moment.

Tiens, thought her sister-in-law. I've been so occupied wondering how Charles put up with her I haven't wondered enough how she put up with him. A picture flashed into her mind of Louella as a red-cheeked girl, her black eyes snapping with vitality, her body firm with the iron health of certain European peasants. "The Auvergnate," they used to call her till they found out that she minded. Where had all that life gone? Into women's clubs, into being an executive . . . into the microphone. Ah, she thought for the first time with pity, he didn't love her. . . . Quite soon, I suppose, he didn't love her at all.

"And now you see"—Louella folded her hands—"why I don't want Nancy to travel or come out in Washington or any of those things you're always suggesting. It's high time for Jonathan to marry again."

"Don't you propose to let her have a choice?"

"What does a young girl know?" She held up her hands. "She could travel everywhere and come out in a dozen places and not find a man to equal Jonathan. Proud as we are of our New England blood you know very well a lot of it has run thin." She carefully didn't look at her husband. "But Jonathan is just as strong as his ancestors!"

A light broke for Miss Ann. She's in love with the man herself and doesn't know it. "But Nancy is so very young," she said gently.

"Once she was settled down," her mother said, "she wouldn't be impossible. . . . I could teach her. I could show her things."

"I think you have the wrong estimate of your material."

Though it was said reasonably, with hesitation, Charles turned toward her and raised his eyebrows. It was a sign to stop.

Louella's eyes were glittering. "Don't you try any inter-
ference," she warned. "I have enough to contend with in
Charles. Putting a spoke in every plan I make. It's not as
if he ever thought of anything himself, anything except his
old essays . . . or any person either except those that are
dead and gone. I've had to bring up Nancy all alone and I
intend to continue."

"But, naturally, Louella." Miss Ann rose. "I'm only the
maiden aunt and quite harmless. . . . Good night, my dear.
Good night, Charles."

She made her usual exit mechanically, her mind whirling. How old was Louella? Somewhere in the forties. The
time to crack if she were going to. Did Charles suspect;
was that why he humored her? Or did he let things go
just to avoid the bother? She felt as if the solid earth had
opened.

And yet she should have known. These practical, efficient people were the ones who had no release. They
couldn't ride the imagination. When things became unbearable there was no escape. They had to go all the way
off the deep end.

10

A sort of pounding sounded far away, as if it came through water. Then there were other noises near, deliberate—silver rattling, the shush of a curtain being pulled back. Sunlight fell on Miss Ann's closed eyes; she screwed them together.

"Hannah, what in the world? It isn't time to get up!"

"You said you'd always see that Ezra Gates; he's here." In spite of the disapproving tones, one could feel she was moving deftly, with sympathy. This early-morning helplessness touched Hannah. She was pouring out coffee; the hearty, bitter smell wafted across the bed.

"Here," she said. "Drink this. It was all I could do not to let him come tramping upstairs. And he was here last night. Said he was going to wait till you got home. Then he went pussyfooting round all by himself. He needn't think I couldn't hear him. All of a sudden, bang, the front door slams and he's off in his car. I had to go down and turn off all the lights. . . . And this is what our tax money goes for!"

Miss Ann, propped on one elbow, swallowed her coffee in long, grateful draughts. "Did he say why he came?"

Hannah waited on one foot, then the other, till the cup was finished. "Oh, yes, he said to tell you he had found the murderer."

Miss Ann was out of bed and in the shower before Hannah could stoop to pick up the first flying garment. With great deliberation drawers were opened; she made a creaking trip to the closet, returning with a house coat in the grand style.

"No, no." Her mistress' head emerged above a towel. "My old tweed suit. I'm not the prefect of police of the Seine. . . . I suspect there'll be work to do."

In five minutes she was descending the stairs, leaving all trace of hurry behind her.

Ezra had worn a path in the rug. On an ash tray there lay a pile of matches he had used lighting his pipe only to let it go out.

"Oh, here you are," he said. "It's all over. . . . Thanks for that tip about Fern Ellyn. She did it all right."

Miss Ann sat down. "You astonish me."

"It was a setup. I came here to tell you last night but you were out." He sounded very sure and stubborn, but there was that pile of matches. . . . "She admitted she came here to see him. She had a motive like you said—crazy about Mr. Lawrence. But there was more than that. Tony Bayne was just writing something dirty about her—see? She came here to make him stop. Went to see him that night. . . . It's all here. She signed it." He drew out his notebook.

"You mean she confessed?"

"No; but so near there isn't any difference."

She let out her breath. "I fail to see how a statement can be *nearly* a confession. Either she said she was innocent or that she was guilty. . . . Which was it?"

"Well, but . . ."

"Don't you see, Ezra"—she leaned forward—"this murder would be the last thing Fern Ellyn could want? The truth would be bound to come out. The newspaper publicity is going to be far worse than any book."

"I don't say she *meant* to do it. She just lost her temper; got in a blind rage . . ." He gestured.

"Ezra." She looked at him keenly and put out a finger. "If you were quite convinced you wouldn't have come here to see me. You *want* to be convinced, to stop the papers. . . . Have you arrested her?"

"I was going to—as a material witness." As the last words came out he knew they weakened his stand. "I went to the Inn this morning. . . . I was too late."

"What do you mean?"

"She committed suicide!"

"Oh," Miss Ann cried, "I've done this!" She shrank back, a picture of woe. "Why did I tell her to talk?"

"Don't you go taking on." He rose. "You had to quit obstructing justice some time." He stood above her clumsily. "She's no worse off than sitting in a cell and waiting for the chair!"

"Poor little thing, poor little thing!" She rocked back and forth. "I misjudged her. She's been through so much. I thought she had the greatest courage. I thought she was the kind that would bend but not break!"

"Get an eyeful of this." He thrust a paper under her nose. It was a torn scrap that said, "I can't stand it any more. Life is just a long torture. I thought you would have to stop when everything was over but I see you will go on until . . ."

Miss Ann stiffened like a retriever on the point and became quiet all over.

"We found it on the floor beside her bed."

"And it looks like a confession to you? It doesn't to me."

She rose so that her eyes were more nearly on a level with his.

"Ezra, suppose for a minute she didn't do it. Suppose she just committed suicide from hopelessness. What a break for the murderer. He goes scot-free. He is pleased with himself, exalted. He thinks murder *works.*"

He said with feigned politeness, "You have a reason for this? Some little thing you've kept from the police?"

One corner of her mouth turned up but it was not a smile. "I have. Now please don't bother to be angry about this. There'll be time for that later when the case is finished."

"Yeah?"

She took a cigarette and looked at it helplessly, expecting somehow a match to appear. After a while one did, and his hard lips unlocked. One could feel that telling about it afterward he would say, "Women!" shaking his head.

"I didn't tell you about the weapon," she said then. "Gubby Lawrence found a stone beside the body. It happened to be *his* stone, the one he used to mark the grave of his dog. He washed it off—there was a little blood—and put it back in his cemetery. I didn't tell you before because I didn't want him questioned unless it was necessary."

"So that's the story!"

"Yes. The point is it's harder to *throw* something that will kill than it is to hit with a club. You know that yourself. It's not likely that a woman could have done it."

He scowled. "We got the blood grouping on the towel. We knew that it corresponded with Bayne's. The homicide squad was just about to take a sample from you. In fact," he said sourly, "they may want to go ahead."

"I shall be delighted." She looked at him and then lowered her voice to its most friendly tone. "Ezra, you must forgive me for this. A jury would, you know, when it comes to a child."

He didn't answer.

"I *did* tell you, even though not at once." She sounded intimate and warm, full of sad trust that was not quite reciprocated. In fact she had shed the old maid. There suddenly appeared that legendary charm that always conquered just because it didn't try. She was again the clear-eyed girl who had astonished Europeans, straight as an arrow yet not obvious and never, never naive.

"I always *shall* tell you everything," she said as if to herself. "How I wish you would tell me a little too. For instance, how her room looked. Was it disordered? Chairs pushed back, you know, as she walked around trying to make up her mind, perhaps crying? Her toilet articles, were they used? How was she dressed?"

"They're taking photographs," he said, like a man hypnotized. "And fingerprints, of course. . . . It was neat as a pin as far as I could make out. She had on her pajamas. Slippers and bathrobe on the foot of the bed."

"Poor little thing." She leaned forward, clasping her hands, and she could see by Ezra's face, like the ringing of a once familiar but now rusty bell, that he was noticing her looks. "Do they know," she asked, "what the poison was? How did she take it?"

"There was a box that had held capsules by the bed. Some ordinary sleeping stuff. It was empty."

"And the poison?"

"We'll have to wait for the autopsy. But we found in her wastepaper basket a little white powder that the doc says may have been taken out of the capsule to put poison in. It's being analyzed."

"I don't like it, Ezra." She pushed one fist in the other hand.

He shrugged. "I can't help that. It's open and shut. Oh, and her door was locked, on the inside. We had to break it."

"She wasn't that *kind* of woman!" she cried. "Murder is the act of a coward and this woman took her smashed up life and patiently put it together again. She must have had worse moments with Anthony Bayne *before*—before last week. . . . And she *couldn't* have thrown the rock."

"A lucky shot," he said. He was frowning. "I'll take a look at your rock, though."

They went through the dining room where the trim breakfast service lay forgotten. The early-morning shadows streaked the grass just as they had when Gubby walked through them with blood on his hands.

The sheriff's eyes looked down indulgently. "I'll admit," he said, "when I came here last night I didn't have a mite of evidence. Oh, I knew who *did* it. But my case would have been nothing for a jury if she had had a smart lawyer, with that innocent actressy way. While I was here I found something. That changed it."

She stopped. "What was it? Tell me!"

He fished in his pocket and held out his hand. It opened, large and calloused, round a small gray pearl button.

"It's off her dress," he said. "The dress she wore that night. I checked it while the troopers were doing *their* stuff, up in her room. This is *my* evidence. It just belongs to a poor country sheriff."

She stayed perfectly still. "Where did you find it?"

"Oh, back there in your posies." He waved his hand. "Something the homicide boys overlooked. Too small for state troopers. Or maybe they had to go back for their dinner and didn't have time to look real good."

"Do you know where you found it?"

"Sure."

"Then show me." She was off.

He swung along with ease at first but had to lengthen his strides to keep up.

Under the plum tree the chrysanthemums were still in shadow, heavy with dew. It was like wading into a pool. He put aside a couple of plants with his big hands.

"Looking for my stake," he said comfortably. "There!"

Miss Ann dropped to her knees. She stayed there so long, her hands on the plant, he began to wonder. Could she be praying, out here in the wet?

At last she turned around her face. It might have been a stranger's. He could only stare.

"You'll have to take me to the Inn at once," she said in a toneless voice. "I'll have to see that room. . . . I won't bother with breakfast."

"What's the matter?"

"This plant is a Korean hybrid. . . . It's the only one I have. I looked at it as soon as the body was moved, at every branch. I straightened it up. There wasn't any button there then."

Ezra scratched his head. "I put the stake right in," he muttered.

"Of course you did." She gave a long sigh and rose to her feet painfully like an old lady. "That button was planted. . . . You see what it means?"

He was to remember her face, as it looked then, for years.

"Somebody fixed the sleeping capsule, too," she said. "Fern Ellyn was murdered!"

11

Miss Ann felt that the sheriff was listening too silently, watching with a too noncommittal eye. "What do you
think about it, yourself, Ezra?"

He sat down on the small cane-seated chair in front of
the table where Fern Ellyn's toilet articles were spread out.
The body had been taken away for the autopsy. Traces of
fingerprint powder that lay here and there, a burnt-out
photo-flash bulb on the floor showed what a storm had
gone before this calm.

"It's a possibility," he said. "That's all we've got in this
case anyway."

His hand idly engulfed a dark-blue leather brush, a
matching comb case stamped in gold, fingered the man-
icure tools in the set, the mirror, the photograph frame.
His harsh manner of the day before had vanished; he was
starting again patiently. He said, "Aren't these things too
expensive for a stenographer? Do you think he was . . .
helping her out?"

"They're good, yes, but she was more than a stenographer. She was his secretary. Well paid, I should think. She'd
worked there five years. And she was the saving kind."

Miss Ann picked up a chiffon stocking with an exquisite darn at the heel. "Most women who could have afford-
ed this in the first place would have thrown it away in the
second." She pointed to the snapshot in the frame—several people on a beach, among them Mr. Lawrence. "That

has for me the earmarks of an office picnic. See how ill at ease they are, yet trying to be very jolly. She could keep it around without embarrassment. But look, he's in the foreground and there's no Fern Ellyn. She had to take it herself." She added gently, "It was the only way to get a picture of him."

He said, "If it was murder why was the box of capsules empty? According to you somebody got in here and doctored these *before* she came up. The locked door proves that. Then why did she take them all? That looks like suicide to me. I think she fixed them herself and took all she had—to make sure."

Miss Ann examined the prescription number pasted on the box. "The homicide squad is checking this, yes? If they're what I think, they are pretty strong. She could only have got a prescription for three or four . . . expecting a bad time with Tony, of course. She was here three nights. Yesterday there were two left, at most. Just right for the murderer."

Her gaze traveled over the empty bed, hardly dented by the light weight that had been on it, the sewing bag on the bedside table, a well-worn Book of Common Prayer, and a stack of brand-new children's books beside it.

"Scarcely the relics of a scarlet woman," she said. "I don't know whether she loved Jonathan or only safety but it doesn't matter. She was such a hurt, harmless little thing! It was fiendish to kill her."

"Sure," Ezra said. "*If* anyone did. And *if* she was all that harmless. And what about the note?"

"Where was it?"

He said reluctantly, "Under the blotter."

"Suicide notes are left in plain sight. You know that better than I do. . . . It was just a torn piece of an old letter."

"Then where's the rest of it? . . . It's written on typewriting paper. People don't write letters on that."

"Yes, they do. Literary people. Remember she'd lived with Tony Bayne. The letter was obviously to him."

"But he was dead."

She held out her hand. "It's really her writing, I presume?"

He nodded.

"'I can't stand it any more. Life is just a long torture. I thought you would have to stop when it was all over but I see you will go on until . . .' Notice where the thing has been torn off. The rest of the sentence wouldn't have been useful to the murderer. Or perhaps it was meant to look like a threat, written before the Bayne murder, to show she intended to do it. Also torn off before she said anything definite, because what she did say wasn't a threat. No, no, I think this was just a scrap of a real letter she wrote him some time ago. The murderer happened to lay his hand on it and thought it might give color to a suicide theory. Not a well-planned crime. It was done in too much of a hurry."

"Why?"

"So she wouldn't give the murderer away. . . . You see she was *there* that evening, roaming around. I got the impression from your notes that she saw someone and for some reason concealed it."

He dug them out and flipped over the pages. "Here it is. When I asked whether anyone had seen her at the Baynes' she hesitated. I had to ask her again. Then she said, 'No,' but in a low voice, I remember."

"I noticed that double question. . . . And besides, the murderer thought he could get her suspected of the first crime and make himself quite safe. He must have known her identity and that she had a motive. . . . Did you make sure she was wearing the dress the button came from that first night?"

He opened the closet door. "Any time you want a job on the force," he said, "it's yours. You think of everything. But then, so do we."

In the closet only two hangers were in use. One held a suit, the other a gray dress. They swayed a little, looking small and limp in the draft from the door.

"I see." She nodded. "She was wearing the suit yesterday. That dress was the only one here so we can't be sure whether the murderer really observed it the first night or took a chance. That might mean that the murderer was a woman. More likely to notice."

Ezra unhooked the dress and brought it over. "I'm listening to you," he said. "The words sound all right but I don't know about the music. I do detecting myself. Look at this." He showed her the frayed, uneven threads where the last button on the skirt should have been. "It wasn't cut off."

"No." She moved the other buttons delicately. "The cloth hasn't been torn or even weakened either. Do you mind if I try pulling one off?"

"Go ahead."

She pulled steadily quite hard but nothing happened. She chose another, gave a quick yank, and it was in her hand. The ends of thread looked as the others had; the cloth was intact.

"Good quality," she sighed. "Like all her things. Few but the best. A thoroughly nice woman." Her brow wrinkled. She said tentatively, "One of her leading traits was neatness. Now if she'd lost this night before last wouldn't she have sewed another on?"

"No," Ezra said. "I spiked that. She didn't have one. I looked in her kit bag." He stood over her triumphantly. "You wouldn't expect her to go hunting around for it, would you, at the scene of the murder?"

She looked suitably crushed. But really a disturbing picture had flashed into her mind of Fern Ellyn at the back of her garden only yesterday afternoon. Was she looking for her button? Did she bend down and pretend to admire the plants while she was talking with Paul Augustine? I must ask Gubby, she thought. He was in the tree.

She summoned that man-to-man air she had herself invented, but it was so different from its crude imitations that it seemed made that moment.

"Ezra," she said, "I have nothing to base this murder on but my own observation—that the button was not there two days ago. Plus what appeared to be her character. But we've discovered nothing to disprove it either. I don't blame you for doubting me. Let's have breakfast."

The manager of the Inn was in the lobby. He had been badly flustered by the publicity. Now he saw a chance to give "service" to the sheriff, and maybe fix everything up. "Right this way," he said, his eye gleaming. "There's a private parlor. Here back of the desk. I use it myself but in a case like this . . . You'd rather be undisturbed, I am sure."

He swept off a book on old glass and some pewter candlesticks. In record time the cloth was laid, trayfuls of willowware dishes took their place, all covered to keep hot. The waiter, the manager, and the cook, who had been running something like a relay race from the kitchen, withdrew.

Perhaps ten minutes later Miss Ann was inhaling the perfume of her second cup of coffee and the cigarette that smoked in her hand. If I'm relaxed, she thought, looking across the table, Ezra is too. There may not be so good a chance again.

She asked, "May I borrow some sheets off your notebook?'"

"Sure. . . . Got a pencil?" He grinned. "When women have one the point is generally busted."

She had been going to use her fountain pen but she decided quickly to take the pencil.

"This is the sort of chart I'd make with my view of the case," she said, adding sadly, "I know it isn't yours." She put down three headings: Wednesday—Murder of Anthony Bayne; Thursday—Attempted Shooting of Adam Carthage; Friday—Murder of Fern Ellyn (Bayne). "Under each one I'm going to put Time and Means, also Motive. Then I'm going to see whether any of the suspects can be made to fit under all the heads, or even the majority of them."

"All right," he said. "You may get something."

She took a deep breath and wrote, "Gubby Lawrence." Under Murder of Anthony Bayne, Time, she wrote, "Impossible for the child to be awake at midnight."

She shot Ezra one of her clear glances. "I'll admit when I first saw the man dead it gave me a dreadful start because I thought it had been done about six in the morning and Gubby could have been around then. But he's never in his life waked up in the middle of the night, not even when he had the whooping cough so badly last spring. He just threw up in his sleep. I know. I did the night trick and admired it greatly."

Under Means she wrote, "Unlikely to have been able to throw the stone." She would suppress the tree for the present. Decidedly. Under Motive, "Bayne disliked animals. Weak."

Under Attempted Shooting of Adam Carthage she wrote, "Could not have been up then. Could not have taken, shot, and replaced revolver. Motive, none."

Under Murder of Fern Ellyn, Time, she wrote, "His father was going to take him to see her that evening."

"He did," Ezra said. "And the kid was up in her room alone. He was there when I came in and found the two of them in the parlor."

She shrank under this unexpected blow, but wrote Means, "Impossible for him to have understood sleeping medicines or possessed poison. You admit that, don't you?"

"O.K."

Under Motive she wrote, "Didn't seem to like her."

Ezra looked at her this time with frank admiration. "That's right," he said. "That's putting the cards on the table. He's a funny little cuss."

After surviving this, Miss Ann decided quickly it was useless to drag in Nancy. She didn't belong."

"Paul Augustine," she wrote with relief. Thank God for a stranger. Under Murder of Anthony Bayne, Time, "Did not arrive in Middlebury till 2 a.m. That's two hours after the last time the murder could have been done if the doctors are right." She paused. "Have you verified that, Ezra?"

"Yes. Plenty of people heard him with that busted exhaust. We've found the gas station where he hit the pump, backing up to it. It's about forty-five miles from here. The old guy remembers fine. It was just midnight and that's right for time; it would take him two hours with his car in that shape. The filling-station man recognized Augustine; he'd stopped there before on his way from New York. Besides he wasn't likely to forget the cursing Augustine gave him for not having more light. What made it worse was that the old man hadn't anything to hitch it up with, only picture wire. No wonder it came off."

"When did Augustine leave New York?" said Miss Ann. "Why was he driving So late?"

"About eleven. He went to a movie by one of the Huntington Reed authors, *Death March*, by . . . well, it's a Polish name. Says he discovered the guy though Huntington Reed didn't give him the credit for it. That's why he was so interested. It was his first chance to see the film and he couldn't wait though he knew he had to contact Bayne in the morning."

"Kuczinski," said Miss Ann. "He is a good writer, a different pair of shoes from Mr. Bayne. I don't blame Augustine for being interested in the movie; I am myself. But did he go with anyone or see anyone there?"

"Yes, lady. I thought of that, too. He said he sat quite near the author. So I had the New York police go see this author and he remembered O.K. He'd come in very quiet like himself, to avoid publicity, and sat in the back and Augustine was the only person who recognized him and spoke to him. Says Augustine was right there, in a stone's

throw of him, all during his picture. He didn't know
whether Augustine stayed for the second feature because
he left then himself. Of course Augustine didn't. Driving
out of New York it would take him that hour to get to
Hood Corners. They sent me a copy of the affidavit."

"All right," said Miss Ann. Means, "Possible," she
wrote. Motive, "None known. . . . I don't think Augustine
cares about Rosa Bayne after all, do you?"

"No." Ezra grinned a little. "Looks like he favors your
niece right now. That doesn't mean Mrs. Bayne wasn't
fond of *him*. I got a warrant and had the New York police
go through his apartment. They made a list of everything,
mostly the contents of his desk, and sent me copies of
his letters from the Baynes. Tony's always began, 'Dear
Augustine,' but his wife's said 'Dear' or 'Dearest Paul.'
Sometimes it was spelt funny, 'Paolo.' One letter began,
'Darling' but all there was in it was a recipe for chops
baked with onions!"

"Some women call everyone 'darling,'" said Miss Ann.
"On the other hand, some don't. May I see the copies of
the letters and the affidavit and the list of what was in
Augustine's apartment?"

"Sure, sure," he said indulgently. "I'll send them all
over."

Under Attempted Shooting of Adam Carthage she
pointed to Time. "Do you know if he has an alibi for that
evening?"

He said slowly, "I could find out but it don't hardly
seem worth while. Look at your next place." He put his
finger on it, Means. "He couldn't have taken the revolver.
Jake was right there with him every time he came to the
house. There's others that could, though."

She put a question mark under Time, the word "None"
under Means and Motive, and came to Murder of Fern
Ellyn. Her pencil paused at Time.

"There's the difficulty," she said. "We don't know when
the poison was substituted for the sleeping medicine. They

don't keep bedroom doors locked here consistently. Since he's staying here himself I should think he would have had plenty of opportunity."

"His room's in the wing," Ezra said. "Yes. . . . Put down 'Possible.'"

Under Means she wrote, "Possible."

Ezra said, "But put 'Unlikely.' He hasn't bought any drugs in town. I've checked the drugstores and the doctors. Nobody has. And he hasn't been anywhere else. Car hasn't left the garage. We all agree Bayne was murdered on the spur of the moment. It isn't likely just a visitor to town came bringing poison. Not when there's others here had it under their hand all the time."

She wrote, "Rosa Liederstraum Bayne," under Murder of Anthony Bayne—Time, "Possible"; Means, "Possible, if a woman could have done it"; Motive, "Hasn't shown much grief. Might have been in love with Paul Augustine. Investigate." Under Attempted Shooting of Adam Carthage—Time, "Possible"; Means, "Possible"; Motive, "None known."

"By the way," she said, "Ezra, can we assume that the person was a bad shot because the bullet went wide?"

"That's one explanation."

The next heading was Murder of Fern Ellyn, Time. She was writing, "Impossible," when Ezra said, "She was out riding with Carthage that afternoon."

"What?" Miss Ann cried. "But he was here!" And then could have bitten her tongue off.

"Was he?" Ezra sat up. "Was that where the reporters got him? . . . Why? You put 'Investigate' for her. Maybe she was here, too. And now Means. When I found that revolver in his room with one cartridge gone I searched the house over again and there are enough drugs to poison an army. Bayne was the kind that liked to take medicine. He experimented some too. The widow admitted it; had to when I found morphine and snow and that Mexican stuff.

We'll wait for the autopsy." He glanced at his watch. "But it's a case of 'You name it, they've got it.'"

"She may get rid of them in the meantime."

He gave her a pitying glance. "I've got a list. I took all the poisons."

"I beg your pardon," she said meekly. "Motive. . . . How about jealousy? Perhaps she didn't take Tony's affairs as easily as she pretended to. And she knew the first wife had a motive for the crime; it could be palmed off on her. She must have known about the new book."

"Yes," he said. "But you've got to prove Rosa knew she was here in Middlebury."

"I forgot that. . . . Now we come to Fern Ellyn Bayne, poor little thing." Murder of Anthony Bayne—Time, "Possible"; Means, "Possible, if a woman could have done it"; Motive, "Admitted." ("We'd better look at that manuscript to see just exactly. . . .") Attempted Shooting of Adam Carthage—Time, "Not known." ("Perhaps the Inn could give her an alibi,") Means, "Impossible." ("She couldn't have got the revolver.") Motive, "None." Murder of Fern Ellyn. ("Where am I? Oh, suicide!") "Possible, in fact probable, except for one button and the fact that she had guts."

"Don't mind me with the language," Ezra said. "And notice the drug she took was the kind that wouldn't hurt or disfigure, in other words was typical for suicide. That's what the coroner said, 'Atropine group.'"

"That's a point, though it's not decisive. It would be equally good for a murderer who wanted to make the thing look like suicide." Motive, "Despair at loss of Jonathan Lawrence or, if you assume that she murdered Tony, fear of discovery."

"Fair enough."

"Adam Carthage," she wrote with a steady hand. Murder of Anthony Bayne—Time, "Possible"; Means, "Possible"; Motive, "None known."

"Put that they had a quarrel," Ezra said.

Persons Near the Bayne House the Night of Anthony Bayne's Murder

Time	In the House			Fern Ellyn (Bayne)	Outside	
	Mrs. Bayne	Mabel	Adam Carthage		Louella Thorne	Unknown?
10:15		Doing dishes until "after ten."				
10:30	Saw a strange woman (Fern Ellyn) in front of the house (from upstairs window—bathroom)—was putting out towels for guest.	Overheard quarrel at end of which Mr. Bayne went out and slammed the front door.		Said that she arrived about 10:30, heard quarreling and did not go in.		
10:45		Did Mabel really then go to bed?	Says he went right to bed when his host went out in a rage, and heard nothing afterwards. (No proof.)	What did she do when Tony Bayne came out and slammed the door? Did she meet him on the path, walk to Miss Thorne's garden with him, and kill him (all in 15 minutes), or did she see someone else go to meet him and hang back? If the latter, why did she hesitate to tell the sheriff?	(No proof that Louella didn't arrive sooner than she said.)	Someone else could have arrived during this 15 minutes and been seen only by Anthony Bayne and Fern Ellyn, both now dead.
11				Seen by Louella, two or three minutes after eleven, walking away.	Says she arrived only to see Fern Ellyn walking away—no one else. The house was dark. *Who put the lights out?* Did Tony Bayne go back and do it? If so, why?	

"All right." Attempted Shooting of . . . himself? Time, "Possible"; Means, "Possible"; Motive . . . She was starting "Unknown" when Ezra took the pencil and wrote "Red herring."

Murder of Fern Ellyn, Time. She went on, "Probably possible. Investigate; i.e., find out whether he was alone here at the Inn long enough to have gone to her room." Means, "Possible." ("He could have taken the Baynes' drugs.")

Motive. She was beginning a *U* when Ezra took the pencil and said, "All the motives anyone had, fear of having been discovered doing the first murder or, anyway, near the place, knowledge that she was the logical one to frame. He could have picked that up easily in the house, probably Tony told him about the book. And having studied medicine he knew what drug to use."

"Yes, but how did he know Tony's first wife was here?" she cried triumphantly. "If Rosa didn't know, how did he?"

"If she found out," he said, "she would have told him, and I have an idea she found out. It was dangerous for Fern Ellyn Bayne to come here, like you said. It's too small a town. That is, if she meant to kill him. And if she didn't, it was just as dangerous, hating him as she did. It gave someone else a swell chance to do it and blame it on her."

"She must have been desperate," said Miss Ann. "I wonder what was in that book?" She seized a moment of quiet like the heart of a cyclone to brood in. She couldn't take long. Ezra would not keep his thoughts suspended as she did; he had to have a suspect. She was jerked into the blast.

"Look at your own map!" He jabbed it. "Look who has the most 'Possibles' after his name, your friend, Adam Carthage! I was betting on him from the first. He's a cool customer. That's the kind you never know what they're like, so cool and polite. . . . You put me off with Fern Ellyn. She looked funny; I admit that. But you don't even

think yourself she did it. All that's happened since yesterday is the girl is dead."

Miss Ann's heart skipped a beat. It startled her; it had
ticked regularly for so many years. But she remained upright, her eyes unblinking.

He leaned over the table. "You believe she was innocent," he said. "You say she didn't commit suicide. It all
rests on your word. Well, if you're right we're back just
where we started from. And that's Carthage. . . . And he
has one more murder to his credit."

12

Adam Carthage took the stairs to his room two at a time and tore off his black tie. He felt like bolting but he hadn't any hole to bolt to. He locked the door; that he could do.

His room was only half a flight from the Bayne living room, eight steps. It had been built on as an afterthought above an attached garage and it never gave him any sense of privacy, voices and footsteps rose so clearly from below. On the other hand—he looked out the window longingly— he had invented a capital exit. That was one of the things that had made the sheriff suspicious. He hadn't explained. He had let Gates assume that he'd walked through the living room twice the night he'd been to see Ann Thorne although Jake swore he hadn't. The sheriff had prowled gloomily around outside looking at the walls, deciding that no, the drop was too great, especially with concrete below.

The Bayne house—cottage, they called it—was distressingly picturesque. God knows he'd suffered enough from the owners' characters to be entitled to profit by them too. The point was: the garage doors, instead of being toward the front where they'd be handy, were at the side where they weren't, in order not to spoil the rose-covered-bower aspect. Above them were the only windows big enough to get through, thoughtfully out of sight of the rest of the house.

The garage was kept locked, but when he learned who lived behind that row of trees his mind had been quite active enough to discover the key, to think of propping one door open with a stone, enough to give a toe hold. His body had enjoyed shinnying down, yes, in every one of his thrilled and now somewhat sore muscles. He'd locked the door and put the key back early in the morning.

How boring it had been several years back when his son used their garage doors to climb on! Now it all came in handy, even making him remember to oil the hinge. Margaret complained that he never paid the boy any heed. Well, this proved that he had. But he could never tell her. The last thing Margaret understood was whimsey.

It was his fate to be surrounded by women who wanted him rather than ones he wanted. Margaret, poor girl, was only the chief example. But had he ever wanted anyone since Ann? Well, he was interested at first, he sighed, and then so quickly sorry for them. Never anything else. But not, he thought, coming back suddenly, for this overripe houri of Bayne's.

He'd gone to the funeral with her—it seemed the decent thing to do—without a thought of photographers. When they surged up he'd tried to get away, but she clung to him like a big, scented, repulsive limpet. He would have had to hit her to get loose. The strength of the hands and arms struck him as curious even through his rage. The piano, he thought. She'd draped herself in a number of coy poses, but if the cameras got his face, between the hunched shoulders and ducked hat, it would show a glare that would ruin everything. The right word, he thought soberly, was murderous.

Feet sounded on the stairs. He sat rigid, pipe clutched in his teeth. I can't stand any more of her, he thought.

Knuckles rapped. A voice said mildly, "It's just Augustine. . . . But I don't want to bother you."

Relief loosened his cramp. He opened the door. "I'm glad to see a human face."

While he was holding out his hand he thought, This is known as sex solidarity.

He said, "You're not a policeman, you're not a reporter, and, above all, you're not a singer with two hundred pounds of anguish to throw at a camera."

"I saw it," said Paul Augustine. "In fact, that's why I came."

"Do you know this woman? Is she like that usually? If not, what is all this about?"

"Yes, I know her," he said slowly. "I'm going to light a pipe, too." He found a chair and settled down deliberately. "Have you heard her sing?"

"No."

"Then it's hard to explain. She has a lovely voice—not big enough for opera. She's a lieder singer. Her manager made her do concert tours in small towns to work up a reputation. She made a hit with musical people, but she hated it. I imagine she came into competition with too many pretty girls. It's not enough to have a good voice any more. Five years ago she quit and married Bayne."

"It sounds perfectly normal. But then why"—Adam leaned forward—"why does she throw herself at me?" He felt drawn to this young man who had showed up so providentially just when he needed somebody to talk to. "Really she doesn't even like me. There's no *feeling* at all. That's why it's creepy. I can't help thinking she's trying to get me arrested for the murder."

"Good Lord! Why do you think that?"

"She tried to make me look like the third angle of the triangle, the surviving male. That was today. And yesterday a curious thing happened. She suddenly arrived at the door, dressed to go out, hat, heavy black veil, everything, a wild glint in her eye. She had just remembered, she said, that the night of Tony's death she had seen a strange woman in front of the house. She was the only one who had seen her, she thought. She'd just happened to look out from an upstairs window. So now she must go out and

look for her quick, quick before it was too late. To humor
her I told Jake I would drive her to do some errands. We
drove slowly. I thought the air was doing her good; it was
hard to see through the veil. Then she saw a lot of cars at
the curb and made me stop. We went up the front steps to
the Inn. The hall was deserted. She made for the bell but
when she got to the desk she leaned on it, put her hand to
her side. "I'm going to faint," she whispered. "Help me,
Mr. Carthage." She could hardly stand. It was like the last
act of *Butterfly*. . . . Finally I got her to the sofa in the
parlor. I rushed into the café to get brandy; that was what
she asked for. A mob of reporters caught me and I had
no more chance of getting brandy than of making a first
down against Yale and Harvard combined. It must have
been twenty minutes before they let me go. I got it and
went back and where was the sick lady? Vanished. *And* in
the car. I had to walk back. Not that I minded except that
one hates being used . . . maliciously . . . for God knows
what."

"You've no idea why she did it?"

"I think she threw me to the reporters like a bone to
dogs."

Paul Augustine took the pipe from his mouth. "Could
she have seen the register," he said, "when she went up to
the desk?"

"I didn't notice. I only thought afterward that it was
odd she didn't ring the bell when that's what she'd started
to do."

"It is usually there," said Augustine slowly. "There are
so few guests the page wouldn't be turned. It's possible she
saw the name of Miss Fern Ellyn, Tony's first wife."

Adam's brows shot up. "That's something I hadn't
heard." He laid down his pipe.

"Then you haven't seen the afternoon papers. I wonder
if Rosa has? There was not much in them except that a
woman named Fern Ellyn was found dead in the Inn. They
didn't mention her connection with Anthony Bayne. But I

used to know her. I saw her here in Middlebury yesterday. She died last night."

"How? . . . Why?"

Augustine sighed. "It's a long tale and not at all amusing. Would you like a drink and a sandwich? That's what I came to ask you. I know a rather decent lunch counter where we won't be disturbed. I thought the meals might be getting dreary here."

"That's an understatement. . . . I don't mind saying it would save my life."

"You don't need to thank me." He gave him a shy look. "I dabble in writing. That is to say, I read books . . . I mean if you write them."

Adam said quickly, "Mrs. Bayne doesn't appear at meals." He got up and picked out a necktie with spots. "The sole source of conversation is Mabel."

"I fear even that would give out tonight."

"Would it?" Adam found his hat.

"Remember that smothered cry in the middle of the church service? . . . Followed by hysterical sobbing?"

"I do indeed." The thick eyebrows went up.

"That was Mabel."

"Good God!"

"That's why I had the nerve to offer you a meal."

"Poor Bayne! . . . I suppose one is known by the type of women who mourn for one."

Paul Augustine gave him another approving glance as he lowered his head to go down the stairs but Adam was too occupied to notice.

He was saying grimly to himself, I can think of one who has mourned for me very little in the past twenty years.

The lunch counter even smelled masculine. It was a truck drivers' stop on the edge of town, one of the few places, since women had invaded saloons, that belonged to men alone. Two enormous roasts, one beef, one ham, were enthroned on the hot plate to be cut for sandwiches. They were flanked by dill pickles and onions. Farther along lay rye bread, cheese, and pretzels, over the draught beer which was piped under the counter. From behind comfortably propped elbows, thick shoulders, came the slow words, the grunts and chuckles of male talk, chiefly profane. Augustine led the way to a dim corner out of ear-shot. Beer and then roast beef sandwiches appeared before them.

"This is the first meal I've enjoyed in days," Adam said.

Augustine flushed with pleasure. Tainted with hero wor-ship, his companion thought, otherwise not a bad youth. If you've had to consort with Tony Bayne for a livelihood anything's a change. Like a dog that's been beaten so much he wags all over for one pat.

He said, "How is the cheese here?"

"I'll get you some."

Have to be careful or he'll call me "sir," thought Adam. Why do I feel that like the serpent's tooth?

Augustine said, "I suppose we'd better not spoil the beer with crime?"

"On the contrary. . . . You promised to tell me about Tony Bayne's first wife. Her death in the same town right afterward looks strange, to say the least."

"All right," Augustine fixed his eyes on distance and the boyish look was gone. "I'll try to be impartial," he said. "But it's all pretty terrible somehow." He began with his astonishment at finding Fern in Miss Thorne's garden. She had begged him not to tell anyone she was Tony's ex-wife. He had been stupid, he said, to have missed her at the Inn but actually arriving so late, rather so early in the morning, he hadn't signed the register at all and hadn't happened to see her. He'd heard afterward that she had come with Mr. Lawrence. The whole town knew it. Fern had told him—they only had a moment alone—that she'd wanted to see Tony and stop him from publishing some stuff, but hadn't been able to. That was all he knew until this morning when he'd heard she was dead.

"What was the stuff?"

"Well, it was principally an abortion. He spared no detail. The wife was forced into it by her husband. He was one of these Byronic lads who loved freedom. Said he'd leave her if she had a child. So she didn't—three chapters of obstetrics—and he left her anyway. . . . Because he couldn't stand a person not sticking to her convictions!"

"Jesus, how that resembles him! . . . You bring the man to life again."

"Well, I don't want to particularly. It's different about poor little Fern. Do you wonder that she couldn't stand it?"

"But how foolish! Nothing's the same when it's written down. Very few people would have suspected and they would have forgotten the next day. Women who are made into books," he went on absently, "walk into drugstores to buy tooth paste just like anybody else and sit down to tea and nobody remembers, least of all," his voice died to a murmur, "they themselves."

Augustine had that Boy Scout look again. Really as if he knew what one was thinking, though he couldn't, of course. "But you see," he said deferentially, "remorse might have entered into it. I knew them at the time and Fern felt awful. But instead of making up to Tony she began to hate him."

"I still don't see," Adam raised his heavy brows, "a motive for suicide. . . . How did she do it?"

"Poison."

"Taken how?"

"The paper said with sleeping medicine."

He frowned. "It sounds all wrong. But one would have to know the characters. For me the second wife is the deadly one. She's certainly trying to do something to me. I shouldn't put it past her to have poisoned the first wife if we could discover any reason for it. Why did she go to the Inn yesterday afternoon? She got me there under false pretenses and got rid of me with a ham dramatic trick. It was all of a piece with her sham fainting when Tony was killed. She hasn't acted natural since that first night when she cooked dinner." He hunched his shoulders and peered out the window into the black night. "No matter what she's like I've got to go back."

As they walked up the empty street, their footsteps echoing, he said, "You may be sure I'll lock my door tonight."

They turned in at the Bayne gate. The sound of a piano floated from the house as if someone had unexpectedly turned on the radio. Then Adam remembered; that was one of their principles; they hadn't any radio. The notes separated into a clear patter like the beginning of rain. A low beautiful sound joined it. It might have been a flute or a cello; it was too impersonal for a voice. But as it rose and skimmed, dipping like a swallow, he knew that it was—a voice so pure that it wasn't singing itself like other voices, more or less clogged with character. It sang only the music.

They stopped. The sound so absolutely clean of double dealing, so abstract, dropped straight into the heart.

The moon, suddenly sliding from behind a cloud, showed Jake on the porch, his nose pressed to the door.

At the end Adam turned. "I feel like taking off my hat," he whispered. "Can it really be?"

"Yes," said Paul Augustine. "It's the same woman."

13

Half an hour later Adam was sitting in his room in the dark. He had managed everything all right he was pretty sure, and yet inside his ribs he could feel a pounding like a big alarm clock. That aged muscle, he thought, was not used to the antics he required of it. He had walked to the road and said good-by to Augustine loudly for Jake's benefit. On the way back, the moon had slipped under a cloud, he had left the path instantly, sneaked to the garage door, and opened it with the key in his pocket. He'd propped it with a stone and got back before the moon did.

Lucky that Jake had no high order of intelligence. Otherwise—he put one leg out the window cautiously—these juvenile proceedings wouldn't have a chance. He swung down, locked the garage—he hadn't done that the first trip and it worried him afterward—and threaded a familiar way through the shadows. He stole up behind the grape arbor to the French door. His heart beat more loudly. So it was not the exercise. . . . No. . . . His soft rap wasn't answered. He turned the knob—it had been arranged—and went in saying just above his breath, "Ann?"

"Here I am."

He crossed the dark hall quickly toward a dim light in the parlor. There sat Ann Thorne beside the fire with a child on her lap, a child who was asleep. She couldn't get up; she couldn't even move. Her left arm was under the child's head; her right hand was closed around the muzzle of a little dog so that he wouldn't growl. "Come here and let him smell you," she commanded.

Adam went up but did not stoop or try any premature advances. The puppy smelled first one foot, then the other, and the trousers up to the knees. He began to wag his tail.

"Thank the good Lord," said Ann. "I didn't want him waking the house."

Adam sat down and bent, in the firelight, to read her face. "My dear, you look tired."

"I've had a long day. . . . There was the sheriff before breakfast, then I had to go to New York to look up one or two things, and just got back in time for the funeral. That blockhead, Ezra, insists on making you the principal suspect. Really, Adam, it's time for you to take a hand."

"How can I?"

"What have you found out?"

"Well, that my hostess sings like a whole choir of angels. . . . And in spite of it, I have a horror of the woman. I suspect her—of almost everything. But clews? No."

"Tell me about it."

He described Rosa's taking him to the Inn the day before, pretending to faint and vanishing before he could get free from the reporters. "And that's not all," he said. "You went to the funeral?"

"I had to," she sighed. "Nancy insisted on going. To stop a family row I took her."

"Did you see the photographers?"

She nodded, concealing a smile.

"That indescribable woman dragged me up there and made me pose beside her . . . me! . . . What I have suffered for you, Ann! You know quite well I stayed there on account of you. Well, yes, it would be funny if it weren't sinister. Why did she do it? It's quite simple. To give the impression that I'd murdered Bayne. . . . To make me look guilty, and by God I did."

"It wouldn't matter except that the sheriff thinks already that you did it."

"Do you suppose *she* killed her husband, or is she trying to protect someone else?"

"I don't know. . . . I dislike maternal women," she said thoughtfully. "I'm not fair to them."

He took in the tableau. She sat erect as ever, Gubby's tousled head heavy in the crook of her arm, his small relaxed limbs in their flannel pajamas sprawled over her. *The Wizard of Oz* lay open on the floor.

"Yes," he said, his eyes dancing, "maternal women are trying indeed. No excuse for them. None at all. . . . Why, Ann!" He knelt in front of her. "You've hurt your hand!"

She tucked the finger with the gouge in it hastily under Gubby's sleeve.

"It's nothing. . . . If you'd get hold of Tony's manuscript and read it I believe you'd solve the crime."

He shrugged his shoulders. "But I'd rather go to jail."

"Of course, if you won't . . ."

"Would you come to see me in jail? . . . If you would I'm sorry I didn't think of it years ago."

Something moved in a corner. Ann jerked. It clattered, a dry rattle like old newspaper, but alive. She turned white.

He sprang to his feet.

"It's only that damn fowl," she whispered.

"What fowl?"

"A crow belonging to this thing on my lap."

"Ann, you're afraid! I had no idea . . . I didn't know you *could* be afraid. My dear, forgive me. I *will* try to help you."

She didn't look up. She said briefly, "I can use it. . . . Will you begin by carrying this child to bed?"

"Of course."

"I'll walk the pup and bring him, too."

"You'll not set foot out of the house. I'll walk the pup."

"But if someone sees you?"

"Nobody will. . . . I've not played Cops and Robbers with your Jake three days for nothing."

"All right, Adam."

He came back, the dingy puppy trotting behind him on a string, handed the loop to Ann, slid his hands carefully under the limp child. "You lead the way."

She seized the crow's wobbly cage, covered with a cloth fastened with safety pins.

"I promised him," she explained. "He dotes on Jimmy. . . . Go quietly. I've got Nan here too. She'll be a nuisance if she should wake up."

They made a procession up the stairs, along the hall past two closed doors. Ann stepped first into her room and put Jimmy's cage as far away as she could. Then she turned down the covers of a cot that had been placed beside her own curved bed. Adam slid Gubby in. They left the puppy draped over the small mound of his feet.

All the way back in the dark he struggled with his too expressive face. Downstairs he had it straight again. "Just why are you running a Children's Home," he said, "a woman with no maternal instinct like yourself?"

She took a cigarette and held it out. "For good reasons." She sat down. "You know, I suppose, that Tony Bayne's first wife is dead?"

He nodded. "Augustine told me. I had dinner with him. It sounds very odd. . . . Suicide, he said."

"Odd isn't the word. . . . Did he say why?"

"Oh yes, on account of Bayne's book. The sheriff told him when he came and asked for the manuscript. She had an abortion done some time ago apparently and Bayne was just setting out to immortalize it. This drove her to a panic. She was trying to appeal to the father of your animal trainer here as the perfect mother."

She settled deep into her chair. "It's plausible, clever, in fact. Only not true. . . . She was murdered."

"Good God!"

"I'm sure of it, though Ezra isn't quite. He's going to let the papers think it's suicide and pin Tony's murder on her. Poor Fern, it can't hurt her now."

"Why do you think she didn't do it?"

Ann told him about finding the button. "But let the papers have their holiday. It will shut them up and put the real murderer off his guard. . . . In Ezra's eyes that's you, Adam."

"This is all perfectly unreal."

"Oh no, my dear, it isn't." She sighed. "I do need help. Listen to this. The sheriff came for me before breakfast. By the time we'd finished going over the ground it was ten o'clock. And then we realized Mr. Lawrence hadn't been to the Inn. He usually called for Fern every morning. I rang his office in New York and he hadn't been in; they didn't know where he was. I went to his house. Mrs. Hodges said he'd had breakfast as usual and gone out quickly, telling her to leave Gubby with me."

"What does that mean?"

She raised her shoulders. "I haven't an idea. . . . It looks as if he knew something."

"How could he have known unless he'd been there? And, if he'd been there, doesn't that mean he did the murder?"

"Jonathan?" She rested her chin on her hand. "At first sight it's ridiculous. He is New England to the bone, conscientious, conservative, spare—what the French call *sec*—in body and mind. He's a good businessman. And he's accidentally very handsome. But he doesn't seem to profit by that . . . or even to like it. Of course, he's pretty morbid. You only have to look at his garden to see that, all dank and overgrown. I'm sure it's just a nuisance to him to have women pursue him."

"Was Tony Bayne's first wife pursuing him?"

"Oh yes. Gently but inexorably. Had for some time. She was leading the field."

"A man can get angry with that sort of thing. Particularly if she tried to force him. Had she been his mistress? Did she have any sort of hold?"

"I don't know." Her chin sank deeper in her hands. "The actions of an unsophisticated man are baffling to me. There's nothing I distrust like inexperience."

"Dear Ann." He smiled. "I'm so glad to know you've kept up your standards."

She said impatiently, "You never can tell how they're going to react. He strikes me as like Jane Eyre's Mr. Rochester—just something to appeal to the untutored female mind. . . . But even supposing that he had a reason for murdering Fern Ellyn—we don't know what it might be, but it's possible—the point is *why* should he have murdered Tony Bayne?"

"Oh . . . so one person did both crimes?"

"Nothing to prove it, but it's probable. Fern admitted she was hanging round the house that night trying to see Tony. One assumes that she saw the murderer and he killed her so she couldn't tell. There's a bit in the evidence she gave to Ezra that's suggestive. She hesitated when he asked if she'd seen anyone. . . . I myself assume that the murderer left her button some time afterward just to make himself safer."

"That certainly makes sense. Now as to motive. . . . Will you forgive me if I say that it was only necessary to know my late host to have a reason to kill him? . . . How well did this Jonathan Lawrence know him?"

"I can't tell you. He'd been there to dinner. Louella, my sister-in-law, heard about it and was furious."

"If he knew him at all well there are possibilities. First"—Adam held up a finger and tapped it with the other hand—"your New Englander might have admired Mrs. Bayne." He shrugged his shoulders. "Hard for me to imagine but it would explain his going to dinner. The host certainly doesn't. It might also explain some of her actions afterward. She might have preferred to throw me to the lions—Caliban that I am—and shield the handsome one. As you describe him he appealed to women . . . to all but yourself?"

She took a deep breath. "I may not be fair to Jonathan. I'm prejudiced because he doesn't spend much time with Gubby. He leaves him to that tiresome Mrs. Hodges."

Adam held up another finger. "Second—and this is more likely—Tony may have found out his ex-wife was interested in Lawrence. It's likely that he knew where she was working. Especially when she begged him not to publish this book. He must have known by then she was in love with someone else. He could have found out whom; he could even have guessed. And then, knowing his malice, can't you see him playing cat and mouse with her reputation? . . . Oh, throwing out hints, you know, reminiscing, just to watch Lawrence squirm?"

"The novelist's imagination!" said Ann. "I should never have thought of that and as for Ezra Gates' thinking of it he would as soon think George Washington did it or John Quincy Adams."

She's approving of me, he saw with wonder, really approving. He felt the warmth of the fire and stored in his mind its rosy glow in the glass pendants of the chandelier (like a bright shower caught in mid-air) and on Ann's hollow cheek. It's something to know one's moment of happiness when it comes, to put it away forever. It was a short moment after twenty years.

"But why did he shoot *you?*" she said. "We mustn't forget that. It's the crux of the matter. If we could explain that we could explain everything."

"I don't agree with you at all. It was pure hysteria. And much more like a woman than a man."

"Don't make light of it."

"I'm not. It would have been quite easy to pot either of us that night if anyone had really wanted to. And so nobody did. He or she just let fly and then thought better of it."

She clasped her hands. "Who? . . . Why?"

"I don't know. I certainly didn't hear anything the night Tony was murdered; I went straight to bed. . . . I'm not dangerous."

"The person who heard things," she said in a low voice, "was Nancy. She was outdoors though some distance away. She heard one more person walk past, somebody not accounted for. Maybe it was an innocent passer-by. But I'm trying to impress that immature mind with the fact that she mustn't mention it. The murderer might get hysterical again."

"That's why you've kept her here?"

"Partly."

"You've too much on your hands. How can I leave you with all this?"

"What else can you do?" Her voice was dry again.

He held his hands to the fire. "Nothing. . . . But my impulse is to lie down across your doorstep like Peter Pan."

"It would be more to the point," her tone had sharpened to its cutting edge, "if you found but who stole your revolver."

"But I'm no good at that."

"Nonsense. . . . We know already Rosa could have taken it, or that apology for a domestic, Mabel. Paul Augustine was in the house a lot but Jake was always with him, wasn't he?"

"I can find out."

"Well, do. . . . And Mrs. Bayne must have had callers. When the news of Tony's death got out didn't people come round? It's the custom."

"There was a lot of coming and going. Perhaps Jake didn't keep track of them all. I'll see about that too."

"And after you went up to bed the night Tony was killed did you hear nothing? What time was it?"

"Not a sound. Your sheriff asked me that too. It was ten-forty-five as near as we can figure."

"One last thing—will you read the manuscript?"

He got to his feet slowly. "All right, Ann, for you. . . . But it's far from the reason that brought me here. Won't you relent?"

"No." She gave him both hands. "It has become a game we have to play, with life as the stake. My favorite writer*— except you—talks of a great love ending in a game. . . . Didn't we have a great love, Adam?"

---

* Letters of Mme de Sévigné. The one to Mme de Grignan, July 14, 1680.

14

Charles Francis Thorne could not remain at his desk. Usually the books he always left open, the piles of yellowed manuscript held down by curios brought back from China, drew him like a magnet. But now he saw them through a haze. The squares of early sunlight on the carpet, the rather tinny clash of old church bells, gave him no Sunday-morning mood. He got up and began to pace back and forth like some ancestor on a clipper's bridge.

He had attained a false peace long ago by ignoring some things. He'd even justified it to himself. He couldn't change them; why become neurotic? It had seemed better manners to withdraw. But now he wondered sharply if it hadn't been pure cowardice.

First there was Nancy, that most lovely child. He'd doted on her so when she was little that he'd been afraid of his own feelings. Bad for her, these psychologist fellows said. His greatest effort of late years had been to keep from showing it so as not to spoil her. The ambassador, he'd always felt, must have spoiled his sister Ann in some obscure way. Otherwise why had she never married? He was aware that he left Nancy to Louella, but he had trusted that no child of his could take Louella seriously; anyhow she saw a great deal of Ann. But now he wondered if he hadn't been mistaken. His pipe had gone out; he bit the cold stem.

Ever since that distressing night at the country club he'd been shaken. Louella made him go—it was the first

time in years—and try as he would, talk as he would determinedly to the old ladies, he couldn't help noticing.
His child, the prettiest creature there, who could have
had anybody, danced the whole evening with a married
man! At first the nice boys cut in, the boys her own age,
but Bayne always cut back. And then they went outdoors
together . . . oh, interminably!

When they appeared he cut in himself. Nan hadn't
seemed to mind; she clung to him rather. After a decorous
interval Bayne walked up, his black eyes gleaming in that
objectionably Latin face. He tapped him on the shoulder,
but Nan's father said, "I'm sorry. It's time for us to go
home." He gathered together the Thorne manner—there
was plenty of it. "I trust Mrs. Bayne is well?" He stared
carefully, too long. "We're sorry not to see her here. We
miss her."

And then, the day after Bayne was murdered, he'd found
that book, *Madeleine Pigor,* in his daughter's room! What
memories it brought back. He'd never told anyone about
knowing Bayne years ago. Since Bayne hadn't seen fit to
bring it up there was no reason why he should. But he'd
taken the book and hid it very safely.

His feelings astonished him; he was glad the man was
not only dead but buried. Six feet of earth over that pasty
face was a pleasure. And he'd always thought of himself as
even-tempered, thought he could control any tag ends of
savagery. What a mistake!

He lit his pipe and started pacing again. Ezra would
pin this on someone; he'd have to. There'd been that other
murder too, or perhaps suicide, of a woman Louella said
was guilty but Ann said was innocent. It was like a storm
rolling up and thunder sounding.

Nancy had told him Ezra Gates was after that writer
staying in the Bayne house. What sort of fellow was he?
He tried to recall. He'd been made to go to a movie once.
. . . He pushed round the little stepladder and climbed to
the top shelf in the farthest corner where he put modern

15

Miss Ann was resting her mind in the garden. She had sent Gubby to Sunday school in Nancy's charge to get rid of them both. Like her brother she failed to heed the homely clatter of church bells, though the sound soothed her unconsciously as did any fragment of childhood lodged in the memory by accident and then glozed over by the years till it assumed a peacefulness quite absent from the first impression. She was meditating, sleeves rolled up, one foot on her spade, when the French door burst open to emit Louella.

Her sister-in-law's costume was at the opposite end of the scale from her own. To begin with, her figure—not a bad one—was produced less by gardening than by a corset. Over that was the print dress described by thousands, perhaps millions, of middle-aged American women as "summery." A prayer book was held in one gloved hand—the only kind of glove that had ever touched it, white kid. From the brim of the expensive (and really good) hat hung a veil. Behind it gleamed pince-nez. . . . Miss Ann sighed. This was one of the reasons why she hadn't gone to her class reunion; she felt strongly about the subject of glasses and veils. I must try to find it pathetic and not ludicrous, she thought.

Louella came straight up to her and stood a moment without speaking. Behind the veil and the lenses her eyes held a gleam that made Ann, though reluctantly, take her foot off the spade.

"So they have found the murderer!" Louella said.

"Have they indeed?"

"Stop pretending, Ann Thorne! You know as well as I do that that woman did the murder! . . . She proved it by committing suicide."

"Did the sheriff say that?" Ann was playing for time, trying to remember what had been in the papers. Only that a woman named Fern Ellyn had been found dead. There'd been nothing about suicide or about her having been Tony's first wife. Ezra was waiting for the right moment to spring it. (She ought to tell him not to wait too long. The tall reporter might remember where he'd seen her and with whom.)

Louella was panting. She must know something . . . . something that she ought not to know.

"Have you found a connection," Ann said carefully, "between Fern Ellyn and Tony Bayne?"

"Not yet," Louella said. She lowered her voice. The triumph in it was struggling with caution. "But she was there that night in front of his house."

"How do you know?"

"I saw her."

"Louella!" It was Ann's turn for control. "What were you doing there?"

"I had the best of reasons for going. I had found out—no matter how—that Mr. Bayne had an appointment with my daughter. You can imagine I had no intention of letting *that* go on. I heard Nancy slip out the back door. . . . Now do you see why the child has to be guarded? . . . I went out the front. I intended to meet him on his way over. I was not going to mince words; I was going to tell him. It's better to catch these people in the act!"

She was taking short steps back and forth. The glove that gripped the prayer book burst its seams.

Ann stayed perfectly quiet. "And did you tell him?" she breathed.

"No, no!" Louella tossed her head impatiently. "The house was dark. I didn't like to go in; my informant might have been wrong. Besides, there was a car parked somewhere near; somebody might have come out to it any time. I scarcely wanted the neighbors to see me calling on the Baynes! . . . Well, as I was saying, when I came this Ellyn woman was walking away. . . . After she'd killed him, of course. I didn't know that then."

Ann said very slowly, "I can see why you didn't like to tell the police."

"But I *should* like to tell the police! I just didn't think of it at first, not until I heard she'd committed suicide. Then it came to me all of a sudden that she'd done it."

"What time did you see her?"

"I stayed at home until eleven—that was the time of the appointment. It only took a minute to get to the Baynes'. . . . There she was, walking away!"

"Did she see you?"

"She didn't turn around, if that's what you mean. She just wobbled away on those high heels with that big hat flopping."

"How do you know," said Ann, "that Anthony Bayne instead of being a corpse was not at that moment in your garden with your daughter?"

"Because I watched!" Louella said. "I watched the garden all evening, sitting in my room with the light out!"

Ann said gently, "How tiresome for you! I know for another reason. Nan told me."

"What do you mean?" Nan's mother cried. "You knew this and you didn't tell me? That's of a piece with what you've always done. Going your own way, never thinking of others. You could have made the whole thing right in the beginning. But would you lift a hand? Not you!"

"I don't understand."

"Jonathan Lawrence comes here . . . to your house. But he doesn't to ours and you know it. You could have had Nan here at the same time, thrown them together. You could have had us all!"

"Jonathan comes to talk about Gubby. That's his only reason. . . . Nancy's just at the age when she finds children boring. It wouldn't work at all, I assure you. On the contrary . . ."

"Then you could ask *me!*" She had stopped pacing and fixed her sister-in-law with glaring eyes. Only her hands, clenched tightly, trembled. "I know my way around. I could manage him. . . ."

Ann thought uneasily, This is madness. Then she thought, But how hard for a woman to see that her charm has gone, that biology's through with her, when she was young and passionate not long ago and, alas, feels the same!

"Louella," she said earnestly. "Did you see anyone else near the Baynes' house that night? Did you see anything else?"

"Don't try to put me off!" Louella cried. "I want to know why you don't help me? Why you don't arrange things between Nan and Jonathan?"

"In the first place he's out of town just now. . . . Will you answer my question?"

"No, I won't! Why should I? What difference does it make? That woman's out of the way now. That's the important thing. Why do you have to start making difficulties? . . . Don't you do it, Ann Thorne. Don't think for a minute I haven't got my suspicions of you. If I had to I could get you out of the way too!"

Ann could only look at her, the habit of control keeping her face a mask. Bits of Louella shook, the ornament on her hat, the large, loose forearms under their thin sleeves, the top of the bosom pushed up to resemble youth.

Could she have done it? She was strong, the Auvergnate. Could she have killed them both? Was she crazy

enough and clever enough too? Certainly she was there at
Tony Bayne's. Instead of her seeing Fern Ellyn walk away,
Fern Ellyn might have seen *her* and so become a danger.
Mrs. Charles Francis Thorne could have gone to the Inn
any time. She could have changed the sleeping powder,
dropped the button in the garden. Above all, she had the
huge self-confidence to believe murder might be a right,
indeed only an incident in her plans.

Shivering quietly inside herself, Ann said, "I'm glad
you told me this, Louella, but don't tell the police. If they
knew you were there that night you'd have to answer a
great many questions. You don't want your name dragged
through the papers, or Nancy's either. . . ."

"I'm not afraid of answering questions."

"You don't know how hard it would be. And think,"
she said, inspired, "how Jonathan would hate it, hate even
seeing your name as somebody who was questioned. He's
the kind to believe you can't touch pitch without being
defiled. He's so very old-fashioned."

A shade crossed Louella's face; her sister-in-law took
her arm. "And when all this is over I'll do what I can to
see that he and Nancy meet, at least." She was steering her
toward the door.

Louella said suspiciously, yet with an eagerness she
didn't bother to conceal, "I'd have to be there."

"Of course," said Ann. "The bells have stopped ringing. If you don't hurry you'll be late to church."

As soon as the door had closed she found a large sheet
of paper, a pen, an ash tray, and sat down. It was time to
figure who could have seen whom that night. She wrote
across the top—

"Persons Near the Bayne House the Night of Anthony
Bayne's Murder."

The first column was for the three people in the house,
Mrs. Bayne, Mabel, Adam Carthage, the next Fern Ellyn,
then Louella, then Unknown with a question mark.

Half an hour later the ash tray was full, the chart had led to no conclusions. It did show a fifteen-minute gap (if witnesses could be believed) that was important.

It showed quite plainly that Fern Ellyn knew, must have known all along, whether she'd realized it or not, who the murderer was. If she hadn't killed Tony herself she had obviously seen the person who had. Wait a minute. . . . If it had been someone in the house, would she have seen him or her? Yes, very probably. That person would have come out after Tony or called to him before Fern Ellyn had a chance to get to him herself (that is, if she had told the truth).

Then either it was someone whom she suspected and wanted to save even at the risk of being accused herself or it was someone she thought must be innocent and so didn't want to involve. The only person she would save at all costs was Jonathan Lawrence, or else . . . or else (this cost Ann a wrench) little Gubby. But no—she took hold of herself—he couldn't have been wandering around at that time of night. *He could not.*

As for people Fern Ellyn would have thought innocent? Well, she had met Louella and without doubt been impressed. Would she have been so overcome with awe that she failed to mention her presence at the scene of the crime to the sheriff? Or did she remember so vividly being snubbed by the lady that she was afraid to mention it for fear Louella would make things even worse for her? Louella would have tried, Ann thought grimly.

From now on, whatever way one looked at it, her sister-in-law was a principal figure. If only she'd been in a mood to answer sensibly about what she'd observed! She might very well have seen something dangerous. That one item about the lights being out was sufficiently odd. If she had noticed more and if the murderer knew she had been there *or should come to know,* her life wouldn't be worth any more than Fern Ellyn's.

	Wednesday MURDER OF ANTHONY BAYNE			Thursday ATTEMPTED SHOOTING OF ADAM CARTHAGE			Friday MURDER OF FERN ELLYN (BAYNE)		
	Time	*Means*	*Motive*	*Time*	*Means*	*Motive*	*Time*	*Means*	*Motive*
GUBBY LAWRENCE	Impossible for the child to be awake at midnight	Unlikely to have been able to throw the stone	Bayne disliked animals (weak)	Could not have been up then	Could not have taken, shot, and replaced revolver	None	His father took her to see that evening	Impossible for him to have understood sleeping medicine or possessed poison	Didn't seem to like her
PAUL AUGUSTINE	Did not arrive in Middlebury till 2 A.M.	Possible	None known	?	None	None	Possible	Possible but unlikely	None known
ROSA LIEDERSTRAUM BAYNE	Possible	Possible if a woman could have done it	Hasn't shown much grief Might have been in love with Paul Augustine Investigate	Possible	Possible	None known	Perhaps she was at the Inn the afternoon before the murder. Investigate.	Possible	Jealousy. To palm off first murder on her
FERN ELLYN (BAYNE)	Possible	Possible if a woman could have done it	Admitted	Not known	Impossible	None	(i. e., suicide). possible, in fact probable, except for one button and the fact that she had guts	Possible	Despair at loss of Jonathan Lawrence or (if you assume she murdered Tony) fear of discovery
ADAM CARTHAGE	Possible	Possible	None known. They had a quarrel.	Possible	Possible	Red herring	Probably possible. He was at the Inn. Investigate.	Possible	Fear of having been discovered doing first murder. Knowledge that she was the logical one to frame

I shall have to tell Ezra, thought Ann, in order to get her some kind of protection. . . . But suppose she killed Tony herself, am I to be the one to give her up? Or suppose she can't prove she did not, am I the one to get her suspected and put through all the ghastly business of a trial? She would convict herself a hundred times, her mind is nearly unhinged already.

She was sitting with her head in her hands when Nancy floated in like a leaf on a breeze. Her aunt collected herself and looked up. "Where's Gubby?"

"Just having a Sunday fight with the choir boys. . . . They do look angelic in those white collars, pulling each other's hair out!"

Her aunt regarded her dispassionately. It had been a mistake sending those two together.

"Nancy," she said with care, "those footsteps that you heard the night of Tony's murder, the ones we can't account for, where did they begin?"

The lovely eyes opened. "I told you they walked past our house and down toward the Baynes'."

"But where did they come from? How far away were they when you heard them first—two blocks, one block, or a shorter distance?"

A tiny, unaccustomed frown knitted the young forehead. "I only heard them in front of the house. Then they went toward the Baynes'."

Miss Ann sighed a long, heavy sigh. "Then they could have come from your own front door."

"I suppose so." Nancy was interested, even pleased at explaining something. "There's the grass matting on the porch steps. I wouldn't have heard them till they hit the sidewalk. . . . Who in the world could it have been?"

"Tell me again what time you heard these footsteps?"

"Before eleven. It was right after I went down."

"And, child, you said it was a heavy tread." Ann fixed her with her eyes. "I told you before not to mention this

but now it's more important than ever. Her very life may
depend on its being kept a secret. . . . It was your mother."

"Oh no, Aunt Ann." The blond curls shook from side
to side.

"She treads heavily."

"That's only when she's wearing high-heeled shoes. She
just wears them for special occasions. Her oxfords are rub-
ber-soled and you can't hear her any more than a cat. . . .
I have reason to know."

"But was she wearing rubber soles that night?"

"Yes. I remember. She went upstairs early to put them
on because her feet hurt her."

And to spy on you, thought Ann. That I shall never tell
you.

"They didn't sound like Mother's steps," said Nancy.
"They were longer." Her face cleared. She said brightly,
"I'll tell you who it might have been. It might have been
Father!"

16

Gubby had come in then with a bloody nose and the bright eyes of anger. Miss Ann had to leave her older charge to take her younger to the lavatory.

"What was it about?" she said, applying cold water.

"That Butch," he said. "Butch Hamilton, the dirty . . . you know what . . . he said it was my father's fault."

"What was?"

"That lady, ump . . . that died in the Inn." Between his feelings and the washcloth, words came out in jerks.

"How was that any concern of your father's?"

"He said my father . . . fttt . . . shouldn't have brought her here. He said Mrs. Thorne told his mother. . . . And he said . . ."

"It's all a pack of lies."

"Thad's what I said." His eyes beamed thankfully though one was partly closed. "Bud why?"

"Now come and put your mind on Sunday dinner," she said hastily. "I'll tend to the eye afterward. It's chicken and ice cream for the first time in years. Nancy will find it very unsophisticated."

It was evening before she had a chance to speak to Nancy alone. Gubby had gone to bed and the early fall darkness closed them in. That was the only sign of the end of summer; it wasn't cold enough to light a fire. But Hannah had closed and locked all the windows, while her mistress looked on, and drawn the pale-green curtains over them.

The old brocade had faded to a color which a visiting decorator called "Twilight at Fontainebleau" (and then Miss Ann refused to let him see the upstairs) but the stuff was still thick. She ran her hand over it, no rents or tears; no light would come through.

Nancy flopped down—it was hard to do in those chairs but she managed it—and said, "About those footsteps that I heard that night, I still think they were Father's."

"I never heard such nonsense."

"But why shouldn't Father have gone out in the evening if he felt like it?"

"Your father is a creature of habit. It was not his habit to do any such thing."

"I think you're wrong, Ann. Father is a man of mystery." She was warming to her work, forgetting the uneasiness she had felt at first. A faint pink stained her cheeks. But though it was unfair to Nancy there was something slightly absurd in her effort, as if a flower or a baby were trying to reason. "I don't mean he went to the Baynes'," she said. "That's absurd. I never realized it until the other night but Father likes to go out. You should have seen him dancing at the country club. He's really good—for his age, of course. . . . He's been so absent-minded lately that it isn't any joke. The more I think of it the more I think he's got some interest we know nothing of!"

Miss Ann crushed out her cigarette with more force than was needed. She had been trying to decide all afternoon whether to tell the sheriff about Louella; she forgot to be diplomatic. "You must really curb this schoolgirl imagination!"

"Just because I'm young is no reason I can't have an opinion!"

"True. But it seemed to me a wrong one. For years your father has been finding his recreation in books and on the whole that's pretty satisfactory."

"Oh, do you think so?" She sat bolt upright; the pink in her cheeks spread out determinedly. "I don't and I'm

Father's daughter. . . . I never agreed with you about Tony either. . . . I'm sorry to say this, Ann, but you brought it up. I just don't think you know much about men!"

She misunderstood the expression on her aunt's face. "How could you," she went on, "living all alone here?"

There was a guarded knock on the French door.

Miss Ann flew to open it. Hannah had gone upstairs. There were a few words spoken in low tones. A familiar figure followed her into the room, familiar to all readers of literary magazines. It was often photographed for the back or front pages behind a typewriter with pipe, or taking a trout off a hook. The wizened face, with its deep wrinkles like a gargoyle, was very ugly and very distinguished. The light-blue eyes twinkled amazingly out of the dark tan. They twinkled at Nancy, briefly however.

Her aunt said as briefly, "This is my niece. . . . Mr. Carthage." Then she said, "Adam, it's too risky. . . . I don't like your coming. Suppose the troopers ever found it out, that you could come and go secretly?"

"They would arrest me for two murders," he said promptly and sat down with the air of a man intending to stay for some time. "But they won't. . . . The first night, it's true, I made a mistake. I left the garage door open. But nobody saw it. That was pure luck. Since then I've closed and locked it every time and before going up I sleuth around to see what Jake is doing. Don't you see, Ann, the beauty of the system? Of course I can't close and lock it after me when I climb up, but then, if Jake should see it, I'd be in my room. They couldn't prove I knew a thing about it."

"Just the same, it's dangerous. . . . Being arrested would not be amusing."

"I never thought so." His voice had a deep purring sound like a large wildcat unexpectedly settling down on a hearth. "Wouldn't you come to see me in prison? It might, after all, be easier than the expedients I have to use now."

"You know what I think of the romantic attitude," she said. "Nancy, I fear it is your bedtime."

Nancy had hardly been able to keep her mouth from opening like her eyes. She got up with a jerk.

"We trust you will not mention seeing Mr. Carthage," said her aunt. "He chooses to come here—he's an old friend—but it's quite true the sheriff would arrest him if he knew."

"Of course I won't mention it," said Nancy. "But I'm glad I saw him—if you don't mind my saying that much."

She smiled at Adam, gave her aunt a cryptic glance over one shoulder, and walked lightly out of the room.

"How pretty," Adam said. "She might be your daughter."

"I suppose so. . . . Children so rarely resemble their parents."

"Ann, you don't do her justice. . . . There was just your kind of intelligence in that eye."

"Perhaps . . . but I like to think I should never have been attracted to a fourth-rate writer."

"What! Was she one of Bayne's conquests? No. I don't believe it."

"Well . . . she was experimenting. It hadn't gone far."

"Is she the daughter of that brother you used to worry about?"

"Yes. . . . But I don't remember worrying."

"You did. He was trying to be a painter and your father wanted him to go into politics. They used to write each other angry letters."

"That was a short phase, I remember now. My brother couldn't hold out. Poor dear, he never could for long against anyone. . . . He was sent to Washington and made to have a career but, of course, it failed. Now he's lost himself in the past, New England history. He's writing."

"Writing!" Adam sank back in his chair; the wrinkles deepened round his mouth. "I've read the manuscript," he said abruptly, "that last one of Bayne's."

Ann leaned forward.

"It was indescribably bad, indescribably."

"And then?" She was holding her breath.

"Worse than pornography," he went on, disregarding her. "It was a parody of serious work. He'd read *An American Tragedy* all too well, but instead of treating the subject with that heavy pity that you have to respect even if you can't admire, he made it into burlesque."

"And then?"

"I copied out a sentence or so for you. You can see."

"And after?"

"*Et après? Et puis alors?* You're still translating." The corner of his mouth quirked tenderly. "And also you knew what I'd do. . . . I did."

"And what was that?"

"I read *Madeleine Pigor.*"

She waited.

"Right after I'd read the manuscript. They're not by the same person."

She gave a long trembling sigh. She relaxed for the first time and moved back into the depths of the bergère. "I was never *quite* sure. . . . I do thank you, Adam."

"Here is the evidence." He fished into his pocket. "I expected to surprise you, fool that I am. But listen, anyway. This is from Tony's manuscript, the one Fern Ellyn worried about, poor thing. 'Up till then my senses had been so numbed by shock that I'd only been vaguely aware of the drama in which I, myself, had played so large a part. Out of the welter of confusion that fomented in my tired brain one fact emerged with terrifying finality. Whatever it was that he was accusing me of, I couldn't be guilty.' And a little later we have this gem, 'I would have infinitely preferred to have been allowed to see "the other woman" (in quotation marks) with my own eyes.' You see, Ann? 'Terrifying finality!' 'Infinitely preferred!' And the vulgarity of those quotation marks. . . . Whoever would read stuff like that?"

"Plenty of people," Ann said, "if the abortion was really in it. . . . What's the other paper?"

"This is from *Madeleine Pigor,* not a specially good bit, just picked at random. It's when Ewald begins to get sick. 'You know how it is there in the ward in the morning when you wake and remember that you can't move all day? I'd shut my eyes and step into my car, the little boat I'd bought for nothing just to work on evenings when there's not enough light to paint. Off she would go on a smooth road and through the shadows of the trees like bars across it and we'd pick up speed, the engine humming, the wind going like silk past my ears. . . . I'd never even hear the nurse till she stuck a thermometer in my mouth.'"

"I see your point," said Ann.

"And then an idea struck me," Adam said, "that *Madeleine* might have been written by a woman. It's very sensitive; one could say ultrasensitive. And all about jealousy. . . . Is it possible Fern Ellyn could have written it? She must have had occasion to be jealous of Tony during their marriage and nothing is easier than to reverse the sexes."

"Yes," she said. "Yes. . . . I've always felt that this discrepancy in Tony's writings was a crucial point in the case. . . . I don't know how yet. I never believed in him." She murmured, smiling, *"On n'a jamais pris longtemps l'ombre pour le corps; il faut être si l'on veut paraître. Le monde n'a point de longues injustices."**

Ann started to get up as if their talk were finished, as if it were time for him to go.

He said quickly, "But you haven't told me yet what you've found out? Surely something . . . in twenty-four hours?"

This sounded reasonable, not just an excuse. She took another cigarette. He was careful to light it quickly and

---

* Letters of Mme de Sévigné. One to Mme de Grignan, September 9, 1675.

casually, not lingering as he might have so easily . . . oh, no!

"I've found out only what I wish I hadn't. My sister-in-law, Nancy's mother, is mixed up in this. I never told you that my precious niece—that replica of me, Mr. Carthage—had a date with Tony the night he was killed, something I shouldn't have done at seventeen or even at seven, I'm sure. Her wretched mother, who at best is difficult and at worst—she's at worst now—very nearly insane, found out about it and barged off to stop Tony. Oh yes, she was there in front of the Baynes' house at eleven o'clock that night! . . . All day I've been wondering if she killed him!"

"Poor Ann! . . . What's she like?"

"Yes, that's important. . . . In her youth she was handsome, full of vitality, rather common, the high-cheek-boned peasant type, the Auvergnate we used to call her. She reminds me of somebody in a book as she was in those days. . . . Good Lord, can it be?"

"Yes?" he said. "Better go on."

She shot him a quick look, almost scared. Then her chin lifted. No one had ever accused Ann of cowardice. "You're clever, Adam, you really are. And quite right. . . . She was like Madeleine Pigor. . . . Of course, it has no connection . . ."

"Your brother didn't have a long illness," he said lightly but definitely, "and worry about whether she was faithful to him?"

"Lord no! . . . Never been ill in his life. Just the wrong type for her, that's all. An introvert, he's turned out to be. And she's never been unfaithful to him. That's the trouble. She's turned her energy to being an executive, runs the town—all the good works, you know—with an iron hand. And no nonsense about a velvet glove. . . . But it doesn't make up for things. Now that she's getting on she's begun to feel it. The poor Auvergnate. She's like a piece of elemental force lunging about, blind."

"Nancy has quite a heritage, I see. . . . And where does she lunge to, your sister-in-law?"

Ann wrinkled up her forehead. "In the direction of Jonathan Lawrence. Not consciously. But she's been trying to throw Nancy at his head. I didn't understand till suddenly I saw that she's crazy about him herself. . . . The word crazy is used advisedly."

"Ah, now we're back to Mr. Lawrence." He put his brown finger tips together judicially and spread them out fanwise. "Has he returned? Have you heard from him?"

"No," she cried. "No! It's just one more mystery. The whole thing is almost too much to bear. . . . Only a single ray of light have I seen today and just when things were at their worst."

"And what was that, my dear?" He was purring again. She hadn't mentioned his leaving in some time.

"I've felt pretty desperate about Louella. You see, she was there. . . ." She ticked off the points with her hand. "She's unusually strong for a woman. She had a motive to kill Tony Bayne. Half mad as she is, she would have done it, I thought, without turning a hair. As for Fern Ellyn, Louella hated her as a rival actually though she put it on high moral grounds. She would have poisoned her with pleasure!"

His eyes glowed at her like pale lamps. "And then you found some reason why she didn't do it?"

"Not quite. Nothing as good as that. But I remembered that the crimes are three, the third one the attempt on you. And I knew she couldn't have done that." She said triumphantly, "First, she had no motive. Second, she couldn't have got your revolver!"

His eyes shifted to the ground. It was as if shutters clicked over them.

"Adam, what is it?" she cried.

"I'd better go back."

"Not before you tell me!"

"I was pleased with myself," he said, "for doing every single thing you wanted. . . . I thought you'd be pleased, too."

"But I am. I will be."

"No. Ann. . . . Do you remember what you wanted?"

"Of course. To find out who could have taken the revolver, besides the people in the house. To find out whom Jake watched and whom he didn't watch."

"Right. Well, among the outsiders Jake kept his eye on Augustine. The sheriff told him to. Augustine wasn't alone there a minute. He couldn't have taken it."

"And then?"

"Jake didn't watch the callers. He thought they were . . . just callers."

"Who were they?"

"I brought you the cards," he said reluctantly. "You always used to like to see for yourself."

He laid the small white heap in her hand slowly, as if the gesture hurt him. The top card said, Mrs. Charles Francis Thorne.

17

Breakfast was going more briskly than usual in that house. A child had to be sent to school on time. They were already late because of arguments about taking various animals; at the last moment a small toad had been extracted from his pocket. Far from resenting the bustle, Hannah enjoyed it. She picked up Gubby's napkin when it had fallen on the floor for the third time and tucked it expertly into the neck of his shirt. "Mind if I comb his hair, ma'am, afterwards?"

"It *is* combed!" Gubby said indignantly, his mouth full of toast. The front lock was plastered damply back on his forehead; the rest waved in all directions like a storm at sea.

"What that old Susan Hodges would call combed," muttered Hannah, under her breath.

Even more surprising was Nancy's appearance, exactly on time and shining with that exquisite neatness which is supposed to take hours. She wore a short white tennis dress, quite vigorous for so early in the morning. She had been reading late last night too, her aunt noted. She herself had slept little and when she got up to look out of the window, listen, smoke a cigarette, there was that crack of light under her niece's door.

Miss Ann was breakfasting mechanically, using the discipline she had learned long ago. Her mind was made up;

the long hours of the night had seen to that. She would wait for the children to leave. Then she was going to tell the sheriff about Louella.

Still, unaccountably, when they had gone—Nancy vanished as if she'd heard a school bell too—Miss Ann lingered. She pushed her chair back, her eyes absently fixed on the newspaper unread in front of her. A shadow fell across it.

There stood Jonathan Lawrence in the French door, taking his hat off most correctly.

"Good morning, Ann." He gave her a formal smile and there was nothing she detested more. "I believe I have a child here."

"If you were more acquainted with the ways of children," she remarked, "you'd know that school has begun. . . . That's where he is. It's after nine o'clock."

"Oh, I'm so sorry." He wavered, his shoulders stooping, his face very pale with circles round what other people no doubt thought fine eyes. To Ann they were like eyes in an historical engraving. They scarcely belonged to him; they were an hereditary trait.

"Come in," she said after a little pause and led the way to the parlor.

She couldn't help feeling awed by his looks. Her memory in a flash went back to a sentence of Adam's. If the person Louella had seen at the Baynes' the night of the murder was Jonathan Lawrence it was the one name that would never pass her lips.

Hannah had drawn back the curtains and opened all the windows before breakfast. The room was as fresh as the garden and smelled of new-cut grass. He sat down gratefully.

The morning light showed up the tired gray color of his skin. Yes, for some reason he had suffered, though she preferred men who did it without remaining impeccably groomed.

"Where have you been?" she said sharply.

His long fingers propped his forehead. "I suddenly realized Gubby ought to go away. He ought to go at once. . . . So I've been trying to arrange it."

"What do you mean?"

"I've been visiting boarding schools."

"You picked a strange time!"

Her heart had contracted with fear, with new worry, but she forced herself to say, "Didn't you know about Fern Ellyn? Wasn't she your friend?"

"I knew," he said. His voice was very tired. "She was my friend, a charming friend, but not a relative. . . . Of course I read the papers but I knew before that."

"And you didn't even come to inquire, to tell us who her relatives are? . . . The sheriff has been looking for you everywhere."

"There are always people to do those things," he said heavily. "But no one can do anything when a father fails to take care of his son."

Oh, she thought, the New England conscience is mixed up in this. She merely said, "Are you quite sure you know about it all? A great deal has happened."

"I knew it," he repeated, "before I went. . . . I'd better tell you from the beginning."

"You had indeed."

"It was that morning, last Saturday. I was just finishing my breakfast. Gubby had had his long before and vanished with some animal or other. Mrs. Hodges answered the phone and came in very excited. Her nephew is one of the sheriff's deputies and he'd called her up—you know how it is in this town—to tell her that poor Fern had been found dead. I was terribly shocked. I didn't notice Gubby had come back and was there in the doorway. I didn't even see him till Mrs. Hodges went back to the kitchen.

"He came in and sat down, 'Oh, she died, did she?' he said like one who expected it. Distracted as I was I couldn't fail to pay attention to him. '*Before* you married

her. I thought she would only after. That's why I didn't
want her round.'

"You see we'd been having a set-to because he'd been
rude to her.

"'Why should you think such a dreadful thing?' I said.

"The answer was burned into me. I shall remember it
always.

"'Mrs. Hodges told me I killed my own mother. . . .
I don't know why. That's why you don't care much about
me.'" (Jonathan winced, bringing this out.) "And then he
said, *'I thought I might again. . . . Why is it, anyway? I'd
like to have a mother like other boys.'*"

Miss Ann's eyes filled with tears. "I never suspected.
. . . I thought I was rather replacing . . . in a way . . . . But
it was just an old maid's vanity. . . . And all this time the
poor child had that burden on him."

The tears ran down.

Jonathan Lawrence stared a moment, then he seized her
hand. "Oh, Ann! If you could ever feel toward me as you
do toward Gubby! . . . I'd be so happy . . . so more than
happy. . . ."

She sat quite still, unable to take in the change. Looking at him again she saw that, yes, it was true; she'd heard
aright.

"Nonsense," she said briskly. "Don't make a fool of
yourself just because I have."

She shook her head so violently the little drops danced
off. . . . Though most astonishing, this was familiar
ground. She could handle a man's feelings whereas she had
been wholly unprepared for Gubby's.

"I'm twice your age," she said severely. "Once and a
half anyway . . . and as set in my ways as a steam roller.
. . . Give me your handkerchief."

He did, rather bewildered. She wiped her eyes and then
blew her nose vigorously. Ethel Barrymore, she thought,
one of her best parts. Glad I remembered it.

"There now. . . . Admit you never thought of it until
this moment . . . and are already quite relieved . . . ?"

The constraint of good manners struggled with other
emotions in his face. Since there had been five generations
of constraint in his family it was strong, but he couldn't
conceal the other feelings entirely or his shame at having
them.

She returned the handkerchief and left her hand in his
with pity.

"There are certain situations," she said, "that lead to
proposals of marriage . . . well, geographically . . . just
as certain terrains in Europe invite battles. It's nobody's
fault. . . . You have to know your history, though, to see
they come from circumstance alone."

She twirked one eyebrow, the left. It had been the most
famous one. "I know mine."

He couldn't help looking grateful. Partly to conceal it
he bowed his head and kissed her hand.

Mrs. Charles Francis appeared in the doorway.

18

Nancy was walking back to her aunt's with Paul Augustine. She yearned to get back to some sort of normal activity and yet she didn't want to face her own crowd, not yet. She had finally persuaded him to try a set of tennis with her at the club.

"I can borrow everything you'll need," she explained.

"I shall be shockingly bad," he said wryly. "I haven't played in years. I want it understood the reason I'm going along is merely to oblige you."

"A visor here," she replied. "Racket from Johnny Ames—he has the best ones—and shoes out of somebody's locker when we get there." They had turned in at the gate and walked a few steps up the path. Even on the road (they hadn't paid attention) strange noises had seemed to come from somewhere in front, noises nobody could associate with Ann's house. But now a voice hurtled at them out of the drawing-room window, a hoarse voice, "Don't try to explain! I don't believe a word you say. Of all the under-handed treachery . . ."

"Why, it's Mother!" said Nancy, stopping in her tracks. She had been hearing it for several minutes but it was so queer and cracked she hadn't known what it was.

A voice said slowly and distinctly like cold water dropping, "I tell you again, Louella. . . . Jonathan was simply thanking me for taking care of his son. These threats, these accusations, are ridiculous."

The strident tones went on. "So this is what you do, living all alone here! . . . Why, it was only yesterday you told me . . ." She squeaked an octave like an adolescent boy and stopped.

The other voice said icily, "Jonathan came in on the train not half an hour ago. Look at him. You can see he's tired. If you have no regard for me you might have for him."

"You mean you two want to be left alone." The sound that must be coming from her mother cracked again. "Oh, *very* well. I'll see you later, Jonathan, don't worry. I shall come to see you . . . this very evening after you've had time to think it over. You'd better be there if you don't want me to take steps at once!"

"What in the world is this?" whispered Paul Augustine.

A door shut with a muffled bang inside the house, feet stumped along, the outer one burst open, and out came her mother almost falling; she didn't see the familiar step.

Nancy jumped to help her. Mrs. Thorne jerked back. Nancy stared at her, really frightened. The usual semblance of her mother was there, hat mathematically straight, iron-gray hair held tidy in a net, but the face, even the neck down to the V of her blouse, was mottled with queer blotches, red and white. Behind the trembling glasses her eyes were deep wells of pain, undeserved, not-understood pain like an animal's.

"Don't touch me," she croaked and then saw Paul Augustine. "What are *you* doing here? You go away, young man. Go right away at once!"

She stumbled off along the path, not looking back, and disappeared behind the bushes at the gate.

For a moment Nancy stayed poised. She did not wait to see her mother on the road, but sighed. "I suppose we'd better go in."

"Is it wise?" Paul said. "Somebody wanted to be left alone."

"I can *always* go to see Aunt Ann."

Mr. Lawrence was coming toward them in the hall. He looked strange too, frightening, like her mother. Giving them a quick nod he stepped out through the dining-room door.

Nancy went straight to the parlor. "We didn't mean to overhear," she said. "But oh, Aunt Ann, what is it? . . . Mother looks so awful!"

"How much did you overhear?" said Ann urgently. "I know you couldn't help it but *how much?*"

"Just a few words. We were coming up the path."

"The first words I heard, or at least noticed," said Paul Augustine, "were 'underhanded treachery.' Does that help?" He spoke with the extra consideration he always had for her.

"Thank you. It does." He was rewarded with the quick appreciation she always gave back. "Nancy, your mother's under a great strain. I'm afraid she's near . . ." She hesitated and then found the words, "A nervous breakdown. Complete."

"But what made her like this?"

"A pure misunderstanding. Mr. Lawrence was thanking me somewhat emotionally. . . . Your mother thought she'd discovered"—she lifted her shoulders and her eyebrows both—"a secret passion."

"That's not unlikely," said Paul Augustine. "On the part of Mr. Lawrence or anyone else. I could point to better men, far better, who've felt such a passion, and still do!" He smiled. "One doesn't have to be crazy to think that!"

Nancy whirled on him. "My mother isn't crazy! And besides, so would you be if you'd walked right down to the Baynes' the night of the murder!"

She stood with her fists clenched. Miss Ann put a hand on her shoulder. "There, child. . . ."

"You're not being fair," said Augustine quietly. "You know I didn't mean that."

"Nancy, apologize," said Ann, pressing down her hand.

"I do. I'm sorry, Paul." She collapsed into a chair. "But somehow I don't feel like playing tennis." She twisted her mouth miserably. "This morning I tried so hard to forget all about it!"

A shadow crossed his face, his too-sensitive face that showed so quickly every disappointment. "Perhaps you'll feel like doing something later, a walk this afternoon, dinner tonight?"

She still looked stricken. "Call me up," she murmured.

"What a child it is!" said Ann. She linked her arm through Paul's and led him toward the door; the friendly gesture brought an answering smile.

Nancy wasn't too far gone to notice it and think, He'd be about as well satisfied if she'd have dinner with him.

When Ann came back she said, "I've had to phone the sheriff. . . . Do you mind?"

Nancy got up and started for the door. There was a long crunch on the gravel outside, a scream of brakes, and then a shudder of loose metal flapping.

"That can't be the sheriff," said Ann. "It's too soon. Wait, child. I may need you."

Over Hannah's slow disapproving head another one craned in the doorway. It was the tall reporter from the Inn. He looked more loose jointed than ever. Even his face looked that way. Like an old-fashioned kaleidoscope it fell with a clack from one set of patterns to another.

"Good morning, madam," he said. "I've just had a hunch, and that's bread and butter in our trade. I thought you could save me a lot of time. I thought you'd know. . . ."

He had got entirely into the room and his face changed abruptly. All the bits of expression flew round and stopped in a new shape—astonishment.

"Hello," he said. "Nice decorations . . . very." The survey pointedly included Nancy.

He caught himself up. "I've just remembered . . . or thought I remembered," he said, "that this second corpse—

pardon me, ladies—she called herself Miss, but wasn't she the first Mrs. Bayne?"

Nancy looked at her aunt for a cue and then she had no eyes for the reporter.

Miss Ann had been leaning back, tired, relaxed, for the moment even older than her years. She gave herself a little shake and seemed to slip into harness. When she leaned forward her eyes shone with a flattering light.

"Now *isn't* that interesting!" she breathed.

The reporter had a new feeling that he was a clever boy indeed. It took the edge off his curiosity.

"It would make everything fit in so wonderfully," said Miss Ann. "I'm sure you play chess."

"A little," he said modestly, "I don't remember clearly enough meeting her with Bayne to swear to it. I have to have proof. . . . Could you give me any?"

She shook her head. "The first time I ever met the poor thing was that afternoon when you saw us. But you must be right; it would explain so much. The sheriff's office is bound to have looked her up. Why don't you ask him?"

"And have him give a statement to the other papers? No, thanks. This is *my* brain child."

"While you're here," she said, "wouldn't you like to look at the scene of the crime? I know you saw it with the troopers but they herded you around. My niece could show you more at leisure."

"That's a fair offer," he said looking at Nancy, getting to his feet at once. "Chip off the old block. . . . Compliment, decidedly."

They had hardly started down the lawn when Nancy thought she heard the sheriff's car, but the reporter was talking. He talked a great deal, calling her "sister" frequently. It was fortunate because on the way to the door her aunt had murmured, "Keep him as long as you can."

She felt as if she were holding a string of firecrackers and somebody had lighted the one on the end. He seemed to feel quite otherwise. He measured things with a pocket rule and then sat down on the grass and told her about other murders he had covered.

When they came back they met no one. She saw him to the door and hurried to the kitchen. "Hannah, where's Aunt Ann?"

"Gone out."

"Where to?"

"She didn't say."

Feeling absurdly lonely Nancy climbed the stairs. The reporter's stories had shaken her more than she cared to admit. She shook her head; she just couldn't take it. She was not used to being afraid!

"The thing to do is figure it out," she remarked firmly then. The first point was to change her opinion about her whole family. Mother now—she had been unreasonable before, heaven knew, but always commanding, wielding a high hand. It was incredible to think of mother at a loss. And she'd been crying, sort of shattered. *What had she done to make her like that?*

Nancy tried then to think about the footsteps. She couldn't be sure. What had possessed her to bring Father in? Well, she had hated to be the one to tie them to her mother.

All she knew really about the case Aunt Ann had told her. There was a subject for you, right there. Just an old maid with a sharp tongue until last evening, pottering about with chrysanthemums. And then the famous Adam Carthage appeared out of thin air and sat down in her parlor.

She reached out her hand for the book she'd started last night, the only one by Adam Carthage upstairs. She'd learned in an English course that he was a Classic. That prejudiced one; besides, of course, one thought a Classic was dead. If she had only known he was alive and had those queer pale eyes and that deep purring voice!

This book was called *Spring in Savoy* and it wasn't bad. . . . She'd always thought the First World War too boring. She'd been made to look at so many pictures of Aunt Ann getting the Croix de Guerre, that long skirt dragging in the mud and that hat, much too big, sitting on top of her head like a pancake. They certainly cared nothing about appealing to men in those days.

Yet this book was like Romeo and Juliet—love, and death waiting round the corner, love never safe a moment from death. . . .

Hannah startled her a great deal by saying it was time for lunch.

She had an unsatisfactory meal with Gubby. The only conversation was halfhearted attempts to improve his table manners but Hannah recommended harshly in her ear to let the poor child alone.

"Well, if they want to spoil him, let them!" she said to herself and was about to add, "A couple of old maids," when she stopped, an odd expression crossing her face. She got up quickly and went back to the book.

19

When Ezra came into the room Miss Ann had the feeling that they were measuring each other with their eyes like duelists taking up positions. Tut, tut, she said to herself, this will never do, and rushed into speech.

"Ezra, it's hard for me in one way, yet I've got to tell you. . . . Mrs. Charles Francis Thorne was near the Baynes' the night of the murder."

"Oh yeah?" said Ezra. "She just happened to remember it?"

"I quite agree with you," Miss Ann said soothingly. "She says she didn't want to mention it unless it was necessary. She was in front of the house about eleven o'clock and saw Fern Ellyn walking away. Then when Fern Ellyn died she jumped to the conclusion that she'd done the murder and committed suicide. You see she didn't like her. . . . You know my sister-in-law, Ezra."

"I know all the family," said Ezra with meaning. "When did she tell you this?"

"Yesterday." This sounded weak. She added quickly, "A great deal has happened. Mr. Lawrence got home too and came to see me."

"And what's *his* story? Did he get home *yesterday* too?"

"This morning. . . . You won't believe his story unless you understand the way he feels about his son. Gubby's mother, you remember, died in childbirth and Mr. Lawrence—old-fashioned as it seems—never quite forgave the

175

baby. He didn't mistreat him, of course, just paid him very little mind, stayed away from home a good deal, and so on."

"The whole town knows that," said Ezra. "You been bringing the kid up."

"I didn't do much of a job. . . . When Fern Ellyn died— the housekeeper told them about it—Gubby showed his father how badly he felt at not having a mother. That upset Mr. Lawrence. His conscience started to work. He saw he'd been neglecting the boy and he rushed right off to find an expensive school that would somehow make it all up to him." She sighed.

"Hum," said Ezra. "It might be true but it's not much of a story."

"You can check with the schools."

"But that's all afterward. . . . He would have had plenty of time to poison the girl friend."

"Why should he? . . . And we can't connect him in any way with the murder of Tony Bayne, neither motive nor evidence."

"Nobody's worked on it," said Ezra. (She was, of course, unable to tell him Adam Carthage had.) "I'll see him," he stated firmly, "myself."

He had lighted his pipe and it was drawing well.

"The one that worries me," she ventured to say then, "is Mrs. Thorne. I've been trying to figure out who could have seen whom the night of the first murder. . . ." Her hand, which was resting on the table, absently played with a piece of paper.

"I'll take a look at it," Ezra said, but with a manner that did not commit him.

She pushed over the sheet headed, "Persons Near the Bayne House the Night of Anthony Bayne's Murder."

His eye went down the columns under "Mrs. Bayne" and "Mabel."

"I saw Mabel again," he observed. "I can't break her down."

Persons Near the Bayne House the Night of Anthony Bayne's Murder

Time	In the House			Outside		
	Mrs. Bayne	Mabel	Adam Carthage	Fern Ellyn (Bayne)	Louella Thorne	Unknown?
10:15		Doing dishes until "after ten."				
10:30	Saw a strange woman (Fern Ellyn) in front of the house (from upstairs window—bathroom)—was putting out towels for guest.	Overheard quarrel at end of which Mr. Bayne went out and slammed the door—the front door.		Said that she arrived about 10:30, heard quarreling and did not go in.		
10:45		Did Mabel really then go to bed?	Says he went right to bed when his host went out in a rage, and heard nothing afterwards. (No proof.)	What did she do when Tony Bayne came out and slammed the door? Did she meet him on the path, walk to Miss Thorne's garden with him, and kill him (all in 15 minutes), or did she see someone else go to meet him and hang back? If the latter, why did she hesitate to tell the sheriff?	(No proof that Louella didn't arrive sooner than she said.)	Someone else could have arrived during this 15 minutes and been seen only by Anthony Bayne and Fern Ellyn, both now dead.
11				Seen by Louella, two or three minutes after eleven, walking away.	Says she arrived only to see Fern Ellyn walking away—no one else. The house was dark. *Who put the lights out?* Did Tony Bayne go back and do it? If, so, why?	

His finger stopped on the space labeled "Adam Carthage."

"'Ten-forty-five,'" he quoted. "'Says he went straight to bed when his host went out in a rage, and heard nothing afterward.' It's a good thing you put 'No proof.' There certainly isn't. Since he was wandering around the next night in the dark, why wasn't he that night too?" He looked her in the eye. "I've never been satisfied about why he went out the second night. Couldn't have been just to pretend to shoot himself. That's thin. Suppose he wanted to plant that little button you set so much store by? Makes a lot more sense."

"He couldn't have *got* the button."

"Neither could he get out," Ezra said, "without Jake seeing him, only he did. The guy's talented."

"Most people use a stronger word," murmured Miss Ann.

His thick finger traveled to Fern Ellyn's row. "'Ten-forty-five,'" he read. "'What did she do when Tony Bayne came out and slammed the door? Did she meet him on the path, walk to Miss Thorne's garden with him, and kill him (all in fifteen minutes), or did she see someone else go to meet him and hang back? If the latter, why did she hesitate to tell the sheriff?' I've thought about that. Let's suppose things are your way—that is Fern was murdered. Maybe she saw someone meet Tony, someone she didn't suspect; that person saw her and they made an agreement not to tell just to avoid trouble. Remember Fern was very anxious nobody should know she'd been married. Then you call up and say to be 'frank,'" He accented the word. "She tells everything except about the other person being there. . . . She's waiting to get his or her permission. But the party's too smart for her; he knows what's going to happen. So he kills her."

Miss Ann's shoulders had drooped. "I'm afraid you're right."

"Let's see the new number," he went on more kindly. "Mrs. Charles Francis Thorne. 'No proof that she didn't arrive sooner than she said.' Why do we have to have proof when there's so much else that's doubtful? 'Says she arrived only to see Fern Ellyn walking away—no one else. The house was dark. . . . Who put the lights out? Did Tony Bayne go back and do it? If so, why? . . .' Well, there you have a funny one. Did you ask her if she'd seen anything suspicious?"

"I didn't have a chance," Miss Ann said. "She was all to pieces. She's due to have a nervous breakdown, I think. . . . I wanted to ask her . . . oh desperately . . . and then I suddenly realized it wasn't necessary. I could deduce it."

"How?" He took his pipe out.

"You see I know who did the murder."

"Oh, you do, do you?" He pointed to her last column, where it said—between 10:45 and 11—"'Someone else could have arrived during this fifteen minutes (the fifteen before Mrs. Thorne got there) *and been seen only by Anthony Bayne and Fern Ellyn, both now dead.*' Do you mean to say you were there too and only just got around to mention it?"

"Oh no," she said. "I wasn't there."

"Then you're concealing evidence again. What is it?"

"That's the trouble. There isn't any evidence. I've got to have some. That's why I need your help."

"No, lady, not this time." He shook his head. "You put me off once that way with Fern Ellyn. Look what happened. She's dead. I pity the person you're suspecting now!"

He started to get up.

"But, Ezra!" she cried. "This time we know where the lightning will strike! It's Louella. There are just two possibilities. Either she did the murders or she knows too much and is in danger herself. You've got to protect her!"

She looked at him with anguish. He stood there, the dead pipe clenched in his teeth.

"I hate to tell you," he informed her, "but I know who the murderer is, too."

20

She stared at him helplessly. How could one get through this blank wall? Ezra had been so kind at first but he had turned against her on account of all the things she just couldn't reveal.

"We're keeping a close watch," he said, "on Mr. Adam Carthage. No more little trips to the village. And that's going to stop the crime wave."

He looked at her expectantly. She couldn't argue this time. Nothing that she could say would convince him. Even if she could bring herself to tell him he wouldn't believe it. The knowledge sank into her mind like a stone. It all depends on me, she thought, with something close to panic. The essence of the thing is time. I must be quick. If he won't help me he must get out of the way.

"There's a reporter in my garden," she said, coming close to Ezra. "From the *Star,* I think. He's just remembered meeting Fern Ellyn when she was Mrs. Bayne. If you don't want the *Star* coming out with it and knowing more than the sheriff you'd better hurry back and give a statement to the press."

"What's a reporter doing here?"

"Being detained by Nancy on account of my friendship for you."

He was impressed and yet in the hall he had a flash of suspicion. "How did you get to know him?"

"I picked him up in a bar," she said wryly, showing him the door.

Miss Ann had her hat and gloves on before the sheriff's car had crunched out of the driveway. Hers had been left at the side for Pete to wash. Walking rapidly toward it, busy with her thoughts, she was entirely unprepared for what met her eyes. Large A's had been scratched on the doors and, to make it quite plain, little obscene pictures. She couldn't help shivering. She made herself say, Imagine anyone thinking I should miss a literary allusion.*

She raised the hood and looked in, thankful that she had lived in other places too long to have acquired the trustful habits of the village. She always locked the ignition and took the keys with her. Everything seemed all right. Well, she said to herself, it's an excuse to go to Ellison's garage, where I was going anyway. I'm glad I have friends there. I'll tell them children did it, but it wasn't children. She drove with new, uneasy caution, paying more attention than usual to cars suddenly coming out of side streets. Luckily Ellison and his son were there and nobody else.

It was a long time later when she walked home still alert—even more so after what she'd found out—but taking time to wonder what mood Nancy might be in. The child had been shaken that morning; her mother's trouble had been too much on top of the murders. But she would probably be back to normal by now. She would have formed her own theories and become hostile again to grown-up advice.

The parlor and the garden showed no trace of a white tennis dress. Doubtfully Miss Ann climbed the stairs; slowly she raised her hand to knock at her niece's door. She got a quick answer. It was already odd for Nancy to be in her room sitting down quietly at that time of day. Her

---

* Readers will scarcely need to be told that she meant Hawthorne's *Scarlet Letter*.

aunt was too preoccupied to notice it. She went in, took off her hat, and pushed back her hair, the same gesture—she didn't notice that either—that the heroine of a certain book had made coming out of a little mountain station, watched by the blear-eyed hero from above.

"Can I trust you?" Miss Ann asked abruptly.

"You certainly can!"

The fervor of the words astonished her. She brought back her absent gaze and concentrated it in front. "What's that you're reading?"

"*Spring in Savoy.*"

There was a moment's silence while ideas were rearranged. "I congratulate you," Miss Ann said quietly. "A very good book."

"Aunt Ann, I'll do anything you say, anything!"

Her aunt smiled, not without sympathy. "It isn't exciting . . . just an errand."

"I've missed you so all day! Where have you been?"

"Having my car fixed."

"All this time? Did you need to stay?"

"I've always liked monkeying with cars and I invariably find the conversation of garage men interesting."

The younger pair of shoulders shrugged. "And what's the errand?"

"I've reached the point with Ezra Gates where he no longer believes me. I do need somebody to help. . . . So I shall have to call on Mr. Carthage. Will you take a message to him?"

Nan's eyes rounded. "I'd love to! . . . And that *is* exciting."

"I hope it won't turn out that way. You know this has to be most unobtrusive. The deputy on guard there, Jake, mustn't know you're delivering a message, nor that impossible servant nor, of course, Mrs. Bayne. I shall give you some flowers for Mrs. Bayne. Be sure you go inside—don't stand at the door—and when you give the flowers to Mabel talk in a loud voice. I hope Mr. Carthage will hear and show up somehow while Mabel is taking the flowers to her mistress."

"Good! . . . I may have to use my ingenuity."

"Be sparing of it," her aunt said. "Though you did a good job with the reporter this morning. Remember you're not supposed to have met Mr. Carthage. A pretty confusion is indicated if there are witnesses. I'll give you a little note in a card envelope to put into his hand in case Jake stays in earshot."

"What shall I wear?" said Nancy, her eyes shining. "Black?"

"Hardly. . . . Mrs. Bayne's the widow, not you. Besides, I think that phase is over, isn't it? Now that you've met Paul? It would be nice to have one piece of pleasant news."

"Yes, actually it is." The lovely face was filled with frank though momentary wonder. "I know it's not a week yet but so much has happened! I don't have time to think of poor old Tony now. . . . Shall I pick the flowers?"

"Please do. Dahlias unless you can find something bigger and brighter. . . . And afterwards I want you to take a note to your father."

Nancy was startled. "Why don't you call up?"

"There are things," said her aunt with a slight air of the conspirator, "that are better not said over the telephone."

The child lilted out and through the open windows came the sound of humming. It struck Miss Ann as something from a past that was far away now. The garden had become a scene laid for the tragic and sinister. It did not belong, as it had for ten years, to bees and sunshine and her well-tempered thoughts. It had joined the dark chaos of the outside world.

Her long fingers left off propping her chin and took up a pen. The note to Adam was brief and in French—for the purpose of giving a few moments' pause to the sheriff should it fall into his hands. To her brother she wrote,

Dear Charles,

Louella has unwittingly become involved in the crimes as you doubtless suspect from her manner. I believe her to be in grave danger and hope you will watch over her.

Could you manage to keep your child in her room tonight? I have been worried about her from the first and have been standing guard without her knowing it but I can't any longer. Please don't let her go out *under any circumstances*. In case you're not going to be there remember the lock Louella had made for her door.

After the quarrel your wife and I had on that subject you can be sure I should not suggest your using it without reason.

Always,

Ann

21

With Nancy gone, her aunt had a strange impulse to lie down, to take a nap, to rest, forget it all; she was feeling her age. Then Gubby's little voice came floating up the stairs.

"I'm home from school," he shouted with complete lack of necessity. "I'm taking my dog for a walk." Six small feet skittered across the hardwood floor accompanied by a series of bumps that could only be the crow cage. Jimmy, willy-nilly, was going too.

Miss Ann rang for Hannah. "I need coffee today, not tea," she said. "And then pack Gubby's things, will you? I have to take him home."

Hannah knew her employer well. She brought the breakfast tray with the large silver pot and even ventured to put a shawl around the drooping shoulders since they were by an open bedroom window. "Just like that horrid statue of Voltaire" came from beneath the shawl, but it was not jerked off.

A hand reached out and took a very small and dainty napkin embroidered with daisies. The Dames de Nevers had made it for Miss Ann because of the help she had given their Garderie des Enfants and her many visits to the convent with its swept cobblestone courtyard. All these years it had pleased her after evenings "in the world," as the good sisters would say, to wake up to daisies and that innocent, embroidered "Bonjour." Ah, the "world"! Especially that winter she devoted to forgetting Adam! That was when she'd acquired the Garderie just to keep things balanced.

She laid the little square of convent linen on her knee and poured a cup of black coffee. There's no one else to do it, she kept saying to herself. . . . I've got to. And there's such a lot of other people's business to attend to first. . . . I've got to get ready.

The cabbage rose now, Mrs. Bayne. She needed attention, oh, badly! Her actions had been far from clear all along. What was the motive that transformed her, at her husband's death, from a French cook to a German siren? Was she grateful to somebody unknown who'd rid her of the unspeakable Tony, more grateful than that pale Fern Ellyn had dared to be? Either that or she might have taken things into her own strong hands. In any case, what was her motive? Had she loved their visitor, the young-old, withered, but still boyish Paul? Did she mind now his leaving her for Nancy? Nancy's extreme danger had always been present in Ann's mind; she'd taken steps to keep her safe that evening. Going back, did Rosa by some strange quirk mourn for Tony? Or did she reach out blindly in all directions at the first chance? Had she been thwarted? On the whole, Ann thought not. She remembered her last summer among her vegetables with her corsets off.

Adam now, one could understand Rosa's turning to him, the man in the house, at Tony's death. But Jonathan Lawrence! Here she came up against her usual stone wall, her neighbor's unfathomable naivete. It was beyond her to imagine what Jonathan thought. Why, he might even think Rosa a fine figure of a woman! Gubby wouldn't. That was what mattered.

Why was he sending Gubby off to school? For the reason he gave or a quite different one? She hadn't been satisfied with Jonathan on his return from that mysterious trip. Or any other time, to put it bluntly. Why did he want such a small child to go away? Wasn't it really to get rid of him?

She took a second cup of coffee, then a third. I must not be pale, she said to herself. How restful not to have to be attractive! But there was nothing else for it right now. Back into harness. After all, he'd proposed to her—was it only that morning?

She tossed off the shawl and then her clothes like last years' leaves, stepped cringing into a cold shower, wrapped herself up to brush her hair hard, and then got out her best tweeds, only two years old. The shop where she'd bought them in London had been flattened to the pavement by a bomb; she was pretty saving of them. Then came the lipstick made especially to match her mouth—no one but Hannah ever knew she used one—and exactly one drop of the sharp powdery essence of mimosa that Monique de St. Hilaire had sent her just before the fall of France, as she had done every year before that for twelve. This was in gratitude for having got back her Marquis whom Ann had wrapped up and delivered on his proper doorstep. Monique was an intelligent woman otherwise, thought Ann, but the Marquis wasn't worth the perfume. Had the Germans taken him prisoner? she wondered. If so, he was doubtless trying to like blondes. He was nothing if not adaptable. A contrast to Jonathan.

She then took Gubby's little suitcase, a stray jar with holes punched in the top, and went to tell him that he had to go home.

"How about leaving the puppy with me?" she said, on an impulse. "Just overnight?"

"All right." He made no other comment, but in spite of the crow cage, the suitcase, and the glass jar he managed to put his hand in hers.

She held it firmly while they went down the path. It was dark under the trees, even darker by the front door under the pines. That was where they went. They needed a ceremonious entrance. She pulled back Gubby, who was for bursting in, with one hand and, putting down the baggage, knocked with the other.

Jonathan, after an interval, opened to them. Behind him, through the door to the parlor, she could see a large bulk overflowing one of the prim chairs, a bulk dressed in widow's weeds. Father and son greeted each other briefly.

Miss Ann crossed the hall. "Good afternoon," she said in her clear voice. "I haven't seen you, Mrs. Bayne, since the morning after your bereavement. I hope you got my messages of sympathy?"

"Oh, yes, yes! Thanks, Miss Thorne. And thanks for the flowers." Rosa put one hand to her bosom automatically as if to go into a routine for grief. A strange collection of expressions chased themselves over her face; slowly the plump hand fell.

"That seems long ago now," she said frankly, giving the whole thing up. "At first I didn't know what I should do. A lady like you, Miss Thorne, you don't know what it is not to have any job. Artist or not, a person has to eat. A person gets hungry. With Tony gone I thought I was going to starve. Me! A woman that understands food like I do."

"He left her nothing," said Jonathan quickly—too quickly.

"I see."

Somehow Gubby's hand had returned to Miss Ann's.

"Nothing," said Mrs. Bayne. "Only a manuscript. We always spent it all. I was afraid I couldn't get much for that; Tony's books weren't doing so well lately. Of course, with Mr. Carthage staying in the house there's hope. Tony told me a good word from him would sell anything!"

How simple it had been. Miss Ann lashed herself secretly. The heavy allurements had been just for cash.

"But now," Rosa beamed with a watery light, "Mr. Lawrence has fixed it all—oh, so beautifully! He heard me sing, long ago when he came to dinner. You never did, Miss Thorne. He's a businessman. He knows I am an artist, a great artist. He asked why I didn't go into radio. Tony was always jealous of that. He refused to let me. Now Mr. Lawrence has made for me an appointment with a friend of his in NBC. It is all settled, my whole life!"

She turned on Jonathan a smile that had heat like a hundred-watt bulb.

"I'm glad," said Miss Ann. "I only hope you won't be disappointed, that you're sure . . ."

"Of course," said Rosa superbly. "Because in radio they can't see me! That," she added, "is business. Gentlemen understand it. Ladies don't."

"You are fortunate in your friends," said Miss Ann.

Jonathan was still standing awkwardly. He moved a chair forward. "Won't you sit down?" He was almost pleading.

Perhaps if she did, she could find out, get some idea of what the situation was. Besides, there was that hand still clinging to her. She'd have to dispose of the child somehow. She went toward the chair. But just by chance it happened to be near a window. She saw with a stab of fear the light was almost gone. What if the dark should overtake her? What if it was a trap?

She gave Gubby a quick squeeze and tore loose her fingers. "I can't stay now," she said. "But will you come to see me, Mrs. Bayne, later this evening? I shall be at home."

She'd reached the door before her host could open it. She was out like a wild thing and the next moment hidden in the trees. There she could stop to listen. Nothing. A leaf fluttered down. The thick growth by the house had been deceptive; outdoors one could see, even in Gubby's creeper-covered path.

None of her plans were made—that was the trouble. She didn't know where Carthage was, or anybody else. She had no weapon. The attack, in spite of her calculations, might come any time . . . anywhere.

Gauging with straining eyes the width of every tree trunk, every concealing bush, she slipped along, careful not to snap twigs. It took am age to reach her garden. Even there she hung back; the open stretch might be a menace.

Out of her barn lumbered the heavy form of Pieter Puyster.

She gave a sharp gasp of relief. "Wait," she called. "Wait, Pieter! I need you. . . . There's some work to do tonight!"

She thought to herself, And you are just the man to do it, mixed up in this as you are.

22

Ezra felt irritable even while he ate his supper. The reporters should have acted pleased, but did they? Hell, no. Why hadn't he told them before about Fern Ellyn? What else did he have up his sleeve? The big fellows knew enough to cooperate with the press, city policemen. Only hicks were clams. Who did he think he was—Lindbergh? All this while they were fighting to get New York on the phone.

He jammed his hat farther down on his head and got up stiffly. He would stroll down to Mr. Thorne's to calm himself. And incidentally try for a little more information. The pickings had been mighty few on Sunday in spite of Mr. Thorne's promise to help.

The very sight of the Thornes' reassured him, that gleaming front door, the perfect arc of the fanlight above, the tidy, respectful way Deborah let him in. Nobody would have guessed she went to Sewing Circle every Thursday night in the world with his wife. The Baynes' Mabel usually said, "Hi, there!"; Miss Ann's old Hannah sniffed as if he were the garbage man got round by mistake to the front, but Deborah bowed her head at what he felt was just exactly the right angle saying, "Come in, Mr. Gates. . . . I think Mr. Thorne is in the library. . . . Will you wait a moment? I'll see."

Then he was following her back, with its crisscrossed white straps, into the high, book-lined room.

Mr. Thorne rose from an easy chair by the fire, pushing aside the coffee table with one hand, holding the other out. The way a gentleman welcomes another gentleman, Ezra thought. If that whole mob of reporters could see it, it would be a lesson to them on how to treat officers of the law. Never mind Mr. Thorne's velvet coat. He might not be doing much now but he had been in Congress when his dad was alive. He had friends in high places still. Let's see, the ambassador bought the seat by raising the tariff on . . . was it leather?

"Won't you join me?" Charles Francis said. "I'm being deserted. . . . My daughter has a studious streak."

He nodded toward the corner where Ezra made out Nancy climbing down a stepladder and saw with amazement that she had a pile of books in her arms. She struck him as anything but a scholar.

"Good evening, Mr. Gates," she said. "I was just going up to my room. I know that you and Father want to talk. . . . Be sure to solve the case!" She gave them an odd little smile.

He hurried to open the door—it was ajar; she could have done it with her elbow—and managed to see the title of the books. They seemed to be the complete works of Adam Carthage.

"My wife, I am sorry to say, has a headache," Charles Francis went on. "She usually attends to this. But I think the coffee's still hot."

He had grasped the silver pot when Ezra said quickly, "No thanks." He really couldn't go those little cups, certainly not without women around.

"Oh, I see. Would a highball be of more use . . . after what I feel sure has been a trying day?"

"It would. . . . . And trying isn't the half of it."

Deborah came again, in answer to the ring, and brought another tray, clinking this time with ice cubes and White Rock.

"Has Mrs. Thorne's medicine come yet?" her husband asked.

"Yes, sir. . . . It must have come quite early in the afternoon but I didn't see it. When I phoned the second time they said the boy had left it on the hall table and there it was all right but it wasn't me that opened the door for him."

"Well, anyhow, she has it by now." He turned to the cabinet where his bottles were kept and poured brown liquid into a tall glass, mixing it carefully with ice cubes and White Rock. "Take her this, Deborah," he said, "with my usual sermon on the medicinal value of brandy."

When she had closed the door he went on, "Confidentially, it's the brandy that does her good but you wouldn't expect my wife to admit that. She always waits until she's sent for the prescription. (A confounded nuisance! It has to be made up each time.) Then, you see, when she's taken both she can avoid saying the brandy helped her. You know your Middlebury, Ezra." He touched his glass to the sheriff's. "The ladies, God bless them!"

Ezra drank without much attention to the age of the whisky. He couldn't help thinking what Miss Ann had told him—that her sister-in-law was near a nervous breakdown because she'd seen something or other. Maybe he should be talking to her instead of her husband. The husband seemed remarkably easy. Didn't he know about his wife's experience, or was it a pose? Well, anyhow, better remember what he came for. One Thorne at a time.

But for a moment a doubt crossed his mind. Those brown eyes in that dreamy face above the coffee table weren't at all absent-minded; they were remarkably sharp. As for the face itself, it was the mustache—just a little too long—that made it seem artistic. It made him look like that painting of that guy that wrote *Treasure Island*. Shave him and cut his hair down close and he'd look like somebody else. A little like his sister or—hold on—the ambassador! . . . And a foxier man never came out of Connecticut.

"You didn't like Bayne, did you?" Ezra said suddenly. "I remember when the Chamber of Commerce got him to write that piece about Middlebury you phoned in and raised—between the two of us—you raised hell. Maybe I better know why."

"I dislike vulgarity," the other said.

"Did you know him before he came here?"

Mr. Thorne sighed. "In my salad days I knew everybody. That's why it's such a relief I don't have to now. I met the late Mr. Bayne in Greenwich Village when I was too young to know better. Why is it youngsters don't learn earlier to be particular about where they do their drinking?"

Ezra grunted. "How about this motive you were going to find for me? This motive Adam Carthage had to do the murder?" He spoke truculently.

Mr. Thorne raised an eyebrow.

"No, it's not the one highball talking," Ezra said. "You made a promise. You as good as accused a man. How about it?"

"I haven't forgotten." Mr. Thorne set down his glass. "As a matter of fact I went to New York yesterday to look Carthage up in the library. I brought back a lot of articles I've been reading today. . . . I told you Sunday it wouldn't be easy; there's nothing definite. I just have reason to suspect his whole character."

"Why?"

The film came back over the brown eyes, made them as hazy as if the owner were wandering in a fog.

"There's an evil streak in the man. It's hard to explain. In the first place, why did he study medicine and then never practice? . . .The art of healing surely is a better life than this scribbling. It takes a grueling preparation; he did all that."

"The war is supposed to have hit him," Ezra said. "The World War. I looked him up in *Who's Who* myself. He's supposed to have started writing in the trenches. Publishers ate it up so he kept on. . . . Maybe you would yourself!"

"Oh, I'm familiar with the legend. . . . But there's the short story about the young doctor who killed a man by mistake and covered it up so nobody ever knew, but he couldn't rid himself of the memory and at the height of a brilliant career he suddenly stopped, went into retirement."

"Stories, stories!" said the sheriff. "What I want is evidence."

"You have to have patience." The voice was very suave. "This Carthage was an expatriate for years. He gave the impression America wasn't good enough for him to live in. That in itself is suspect. What did he do here? Something to make the place hot for him, I'll be bound. His cynical attitude had a bad influence on young people, especially writers. . . . There was an article about it in the *Transcript*. . . . After that, he got mixed up in republican Spain. Took to doctoring among the prisoners who were in concentration camps in France. He didn't do that kind of thing at all in the World War."

"All this," said Ezra, "doesn't tell why he murdered Bayne."

"My sister," Mr. Thorne let out, "used to know Carthage." He stopped.

Ezra looked at him keenly. "So she told me. . . . She doesn't like to talk about him." He added to himself—And you talk about him too much, without saying anything either. What's the idea? Covering up some trick of your own?

"Tell you what we'll do," he went on easily. "Go and see him together. Maybe you can find out more than I have. Find out why he really came here."

"I've never met the man, you understand."

"That won't matter. I can introduce you." Under cover of this irony he thought—And maybe, even if we don't get anything on him, I can find out your little game.

Charles Francis Thorne twisted in his armchair. "I have a note from Ann," he confessed, "telling me to take care of my wife and daughter. . . . I don't like to leave them."

"She told me the same thing," said the sheriff, watching the uneasiness with interest. "And for the same reason—to get us out of the way of whatever she's doing."

"If you think it's quite safe . . ."

"As long as we keep Carthage under observation we don't need to watch anyone else."

Mr. Thorne still faintly objected. "There were all sorts of young men here this afternoon wanting to see my daughter. . . ."

"That's quite natural," Ezra said patiently.

"Deborah didn't know them. . . . I think I'll just make sure—as Ann suggested—that she stays at home."

He got up, more confident on his feet, and strolled out of the room. Since the door was left open and the house was quite still, Ezra couldn't help but overhear, nor—to do him justice—did he try not to. Dignified steps went up the stairs, paused. There was a knock, a murmur, "Still reading, dear? . . . Goodnight." Ezra distinctly heard a key grind in a lock. The footsteps paused, perhaps outside another door, but now there was no knock, no greeting. They resumed, came down.

Charles Francis hesitated, with that shyness that made you want to help him, in the doorway. "Do you really think there's any need to protect my wife? She usually goes to sleep after one of her headaches. I didn't like to disturb her."

"Of course there's no need." The sheriff had got up impatiently. He put on his hat and strength returned to him. Without it he was like Samson shorn. "Nonsense," he rumbled. "She's right here in her own home."

"I must say," said Charles Francis with his quizzical smile, "if there's any woman in the United States able to look out for herself, it's Louella."

He led the way to the door.

Upstairs Louella crouched in front of the mirror, her face covered with cold cream. She'd held her breath while Charles was outside. But even if he had seen her, had been astonished, she would have lied, got out of it somehow.

She wiped the cream off—a pack, it was called. Yes, the mottles were better. With plenty of powder her skin looked all right. Her eyes had improved too with the compresses and drops. They burned back at her with a fiercer fire than youth knew anything about. She sprayed perfume on her curled hair.

If Jonathan could be attracted by Ann who was at least a year older than herself . . . I must have made mistakes, she thought, been hopelessly conservative. I've become too New England, overdone it.

She took a box of rouge and put some on her cheekbones. After all, she was the full-blooded type. And then mascara to bring out the eyes. There, that bore some resemblance to the girl who had mowed down the stag lines at parties in Chicago till one day Charles Francis Thorne came to one by mistake.

She peered with satisfaction; without glasses Louella was very nearsighted.

Her head still throbbed. She took a stinging gulp of brandy. No, not when Jonathan was waiting for her; he'd smell it. She'd have to depend on the medicine. That smelled too—worse than usual, much worse. She took a mouthful; it was awful! Tonight Louella wasn't bothering about being refined. She spit it out, right back into the glass. And saved her strong, unhappy life in that quite vulgar way.

23

Charles Francis did not favor this expedition. He merely saw no graceful way of getting out of it; in fact, no way at all. He had felt the sheriff's manner change from pleasant deference to suspicion. Damn his own rashness at putting a knife into Carthage when he couldn't, of course, back it up without hinting about Ann which he'd be hanged rather than do. Damn the sheriff for coming in as he was finishing that cursed book. If it hadn't been just that moment when he hardly knew what he was saying, he wouldn't have said it! . . . One got along so well with a fixed policy of silence. People let you alone then; they let you stay by your fire with a glass of old whisky, an old book. Damn his own damn asininity.

He touched his hat with the brim a little too wide—the same calculated fraction by which his hair was too long, a fraction that avoided conforming but stopped just short of eccentricity. He pushed it to the back of his head and endeavored to stroll. This was made difficult; the sheriff was hurrying. One would have to divert him.

"I declare," he remarked, "if there isn't the old character who gardens for my sister. I've never seen him up so late."

The long block between his house and the Baynes', lined mostly by the backs of gardens and high fences, was unlighted. Louella had often urged him to take it up with the town council, but his inertia was immense. He'd made

an art of it, he admitted. Ann hadn't. Her road, now, from
the Baynes' corner on, was lighted brightly. He hadn't really seen Pieter; he'd recognized the gait, that elephantine
roll.

"You can't imagine what hours he keeps," he told the
sheriff. "Rattles around with wheelbarrows long before
dawn. Then when you chide him for it he says sternly,
'Time to get oooop.'"

No answer from the sheriff, no amusement. When they
were up to Pieter, Gates flashed on his torch. It showed
the pink impassive face, the curving bulk, and far below to
the rear a small, dingy puppy of no breed at all with one
ear pointed up and one which would have been except that
it hung in shreds.

"Hump. . . . Going to the pound?" said Ezra.

"No, mister. . . . Gubby's dog."

"Where *are* you going?"

Pieter said solemnly—he was imperturbable—"Little
dog likes to walk."

The dog sat down wearily; he laid his head in the dust.
Pieter's blue China eyes stayed moveless in the glare as
hard as marbles.

"You watch your step," said Ezra, snapping off the
torch.

They moved on.

"That's the guy that found the body," Ezra muttered.
"He better stay out of the case. Or else it won't look good.
. . . Foreigner!"

Charles Francis by this time had given up trying to
change the sheriff's mood. He was aware that there were
situations where charm had no place. Hadn't he been in
Congress?

The dark road, the muffled thud of their own steps,
wore on him. Everything was too hushed, too muted, waiting . . . for what, in God's name? The shadowy figure of
Carthage that he didn't really know, that he only imagined, crouching to spring out? Had that figure pushed

someone off a cliff (or tried to) . . . Ann, for instance? Poisoned someone else? And then, not being punished for it, making capital in fact, gone on cleverly—the man was brilliant—quietly, obeying no law, making his own?

The lamps of the Bayne cottage (a gimcrack place by day) shone out mercifully like a harbor. Walking up the flagstone path they could see a stolid shadow in the entry—police, he supposed. A reassuring sight. And it was reassuring to hear the sheriff's gruff voice, "Everything quiet, Jake?"

"Yes, sir."

"Mrs. Bayne in her room?"

"No, sir. She's gone out."

"Gone out? Why didn't I know? Did you phone me?"

"She just went calling on some neighbors, Mr. Gates. But she's been gone quite a while now and I thought I'd report. I been trying to phone but this here's a party line and they been changing the date for the church supper down to the Methodist church."

"I got you that time," said the sheriff angrily. "We've seen your shadow for at least five minutes and you've been sitting right here."

"But Mabel's using the phone now!"

Words failed Ezra. A dull red crept upward from his leathery neck and filled the little veins in his face.

"You told me," Jake stuttered, "that this Carthage was the guy to watch and I ben doing it. Kep my eye on him all afternoon and when he had visitors and through dinner and when he offered me a drink of whisky I didn't take it and here I ben setting with my eye on his room."

He gestured to where a half flight of stairs swung upward from the living room to a small balcony that formed an entrance for one door.

Ezra didn't deign to answer. He jerked sidewise with his head. "Come on up, Mr. Thorne. If I stay any longer with this flat-foot I'm liable to commit murder myself."

He stalked up the half flight of stairs, his hat still firmly planted on his head. Charles Francis took his off quite
pointedly as Ezra knocked; the sheriff failed to take the
hint. He merely knocked again impatiently. Then he tried
the door. Locked. He knocked a third time, shouting,
"Carthage, open up!"

Silence. He put his shoulder to the flimsy wood and
burst it in.

They could see all around at once. The room was empty.

Ezra turned on his heel, snarling, and charged the helpless Jake. Charles Francis followed, but at a distance, as he
would a wounded tiger. Ezra was spitting out descriptions
of Jake's ancestry, his make-up, what he had been doing
while Carthage escaped. He went on to Jake's future now
that he was fired. By this time they were down the stairs,
Charles Francis creeping along the wall.

Another time he would have found it all very fascinat-
ing and novel. Now he was as worried as the sheriff and
far more collected. He gathered from the orders showered
out in the profanity that Ezra's idea was to go back after
all and watch Louella. His was different. He thought that
Carthage, once free, would go straight to Ann. He hadn't
read *Spring in Savoy* for nothing. But he couldn't compro-
mise his sister. He'd have to get out unobserved.

He was in front of the door; Ezra's back was toward
him. Would they go up the stairs to search the room? A
window—he'd seen at a glance—was open but, so far as he
remembered, there was a straight drop beneath. Perhaps
Ezra wouldn't bother, wouldn't think there was time. Jake
faced him directly. But there was no more life in the face
than in one just hit with a club. The eyes were glazed.
He'd take a chance. He slipped out of the door.

Crouching a moment in the bushes by the entrance he
heard them pound upstairs. Then he was off around the
house like a hare. His own speed and sureness astonished
him. He remembered in his checkered education that brief
public school in England where he'd been Good at Games.

He found, steering—he said to himself—by the stars, a way through the Baynes' back garden to his sister's.

Unexpectedly his feet weren't entangled; they must be on a path. He came to thick trees, tall and rustly. He could see nothing but the path ahead. The other side he caught sight of something familiar, the outline of Ann's plum tree on the not quite black sky. Stopping to catch his breath he also took his bearings by the dim shapes of her orchard, the boughs that must hide her roof. He stole along beside the grape arbor, just touching now and then the sprawly heart-shaped leaves with his hand.

The darkness he was grateful for; he didn't trust it. The man he was after might be anywhere. He stole as silently as if he were in the midst of a hostile army.

A quite small noise stopped him, Ann's door opening. For a moment, against the light behind, he made out two figures. It closed and he could only listen; he was not twenty feet away.

"Let me take the revolver," said a man's voice.

"No," said Ann.

"Oh, very well. . . . I forgot you were not as other women." The voice was quite unlike any he knew. It purred like a hive of bees.

"I don't know," said Ann, "if the murderer has a revolver. I think not. But anything is possible, I might need this; you have your fists. . . . I hope you're as athletic as you look, Adam."

"'Before we start," murmured the man, "tell me just why you're doing this. I've never thought of you as tracking down a murderer. I've never thought you were ruthless, though God knows you were always severe. Tell me this much—is it for me?"

Ah now, perhaps he'll confess, thought Charles Francis, perhaps he'll stop her going by confessing. I'm the only witness. Whatever they do I'll stick close to them. It's my only chance to find out what it's all about and I'm the only one who has even that chance.

His sister laughed softly. "No, Adam. I've always gone on the assumption that you could take care of yourself. And life has justified me. I'm worrying now about a child. He can't have these murders weighing on him, not with all the rest he's had. . . . It doesn't matter what happens to grown people."

He couldn't hear the answer; he just caught the words, "Why do you think she will be attacked?"

"Because I called her up and asked her if she'd seen a certain thing and she had." Ann was whispering but the sound carried as far as speech. "I'll go ahead to show you Gubby's path. You have to bend double."

Who was called up for what? thought Charles Francis. Gubby's path, that must mean to the Lawrence place. He followed, glad to have heard the first words they had said also. Ann kept the revolver. She suspected Carthage too, did she? He had to hurry, crouching over, making no noise. It was lucky that he'd heard that about bending double. Otherwise—he put his hand up to feel—he'd have had many a crack in the face and would have given himself away by the noise. Now if he made any by mistake it was covered up by the tiny sounds they also made. Alert as a dog pricking its ears he had to sense where they were going to step and do it first.

The night was perfectly still—no breath of wind to divert anyone an instant—and black in the leafy tunnel. Even when they were through (he felt it by the cushion of pine needles underfoot) he was surrounded by deep gloom. Above, one could just see, against a light place in the sky, the cone-shaped tops of pines, Lawrence's place. Why, in God's name, did the man keep this graveyard grove in front of his house? Why didn't he have a lawn like other people? The trees made a tomb full of dank air, a trap.

He heard a whisper, a ghost of footsteps going toward the house. A twig snapped on the other side, the right. It must be Ann near the house. The heavier steps, he guessed, were crossing the path; that would be his man. He must

keep near to watch him, to prevent whatever dreadful
thing he was getting ready to do. Ann didn't carry that revolver for nothing. With infinite caution he stepped over
the path. His foot slipped on a stone; it grated.

Something dark and tight fell on him, hugged him. He
struck out. He hit again with gritted teeth, silent instinctively. Then he was down and at last gathering his wits
to call out, to tell his sister where he was and who. He
opened his mouth.

Something slid into it, neatly, hugely, muffling him,
holding his tongue, his throat. . . . He couldn't even gag.

"Don't try," said a purring voice right in his ear. "I
learned this in Spain . . . in the school for sentries."

Charles Francis gave a great heave. All that happened
was that hands like iron peeled his coat down to his elbows, tied it, held his legs. He was trussed up like a package, how he couldn't tell.

"I can't have you making any noise to disturb the
ladies," the cat's voice hummed again silkily in his ear.

24

When Adam heard a foot slip on a stone he hurled himself with a blaze of anger as well as the sureness of his years of practice. He knew who it was. His arms squeezed that soft body like steel hoops. He'd had the gag ready when they started. He pulled it tight.

Ann had been obliged to tell him about Lawrence's "ridiculous," as she called it, proposal to explain why Louella was bound to come here. She hadn't said much. Ann never mentioned other men's feelings for her. You would have thought, in the old days, he was the only man alive in a world like a desert island. But once, after she'd thrown him down, he'd taken a flat near her impressive doorway with its lighted columns, its butler. He'd watched her go out night after night with young men in top hats. One wore a cloak—he hated that one the most—and a ribbon across the shirt front. Quite soon he gave the key back to the landlord with a shudder. Besides being morbid and unbearable it Interfered with his Work. He was no bloody Russian. He went to the opposite end of the city and started *Spring* beside Margaret's warm fire.

But there . . . he'd done that insane thing, lurked in the street to get a glimpse of her with others! The feeling could stir in him still. If Louella was jealous of Ann, if she'd got hysterical because she came on Lawrence kissing her hands, what had Lawrence been trying to put over?

He sat on him hard. Quite theoretically he'd taken
Lawrence as a likely suspect for both crimes. Now he hated him too. . . . But it was funny the bundle under him
wasn't bigger. Ann had always described Gubby's father as
a tall, lean man. He felt with his hands. My God! Velvet!
Disguised as a woman? No—he felt further—a short coat.
What, the conventional New Englander in *velvet?*

Holding his breath in the dark stillness—he'd been
warned not to make a sound—he felt doubts creep over
him. Suppose this wasn't Lawrence? Then who was it?
He explored—half knowing already what he'd find—the
hair at the back of the gag. His finger went under it. Yes,
by God—his heart sank irretrievably—that portrait like
young R. L. S., Ann's brother. He'd seen the picture in her
parlor every night he'd been there.

How dreadful this would be for her! She could have had
no idea. Appalling! Perhaps he'd better let him escape? He
put his hand down to untie a knot.

Far off he heard a woman's heeltaps on the sidewalk.
This was what he'd been waiting for; he froze. They came
still nearer—sharp, nervous in the breathless dark—Louella. . . . Could this man have been waiting to attack his own
wife? Perhaps kill her? No, no, it didn't bear thinking of.

As for the other crimes, he tried to imagine excuses.
Bayne might have gone farther with that little Nancy than
anyone thought. Even if not maybe her father had been
roused to frenzy at the very idea. Or wait, this frail guy
was a writer of sorts as well as a painter; plagiarism might
come into it. Could he have written *Madeleine Pigor* and
had it stolen from him? Ann had hinted something like
that. Oh, any reason to kill Bayne was a good one, but
Fern Ellyn! That must have been pure cowardice. . . . That,
come to think of it, was what Ann had always rather worried about, his stamina.

But what exactly should he, Carthage, do? If Thorne
had come there to make an attempt on his wife it was

ghastly, but how were they ever to know now that he was trussed up?

His ears that had been living on the sound of heeltaps suddenly knew a strange sensation, silence. . . . She had got in between the trees halfway, at least, up to the house. And then his straining eyes had a reward. The dim light in the hall that was just visible through the fan-shaped window shone out a moment in another place. Someone had opened the door.

In the new darkness he relied on his ears again. . . . Nothing. What could Mrs. Thorne be doing? Waiting? But for what? The silence was worse than any noise he had ever known. He heard a little thud, a very small one, then a revolver shot. There was a crashing through the bushes to the right. Instinctively, he set off in pursuit.

It must, it had to be Lawrence, but he wasn't on a path. He was going it blind, crackling and lunging any way at all. Lost his head, thought Carthage while he ran. He wouldn't do that. He'd marked the exit from the path Ann showed him by the feel of two big tree trunks, the curve of stones beneath. He took time, a half minute extra, to find it again and, bending double, shot through Gubby's tunnels. He made almost no noise and what there was the quarry couldn't hear; he was too busy banging into trees. But this wouldn't last. They were almost into the clear, in Ann's garden. Here, thought Carthage, was where he really knew his ground He'd moved around in it night after night. He knew every foot, every obstacle.

Lawrence stopped making noise, that was the trouble. He was running on grass. The night with no moon, lit feebly by a scattering of stars, didn't give enough light to see really, yet it was better than under the trees. Carthage thought he made out movement in front, a piece of the dark that didn't stay still with the rest of it. There was a clash of leaves. That must be the grape arbor. Halting a moment, he heard the soft thud of feet His man must be running around it on the house side. Carthage knew the grape arbor. The bottom runner was a good two feet from the ground He felt for a free place, dived flat down like a football tackle, wriggled under it, and caught him.

25

Ann had heard nothing but the heeltaps then they stopped. She had seen the Lawrence door open and knew someone else was there, near in the dark. She had no clew to where that person was nor, worst of all, to what Adam was doing.

Leaning against a pine, she'd been straining her ears till she was nearly dizzy, till she heard—louder than all the little crickets—her own pounding blood. Second by second the silence weighed more. Oh, it might be all right. Louella might just be standing there in the path quietly, thinking. But it was the last place where the pines were really thick, on the way to the house. What if the murderer was there too? What if Carthage had failed her, what if the murderer was doing his work so softly nobody heard?

It was a dreadful decision. If she gave the alarm prematurely the killer wouldn't be caught; if she didn't give it quickly enough Louella would die too. Then came the tiny thud. She fired her revolver into the air.

There was a crash and then a double crash through the bushes. Thank God! Nothing had happened to Adam. He was starting in pursuit. She could breathe now; he'd understood. She didn't need to follow, not at once.

She stepped with caution out from behind her tree. A stumbling sort of noise began in front. A frightening noise like an animal dragging itself on the ground. At the same time a flashlight went on.

There was Louella, lying on the path. Her hat had fallen off and her glasses. The rigid waves of hair were loose, for the first time in years. Her lashes were startlingly black, her cheeks, though she must be unconscious, still pink. She looked quite artificial but pathetic, like a doll thrown violently away. But yet, Ann saw, there was one sign of life, her bosom moving up and down on the stones.

The figure holding the flashlight bent over, a tall figure. His face stood out plainly, Jonathan Lawrence. Then he straightened. He'd heard the stumbling noise too; it was almost on him. Into the ring of light there struggled a strange creature, pulling itself on its hands. It was up, gave a yank to a sort of rag round its legs, got clumsily to its feet. She knew by a kind of sixth sense who it was. There wasn't enough light, outside the circle, to see. Besides, there was a muffler round the face. But she knew. She couldn't understand, though, why it drew up, gathered itself together in that way.

An arm shot out. It hit Jonathan's jaw. Though he was so much taller he hadn't made a move. He couldn't have expected. . . . Even now he stood swaying, his arms slack. The shorter figure stepped up close, pommeled him left and right. Without a sound, without a gesture of defense, Jonathan crumpled like a marionette when the string is let go. He fell very slowly. The light described an arc. It showed the other man tearing his gag. It tinkled on stone; blackness wiped everything out.

Ann heard fumbling, shoving on the path. Her brother's voice said, "Poor Louella! My poor little girl. . . ." He seemed to be choking with pity, anger . . . affection. "Where have they hurt you?" he was begging. "Can't you talk to me?"

"Oh," moaned Louella. "Charles, where am I?"

"Perfectly safe," he crooned. "Right here with me."

The Lawrence door opened. A trailing shadow was outlined again a moment—the same shadow Ann had seen before.

"Leave that open!" shouted Charles. There was no response. The door closed quickly. He clattered, cursing, up to the porch and went in.

Amazed, Ann saw that her brother was proving equal to a situation.

No sooner had the door closed than the dim glow on the walk from the fanlight was blotted out a moment. That trailing figure hadn't gone in. It had stayed behind on the porch while her brother charged past. Now it came whispering down the path and that whisper was skirts. The tread was the light one of a fat woman. If their feet don't hurt they walk well, thought Ann. But when a twig did break, it crunched very thoroughly.

Behind her tree Ann listened, marking out in her mind the turns, the large obstacles, to pass on the way to Gubby's short cut. The person she was listening to knew it also though not so well. Perhaps that person was a little careless, not thinking that she had an audience. An audience for the great singer, Ann thought, an audience of one, not listening to a lovely voice soaring up from a bright stage but to small secret noises in the dark.

As soon as Mrs. Bayne was far enough ahead, Ann began to move after her. She had a pretty fair idea of where the singer was going: first, she was going somewhere else fast so as to be nowhere near the Lawrences' when the police turned up; second, she was very likely to be coming to see Ann herself. Without a sound Ann threaded her way. Yes, she was in the tunnel now. How well she knew it! Mostly, to be sure, by day, but she had used it even at night during the whooping cough last year. She passed through at top speed and found herself on the far edge of her own lawn not twenty feet behind Mrs. Bayne.

I must stop here, thought Ann, till she gets well inside, in order not to alarm her. I hope I left a light. Stooping down to get a view under the branches of the fruit trees she was in time to see her French door open and two men go in.

26

Adam was shoving the prisoner in front of him without losing his hold. One hand surrounded both wrists at his back, the other half inside the shirt collar twisted it when he showed signs of being anything but a puppet. These little lessons on technique had come in very useful; that desperate, hard, elastic ex-fencer in Madrid had told him they would.

He hooked one elbow round the doorknob, got a toe in and kicked the door open. Holding his man like a shield he didn't turn him round until they were inside, in the light. Then he dropped his hands.

"Hello!" he said. "What in God's name were *you* there for? You're not the man I'm after."

"I sincerely hope not."

It was Paul Augustine, blinking, rubbing his fingers round his neck. "You hardly gave me a chance to explain," he croaked. "Whoever it is, I pity the poor fellow!"

Adam felt let down. "Tell me what you were doing and be quick about it." He didn't have time to coddle the man though he looked pretty white. "Hurry. I've got to go back."

Paul was massaging his throat; no sound issued except squeaks and grunts but his color was coming back.

"In a minute," he said hoarsely.

They heard a rushing sound outside. The door burst open. There stood Rosa Bayne. One hand clung to the door to keep her balance at the sudden stop; the other brought itself up and clutched at her bosom. She had obviously been trying to slide in quickly, hoping not to find anyone there. The thing to do now was to transform it into an Entrance. It was going to be a struggle.

She was just drawing herself up for the first speech when her eyes took in Paul—his pallor, his hands on his throat.

"Paolo!" she cried. "What's happened?" The breath surged out of her too soon. "What's he done to you?"

"Nothing." Paul smiled wryly. "He made a mistake in the dark. That's all."

"Are you sure it was a mistake?" Her eyes flashed. "He means no good either to you or me. . . . He watches all the time. I don't trust him."

"You can trust him," a cold voice said behind her. "Would you mind stepping aside so that I can get into my house?"

Mrs. Bayne had to move and it was Ann who made the Entrance. Adam noted it subconsciously while he was saying very fast, "I didn't get Lawrence! This fellow fouled the trail. I've got to go back. Lawrence is out there, on the loose!"

"Not any more," said Ann. The words were like a trickle of ice water falling. "He's flat on the ground. . . . Entirely unconscious, I fancy. Let's all sit down."

"But still"—Adam wasn't convinced—"I like to be in at the finish. . . . I'll just go and see."

"I didn't leave," said Ann, "till I saw him in competent hands. You can be sure of that. Let's all sit down and hear what Mrs. Bayne can tell us. I asked her to come."

She moved up to the table, greeted Paul, and placed a chair for Mrs. Bayne.

Adam was still in full cry in his mind after the prey, but another feeling penetrated the first—he was never too preoccupied to keep it out—Ann's unfailing though remote and frozen charm. He'd taught himself to savor every moment. She'd given him no illusions about his time being long.

He sat down with them, absent-minded for a moment, trying to imagine her life here alone. The small round table was polished till it shone like a mirror but it gave back reflections distorted by the grain of the wood—Rosa Bayne's face, plump in odd directions; Paul's, grotesquely long and thin. Ann's was queer too. He glanced up at the reality; it looked curiously tired. . . . At any rate, they were there, cozy enough in the light from the sconces. There were even a few embers of fire in the grate.

"Mrs. Bayne," Ann said formally, "it might help if you would tell us what terms you'd been on with your husband. I don't suspect you of being jealous. Some women might have been but not you. Instead of that I suspect that *he* was. You said his books hadn't been doing well lately. Did he realize that he was a second-rate artist and you a real one?"

Rosa looked stunned; it was as if something always carefully hidden had suddenly been brought out into daylight.

She said after a moment, "Tony didn't know much about music. He liked to hear me sing but he didn't know."

"Not even when you practiced every day? Although I've never heard you sing near by I've often heard you from my garden."

"I didn't practice when Tony was there; I didn't want to disturb him."

"It disturbed him because it was real," said Miss Ann. "Nothing that he did was. . . . He was scared."

Rosa's face worked. "He was worse than that!" she cried. "He was even jealous of my friendship for Paul!"

One touch of understanding, thought Adam, had broken her reserve; the words came pouring out.

"Once a man came to the house in the evening," she said, "and I overheard. He was the janitor of Paul's apartment house. Tony had paid him to bring all the sheets of paper from Paul's wastebasket. I heard that! Only think!

This was a regular arrangement. It had been going on for months. I suppose he hoped to find compromising letters—not that he wanted to divorce me. Oh no! I ran his house too well! But he wanted to threaten me if I should start to sing again!"

"What did your husband do with the sheets of paper?" Miss Ann said. Adam remarked the eagerness in her voice.

"Pressed them with the electric iron," Rosa said contemptuously. "I watched him though he didn't know it."

"They weren't letters from you?"

"Oh no. I wrote very few. Paul and I knew Tony didn't like our friendship; we were careful. And these were stacks and stacks of sheets, all crumpled up."

"What kind of sheets?"

"Typewriting paper."

Adam's eyes traveled around the table, professional now. He couldn't help making notes. He'd read Zola too well. Paul, he saw, hadn't recovered yet; he was looking at Rosa Bayne quite dazed. Ann was gathering herself together dangerously.

"You know, Mrs. Bayne," her voice jumped out. Her hands gripped the edge of the table. "You had a good opportunity to murder your husband and, it seems now, a motive."

Rosa sank in her chair; tonight she was quite different. She wasn't acting. That plump face, glistening with health, that had been open and confiding, crumpled. All in a moment she was shattered, at her wits' end.

"I hate to do this," Ann said. "For your sake too, Paul. She looks like that woman in *Death March,* doesn't she? Do you remember, in the movie, when the bomb killed her baby there in front of her?"

"Yes," said Paul, very low. "But that was chance, the chance of war. You're doing this on purpose."

"And you were in the Inn, Mrs. Bayne," Ann went on, "on Friday afternoon. You got rid of Mr. Carthage by pretending to faint when you saw Fern Ellyn's name on the register. You hadn't recognized her, I think, on Wednesday evening at your house. But you were looking for someone; Mabel or the neighbors had told you Mr. Lawrence's secretary was there. And then you saw the name. You knew she'd be a suspect for the murder. You knew why she must have come to Middlebury—to prevent your husband from publishing his book. You had just time to get up to her room, put the hyoscine in her sleeping capsule, and tear the button off her dress."

27

"It isn't true," gasped Rosa. "It's a lie. Why don't you tell them it's a lie, Paul?"

Paul gave her a glance of pity.

Adam said, "I suppose you mean that Mrs. Bayne didn't see Fern Ellyn out of the bathroom window; she was surprised by her at the scene of the murder."

Rosa shrieked, "No! no!"

"That ought to wake Hannah," Ann said coldly. "Just as well. I'd better search Mrs. Bayne." She took up the handbag that was lying on the table. "And while I'm doing it, Adam, go through Paul's pockets, will you? It will be more regular."

"I'll search him, though I don't see why," Adam said.

"He still has to explain what he was doing in front of the Lawrence house," she answered patiently. "What was it, Paul?"

"Oh, nothing much." He smiled; one hand was moving in his pocket.

"All right, I'll search him," Adam said. He turned—Paul was next to him. "Do you mind?"

"No, I don't mind. I'll save you the trouble."

Augustine took the hand out of his pocket; it held a paperweight. They were all watching him, even Rosa. He laid it on the table.

"A silly weapon, as you will doubtless point out—it was the first thing I picked up at the hotel—and a silly thing I did. I hoped you wouldn't know but I see you'll have to. It had nothing to do with the murders." He smiled ruefully. "The only way I can explain it is the atmosphere around here. It's made people sort of crazy. Rosa, my dear, I don't know about you. I know nothing at all. But Mrs. Thorne! You see, Miss Ann, I saw your car this morning; it was Mrs. Thorne leaving it. She scratched it up. . . . She's lost her mind if she had any to begin with. I'm afraid I'm not quite normal either."

He lifted candid worried eyes.

"Search him, Adam!" Ann snapped in her schoolmarm way.

Adam didn't like it. The man was so pitiful, caught out in some piece of foolishness and trying to be intellectual about it. Why didn't Ann stick to Rosa instead of just sitting there with Rosa's handbag, looking at him? Augustine was a weakling physically—he hadn't put up any fight at all—but he was civilized and agreeable. He was the one—besides Ann, of course—who'd made the last week bearable!

He turned again, repeating, "Do you mind?"

Paul held his hands up then obligingly. Adam went through his pockets, laid the contents on the table, all quite ordinary—wallet, keys, pen, pencils, notebook, handkerchief, also a rumpled big silk one to wear round the neck, a little box of tablets with a druggist's label and marked P.R.N.

"For headaches," said the owner.

"Give them here!" Ann held out her hand and put the lot, including the paperweight, with Rosa's handbag on the sideboard behind her. "Why have you got that paperweight with you?" she said.

"I don't mind telling you." Paul spoke easily as if everything was as usual and he enjoyed being with them. "I can't explain it, even to myself, except, as I said, that the murders made everyone crazy, released inhibitions. . . . It was about Nancy.

"You know what she's meant to me, Miss Thorne. You know everything. Not that for one moment I imagined I was good enough for her. I didn't. I just wanted to be with her every moment, knowing I'd soon have to go away, knowing I'd never be part of her life."

Adam thought, struck with wonder, this young man, so old for his years, thinking about that child what I do about Ann! He noticed Rosa leaning forward, gaping.

"Nancy's mother," Augustine said, "tried to prevent my seeing her. It was she who refused to let Nancy have dinner with me. Today I thought my time was almost up; I might be sent for by Huntington Reed. All afternoon I tried to find Nancy. She wasn't here. I tried going to her house. Each time they sent me away, but I came back. I knew she was there all along. Finally I realized it was that mad woman's orders. I remembered—I'd heard her in the morning raving—that she intended to visit Lawrence. I laid in wait for Mrs. Thorne—it isn't pretty but I'm being frank—to knock her out, thinking it would be blamed on the murderer." He raised his hands to his forehead. "I thought then I could see Nancy!"

"Paul!" Rosa said. "How could you? Oh, it's not like you!"

Adam said, "Childish! Like a vicious child. But God, I hate to hand you over to the sheriff! He's hungry for a murderer." He moved unhappily.

Ann said, "You tied the paperweight in the silk handkerchief and used it like a blackjack. You managed to untie it before you were searched. Watch him, Adam!"

He was amazed at her face. Deep lines had carved themselves from the nose to either side of the mouth. Her eyes had sunk in to dark, somber wells.

She got up and lit the candles of the girandoles behind her. The room had no electric fixtures visible. It was paneled in walnut and suitable for the serene feelings of the eighteenth century. A blaze of light flared up; each flame reflected many times in swinging pendants of glass. Paul Augustine took his hands down and blinked.

Ann said to him slowly, "You are the author of *Madeleine Pigor.*"

"What's that?" said Adam.

"Ten years ago," she said, "Tony Bayne stole it when you showed it to him. You had no experience, no friends, only one copy, and no proof that it was yours, no money, I suppose, for a lawyer. I think you may even have been starving. You'd perhaps given up your job to finish your book. It's likely you'd been ill, you described illness so well."

They were all leaning forward breathless, except Paul. Ann might have been talking about the weather for all he seemed to care.

"It's likely," she went on, "that you'd been left by somebody you loved and were too numb to react properly to this new blow, to fight."

Adam looked from one to the other, stunned. They were both perfectly impassive.

"In order not to make you desperate," she said, "and— if he had a conscience, which I doubt—to throw a sop to it, Tony got you a job. Yes, and he even kept the job for you. He kept an eye on you that way. But, of course, all these years you've hated him."

Purely from habit Adam could still note. What a scene, one part of him was saying, but I must get the details right. Even while he felt, he observed.

Paul said evenly, "A great talent for fiction!"

She said, unperturbed, "You must have planned your revenge. It would obviously not be murder. No! That wouldn't show up Bayne. That's what you had to do. *Show him up.*" Her voice sank lower. "Your plans were all ready and then something went astray. What, I don't know. I can guess. You lost your self-control quite suddenly and killed him."

Rosa Bayne shuddered; the chair under her was shaking. Ann opened the door and there was Hannah with a clean apron tied over her wrapper.

"Take Mrs. Bayne to the kitchen," Ann said, "and keep her there. Come now, Mrs. Bayne," she steered her firmly. "Hannah is going to make you a cup of coffee."

Closing the door after them she sat down.

"And then," she said, "you killed Fern Ellyn. She'd seen you that night at the Baynes' and, besides, you suspected that she might have known about you, might have overheard your quarrels with Tony years ago. Oh, of course, when you met in my garden you agreed not to give each other away. But you feared that when she was accused she wouldn't keep to the agreement!"

Paul hooked his arms over the back of his chair. He was no longer the apologetic man who'd sat down in it.

"A good story," he said with perfect assurance, "only it happens not to be true. You haven't one shred of proof."

"You planned to make Fern out the murderer of Tony," she said softly. "Gubby Lawrence saw you bend over and put something in the chrysanthemum leaves; it was her button. He was in the tree."

Paul allowed himself to smile. "I admire your feeling," he said, "for that curious child. But the law will not convict me out of that little mouth." Adam was watching them breathless as if they were tightrope performers sliding, swaying over emptiness. He didn't think guilty or not guilty, truth or lying; it was too dreadful. He thought, which would fall?

"You forget," said Paul, "I wasn't even in this town till nearly morning the night of Tony's death."

"That put me off awhile," Ann said. "But I read Kuczinski's affidavit. He spoke to you before the movie, saw you take your seat, in the same row three or four seats beyond. He swore that you were there all through his film, apparently because to leave you would have had to pass in

front of him. That convinced the sheriff; it convinced the
New York police. But they've never seen a writer watching
his own film; I have. There's nothing like that complete
absorption. Their eyes seem to be magnetized. They can't
take them off the screen, not for anything, not a minute,
and, of course, they're ashamed of the feeling and try to
pretend it's not there. And I'm assuming that when you
suddenly couldn't stand it any longer—perhaps because
of seeing that man's pleasure in his own work, something
you'd been cheated of—when you decided to leave the film
to see Tony, you did it unobtrusively in order not to offend
the author. Perhaps you went out the wrong way, making
more people stand up or brushing past them. Perhaps you
walked right past the author and he never saw you."

"Ann," said Adam—he couldn't stand it any longer—"I
see why you suspect, but how do you know?"

"He didn't see the film," she said. "There was no incident of a bomb killing a baby. They left it out."

"Is that all?"

"Louella saw his car," she said. "It was parked before
eleven across the street. She peered into it thinking Nancy
might be there with someone. I knew she'd seen it and this
afternoon she told me over the phone that she'd looked in.
Nancy let Paul know this morning here in my house that
her mother had been there that night. That's why he tried
to kill Louella, not for any other reason."

"Mr. Carthage," cried Paul, "don't you see she's in-
venting all this? Mrs. Thorne may have seen a car, but
it wasn't mine. I doubt if she remembers the number or
anything else. She's too hysterical to be a witness. My car
was banged up fifty miles away and I hardly got here at all.
Everyone knows when I rattled in."

"Everyone knows the second time you came," said Ann.
"The first time you didn't make any noise. And I talked
with Ellison's garage about that broken exhaust. It was an
accident you could have made yourself by backing right
into that gas pump that you knew so well. You really left

New York early, by quarter to nine. You got here on the dot at ten-forty-five, in time for Fern to see you, not Louella. You met Tony on his own front path, right after he'd slammed the door on Adam and come out.

"He was in a predicament where to take you. He expected a little unpleasantness and didn't want it overheard though he thought he was ready to handle it. He strolled back with you toward the house. Glancing in apprehensively, he saw that Adam had gone to bed but he didn't ask you in, not with Adam's room separated from the living room by one thin partition. He just went in to turn out the lights, remembering he had a rendezvous afterward and wanting to make people think he'd gone to bed. He was an expert in such matters, Tony.

"But then, where was he to take you? Not walking on the road—that would be too near Nancy's house. She might come out perhaps, if he were late. Instinctively he went the other way, back of his house toward mine. In his anxiety to get well out of earshot he came all the way. My neighborhood was harmless, he thought. He didn't reckon on passing those stones just when he'd driven you that shade too far."

"Will you let her do it?" cried Paul. "It's clever but there's not one bit of proof. She's making it all up to protect you. You see that. You will have to save me!"

"Why should he," said Ann gently, "when you tried to kill him?"

Paul flinched.

28

He buried his face in his hands, that too-sensitive face that had remained so long unnaturally calm in the festive light.

"I won't pretend," said Ann, "that I have anything but circumstantial evidence. That little box"—she gestured toward the sideboard—"contains, I think, the poison that you put in the capsule in place of Fern's sedative. I suppose it's a powder. Hyoscine, they said it was. I suppose too it's in a form you could take yourself. Poor Fern, she went to sleep quite peacefully as you had intended to any time all these years if you made up your mind not to stand your hard fate." Her voice had a caressing quality, rare with her. "Can you stand it any longer, Paul?"

My God, thought Adam, she likes him; she likes him a lot.

Paul put his elbows on the table; his head sank down deeper.

"I'll go on," she said, still gentle. "All these years while you hated Tony there was only one way to expose him— write another book, as good as the first. I had to deduce that. Mrs. Bayne has just borne me out. Then there was what the police found in your apartment—did you know the sheriff had it searched?—a new portable that had seen lots of use, boxes and boxes of typewriting paper, and not a scrap of anything written. You knew if you published something good you'd stand a chance of getting listened to about *Madeleine Pigor*. But hate, corroding hate, doesn't help the creative mood. Tony's face would get between you and the typewriter. He'd given you no chance to forget. The life you led—for security and because you hoped, somehow, to get your revenge—kept your mind fixed on him.

"That's why it took so long. You threw away reams of paper, I expect, in that time." She spoke almost to herself. "You probably kept your manuscript locked up. There's a safe-deposit-box key on that ring. But you never thought of what you threw away. One doesn't somehow. And all the time Tony had paid your janitor to steal the emptyings of your trash basket!"

An unprintable epithet hurled itself out from Adam. "I wish I'd killed Tony myself!"

"If you had," she said sharply, "you'd have done it in a fight, not throwing a stone from behind. And you'd have made a clean breast of it if you had to. You wouldn't have killed other people to cover it up. Poor Fern . . . and then that shooting in my garden!"

Paul's head flashed up. "I'm sorry about that!" he cried. "You must believe me. That's the only thing."

Yes, he had fallen off the tightrope now. He'd smashed to pieces; that face showed it all. But, Adam marveled, she still hadn't any proof.

"I'd finished my book," said Paul in a rush. "I hurried up here to tell Tony, walked right out of the movie. I couldn't help it; it was too strong for me. This was a manuscript he couldn't steal! And then he told me that he had enough notes to put together the plot. He'd talked of it, he said, in 'important quarters.' It was well received. If I came forward with the script they'd naturally suppose I'd got hold of it through being his agent. Then I picked up the stone. . . ." His head rose. "I don't regret it. I should have killed him years ago. . . . I thought it would be stupid for me to suffer for a thing like that. As for Fern Ellyn— what did she matter? A poor creature, bah!" His voice was going first high and then low like delirium. "She must have known I'd killed Tony and she didn't know enough to be afraid! Went out without locking her door! The world is full of characterless women. They're a different thing from an artist, a great artist!" His voice tapered off. "That's the one time I didn't know what I was doing."

He was silent a moment. They said nothing. He went on. "I tortured myself wondering to whom Bayne had talked. Then you told me, Miss Ann, while we were having tea. Carthage was there; it must have been to him! 'Important quarters,' indeed! When I couldn't get into the house I watched from outside. I saw him climb down on the garage door. When he'd gone I went up. My notes were right there in his room, in Bayne's manuscript, and some letters from Fern. Bayne always shoved everything in one pile. Beside them on the desk was the revolver. I took it and went after him, thinking if he was out of the way I'd be safe. Forgive me, Carthage." His voice dropped. "It was I that shot at you. And then Miss Ann came out. I heard what you said. I know *Spring in Savoy* by heart. . . . It brought me to my senses."

"I knew you knew about us," Ann said. "The only way you could was to have been there that night. That's why I suspected you first."

"When I heard you," he said, "I knew Carthage had come to see you, not the Baynes. Tony and his kind dropped out of my mind. He was really dead, at last. I could begin to live. It was magic to be with you, you two and Nancy, people I could talk to. . . . You seemed to like me. . . . I've been very lonely."

Ann said—her voice cut like a lash—"too late. The sheriff will be here now any minute."

Then Adam had to turn away his eyes. He'd seen wounds in Spain; he'd done dressings all day long and never minded. But this he couldn't look at.

Paul whispered, "You're going to give me up? . . . You can't prove I killed anyone. I'll deny it."

Ann said as if to a child, "No, Paul. We can only prove you tried to kill Louella. Adam caught you at that. It will mean a prison sentence. And there's enough evidence for the rest to keep you always under suspicion. Any day something might turn up. You'll get no glory from your books. It will be worse than when Bayne got it. Because now they'll weight the scales in favor of your being a murderer."

He whispered, "Give me my little box."

She said, "First you must write a confession."

Adam fumbled in his pocket. He shoved over a notebook and a fountain pen. There was no sound but the pen scratching. One candle hissed and went out.

Ann seemed to be carved out of granite. "Have you put it all down?"

"Yes," he said like a man in a great hurry, like a man who had a train to catch. "That I killed Tony and Fern Ellyn and slugged Mrs. Thorne, for reasons known to you two. Must I say I shot at Carthage?"

"No," said Adam.

That helped to reassemble Paul's face. It was like a picture puzzle when the last pieces go in. "Tell Mrs. Thorne to throw out her medicine," he said, "the stuff she got today. I put a couple of grains of hyoscine in it." His fingers reached across the table. "May I have the box?"

Familiar wheels crunched on the drive; brakes ground. "The sheriff," said Ann.

"There won't be time," Paul groaned. "It takes half an hour."

Ann was drawing her hand out of her coat pocket slowly as if the motion hurt her. She laid her revolver on the table.

"Thanks," said Paul.

She said, "In the parlor."

He smiled and his serenity was perfect, much better than theirs. "That lovely room?"

She nodded.

Adam held out his hand. "About *Madeleine Pigor*. . . . It's a very fine book. I'll look after the new one."

Paul took the hand quickly and went out. There was a pounding on the front door. Adam and Ann moved toward it sightlessly like sleepwalkers. Only their ears were living, listening. A shot rang out. Then, like breaking a spell, they opened the door.

29

Everything was confusion like a nightmare. As in a dream Ann tried to move and nothing happened, tried to speak; no sound came out. She could hear Adam talking on and on, see him walking from one room to another with the sheriff.

She found herself in the dining room. Adam had raised a glass of brandy to her lips. It burned very nicely. The first thing she was able to notice was that he scarcely looked at her; the sheriff would have nothing in that line to go on. She felt grateful. How nice to be old, to have a long life behind so people knew you, knew you believed the only sin for a woman was *faire parler d'elle*. She saw the candles, guttering, had dripped great gobs of wax. She blew them out.

The two men came in again, the sheriff holding her revolver in a handkerchief. Adam reached behind her and gave him Paul's little medicine box. "You'd better send somebody to the Thornes' for the bottle," he said. "It will be safer, and, besides, confirm it."

Ezra pushed his hat to the back of his head frowning. In front of them on the table the confession lay.

"Look here," said Adam suddenly. "The casting is what's wrong. . . . Suppose you were to take my place for the last hour. Let's see how that comes out."

Ezra sat down.

"We're reasonable people," Adam said persuasively. "Miss Thorne and I don't want publicity. That's the last thing we want. Neither does Mrs. Bayne; she's the one other person who knows anything. You need it in your business. So you take my place. . . . When you left Mrs. Bayne's you didn't go to Charles Francis' house. You followed him to Mr. Lawrence's. You tackled him when he got in your way, heard the attack on Mrs. Thorne, chased the murderer over here, caught him, got a confession. Mrs. Bayne's in the kitchen. I'll fix her. She only knows part of it anyway. Nobody else—that I'm sure of—saw me; it was absolutely dark. Now did anyone see you? Could they prove you weren't there?"

"N . . . no," said Ezra. "I went to watch Mrs. Thorne. There was a light on in her bedroom so I stayed outside, waiting to see if anyone would come. That girl of theirs began pounding on her door, but I knew it was her father locked her in. I didn't pay attention. No more did the help; they were way down in the kitchen. I figured she'd scare anyone away so I went back to Bayne's.

"There in the middle of the road, Miss Thorne, was that fine hired man of yours stretched out on the ground. I thought sure it was another murder. I stopped the car and jumped out. And there he was sleeping like a baby, with that mangy pup beside him!"

"I sent him," said Miss Ann, "to watch that stretch, of road for Louella. It was the only dark stretch."

Ezra said, "When I ran the car round I may have splashed him some. He sat up and rubbed his eyes but he couldn't identify me, not him!

"The Bayne house was wide open and not a soul in it. I called up my office from there. The girl said Mr. Thorne had called in that he'd caught the murderer—it was Mr. Lawrence, he'd tried to kill Mrs. Thorne. The boys beat it out; she gave the call to the homicide squad. Right away they called back to find where the hell was the sheriff. But, you see, I asked them"—his eyes narrowed—"if

either of you two were there and when I found you weren't
I wouldn't bother to go."

"Splendid," said Adam cordially. "For all your office
knows, you made the calls from here where you were busy
catching the real murderer. . . . The only thing that needs
explaining is why you let him commit suicide . . . eh?"

"And then some," Ezra growled.

"That," said Adam, "is where I come in. I entered at
that point and blunderingly tried to interfere. While you
were subduing me Augustine got away, grabbed the gun—
women are careless about leaving them around—and it was
all over!"

Ezra looked Adam up and down, from his head to his
heels. His eye showed his opinion plainly that while the
guy wasn't large (he was shorter than the sheriff) every
inch was wildcat. Ezra enjoyed that part about subduing
him. He took off his hat and scratched his head and they
knew they'd won.

"Have you got it, Ann?" said Adam, not looking at her.

"Yes."

"Then I'll tell Mrs. Bayne, and tell her what to say. The
less it is the better."

"She'll keep still," said Ann. "She has her living to
make."

"I'll phone the boys," said Ezra. "They're waiting next
door . . . with the reporters watching them, I bet, by now."

Somehow they got through the endless repetitions of
the story. Adam stayed in command, second in importance, of course, to the sheriff, who kept glancing at him
curiously. And Mr. Carthage was naturally the target for
the press. Having pumped him dry—as they thought—on
the murder, the reporters tried to get a Sunday feature out
of him: "Would Augustine Have Been Our Greatest Young
Writer Had He Lived?"

Yes, Adam was drawing off the hounds. While he had
them, a baying pack, in the dining room, Ann said to the
sheriff, "May I?" and went with him to the parlor.

There was that dark shape on the floor next to the delicate marble of the fireplace. Plainly, it seemed to her, he'd tried to fall in that one spot in order not to spoil the room.

She had marched in and knelt—Ezra standing above her—by the lax head where it lay almost in the ashes. She closed the eyes carefully; this much could be done by a friend. And then his miserable body would belong to the public like his more miserable life.

"Good-by, Paul," she said aloud for no reason while her tweed skirt soaked up a stain.

30

Miss Ann got breakfast over with and stepped out in the sun. She had to feel it, sniff the dewy air. The great thing, she had learned long ago, was to start every morning new, not dragging the dull weight of yesterday.

There was a thread of worry about Gubby that she had to follow. Even so, keeping her finger on it, she could smell the pines, so warm and pleasant, not like last night, and feel a tingle of pleasure when she came on a small figure industriously collecting cones in a wheelbarrow.

There had never been any sentiment between them. She merely said, "Why aren't you in school?"

"Daddy said not to go." He lifted eyes the color of a mountain brook and just as clear. One could apparently see every little pebble on the bottom, yet she was never sure.

"I'm going away," he said with some importance and only a shade of doubt. "I'm going to another school. Mrs. Hodges is packing my clothes."

"Oh," said Miss Ann, the old campaigner. She kept every hint of *parti pris* out of her voice. "Is your father at home?"

"Yes." Gubby dropped the handles of the wheelbarrow right in the path and went along too. "He's looking for Jimmy. Jimmy's lost."

"Did the cage finally break?"

"Yes, where I mended it with string." He sighed. "Jimmy was never really tame."

"I agree with you," she said, remembering that yellow eye, that vicious beak.

It was a pleasure to find Jonathan not actively searching, just sitting, rather pale, on the steps. He came forward with outstretched hand, a conspicuous bandage on his chin.

"Oh," she said. "I didn't remember about that. Does it hurt?"

"Not so much as what went before." He smiled one-sidedly. "Why didn't you help me, Ann, to get rid of that woman in the afternoon? This will be a lesson to me not to do good deeds. I thought I couldn't refuse to help her; after all, I'd accepted their hospitality. But then she stayed and stayed. It was a relief, finally, when I got knocked out and didn't know whether she was here or not!"

Miss Ann noticed that Gubby hadn't made a move to take her hand. He was standing beside his father.

"I might go away," said Jonathan. "Would you advise it?"

"I *am* going away," Gubby said. "It's a school where they have horses. We are allowed to feed them every day and take care of them and *ride* them." His voice rose from its usual diffidence to pleasure, to excitement. "I hope mine is a gray one. . . . If it is, oh boy!" He yelped, "Heigh-o, Silver!"

"That was my only clew," Jonathan said. "Animals. . . . I hope you approve."

"It's a good clew," she said and bade them good-by quickly. In record time she was going down their walk and along the road to the village. She didn't like to think—in fact, she put off thinking—how much she was going to miss Gubby, but he would have, she knew, more suitable companions, children, horses. . . .

She raised the shiny knocker on her brother's front door.

"They're in the library." Deborah, for the first time in years, was actually fluttering. "Oh, what a narrow escape, ma'am! Mrs. Thorne has a lump on her head as big as your fist but she won't stay in bed, not her! Mr. Thorne is putting the compresses on himself. He wouldn't let me do it."

Nothing could astonish one that morning; Miss Ann viewed with calm the sight of her brother hovering over his wife who reclined on a sofa. Louella reclining! Her hair, due to the bump, was still surprisingly out of its rigid waves. Her eyes—she was, of course, unable to put on her glasses—followed her husband with the pure regard of a woman for a man who has knocked out another for her sake.

Charles Francis should have looked sheepish after his ill-aimed excursion into drama but he didn't. He'd enjoyed it. He looked like a man who was fully capable of capturing a murderer singlehanded. If he hadn't, it was just an error of the Management. There had been other errors, too.

"By the way," he said meaningly, "I didn't know our Ezra Gates had ever been to Spain. Very adroit he was, too—not the awkward fellow he looks in the daylight."

"It will be just as well," Miss Ann said hastily, "not to stir up any questions about last night, otherwise there will be publicity for Our Family. We shall be dragged in, even more than at present. I'm sure we all want to avoid that. . . . And how does Nancy take it? She's at home?"

"I don't think so," said her father. "But wherever she is she's very depressed. I could see that at breakfast. It's depressing to the young to find out that their elders know more than they do."

What elders? thought his sister but she didn't say it.

Louella pointed to a florist's box. "Deborah brought that in," she said, picking up the card. "From Samson to Delilah," she read with a disapproval that showed she'd be back to normal presently. "Who could that be?"

"A nice young man," said Ann and went out rapidly. Good! she thought. I'd forgotten the reporter. There's one admirer alive anyway.

As she'd expected, when she opened her front door there was Nancy huddled in the hall like something Hannah might at any moment sweep out.

"At last!" she cried, rushing to meet her aunt. "Aunt Ann, please tell me why this had to happen. . . . I can hardly bear it."

"There, there," said Miss Ann, patting her shoulder. "Of course, you can bear it."

The small face—she had seen in that rush—was now really beautiful, white, sorrowing, mature. If Paul could have seen it! she thought and suppressed the thought. "You're a Thorne, child," she said. "We don't crack up. That's what it means, not that you do or don't belong to the Girl Scouts."

"But Paul . . . Paul . . ."

"Paul was a murderer," said her aunt sharply. "But he had some justification . . . also great talent, perhaps genius, but he was weak . . . weak."

Through her own words she heard the knock; over the tumbled head she could see the French door opening. "Here's Mr. Carthage," she remarked. "Paying a call, for once, in the daytime."

Nancy drew back. Her distracted face struggled a moment for composure and then found it. "You can tell me later," she breathed.

Bowing to Adam with a new young dignity she hurried past him out of the door.

31

Purely from habit Ann had started toward the parlor. An expanse of bare floor met her eyes and then a starched hummock which she recognized as a rear view of Hannah on her hands and knees.

"I forgot," she said, turning. "The rug had to be dry-cleaned. . . . Let's go out."

Adam followed her without words but so near she could smell his shaving soap and tobacco.

The sun was nearly over them. She stopped and looked at him and it lit very plainly the well-brushed gray hair, the deep lines in his tanned, healthy, but old skin. Bracing as sea water the thought broke over her that she looked the same age.

"You made a good job of it last night," he said. "A good clean job."

"So did you."

"Why did you happen to think about breaking that alibi? I've been wondering. Why did you know Kuczinski would be unreliable at his own film?"

"Because of you, Adam," she said. "It was the only time I've seen you in the last twenty years, at your movie, *Spring Flight*. I sat three seats away and you never noticed me."

"What a fool!" he said. "What a blind fool, but I've made up for it. . . . Ann, you know what I've come for. Won't you marry me? Let me arrange things? Get a divorce? I could so easily."

"No, Adam."

She sat down then on the bench by the grape arbor and patted the place by her side. When he had grudgingly taken it she smiled. "Do you still keep a bag of peanuts by you when you write and skip your meals and throw the shucks anywhere? . . . And leave your ashes in your coffee cup?"

Ah, she remembered. That was something. "My dear," he said indulgently. "Things like that, all one's peculiarities, don't get better as one grows older; they get worse."

"So I notice with mine. . . . One of my peculiarities is Hannah. . . . She wouldn't like it."

"Ann, look at me." He was stern. "I'm talking seriously."

"Look at me, too, for the same reason." She gave him stare for stare. "These children of yours—I learn by the public prints that you have them, two anyway. . . ."

"But they're not like your little boy," he said impatiently. "They're grown up. My son's in college. Margaret Ann's in boarding school. . . . Yes, I was allowed to choose the middle name."

"They're adolescent," she said gently. "That's a sensitive time. I can remember, before I came out, there was an actress who used to come to Father's parties. She had no observable connection with the Department of State."

He shifted on the bench. "Children ought to be kept where they can't observe."

"And then your wife," she went on inexorably. "She's a good sort of girl?"

"Just that exactly . . . poor Margaret."

"She loves the children and enjoys your being famous and puts up with the peanuts?"

"She does . . . quite patiently. But that isn't all a man needs."

"Adam, I remember what a man needs. I used so often to be called that article." She turned her head on one side. "I studied the subject!"

He sighed with what he hoped was a humorous expression; it didn't turn out very humorous. "You did, indeed."

"Your wife puts up with little unexplained excursions like this one? She sees you catch the eye of women she has never met, some of them quite delightful-looking, probably? She knows you get letters, telephone calls?"

"Occasionally. Who doesn't?"

"I shouldn't put up with it."

"But Ann! With you there it could never happen!"

"That's as may be," said Miss Ann with decision. "I do not intend to marry."

Adam's head dropped to his hands. "I knew it," he muttered. "I have every reason to know it. . . . But the thing is I can't bear to leave you."

"It's taken me all these years," she said, "to learn to live with myself. I'm too old to learn to live with another person."

"You don't want to," he groaned. "I know that. . . . You've never wanted to." Then he said as if to himself, "How can I go away? With nothing of you to take with me . . . for company?"

"You know where I live now, idiot, and how. You don't have to think of me flitting from Palm Beach to Pinehurst to Newport to Bar Harbor. Or taking up with younger men, or dieting, or getting my face lifted. Am I very wrong to think you've not been disillusioned? . . . Isn't that something?"

"Yes, dear. . . . But it makes things worse," he said simply. "If I'd been disillusioned I shouldn't mind going; now I do. . . . I shall be so lonely."

"Not if you get to work."

"What work?" He lifted haggard eyes.

"At your age," she said musingly, "with all those volumes back of you, I should think you'd begin to wonder what there was left—as Henry James would say—to 'treat.'" She didn't dare look at him. She was delicately

pulling from her sleeve what she hoped would be the right
card. "You've done war and death and all kinds of disease
and, of course"—she cocked an eyebrow at him—"love. . . .
But you haven't—I read everything you publish, Adam—
you haven't ever done a character going to pieces under
the blows of fortune, turning from something rather fine
to something monstrous. . . ."

"That's so," he said, astonished. "I haven't."

"I suppose"—she hung fire just the right length of
time—"it would be very hard?"

"Harder than hell," he said and his voice hummed
again, that deep vibration it had usually. "But it's a major
subject." He was sitting upright. "Paul Augustine, poor
devil, was handed to me on a silver platter. I made a few
notes at the time from habit; I'd forgotten. . . . Clever of
you, Ann."

He stood up; he paced back and forth, the sun gleaming on the white hair at his temples. And there were people, thought Ann, who said that gypsy face was ugly. Why,
this was how a man *should* look!

"The facts are nothing," he said. "I could change all
that. The process is everything and I saw a little of it." He
stood in front of her with folded arms and the light eyes
shone down. "Good-by, my girl," he said softly. "A book
is only a book. It's not worth you. Don't think you're dis-
tracting me. You only prove my point about the value of
your company."

He wheeled like a polo pony turning on a dime and was
off, almost running.

Miss Ann sat looking after him and then at the place
where he had disappeared through the trees.

The grape leaves rustled behind her. Which of Gubby's
animals, she thought, must I cope with now? They rustled
louder. Nancy's face poked through; she hadn't even both-
ered to wipe off the tears.

"I didn't want to overhear," she moaned. "I had to; I
just couldn't get away." She wriggled through the vines

and came to rest, very disheveled, on the bench. "Oh, Ann, he's so wonderful! I don't understand you. Can't *anyone* be happy?"

Her aunt smiled at her. With a streaky face and hair she looked Gubby's age. "I'm happy, child."

"That isn't what I mean," said Nancy firmly. "Why did you leave him long ago?"

Her aunt didn't answer. . . . After a moment or two she said, "Nan, you've been through a lot. Two men you've known are dead, one murdered, one a murderer. The only way to profit by one's troubles is to learn. I don't begrudge your profiting by mine. So I'll tell you. . . . I've never told anyone."

"Oh, Ann!" Nancy said with awe.

"It was quite simple, banal really. I saw him kiss the innkeeper's daughter. Oh, she was nothing, just a pretty child. He didn't care about her, of course. . . . But I knew he was like that. He'd told me. I knew anyway. . . . By then I knew him quite well."

"Was that all?" Nancy's mouth stayed open. "Couldn't you forgive him?"

"Very easily," her aunt said. "But by then I knew that a woman was only safe in his imagination, not his arms. Only real there, too. With Adam writing is the Substance; what you, my dear, would call 'Life'—the Illusion."

She looked out across the lawn. It was cool. Though the leaves were green one could feel fall in the air; winter was coming. "I've always been vain," she said. "And of nothing vainer than Adam's feeling for me. I wanted to keep it."

"When he was young," said Nancy like a child going over a lesson, "I can see he might have been unfaithful and he wouldn't have been practical as a husband. But think of the way he is now! That's what I can't bear . . . with the books and the murders and all. I can't bear that he can feel the way he does about you and you not love him!"

Miss Ann raised an eyebrow. "But I do, you little ninny. . . . I did and I do."

DEATH IN LORD
BYRON'S ROOM

The characters and situations in this work are wholly fictional; do not portray and are not intended to portray any actual persons. The geography is also imaginary except in its broadest outlines. The locale of the story in Lausanne and Genève, the country around Sir John's villa, the scene of the climb above Caux, the mountains near Genève are fictional . . . Lord Byron's room as here described is an invention although the poet did once stay in Ouchy. Nor does the author wish to be held responsible for any railroads; a resemblance to the real ones, though sometimes striking, is purely coincidental.

1

The fire wasn't burning very brightly; it was choked with ashes. Only a little glow spread on the faded garlands of the rug. Miss Ann Thorne, spinster, poked it absent-mindedly. I've retired to the chimney corner, she thought, like an old Cinderella. Nothing, thank God, will get me out of here.

But the fire wasn't so far gone. It sprang up easily and flooded the still graceful, bending figure. She moved her chair a little and sank down. How pleasant, she thought, to have the coach turn back into a pumpkin! I've been to far too many balls.

She had been thinking of them rather idly because of the man she was waiting for. By the end of the war—how long ago it seemed now—he'd become a general; at the end of the First World War he'd been a young major. That was in the period of the balls. She hadn't seen him for years and had been wondering ever since his telegram what brought him this way.

The doorbell tinkled. Miss Ann rose to light the lamps. She was not, after all, going to receive Breck Summers in a studied twilight so he wouldn't notice that she had gray hair.

The charming room, so utterly unlike New England, with its green silk walls, its low French chairs, surrounded her with the ease of habit. The old gilt mirrors doubled her movements in their wavering depths. She turned to the door.

There on the threshold stood a modern creature, a young girl in a Red Cross uniform. She was crying.

"Aunt Ann," she said. "It doesn't help."

"You mean being on duty every day?"

"It's not enough," she said.

Even the tears failed to disfigure that lovely face. Before this, thought her aunt, the days when she worked in the hospital had been the one way to take Nancy's mind off Philip, first when he and his plane were reported missing and finally when they received the notice he was dead. Not that Nancy had known Philip very well. She had just met him a week before he was sent abroad but then she'd written madly—after all people urged one to—and Philip had proposed to her by letter. All he could have known of the child, her aunt reflected, was that she made a pin-up girl the other men envied.

Miss Ann considered privately that Nancy's grief wasn't as personal as she thought; it was a symbol of what had happened, what was happening to her whole generation. Lately it had failed rather astonishingly to get better. It had got worse. The breakdown of idealism all around . . . Miss Ann sighed. Young people needed such high things to live for.

"Come over by the fire, dear, and sit down."

Nancy advanced, her look just as desperate but beginning also to be a little ashamed.

Miss Ann's heart smote her. She knew that she was the only person before whom Nancy gave herself the luxury of tears. It had always been this way since her niece had been small. And the tears, Miss Ann thought, were actually for the same reason: Nancy's parents. Her mother was a clubwoman, not really at home except on a platform, gesturing with a pince-nez, asking whether those in the back of the hall could hear. Nancy's father, Charles Francis Thorne, had retired from the world as completely as any monk into the crumbling leather of his library. They had early settled into a fixed attitude toward their daughter: they viewed with alarm and said no. Now that she was twenty they treated her as if she were sixteen. And living in a small town helped them, especially when the young men had gone to war. Nancy's mother really thought her daughter's emotional needs ought to be satisfied by being a Girl Scout leader.

Miss Ann had always known she must do something about Nancy, something beside drying her tears every time the child made a vain attempt to scale the nursery wall. She had thought vaguely of a season in Washington, but her own reluctance and then the war . . . Nancy had never really had a chance even to fall in love . . . And she had such a healthy appetite for life! Maybe so much thwarting had been dangerous. It looked now as if the almost totally imaginary Philip were turning into a neurosis.

Nancy looked up suddenly.

"You have on a long dress," she said.

"Yes, dear."

"But I told mother I'd come here to dinner. I just had to get away from the family . . . Are you going out?"

"No . . . I expect a guest."

"Then you don't want me?"

There was a tiny hesitation. Miss Ann said, "Of course, dear, I want you."

She had been rather looking forward to some Washington gossip and wondering, without a thread of information to guide her, what brought Breck Summers here. She couldn't help but think it was something out of the ordinary. But then, she decided, youth suffered the most always and should come first.

"Who is your guest?" said Nancy doubtfully.

"An aged Army officer . . . By that I mean as old as I am."

Nancy sighed. "If you don't mind I'd like to stay. It will be sort of soothing."

If Miss Ann had objected to being patronized she would have forsaken the company of her niece long ago. She did not; it amused her. Besides, she noticed that the tears were drying.

"I'll have to change then," Nancy said. "I wasn't going to but we're not supposed to wear the uniform off duty. With the Army you've got to be fussy. Do you have a rag I could put on?"

"There's that blue thing I used to wear when I took you to New York to the Opera."

"All right."

Nancy's eyes were definitely brighter. Ever since she'd been small she'd loved dressing up in her aunt's clothes. Now that she was the same size they made a welcome addition to what her mother alone thought was an adequate wardrobe. She turned toward the door.

Miss Ann said lightly, "Tell Hannah that I've asked you to stay . . . as a chaperone. She still thinks I need one."

But when the child had gone the room seemed darker. Miss Ann didn't move toward the rest of the lights. The evening paper lay neglected on the table. This war, one couldn't forget, had left the world more prostrate than the last and this time a new generation had to face picking up the pieces. What a failure all the intelligent young men she used to know had made of it! She, too, in her way. They'd have no second chance.

The doorbell tinkled. Hannah's progress, she knew, from the kitchen wouldn't be rapid. There was time to arrange her face in a pattern of personal pleasure, banish the world's sorrows. She hadn't been an ambassador's daughter and official hostess for years in Europe for nothing. Besides, she felt really curious to see how Breck Summers had turned out.

The voice was brisk. Eisenhower had made an end of drawl. The step was brisker. He outdistanced Hannah and reached the room almost at double quick.

"Ann," he said. "I'm so glad to see you." His eyes were as fast as the rest of him. "You can't know," he said, "what it is to find you at last!"

"My dear Breck." She extended a hand from the chair arm. "All you have to have is a road map of Connecticut . . . Hannah, ice please."

He kept the hand a long time, but they all used to in that set.

"I don't know that you need it," he said.

"Why not?"

"A couple of words from you are still enough to ice a cocktail."

They had also made fun of her voice.

Breck wore a dark suit and, of all things, a bow tie, but they fitted him as they only could an Army man or a tailor's dummy. He was not a tailor's dummy.

He was regarding her quite as searchingly as she looked at him, in fact rather more so. She raised an eyebrow.

"Would you like to make a cocktail?" she said. "Or would you prefer to have me do it while you continue to satisfy yourself of my identity?"

"Ann, I'm sorry." He started for the tray on a side table. "You'll forgive me when you hear what I've come for . . . Have a drink first."

He dropped Hannah's ice into a shaker and mixed neatly a large quantity of very dry Martini.

He gave her a glass and said, raising his, "To the United States." Half of the cocktail disappeared and he said, "No, my dear, I had to have more than a road map. I had a change of clothes, a game of hide-and-seek in a department store, a tunnel under a hotel, two cars and four license plates. You may have noticed I signed a nickname to the telegram and arrived after dark?"

"Heavens!" she said. "What for? Are you a fugitive from Justice?"

"No," he said. "More like Justice pursuing fugitives. All the latter part of the war I was in Intelligence."

"Oh," said Ann faintly. "I didn't know."

"You're not supposed to know, not even now when so much has come out about the O.S.S. Not all, however, not by any means."

He was studying her again, but she didn't mind now. She was too occupied.

"One thing," he said, "it proved the value of the amateur. But it left many threads untied. Disbanding the organization couldn't help but do that." He finished his cocktail and poured out another. The fire had blazed up and lit his quick hands. "With the reaction from war there's a dangerous slump. We don't need to go into it all. A group of private persons, including owners of newspapers, has decided to finance an investigation. That's what I've come to you about." He paused. In the deep silence one could hear a door open and then close upstairs. "Rather than wait for Congress to vote funds, we have the money— that's the size of it. Am I boring you?"

"No, of course not."

"What we must ferret out is the financing of the Nazi underground. We know it exists. They're doing things they have to pay for, not only in Germany, everywhere in Europe, but particularly France. With all due respect to Switzerland, whose good faith we don't question, we think the Nazis hid their money there. Every other place is so far away, so awkward. The Swiss are honest, their figures are correct, and naturally, they're very annoyed at us."

He stopped for breath.

Miss Ann said, "And just where do I come in?" She hadn't touched her Martini.

The general looked her in the eye. "I assume I'm talking to the same girl who drove the British ambulance in '18 and got the Croix de Guerre from old Foch?"

"The word 'girl' is misplaced." Miss Ann lighted a cigarette before he got to it. "I'm a quiet old lady. I'm nearly fifty. Otherwise, yes, things happened to me when I was young."

"You still have some faith in your country, in spite of its blunders and Congress and all that? You wouldn't give it over to its enemies? And courage, Ann, we count on you for that."

"What do you want, Breck?" she said sharply.

"We want you to go to Switzerland, my dear. We have an agent or so there, young men who could naturally join the circle round you. But we lack liaison." Hannah's slow feet were plodding back and forth between the kitchen and the dining room. Miss Ann wished she would come in and stop Breck but she didn't. "Washington Osborne," he said, "wants to come home; he's getting old. He sent a message by a friend that he wants to die in his own country, a country he's served well as you'll find out. During the war he was one of the mainstays of O.S.S. in Switzerland, a rich man who owned property there, and he got on the track of German funds that were brought in and disappeared."

The fire had died down again. Ann shivered.

"That started our project," Breck said. "He'll tell you about it; all the threads are in his hands. He sends back brief messages, mostly about what he wants in the way of cooperation. That's what you'd take over."

"It's fantastic!" she cried,

"Not at all. You used to know everyone in Europe. What would be easier than to renew those relations?"

"With the world as it is now? What reason would I have to go to Switzerland?"

"We thought of that too. You'd be writing your autobiography."

"Never," she said.

"You'd visit Europe," he went on—he might not have heard her—"to put in changes that have taken place. And you'd send back reports in chapters of your manuscript to your publishers. Literary codes are the ones that are never broken. No less a person than Adam Carthage* invented this one."

She leaned back in her chair and said faintly, "They don't want tourists. They're not ready for them."

* See *Murder of a Novelist*

"Hah!" said the general. "Wars may come and wars may go but Switzerland always wants tourists. They live on them. May I, Ann?"

He stirred the Martini.

She drank hers absent-mindedly. "I'd have no reason to receive," she said, "in Switzerland, to any extent. There'd be no reason for these men to come to see me."

"You wouldn't need a reason," he said. "There'd be no question but that people would want to see you. We all agreed on that."

"But the men you use will be *young*," she cried.

"What of it?"

"Come in the morning and look at me in a good light."

"You are charming in any light."

Miss Ann leaned forward.

"The Army," she said, "was certainly the right career for you. The tank corps, wasn't it? But you can't run over me, Breck Summers, with your fifty tons. I see it all now. A few men of your age got together in Washington and got sentimental over me. 'Where's Ann?' you said. 'What's she done in this war, or after it? Nothing? A waste of material.' You simply failed to remember, egging each other on, either that you'd grown old or that I had. You hadn't seen me in years, any of you, to begin with."

The general was silent. She'd hit home. But he remained regrettably poised and alert. If she were the enemy, Miss Ann thought suddenly, she'd be afraid of him—too well set up, too jaunty with that bow tie, too grim. Perhaps she was afraid of him anyway. It had been very peaceful here just half an hour ago. The twilit room, the soft shine of the furniture brought across the sea from another life, another world. Yes, she had worried about things, but so vaguely. She'd been miles from thinking she could do anything. Could . . . could?

"Ridiculous, Breck, it's ridiculous!" The words fell out on top of each other. "I'm the exact opposite of a Ninon de Lenclos. We both know the kind of European woman, middle aged, with money, who surrounds herself with young men. A type I loathe and abhor. Do I look like that? I couldn't possibly act like it."

"But, Ann," the general said, "there's no one else for the job."

"I'd be a failure."

"On the contrary, you have gifts. We've heard about the murder you solved single-handed. We had the inside story about that."

"It's not the secret service part of it," she said, "that I'd fall down on. It's the social side. I simply have to be myself. I can't become a dreadful old harpy who ensnares young men. I've spent the last ten years learning to be an old maid and I *am* one."

The general didn't answer.

"I'm sorry, terribly sorry," she said. "I gather this is not without danger. You're right to think I shouldn't refuse that."

He was still on the edge of his chair. There was a light step in the doorway and he turned around. Slowly, very slowly but quite impressively he stood up.

Nancy had stepped inside the room. The blue thing Miss Ann used to wear to the Opera showed her pretty shoulders. She had brushed and brushed her shining hair. She had made use of other trifles like lipstick and perfume.

Breck Summers was struck dumb.

Nancy smiled joyously like a child whose brand-new trick had worked.

"This is my niece, Nancy," said Miss Ann with a clutch at her heart.

Why couldn't he have seen her in the morning, in dungarees, her shirt-tail hanging out? The general brought his feet into position and bowed.

"How much you look like your aunt," he murmured. "I remember . . . oh exactly . . . Are you as much like her as you appear to be?"

"I don't know," Nancy said demurely, thinking what fun, "Am I like you, Ann?"

"Not very, dear. It's lucky for you." Ann's heart was beating much too fast. She said quite casually, "Have a Martini?"

"Allow me," said the general. "I shall make a fresh one."

His motions were too deft; she'd noticed that before. But also his voice was too smooth. This was worse. Yes, now she was very afraid of Breck Summers.

"What a fortunate thing," he said, almost purring, "you happened to come in."

"Was it?" Nancy said with round eyes.

"Almost a miracle," he said. "We see them sometimes in our work. Tell me, Miss Nancy, do you like to travel?"

2

Nancy stood by the window opening on the balcony and looked at Lac Léman. It was all smooth and gray and misty like a moonstone. You could hardly see the other shore. It seemed to be a bank of cloud or of dark evening sky with, slightly to the left, three peaks, the Dent du Midi and her sisters, white on top with snow. On either side of Nancy heavy dark red curtains were caught back with heavy dark red cords.

I certainly don't feel the way I felt in America, she thought. I've never felt this way before. Why, anything could happen in this place. It won't be the same old thing day after day like in Connecticut . . . It will be . . . Oh, I wonder what!

Partly, she thought, it was this room with the gold lettering over the door, *La Chambre du Lord Biron*. Her aunt had cabled for the suite. She had lived in it, she explained, one summer twenty years ago, more than a hundred years after the poet had stopped in Ouchy, the port of Lausanne. Byron was a bad writer, said her aunt, but he certainly knew hotel accommodations. To be sure, the place had run down. The red velvet chairs and the curved sofa in the anteroom were a trifle threadbare but they looked as if they'd been worn only in the service of now a marquise now a comtessa.

The sun came through between the curtains of the balcony with the same slant it always had, Aunt Ann told her, and trembled on the wall with the reflection of the water. Only that morning she'd been wakened by it. The little maid, about her age or even younger, with such red cheeks that were not painted any more than the side of an apple, had said shyly, *"Bonjour, mesde- moiselles,"* and drawn back the curtains. Nancy had propped herself on one elbow and discovered, beside her bed, a tray with fat crusty rolls, not like the thin rolls of France, butter and honey and foamy chocolate. She'd taken one bite, tossed her hair back to see the glittering water and said, with her mouth full, "I like Switzerland." How her aunt had laughed!

Aunt Ann had seemed quite a bit gayer since the news in Paris. Strange that an accident should make anyone gay, even if it was to someone they didn't know though they'd been going to meet him. WASHINGTON OSBORNE, that was the headline, KILLED IN CAR SMASH. At first Aunt Ann had been rather silent. After a long while she'd said, "That *is* a tricky road above Lausanne. Anyone could go over the edge."

Then she had sent a cable. Nancy hadn't been told. Her aunt's idea was to keep Nancy out of it as much as possible, but after all! Did the older generation think one couldn't add up two and two? First, Ann had fussed around with her door shut and afterward there was the ash on her ash tray that didn't come from a cigarette. That would have been the code. Nancy remembered perfectly that Mr. Osborne's was the one name General Summers had mentioned, in fact the only name he said he knew. "Doesn't do to know more than you need at one time in our business." He impressed them with that.

So she had asked her aunt, "Watson would like to inquire, do we have any other contact in Switzerland? Or from now on are we just traveling?"

Her aunt had said, "So far as I know we're just traveling. I admit I like it."

Her voice was gay even now as she talked with the little maid, Lydia Flickinger—Leedia, she pronounced it How fast they both talked. Nancy could barely keep up. She knew the words but they surprised her outside of a classroom. Leedia came from a small village in the mountains. About that size; she showed it with her hands. She had been spreading out a long black dress on Aunt Ann's bed. She turned toward the window.

"And for mademoiselle." She clasped her red hands and said with bated breath, "Is it the pale rose?" After all, the child had pressed all their dresses.

"Yes, Leedia," Nancy said in her halting French, "you have guessed it."

The little maid carried the dress as if it were something sacred in a procession and when she had laid it down stroked one of the folds.

"Is there anything else needs to be done for these ladies?" she said with hope.

"Not for me, thank you," Nancy said and smiled. "I like the pale rose, too." Strange that she could like things again. The days with Philip were a lot farther away now, almost like something she had read in a book and not lived at all. Besides, to be honest, there had been very few of them.

"Oh, mademoiselle, it's a dream!" Leedia ducked her head quickly. *"Excusez, mademoiselle."* With an embarrassed rustle of starched apron she was gone.

"Are you really reconciled to the dress?" Miss Ann said.

"I think so. There's something about it. Even though I was so bored in Paris by being forever treated as a *jeune fille.* All the attractive things I couldn't wear. 'Oh, never, never, mademoiselle . . . When you are thirty.' What is there about being thirty? This dress is so innocent I believe it's sort of overdone on purpose."

Nancy was shoving her feet into blunt slippers with ankle straps. "The heels are high enough anyway," she said with satisfaction.

Miss Ann had finished dressing and sat by the window, her eyes rather absently fixed on the gray lake. "One's first

Paris dress," she murmured. "It's like the little phrase of music in Proust." She seemed to be quite rapt in memories now and then, and they were hard to penetrate.

"Who is this British invalid we're dining with?" said Nancy. "Where did you know him? Was he ever in love with you?"

"Really, you must stop making fun of me." Miss Ann was looking stately, drawing on long black gloves. "You will when you have a fling at diplomacy yourself. Remember you're expected to be pleasant to *all* the young men, whatever you may feel about this or that one. When your grandfather was ambassador, my manners were in the service of the United States. So are yours."

"Yes, dear," Nancy said. "Coming back to Sir John. Do you know him well?"

"I've never met him," her aunt said. "Mary Trelawney was at school with me in Brussels. She was his older sister and quite plain, so, of course, the family lavished everything on John."

"Will she be there?"

"She was killed three years ago."

"Oh," Nancy said. "How?"

"By the Germans," said her aunt quietly. "Like everyone else. Their place, Trelawney Great House, was blown up. Not a stone left on a stone. That may be one of the reasons why Sir John is here. Of course, he's taking the cure. Nobody with tuberculosis stays in England. Too damp."

"But I thought the English couldn't take money abroad? How can he give dinner parties?" Nancy had slipped on her dress and was hooking it up with a twist of very competent shoulders.

"Trelawney money was already here. Their mother owned a big property. And the British always give dinner parties."

"Will it be gay?"

"They're usually gay," Miss Ann had finished with her gloves. "Even though, as I told you, Sir John got his lung trouble in a German prison camp . . . Do you want help?"

"No, thanks. I hear someone outside. It must be Leedia coming back."

"You look very well, child, and do remember, don't be pert."

Miss Ann went to the anteroom. *"Entrez,"* she called, and then, rather impatiently, *"Entrez, donc."*

There was a brushing sound against the door and then a bump that made it tremble on its ancient hinges.

"What in the world?" Nancy was saying. For no reason a little cold wind seemed to blow around her. She remembered suddenly . . . And it was such a funny noise.

Her aunt opened the door. Nancy saw nothing, just the dark corridor. Her aunt was in front. Something heavy crawled on the Turkey carpet.

"This man is ill," said her aunt softly.

Ill? There'd been nothing in the hospital like this. Nothing anywhere, ever.

"If you were the kind of girl who screamed," her aunt said, "you wouldn't be in Switzerland."

Nancy didn't scream but she couldn't move either. Her aunt dropped on her knees. She partly hid—Nancy was oh so grateful—what was on the floor. The man gave one or two long gasping breaths. He raised himself on his elbows, tried to raise his terrible face.

"Monsieur *Osborne,*" he said. "Monsieur *Osborne* was killed. Not an accident. They took out much money afterward. I don't know how they killed him. Or me either. *Ah, ils sont malins.*"

His head fell down between his arms. A long shudder took him, from the shoulders down to his feet, still in the doorway. Then he was quiet.

Miss Ann felt for his pulse through her black glove, then she slid her hand under his coat against the heart. She turned his head sidewise gently, pulled out his pocket handkerchief and put it under the mouth which had fallen open. Nancy backed off. She couldn't look. The dreadful eyes, the eyeballs . . .

"Nancy, collect yourself," Ann said. Her voice seemed to come from very far away. "We'll have to move him. He can't be found here." Everything was swimming. "We'd be compromised," said her aunt. "Don't you see? We'd be useless. Hurry."

"First turn him over," came the urgent whisper, "Take the legs. Just like your First Aid course. Surely you aren't going to turn into an idiot at this point?"

"No, I won't," mumbled Nancy. She reached blindly. The man's legs were limp and heavy and went into strange contortions. Her aunt was struggling with the heavier shoulders.

"You'll have to help me," she panted. "Here, under the back."

Somehow together they moved the body, its legs dragging, into the dimly lighted hall. Past three doors they went, past four, to the head of the stairs. They let their burden slump, his head in the opposite direction, as if he had been going not toward their room, toward the other end.

"Go back," murmured Miss Ann.

Nancy felt like an animal wanting to bolt. She just restrained herself from running. She mustn't even let her long skirt swish.

In a moment Ann was there too, safe beside her with the door closed. She was looking at the carpet.

"It's all right," she said. "It's so thin nothing shows . . . And now how do you look? No spots on your dress, thank Heaven. You need a little rouge though. Put it on at once."

She gave a vigorous jerk to the embroidered bell rope hanging in the corner.

"Oh, not Leedia!" Nancy said. "You can't let her find him!"

"Somebody has to," Miss Ann said. "Somebody except us. And quickly. We can't be late to the party."

"Oh, the party!" Nancy said with scorn.

"Exactly." Her aunt's tone was icy, "You're to be at your best tonight. It's our first chance to meet the young man we were sent to help . . . Then if you want to you can go back to the States tomorrow."

Nancy was dabbing on the rouge. She heard the scream, choked off, and the puff trembled. She knew the maid's chubby red hand had been clapped to her mouth. Leedia may not have been brought up a Thorne but she did her best. There came the sound of many feet, hurrying softly.

Miss Ann nodded. "That will take care of marks on the hall rug."

She was sitting in front of her dressing table, gloves peeled back in balls, touching the silver streaks in her hair with a silver comb. From the glass her eyes watched Nancy without seeming to.

"Calm is desirable in battle," she said. "We aren't just traveling any more. We must be ready to shake hands politely with the murderer of this poor man."

"But who was he?" Nancy said. "How did he know us? Aren't you going to *do* something? What *can* you do?"

"Just keep whatever wits I have about me." Her aunt closed the door to the anteroom. "We have heard nothing through two doors."

She pulled the bell rope several times. When there was a knock she had to raise her voice for the *"Entrez."*

"It's I, *mesdames,"* said the proprietor from the anteroom.

Aunt Ann flung open the bedroom door. Her sable cape was on her arm majestically. "Why has our taxi not been announced?" There was no telephone in Lord Byron's room.

The proprietor wrung his hands.

"Never mind now." Miss Ann reproved him. "Is it there? That's all I want to know. *Voyons, monsieur,* one can't be late to dinner."

She sailed out, followed by Nancy who achieved a kind of sail too with her head high. The hall was empty.

In the taxi her aunt seemed pleased. She pressed Nancy's hand. "I knew you'd be all right."

"Oh, I'm all right. But if it's any comfort to you, I'm not going to be pert."

3

There seemed to be a vast expanse of polished floor like a skating rink and on the other side people with nothing to do but look at one. Nancy was grateful that she didn't have to cross that floor alone. She would have hurried; she couldn't have helped it. Aunt Ann didn't hurry. Her straight slender figure moved as deliberately as if she were walking down her garden in Connecticut. At home that gait had seemed a little stiff and formal. Here, Nancy saw in a flash, was where she had learned it, where it was just right, on these miles of waxed floor.

They even stopped a few feet from the other guests who, by the way, weren't staring after all as she had thought at first. They were drinking cocktails. A thin man with thin hair stepped forward.

"You are Miss Thorne," he stated. "How kind of you to come. Among poor Mary's things that were saved were a few of your letters. They made me see we should have met before."

He looked at Nancy. She noticed with pleasure that he was wearing a monocle and that his dinner coat fitted him as if it were an old tweed jacket.

The monocle came back to her aunt. "I intend to make up for lost time."

"My niece is Miss Nancy Thorne," said her aunt somewhat firmly.

271

"Oh, yes," he murmured. "And there are masses of eager young men . . ." He turned his head and the eye that was not behind the monocle twinkled. "Ah, I see not too far away." Three were standing beside him. He waved at them vaguely, "Monsieur de Pré Morel, the Count von Metsch, and a compatriot, Mr. Lane."

Nancy felt her hand seized and brought up and down in an unfamiliar quick gesture, as different from an American handshake as anything could be. Then it was taken slowly, held in one position and bowed over by a blond head. Is he going to kiss it? she thought. But no, the lips didn't touch. This is Europe, she thought.

"May I get you a cocktail?" said a middle-western voice. "Bill Lane making the offer."

"No, better come with me and choose your own," somebody said.

"Nancy," her aunt broke in. "There's the British consul, Mr. Medway, and his wife, Lady Jane. It was she who kindly told Sir John about our being here. I want you to meet their daughter, Diana." She added in a low tone, "And share the young men."

Nancy felt herself steered toward a group that looked like a picture in *Punch*, a beefy squire, a tall bedraggled woman and a girl her own age who seemed to have too many bones that stuck out in the wrong places through quite the wrong kind of dress.

"I say, how jolly there's another girl," she heard. (It was pronounced gel.) "But oh . . . perhaps you don't care for sports?"

"I do. I care a lot and I like mountain climbing." She was pressing a pathetic young hand whose palm was actually damp with embarrassment. She succeeded in drying it a little before the young men lined up to take it in turn. "That's why Aunt Ann brought me," Nancy said earnestly. "I go in for sports."

A grateful smile rewarded her and then they were surrounded by dinner jackets. Aunt Ann had retreated; she must have felt her niece could manage alone: The English girl's shoulder touched Nancy's; she was going to cling. Nancy was glad of it. They were like two soldiers in formation and in front of them was the enemy, impeccable white shirt fronts and wide glasses, that fizzed a little, held up and so many pairs of eyes! Very inquisitive eyes. Somewhere among them, she remembered, probably was a pair that knew the dead man in the corridor of the hotel, that had perhaps seen him dying.

Nancy didn't know that her fright gave her just the right shyness, took away that American veneer Europeans disliked. Her aunt, looking on, knew it and knew the reason and her heart contracted. How had Breck Summers persuaded her to use this baby to bait his trap?

Nancy was thinking, Can I ever figure out which one? and her fingers closed round the stem of a glass offered to her. Mechanically her lips curved in a smile that she had often practiced in front of the mirror and it was a good one. It was received by the German and did things visibly to his face. He's the best looking anyway, Nancy thought, as she found he was touching his glass to hers.

Monsieur de Pré Morel said just a little sourly to Diana, "Ah ha, *le coup de foudre!* Not only does he get conquered by the American men, but now, if I mistake not, he is conquered by one of the women. Maybe he will be wounded too. Who knows? He's a Boche anyway . . . Your health, mademoiselle." He put a glass in her hand.

Diana murmured to Nancy—their shoulders were still touching—"What about this drink? Isn't it rather strong?"

"I haven't the least idea," Nancy returned. "I think it's wonderful."

Monsieur de Pré Morel looked at them sipping gingerly and smiled under his small mustache. "The champagne cocktail, mesdemoiselles," he said, "is no atomic bomb. Oh, perhaps just a little. One is all right for anybody. If you are thinking of two or three . . . well, one should know oneself."

"I say, that's aw'fly kind of you," Diana said.

Nancy said nothing. She thought, Old Mr. Superior Smarty himself in person. The brandy in the champagne melted her so that her feelings ran together. Since he may also be a murderer, she went on to herself, I shall be nice to him. She gave him a dewy look. He noticed it, he certainly noticed it! He had the stiffest, the most military face she'd ever seen though, and the best control.

The Count von Metsch was saying very low, "You will not like me because of my country. I am only tolerated because I was anti-Nazi and came here early as a refugee. But you'll never believe, you Americans, that we could do nothing. *They* were too clever. It's not German to be clever. We are by nature innocent. That is our tragedy."

His voice flowed like music, like sad, hopeless music and he didn't look at her.

"I'm sorry," Nancy said and she did feel sorry though it might have been the brandy.

"They'd killed so many of us." He looked down at his glass. "They'd put so many in prison . . . they tortured the rest."

"Did they torture you?" Nancy said.

"You can call it that." A kind of smile twisted one corner of his mouth and he looked up.

"Don't think I want pity," he said. "Not for myself. Not even for Germany. It's too late." He raised his head proudly and the chandelier made his hair glisten. His whole head was incongruously beautiful; it was a model for a sculptor above the conventional white shirt and black tie. "The rest of you look forward, I look back. I have only the memory of a country I once loved, before all this. I always know my heaven lies behind me."

"But I say," blurted the English girl, "that's not at all fair."

Nancy herself felt oddly stirred; she must sort out these sensations. She put her half empty cocktail glass carefully on a table. Another man had come up behind Rudolph von Metsch.

"You're too gloomy, old man." He slapped him casually on the shoulder.

What a relief to hear an American! She had been feeling overwhelmed by Europe. She twinkled at the newcomer, Bill Lane, although he wasn't striking like the others. He had brown hair and blue eyes, was neither tall nor short. He didn't carry himself in a way to attract attention, but you could see when he moved that there was a certain amount of muscle under that tuxedo.

He went right on, thumping Rudolph in a most friendly way. "It's not as bad as that. I've been all round Germany for my syndicate. A three-week trip. I just got in this morning. Those Nazis of yours, sure we're all glad to be rid of them. They went too far; they were on the loose. But they were damned efficient. They organized the place so that it's going to shape up mighty pretty. As for the race business, I've always thought we were plenty hypocritical."

Rudolph had bowed his head to listen; you couldn't see his face.

Bill Lane had turned curiously white. He'd not returned her smile. What was the matter with the man? This was not the accent of home; this was crazy. I can't wait to tell Diana, she thought, that Americans aren't like this.

Bill was going right on. "Our methods are different, that's all."

Suddenly it struck her. He must be that fascist writer, that Lane who was so unpopular he could hardly be published even in the worst papers. Fury rose in her.

He was saying, "We don't like the way the Nazis went about it, not a bit, but I must say it's a pleasure to go into town after town and never find yourself in the Bronx."

Nancy took a long breath. She needed it for what she was going to tell him, party or no party. But then her foot was stepped on painfully. She managed not to yelp. She gritted her teeth; the air sighed out between them harmlessly.

Her aunt's clear voice was saying right beside her, "Aren't you Bill Lane? You've no idea how we enjoy your articles. They are the only ones that give us an idea of the New Germany."

Nancy said, "I believe I've mislaid my glass."

She moved away, holding herself quite straight and trying not to favor the left foot. It hurt to be a spy, she thought, in various ways, it hurt. François de Pré Morel held her cocktail in front of her.

"Permit me, mademoiselle." His eyes were more sardonic than ever. "All the heroines do not win their medals on the field of battle."

She was glad that he turned from her momentarily, shaken by a spasm of coughing.

"I haven't any idea what you mean," she said coldly. She wanted to go away from this horrid creature who'd probably seen the whole thing. But no, that was not her job. She would have to get round him.

"I do love champagne," she said, taking a sizable gulp. "But it makes me talk too much, according to my aunt. Why don't you do the talking? Then she can't object. Besides"—she fluttered her eyelashes—"I do want to know. Are you here to climb mountains? Or is it for your health?"

"My cough is just a piece of shrapnel in the lungs," he said. "It's of no importance."

His heels came together and he bowed stiffly, as he did everything. "I have the honor to represent France," he said, "on a civilian mission, quite informal. It's a matter of trade treaties with small countries, the Balkans and so on. We find it convenient to meet here."

"Heavens!" she said. "How ignorant I am. I should never have taken you for a businessman. You are too young, monsieur. You look more like a soldier . . . That piece of shrapnel . . ."

"Those in the service of the Fourth Republic"—he bowed again—"are very likely to be soldiers. That is, they were soldiers only yesterday, doing the job von Metsch was too innocent to do." His words came out like drops of acid.

No mention of the Americans, thought Nancy, or the British. Aunt Ann had warned her that the French would be like that. But at least he might have mentioned Vichy, might have admitted that the French had had a cleaning up job in their own country. Was he really an ex-member of the F.F.I. or just a Vichyite reformed? There were lots of those now. She would try to find out. Meanwhile—she pressed her lips together—how careful one had to be!

Her mouth was still closed firmly when Bill Lane came up.

"I am the lucky guy who takes you in to dinner," he announced.

Before she could say a thing Aunt Ann was there, hovering. "Have you met my niece? I wasn't sure . . . Nancy, this is a man I really admire. He gets to places where no other correspondent is allowed to go. Nancy's not very interested in politics." She turned apologetically. "She's one of the few people who might not know you."

"Relax, Aunt Ann." Nancy gave Bill a brilliant smile. "I'm going to learn right now."

But what a barefaced lie, she thought. They had read Mr. Lane's articles together in what remained of the isolationist press and cursed them one by one. She slipped her arm through Bills confidingly. She understood her job. Would Aunt Ann never think she was grown up? Her foot didn't hurt any more. There was Sir John fussing like an old hen because he couldn't find Ann to take in to dinner.

Nancy curved her lips just a little and bent her head toward Bill. The soup is getting needlessly cold, she thought, feeling the *fine champagne,* while my elderly relative endeavors to extract me from the kindergarten. I'm going to show her. I'm going to find out every last thing about Bill and without his knowing I did, either.

But she was mistaken. All during dinner, however carefully she began, her partner saw the question she had ready and parried it.

"Look here, this is all shop with me," he said rather curtly after a while. "Can't we forget it? Let's talk about you. What you're going to do in Lausanne and so forth."

"Aunt Ann will never forgive me," Nancy brooded. "She expects me to be intelligent and up on things and I'm not."

"Don't worry about the intelligence, sister," he said kindly. "A person can have too much of that around here."

She was still very angry in spite of the smile that she had pasted on. He was actually patronizing and quite ordinary looking. He would be a graduate of a state college out west, thought Nancy, who had never met one. You could tell he was American, that was all. She couldn't imagine him as a secret agent, either friend or enemy. Just too common. Here in this roomful of distinguished faces you wouldn't look at him twice. Even the sour Frenchman had something stony and ancestral about him.

As for Rudolph von Metsch, Nancy was accustomed to good looks in men but not to beauty. He was like a legend of the middle ages; one could almost see a coat of mail. She couldn't tell whether she liked it, but it kept drawing her eyes. Poor Diana was rather tremulously being nice to him. He replied politely but his eyes, when they looked anywhere outside of a dream, looked right across the table at her, Nancy.

With a start she recalled herself to the earthy and quite unflattering creature beside her; she would have one more try.

"My real interest is skiing," she confided to Bill. "Of course, it's late for that, but I like mountains. How are the German places I've always heard about, Partenkirchen and so on? Have they opened them?"

Bill crumbled a piece of bread on the tablecloth.

"I think," he said, "the skiing will be better in Switzerland the next couple of years."

So much for that, thought Nancy, clenching her teeth. He doesn't trust me or even like me, no matter how hard I work. Same to you, Bill, and many of them.

Then he said, "How about going to the flower market with me? It's one of the sights here. Let me see, is tomorrow Wednesday? No, it's day after tomorrow. Ten in the morning?"

"I should love it." She thought, what a liar I'm getting to be. Aunt Ann pretends to like him. Well, let *her* be nice to him. She said, "Is it all right for my aunt to come too? She's crazy about flowers."

He said, far too quickly, "Of course. I'm crazy about your aunt."

Lady Jane, Mr. Medway's wife, acted as hostess. She was glancing around the table busily catching eyes to signal that the ladies must leave. But Nancy intended to put Bill in his place. She aimed a melting look across the table at Rudolph von Metsch. It wasn't hard to attract his attention; it had never left her.

Then she whispered to Bill, getting up, "I think he's terribly good looking, don't you?"

4

On the way home the excitement of the evening began to evaporate. There was no level driving here. Sir John's villa was above Lausanne, their hotel below it, and the city itself was in terraces on the slopes of a mountain. They'd noticed that morning no two streets were on the same level; some even turned into stairs. The automobile roads wound around all this, back and forth over bridges. As the taxi kept going down so did Nancy's heart. The street lights, the shape of the roof tops, everything was strange. They made a series of plunges into a darker and darker chasm.

She said like a small punctured balloon, "Was I all right?"

"Certainly, dear, you were charming." Her aunt's clear frosty voice carried quite well to the cab driver, of course. "And you see now what I meant by Switzerland being the perfect place to write? It's international enough to be amusing but everybody behaves well. It's so peaceful. Nothing happens to disturb one."

"I see," Nancy said.

She was dreading the moment when the cab would reach the hotel. Then she was going to remember. She'd got through the evening by not thinking of that strangled voice, the white eyeballs, the limp weight. She found her hands were clenched at both sides as the driver turned onto the Avenue d'Ouchy. But the hotel looked just as

usual, very placid beside the empty quai. The little cedars
in tubs stood guard so primly round the terrace. Surely
nothing sinister could have happened here.

The night concierge came out of the door as neatly as
a cuckoo out of a clock and bowed them in, took them up
in the old-fashioned lift, wished them good night. He was
so mild, so competent and plump; Nancy felt reassured in
spite of herself.

To her surprise it was easier to forget than to remember. In fact, she had hardly slid out of her clothes, leaving
them just anywhere, and done the quickest wash before
she found herself between coarse linen sheets, her eyes
closing.

It was the first night in months she'd failed to think
of Philip the last thing. She forgot that too—the pillow
that she always had to turn for a dry place, the handker-
chiefs she threw on the floor. The next thing you know,
she thought half in a dream, it would be morning and the
slanting sun darting in again over the balcony.

But it wasn't. All of a sudden Nancy came awake. She
lay perfectly still, tense as a bowstring, in the black dark.
It was two or three minutes before she heard anything, then
just the faintest creak. She thought quickly, wood rubbing
wood. Must be a dresser drawer opening. What should she
do? The sound came again, a soft jerk. Light sprang up.

Aunt Ann was pointing her revolver, saying *"Hauts les
mains!"*

She'd chosen her moment. The man was bent over, his
right hand on the drawer. He put both hands up.

"Ne tirez pas," he mumbled, then turned toward them.
"My God, women."

A slow, delighted smile broke over his young face. "And
such women!"

His eyes rested on Nancy. She made a furious grab for
her bathrobe and shrugged it on, gritting her teeth.

"How to meet people in Switzerland," he murmured,
"the right people, oh definitely . . . *Je demande pardon,"*

he brought out, composing his face though his eyes were dancing. *"Je regrette . . . je ne savais pas que . . . que . . ."* He appeared to be searching for the word in a total void.

Aunt Ann was resting her pearl-handled weapon on her knee thoughtfully, still aimed, even cocked. So Madame X, that revolver, Nancy had thought at home. By the way, how did she get it here, through all the customs' inspections?

"Young man," Ann said. "You may explain yourself in English. It's bound to be difficult. There's no use struggling with a foreign language, too."

"Good God," he said again. "You're American."

He took just a glance at the distance from the dresser to the balcony.

"Advance three steps," Aunt Ann snapped at him. He obeyed. "Nancy, go round behind him and lock the window. Then go through his pockets, remaining behind."

Nancy slid out of bed.

"How long," Miss Ann said, "have you been out of the Army?"

"About a year."

"Who hired you to break into our rooms? What were you told to get?"

A look of surprise came over his face. "Nobody hired me. Fat chance. I've been working for Uncle Sam too long to want to hire out to anybody else. I'm on my own." He paused, then burst out suddenly, "I don't mind telling you it's been damn boring."

"What were you looking for?" Ann said.

"Oh, money, jewelry . . ." He shrugged his shoulders.

"Are you broke?" Ann said.

Nancy was gingerly lifting a stuffed wallet out of his pocket.

"Not exactly . . . No use telling you that with sister here frisking me like my wedded wife." Nancy stiffened and dropped a clasp knife onto her bare foot. "Ouch," she said.

He looked down at the pink delicately painted toenails.

"When you come to that picture in the wallet," he murmured, "you can throw it away. I want a new one."

She swept past him and laid the contents of his pockets on her bed.

"Read me his ration card and passport," said Ann. "Look at his papers to see if there's anything about his Army record."

"I might as well tell you," said the man quickly. "I was a pilot. The government gave me special facilities over here. I was shot down in France and I was looking for a family that helped me. I didn't find them. I know now the Germans got them all."

"Name is Captain Millard," Nancy said. "Ninth Air Force. At least that's what these papers say. The pictures are him, all right." Oh, dear, she thought, there goes my grammar. I hope Ann won't notice in front of a thief.

"Millard, Millard," her aunt was musing. "It's familiar. You must be something special for the government to help you. Did you get a lot of planes?"

"A matter of luck," he said without expression.

"Why did you come to Switzerland, Captain?"

"It's such a safe country!" His face smoothed out and became actually childlike. "More so than America because there they don't know, but here the war boiled all around and didn't touch them . . . It used to be the finest feeling in the world to be safe each time after you weren't . . . But safe every day! That's something else again." His face knotted like the same child very puzzled. "Wake up in the morning with nothing to do but go out and get breakfast! God, I couldn't stand it. Made me too nervous."

He rubbed one foot against the other sheepishly.

Miss Ann nodded, her eyes vacant, as if thinking of something else very far away. "And so you climbed this balcony for the excitement?"

"That's right."

"A likely story," Nancy burst out. Her aunt was acting so peculiar, like a sleepwalker, like somebody lost in a dream. Her age must be getting her; she'd even uncocked the revolver.

Nancy shook out a wadded khaki handkerchief; a little shower of striped ribbons and metal poured on the bed. A bright blush stained her face but she said doggedly, "Probably been stealing these too."

"You missed that time, sugar." The childish face could crease into cynical lines. "When do we start calling the gendarmes? Good old Swiss. They keep a fairly comfortable jail."

"We're not calling the gendarmes," Ann said.

Nancy's heart sank. This was crazy.

"Why not?" He pretended to be injured. "Don't tell me I'm a failure as a cat burglar. It's certainly hard to work into a civilian job."

"I presume," said Aunt Ann, "you can get down by the balcony as you got up that way?"

"But lady." He sounded really disappointed. "Don't you believe I was going to steal something?"

"Of course. That's why I'm interested. I think you might give it up in favor of something more dangerous."

"What!" His forced light expression suddenly relaxed. He gaped like a small boy.

"I'll have to keep your papers," Ann said crisply, "until they're checked. Let me see. There's a good orchestra not far from the Place Saint François. Would you like to take my niece tea dancing at five?"

"Would I not? But who's going to make her go?"

"My niece will accept. Miss Nancy Thorne, Captain Millard. I'm Miss Ann Thorne. Unfortunately, since this is Europe, Nancy must have a chaperone. I'll be there too."

He bowed. "It will be a pleasure."

She makes them behave, Nancy reflected, even when she's in a nightgown, even burglars, although, she said to herself bitterly, this lesson in manners will be at my expense.

At her aunt's direction she gave him back his money, his medals, the key to his pension.

"Would you mind," he said, "turning out the light? I want to look before starting down. I'd hate to be in jail at five o'clock. It's much less good to be picked up without papers. Oh, but then, I could telephone our consul at Geneva." He grinned suddenly. "I forgot about the peace."

He turned and the back of his head showed. It was gray, all gray. Nancy had thought him blond.

"Don't count too much on the peace," Ann said.

She snapped off the light. The curtains parted in a dim streak.

Nancy moved noiselessly on bare feet to the window and saw a shadow round a pillar fade into the shadows at its foot. She padded back.

"Now will you tell me why," she said, "we have to make a friend of a man who breaks into our room? Your pearls were in that drawer. And have you, by any chance, forgotten the murder?"

"You sound a little like your dear mother." Her aunt's voice was tired. "You'll have to go to Geneva by the early train to check Captain Millard's papers. The express makes it in an hour. You remember Geneva, at the end of the lake? Get to bed now."

"I don't think I can sleep a wink."

But she had scarcely pulled the eiderdown up to her chin when a great weight came over her, pressing her limbs flat to the bed. As if I'd been drugged, she thought drowsily. She had to struggle to say, "Aunt Ann, you weren't afraid of him. Why not?"

Her eyes opened just a little, enough to see the end of a cigarette glowing. Smoking in bed! What mother would say.

"That man," said Nancy, "would just as soon be a thief. Why don't you think he's a spy and a murderer, too?"

"Because, dear, people can be driven. We'll know more when we check his papers. I just made a guess about him."

"Why?"

"You see, I knew someone who did the same thing after the last war."

5

Miss Ann's eyebrows went up. "See an inspector of police, monsieur? But why? Our papers are in order."

The hotelman fidgeted, he looked this way and that.

Then he burst out, "To tell the truth, mademoiselle, there was an incident. Very upsetting. In a house like this such a thing *cannot* happen. We have always been such a quiet house." He clasped his hands. "The tranquility . . . the repose!"

Her eyebrows did not come down.

"An incident, monsieur?" she said. "What incident? I am busy this morning."

He looked directly at her at last, his eyes begging like a spaniel's.

"I'm not even allowed to say," he murmured. "It was ah, unhappy . . . The police are examining all my guests in the dining room."

Miss Ann rose from the large carved armchair and pushed her sheets of manuscript together on the poet's table.

"I am not aware of being a witness to any event, either happy or unhappy," she said firmly. "However, if the police of Switzerland wish to see a tourist, one cannot refuse, even at the cost of one's work."

The proprietor rubbed his hands, cringing as if they hurt.

"The niece of mademoiselle also," he said. "The police wish to see also Miss Nancy Thorne."

"My niece went to Geneva by the early train."

And what a splendid thing that was, she added to herself, sailing out of the door M. Dunois had leapt to open. He trotted along behind, not quite daring to come abreast. She had been told by Nancy many times that her back was fully as intimidating as her front. And so it proved. M. Dunois was incapable of a remark until he introduced her to the police officer. Such a nice man, she thought at once, brown eyed and quiet, M. l'Inspecteur Charbonnet.

She hesitated just a second and then did not restrain the impulse to give him her hand. Americans, she thought, are well known to be always shaking hands. He took the gesture quite well, not showing he was startled, not allowing himself to be impressed. In England he'd have to be a gentleman for this. But anyone could be that way here. It was an old democracy. Even police inspectors could afford to be unpretentious.

While his assistant was writing down her name from her passport she gave a quick glance at the other guests of the hotel. They sat along the far wall in armchairs, bored, indifferent (or pretending to be), glazed over with hauteur. They were all refugees from somewhere or other. They'd come to Switzerland with memories or money, or both. Here they were safe (or pretended they were). She thought suddenly with pleasure that probably most of them had something to hide. M. l'Inspecteur Charbonnet would have to delve into the entire lot.

What a harmless picture, in contrast to these tired devious Europeans, was presented by an American old maid and her niece! All honesty and candor, she reflected. Besides, none of the others would have shaken the inspector's hand.

"I don't understand this," she said. "But naturally I'm willing to help. What is it all about?"

"Thank you, mademoiselle," he said gravely. "A few questions."

She nodded.

"Where were you about six o'clock last night?"

"We were in our rooms dressing, my niece and I. We were going out to dinner . . . But what is it? What happened?"

He raised a hand. "Just a moment, mademoiselle. Did you hear anything unusual?"

"No, nothing."

"Can you hear the other guests, as a rule, when they pass by in the corridor? There are cracks round the doors; boards in the floor that creak." He smiled. "The hotel is not young."

"No, we can't hear them. That is, only from the antechamber. When we are in our bedroom with the door closed, we can hear sounds from the lake more readily than from the hall."

M. Dunois nodded eagerly in the background.

"And how long did you remain there dressing, in the bedroom?"

"Oh, far too long, until nearly seven. I was afraid we were going to be late. Our cab didn't come; no one answered the bell . . . That was *most* unusual. The little bonne, Lydia, such a nice girl, always came right away before. And where . . ." Miss Ann turned to M. Dunois, "is Lydia today? Someone else brought us our breakfast."

He started to speak, then stopped, looking at the inspector.

"Oh," breathed Miss Ann. "Don't tell me anything has happened to *Lydia!*"

"No, no," said M. Dunois. "Nothing at all. She received a telegram this morning that her mother is ill. She had to return home for a few days."

"Why are you so worried about Lydia?" M. Charbonnet said quickly.

He must see it in my face, she thought. He's intelligent. She allowed a slow smile to take away the lines one by one.

"A guilty conscience. We really missed her this morning. I promised Nancy to inquire about her. And I forgot."

"When you were waiting for the cab," said M. Charbonnet, "did you not open the door to the antechamber? It would be natural . . . *voyons.*"

Miss Ann wrinkled her brow. "I don't remember. The bell is in the bedroom. I expect I was concentrating on that."

"Pardon, monsieur," the proprietor said. "The door between the antechamber and the bedroom was closed when I arrived." He bowed to Miss Ann.

"Now do tell me what happened," she said pleasantly. "What is it that we should have heard?"

"Only a man dying in the corridor."

"Oh!" Her hand flew to her cheek. "How dreadful! When we were thinking only of our frocks and wondering why the cab didn't come."

The inspector was watching her closely.

She turned to M. Dunois with a puzzled frown. "But you answered the bell and said nothing. There was nobody in the corridor then."

He drew himself up. "It is the *métier,* mademoiselle. Never disturb one's guests. For four generations in our family we have been *hoteliers.* What would you? It is in the blood."

"So much so," M. Charbonnet said wryly, "that he reported it as a heart attack. We wasted a lot of time before getting an autopsy. Then a lot more ruling out suicide. It took fourteen hours to find that this was murder."

"Murder!" She just didn't cry out. She looked fearfully over the room at the other guests. "Do they know?" she whispered. "I don't make such a noise as a rule, but this is *too* frightening. Should we have heard a shot?" She turned to M. Dunois. "There wasn't any blood or anything."

"We wouldn't have had to clear him out so quickly," he said quite resentfully, "if you hadn't kept ringing that bell."

"But, oh, monsieur, how could I know?" She turned toward the inspector. "Who was the man? How was he killed?"

"He was an employee of a bank, the Crédit Alpin . . . He was poisoned."

"But poisoned . . . in the corridor of a hotel?"

"Not there," the inspector said patiently. "Somewhere else. The doctors say the poison must have been taken an hour before he died. All this will be in the papers. We have freedom of the press like America. We do not conceal crimes here, not unless," he fixed M. Dunois with a relentless eye, "we happen to be for four generations *hoteliers.*"

"Why did you rule out suicide?" Miss Ann said.

"Ah, you are interested in the case?"

"Of course . . . At home we read so many detective stories."

"Then you will guess," he said, "that we have been in touch with the bank. There was no error in his books. No trouble in his private life. Georges Évanoui was a happy young man."

"Oh," she said. "It is even more sad."

"Since you read so many detective stories," he said, and for the first time she didn't like the tone, "undoubtedly you know why we are asking these questions? The exact point that we wish to find out?"

She opened her eyes quite wide. The inspector noticed that they were the color of Lac Léman on a cloudy day. She cannot be any older than I am, he thought irrelevantly. Too bad she has that air of the old maid.

"I'm afraid I don't."

If she were happily married she'd be beautiful, he thought quickly and with an unexpected little wave of concern. She's not really old maidish.

"We want to know why he came here," the inspector said, "when he was dying. The clerk saw him force himself up the stairs, hanging onto the wall as if he'd had too much to drink. Whom did he wish to see? And why?"

"How very clever of you!" breathed Miss Ann. "How I wish I could help."

M. l'Inspecteur Charbonnet shook himself. He had never seen eyes that exact color before.

"Thank you, mademoiselle." He sighed. "Now for the lady in Room 22."

The part of him that belonged to the canton of Vaud was urging, Make some excuse to see this charming woman again. The part that belonged to the canton of Berne said equally, Remember your wife and your three children.

His eyes followed her straight retiring back. Nothing would come of it anyway, he thought sadly.

Miss Ann was thinking, A lead to the Crédit Alpin, something definite. How lucky I gave them my letter of credit.

There had been no reply from America to her cable. Believing that there would be, that there must be this morning, had been the only thing that got her a little sleep last night. Now she was forced to admit a possibility. It was that no one, even in America, knew the name of the agent that she ought to get in touch with. Doubtless there'd be some roundabout way of identifying him, but after how long? Mr. Osborne had built the organization here. He might quite easily have avoided sending any names at all. The orders, the money (he was a rich man himself) had gone through him. His contact must have been the bank clerk. Both were dead.

She could only wait for the next link to announce himself. But suppose he hadn't been told who she was? The bank clerk had known. Would he have passed on his information? If he had only fived a few more minutes!

She shivered reaching the door of Lord Byron's room. She went in quickly and locked it. Instead of the American agent knowing her mission perhaps the enemy ones did. Perhaps they'd figured it out from the direction the bank clerk took when he was dying.

That was what made her seize so quickly on the flyer. It was desperation. She and little Nancy were so dreadfully outnumbered. The possibility of the burglary being a ruse counted less than that fear. She was hoping Nancy would find proof in Geneva that Captain Millard was all right. Besides, Ann Thorne felt sympathetic to any strange mental state left by war—here she smiled very faintly—it was more than a trifle nostalgic.

Under the influence of memory she dressed with great care. I have such a horror of wearing anything too young, her thoughts ran on, I sometimes overdo the middle-aged business. No use being quite so rusty. She emerged from the hotel in gray with pearls.

All the way up on the *funiculaire** various openings flitted through her mind. The thing was to find out as much as possible about the murdered man, not just his name and office. That would be in the papers. Who his friends were principally, and where he'd been before coming to the hotel, not to mention the crux of the matter, who withdrew money after Washington Osborne's death. How could one manage this merely as a depositor in the bank?

She did not men see the pretty slopes on either side of the little railroad, did not glance affectionately, as was her habit, at the music box in the station. She marched up the rue du Petit Chêne like a soldier going into battle.

The offices were at the back. She proceeded resolutely behind a secretary to a glazed door, the largest door, lettered with the most gold letters. The secretary opened the door, announced an American client and withdrew.

It was lucky she did. A man and woman stood there frozen. Neither Miss Ann nor the bank president moved so much as an eyelid. The glazed door with the gold letters took an eternity to close. The man moved forward two steps as if he were sleepwalking.

"Is it you, Ann?" he said. "Is it really you?"

He was very tall and thin, *sec* as they called it here. He carried himself like a soldier and he limped, he still limped.

* Cog and pinion railroad.

Miss Ann lifted an eyebrow. "Am I so much changed?"

Even while she gazed at Henri—she couldn't take her eyes off him—she was thinking with fury, Damn Breck Summers! So this is why he sent me! He might at least have . . . No, if he'd told me I shouldn't have come.

"Yes, you have changed," Henri Rambert said slowly. His eyes smoldered quietly just as they always had in their deep sockets. "You are beautiful in another way. You must have had a good life. Has it been good, dear? Did you finally bring yourself to marry?"

"No, *mon ami,* I told you I wouldn't."

"I did," he said. "Remember, you ordered me to. And I achieved a difficult peace by tight-rope walking as we used to say, always conscious of the strain on all sides, like Switzerland *enfin . . .*"

"The tight-rope walking hasn't made you fat," she said wryly. "And your hair, it's all white. Now you can't see that white streak that there used to be among the black."

"*Voyons,* did you expect me to go through two wars with locks like Lord Byron? Even if Switzerland didn't fight we've had our little problems this time, believe me!"

"Yes, and you have one now," she said quickly.

"Do you know about it?"

"That's why I'm here. One of your employees was murdered just outside my room."

"Ah." His face changed; it softened. Its deep lines were less evident; he was young for a moment. "Ann, are you . . . No, you can't be staying in Lord Byron's room?"

"Why not? It's very pleasant. And I didn't know you were here. When we said good-bye you were starting out on a freighter to find an island."

"Yes." He shrugged. "That was the mode . . . freighters, islands. But there were deaths in my family, obligations . . . Is there still that convenient balcony outside Lord Byron's room?"

"A young man came up that way last night," she remarked. "He was very impressed with my niece."

"Oh," he said. "No doubt we are older . . . The young man wasn't my cashier, was he?"

"No, your cashier, Évanoui, came up the stairs. Inspector Charbonnet says that he was already dying . . . I came here, my friend, not knowing about you, to see the president of the Crédit Alpin. May I see him?"

"At your service, madame." He bowed, his eyes twinkling.

She looked deeply into them. "I trust you, Henri. I'll tell you more than I would any other man. There are people in our state department who have known me for years; they want me to help them in a certain matter. It was all pretty vague when I left America. Washington Osborne was going to tell me about it, but when I reached here he was dead. Then last night your cashier just managed to say, before he died, that Monsieur Osborne was murdered. I haven't told this yet to your police. They dislike international complications. So, I suppose, do you. Still, you were serving in the Foreign Legion when I first knew you. I imagine you still prefer the Allies to the Germans?"

"I tried to volunteer this time," he said. "They wouldn't take me on account of my leg."

"The very center of the plot," she said, "seems to be in this bank. It was your man who was murdered. And then my diplomatic friends didn't see fit to mention it, but you and I must have been indiscreet. Just after the last war it didn't seem to matter. I think they chose me because somebody told them"—she smiled quite bitterly—"that I might have some influence with you."

"Don't be angry, my dear. It was very intelligent. It's true I always parry questions of agents. I don't like them. They're too many and too boring and they resemble the kind of cinema one avoids." His eyes were dancing. "I'll answer any of *your* questions."

"So General Summers thought," she said through her teeth.

"Is it so dreadful?" he said gently. "Life might quite easily never have given us the chance to be in the same room . . . Look, here we are."

"You make a funny banker, Henri." She shook her head. "Very funny . . . Have you children?"

"Yes."

"And you adore them and your wife is a lot younger and you make her happy?"

"I think so."

"Just what I wished for you," she said firmly. "And it makes an added reason for us not to see each other."

Some of the light left his eyes. He said colorlessly, "How am I to help you?"

"We need a person who won't be suspected to carry messages."

He frowned. "But who is there?"

"There's only this American who climbed up by the balcony. It will not be difficult to persuade him to see a great deal of my niece. He was a flyer, an important one, I think. We're looking him up. He's at a loose end. Pretty ragged. You know . . . you remember how it used to be?"

"I remember. Yes."

"He's the type," she went on, "to pull himself together in a crisis. That's what we have, a crisis. Could you use him?"

"There's the Tourist desk," Henri said doubtfully. "Georges Évanoui used to spend some time there. Our clients often want information that travel agencies don't supply. As long as the Occupation Forces use us as a leave area, an American might not be out of place. I would have to get federal authorization and it would only be a temporary job."

"Splendid," she said. "Being a flyer, my young friend must have some idea of the map. The rest he could learn. You'll try him?"

"Have I ever refused you anything?" He smiled rather sadly and said, "Yes, one thing. I did not forget you."

"Now is the time," she said briskly, "for the *preuve d'amour,* or rather ex *amour.* We've got to find out who they are before they find out who we are. Otherwise they'll eliminate us, like Mr. Osborne, like Georges. I saw him die yesterday; it wasn't pretty."

"Call it *amour*," he said. "Who are 'we'?"

"My niece, of course, and that's the devil of it, I don't know who else. I must have a cigarette." She took one out. "A match, Henri. You smoke a pipe still and drink tea for breakfast as you learned from the Black Watch?"

"From the Greys, dear. The Black Watch drank whisky for breakfast. Why don't you know who 'we' are?"

"Because of this cursed caution. One agent only knows one other one. With Washington Osborne dead I have no contact. I was supposed to replace him, merely to serve as a means of transmitting information to the States. Some young man was going to give it to me."

"Perhaps that was Georges Évanoui."

"I don't quite think so. He would not have paid court to my niece. Mr. Osborne told Breck Summers—that's why he approached us—to get somebody who could form a social circle, be, as you say, surrounded."

"And are you?"

"We're beginning. We've met M. de Pré Morel, on a French mission but he seems to have headquarters here. Decidedly ambiguous. Then there's Rudolph von Metsch, an anti-Nazi German—in a way not a bad choice because he'd inspire more confidence in the Germans than an American could, get more out of them. Whether our people could ever trust him I don't know. There's one American, a reporter, Bill Lane, quite mediocre, even has fascist leanings whether he knows it or not . . . Writes for our worst papers."

"I've heard of them; and this flyer who flew in at the window?"

"His approach was not one that any secret service in the world would have thought up. Anyone else but me would have turned him over to the police."

"But someone who knew you very well, either friend or enemy, might have thought of it?"

"Nobody in the world knows me that well except you, Henri." For just a moment she wondered if Henri could have sent the American, knowing she was there. He could be very devious, she remembered. This meeting seemed, for a flash, too fortunate.

He was saying, "All the same, I shall be cautious with him. What information do you want him to bring you?"

"Who were the friends of Georges Évanoui? What were his habits, to the last detail, and especially what did he do, whom did he see before he died?"

"The police asked me that last. We found out that he went every day to the Café des Fauconniers for an aperitif on his way home. That in itself is an odd habit for a bank employee. The café is in the Red Light district. No respectable woman ever walks on those streets."

"Oh, yes, we had an argument about it twenty years ago."

"So we did . . . Georges used occasionally to meet a woman. The police can't find her. This time he came alone, the café people say. The waiter served his drink on the terrace, deserted except for him—it was quite cold—and then went inside where he served others from the same bottle. The police have examined the bottle. Perfectly harmless. They're keeping the proprietor under observation. They can discover no motive."

"The police talk to you freely, don't they? Quite different from the old days." She smiled. "It's a help. We shall need it if Nancy and I are to save our necks. The *sales Bôches* are brighter this time."

"Yes, it's astonishing . . . And just what are they doing with my bank?"

"Using your safe deposit boxes to store money to pay their Underground."

"No!" He jumped forward, turning his stiff leg, grimaced and pulled the knee up with his hands. "My child," he said sternly, "that cannot be."

"It is what your own employee told me when he was dying. 'They killed M. Osborne. They took out much money afterward.' I came here to ask you to look up who took the money out."

"I can't believe it!" He was breathing deeply, almost panting. "We investigate everyone who wants to rent a box. That's understood. But I've gone far beyond the legal precautions. My colleagues think I'm ridiculous. In the whole country I'm the man who's hardest to satisfy."

"Perhaps"—she leaned forward in her chair—"that's why the Germans chose the Crédit Alpin."

6

Johnny Millard walked up to the door of the dance place at exactly quarter to five, glancing at his wrist automatically. He was used to figuring time. *Thé Anglais* it said over the door, *Orchestre de danse Rossinière.* He checked himself as he gave up his hat and coat, suit shoddy like all civilian clothes but smelt of the iron, shoes giving back reflection, shirt new and stiff as a board. Feel like a monkey, he thought. The head waiter was bowing even more like one.

"A table next to the dance floor for monsieur?"

"No." Johnny had thought of this, too. "Way back in a corner. I'm expecting friends."

That wasn't a girl you could risk showing off. You'd better try to hide her if you wanted any of her time.

The next impulse was pretty overpowering—to order a drink. But he didn't want his breath to blow the child off the floor. Was it for this, he had to tell himself, that I went to every drugstore in Lausanne looking for a bottle of mouthwash?

"Monsieur takes tea then?" said the waiter patiently.

Johnny shuddered. "Coffee, but not right now."

The band was giving out with something South American, German-Swiss South American. Any time they might quit the marimbas and start to yodel. But it was cheerful; people were bobbing around. Swiss young girls, very healthy looking, either in parties with equally healthy

303

young men or, if a girl was here just with a date, her mama
would be sitting at the table drinking tea.

There were the usual lot of old foreigners looking like
movie extras. Probably had been kings of some little dump
somewhere, at one time.

Several tables just had one woman at them. These were
better dressed, older, not what you'd see on the street, no,
but still not quite right. They were pretty good at pretending to wait for somebody. They'd glance at their watches
while drinking their tea "simple" (not "complete" with
cakes) but they glanced at him too. He hated to be looked
at since his hair had turned gray; couldn't get used to it.
He knew he looked silly with that old man's stuff over his
unlined face. He gritted his teeth. The waiter took pity on
him and laid three places ostentatiously.

At two minutes past five his careful, unobtrusive watch
of the door brought results. Here they were, all right, not
that he'd really know them from having seen these dames
in bed. What he recognized was the type. They were a
couple of women with Class.

This thin old one, walking not slow, not fast, furs dangling off a pair of shoulders any top sergeant would have
been proud to have trained, this had to be the one with
the revolver. And behind her, whee, Nancy looked possibly
fourteen except there were no bobby socks, no indeed. It
must be nylon on those perfect legs, perched on a pair of
heels like stilts. Her hair was just as pretty combed and
the wide-eyed face had an expression as if it had this minute chipped the shell of the egg when actually every eye in
the place was fixed on her and she knew it too.

He stood up. They saw him and smiled. A warm, happy,
new feeling started to roll over him and he forgot his hair.
Best-looking women in the restaurant, in Lausanne, in the
world! Let the old dukes in the corners crane their necks,
the Swiss boys goggle over their partners' shoulders . . .
they were coming straight to him, Johnny.

The head waiter and two others dived to pull out chairs. Miss Thorne kept them waiting while she gave him her hand.

"This is so nice of you, Captain," she said. "Such a good table, too."

Nancy was actually smiling. "Glad to see you," she murmured. "Strange as it seems."

He didn't believe it. He waited till they were supplied with tea, so "complete" that it covered the whole table, and the waiters had vanished.

"Why are you glad to see me?" he said. "*If* you are?"

"Because I didn't have any lunch." She tilted her head sidewise at him and took two sandwiches. "What with going to Geneva to check your papers."

"We had to make sure," Miss Thorne said gently. "What we're about to ask of you is very important."

He turned to her then.

"I forgot. I'm only out of jail for a special reason." The defensive feeling of last night came back. "Something you want me to steal for you ladies?"

She smiled with her mouth but her eyes continued to look very steady. "It may come to that. Do you read the papers?"

"Only the *Paris Herald* when I happen to catch one."

"Then you would not have seen it; it came out this afternoon. There was a murder here in Lausanne yesterday, in our hotel, on the same floor where we live."

"So that's why the gun under the pillow. I wondered if it was a habit. You might really have drilled me!"

He must have let his mouth stay open because she said quickly, "Have some coffee."

"No need to burn yourself, though," Nancy said. "Here, I'll pour in some cream."

"Thanks, helpful." He could rally, too. "And you look every bit as beautiful with your mouth full."

"We can't stay long." Miss Thorne recalled them. "I'll give you the facts. Nancy can fill in details while you're dancing with her."

He bent his head.

"A light for my cigarette," she murmured. "The waiter's too near. They speak every language under the sun, these wretched Swiss. Thank you. He's gone now . . . Georges Évanoui, the man who was killed, worked in a bank, the Crédit Alpin. He looked after tourists and occasionally replaced a man in the vault. I used to know the director of this bank in my youth. He told me the murder might have been the work of German agents; his man might have known something about undercover accounts there that he didn't know himself. He'd like to replace M. Évanoui with somebody who'd keep an eye on things, a man with a desk in the front office."

"Me!" Johnny exclaimed. "Work in a bank!"

"You," Miss Thorne said. "A job stepping into a dead man's shoes. I daresay it wouldn't be the first time."

"Maybe not, but the shoes have to fit." He hunched a shoulder. "All I know about a bank is how to overdraw."

"Your job would be to explain things to tourists . . . Look out, now. Here are some people we know. See if you can tear Nancy away from her tea."

He turned to the other side all too readily.

"I've been told I have to dance with you," he said. "Tough, isn't it?"

"Must you be so romantic?" She pushed back her chair, but the next minute she smiled up at him and slipped her hand into his. "There's no reason why we shouldn't enjoy it. May I call you Johnny?"

He slid his arm around her in a daze. When they had turned, Nancy still smiling at him, she broke off to bow to people who'd come in. So he owed everything to them. Not quite, he was to learn afterward. He owed a great deal to the consul who had okayed his credentials.

He didn't know till Miss Thorne told him a week later that it was the first time Nancy'd danced since Philip's death.

When the music stopped she sighed. "What a shame that you do it so well! I hate talking when I dance. But Aunt Ann told me . . ."

"Relax, little one." He was clapping softly, rhythmically like the rest. "Whatever it is you and your aunt want me to do, I'll do it. You know that. However cockeyed."

They went round the floor, past the table toward which Nancy had bowed.

"Who is your Nazi friend?" he said sharply.

"He's not!" Nancy was equally sharp. "That's Rudolph von Metsch. He's well known to be on the other side. The Nazis had him in a concentration camp; he got tuberculosis. And that's Lady Jane Medway with him, wife of the British consul, and her daughter, Diana."

"I've seen that guy before somewhere," he said. "Or hundreds like him. Maybe you'd better tell me after all what it is you and your aunt have got mixed up in. Why not let the police handle it?"

"They didn't do well," Nancy said. "You see before this man in the bank, Georges Évanoui, was killed, there was another murder . . . of an American. M. Rambert will explain. He's not very crazy about being investigated all the time. He's the president of the bank. You see, he used to be in love with Aunt Ann. Everyone was. Everyone of that period, of course. She went all over Europe breaking hearts . . . So now M. Rambert cooperates."

"I'll say. Anyone willing to hire me is cooperating one hundred per cent. And that's just about all he *is* doing,"

"Let's go back to the table."

"We can't." He turned her in the opposite direction. "Your Nazi friend, so sorry, German, is going over to speak to your aunt . . . Jitterbug?"

"Yes, but not much. Aunt Ann doesn't like me to be conspicuous."

"Neither do I."

He threw her just a short way and caught her. The English girl, a homely wench, was watching them with bug eyes.

"I work for this Swiss?" he said, "Is that all there is to it?"

They were just keeping time to the music, walking with short steps.

"Not quite. You see my aunt's very clever. She solved a murder once in Connecticut. But she can't go to the bank all the time. Lausanne is simply lousy with secret agents. You're supposed to take messages back and forth between her and M. Rambert. The idea is"—she ducked her head—"to have dates with me."

"Rugged. That's going to be really rugged." He whirled her round three times.

Nancy was breathless. "Let's go back. I hadn't finished my tea."

"Can't do. Jerry is cutting off our retreat. I wouldn't want you to dance with him and get tuberculosis, would I?"

Quite suddenly the music stopped. The musicians filed out to the bar to get their periodic beers.

"Come," Nancy said. "Please be nice to Diana. She can't help her looks."

He found himself being introduced to the British Empire.

"An American flyer!" The old lady's voice certainly carried. She pronounced it flahr. "We used to meet so many. You wouldn't have known my son, would you, Leftenant Percy Medway? But, of course not. He was shot down in the battle of Britain. Or my nephew Ronnie, Lord Darts? He was a pilot, too, with Montgomery in Africa, quite a long time for the R.A.F. Killed over Italy in '43. There were Americans about then."

"I'm sorry. No, I didn't." Johnny looked around desperately; he was lost in these titles. There were the musicians filing back, wiping their mouths.

"Dance, Diana?" he said.

She blushed a bright red and stood up at once.

"Remember, Nancy," he warned. "No germs while I'm gone."

Lady Jane sighed. "So difficult to keep up with American slang. He looks very young."

"He shot down fifteen planes and got four on the ground."

Johnny just heard it as he guided a bony elbow. Sounded as if Nancy was his kid sister, quite different from the way she talked to him, all pleased . . . One thing about her friends, they weren't surprised by his hair.

The homely little girl could be worse. She danced well enough so he didn't have to pay much attention. He could keep his eyes on the handsome Jerry who was leaving Miss Thorne just as per contract and going over to Nancy now that the field was open. She wasn't going to dance though, shaking her head and holding a cigarette to be lit. Good Lord, the Englishwoman had a lorgnette trained on him.

"Come here often?" he said hastily.

"Oh, no." The girl raised an earnest face. "It was such a surprise. We just happened to run into Herr von Metsch on the Place St. François. He invited us. We were going to a hotel for tea."

So that was the way of it. He, Johnny, knew a wolf when he saw one. Though this was certainly taking a lot of trouble. Must have seen Nancy going in. No man in his senses would take this forlorn little family dancing.

"It's frightfully gay, isn't it?" Diana said.

"Think so?"

"I'm very keen about Americans," she said, "Miss Nancy Thorne, she's the first gel I've met who's my own age. I like her frightfully."

"Me too, sister." He started to steer her back.

"'Sister,'" she murmured, "How nice! I haven't got any brothers any more."

He pressed her arm and just nodded when he was introduced to von Metsch. The German bowed a lot too low but skipped the monkey business with the heels. No hands were held out.

Johnny said, "Nancy, time to go back to your aunt."
She rose at once, said good-bye formally and slipped her
hand under his arm.

In their corner he took his chair between them and
held out his cigarette case to the old Miss Thorne.

"I'm catching on," he said. "I don't like that German."

"Your privilege, of course." She tapped her cigarette,
"But around here, the ones to pay the most attention to
are the ones who aren't obvious." She poured Nancy another cup of tea, "Please tell M. Rambert that I'm not satisfied about the café. There simply has to be a clue there.
I shall look into it."

"I'll tell him and I'll strike him for the job . . . But is
he going to give it to me? What would he think if he knew
my qualification was robbery?"

"He would think none the worse," she said calmly. "He
did the same thing himself after the last war."

Johnny was looking at her—one naturally would at a
remark like that—when Nancy's voice said, "If there isn't
M. de Pré Morel. Why, everybody comes here."

Thanks to his care in getting a distant table Johnny was
able to observe the man she'd noticed for several minutes
before de Pré Morel caught sight of them. While Nancy
and her aunt were chatting, he saw that one of the women
alone, one of the women who wasn't quite right, a brunette, quietly dressed, had put on a smile of welcome. Oh,
it was inconspicuous, of course. So was the little gesture
of her hand. They wouldn't have let her in here if she
hadn't been able to behave as well as the girls with families. Johnny wanted to remember that face. His airman's
eyes found something special, a scar on the forehead, pretty well covered with make-up.

De Pré Morel looked all around quite leisurely, his face
a blank, a haughty blank, and finally his eyes found the
corner table. He walked straight past the woman who was
waiting for him without a sign of recognition.

"Here's where I'm leaving," Johnny said. "I don't like this man."

"Please, Johnny," Miss Ann said. "We can't. We've had dinner with him. It would be embarrassing."

De Pré Morel was bowing, his hands light on the back of an empty chair. Miss Ann presented him to Johnny who nodded curtly.

"Capitaine Millar," said the Frenchman. "Would you permit? It would be an honor. . . . *Enfin*, would it derange you if I should sit at your table?"

"Whatever Miss Thorne wants," Johnny said stiffly.

"Do join us then," she said. "Only . . . we've almost finished. Do you mind being left rather soon?"

"A few moments of your company is more than I'd expected." He slid out a chair. "*Garçon*, a whisky soda."

This was adding insult to injury. First, the waiter was too attentive; second, the Frenchman shouldn't have ordered whisky, not when he, Johnny, wanted some so much! Johnny didn't trouble to hide his feelings; he glared.

The Frenchman's face looked as receptive as a piece of granite. When the whisky came he said, "Excuse me, ladies, I forgot my beast of a pill." Then he used the good whisky simply as a chaser for a big brown capsule. He pretended to choke so he could take another slug. Still very solemn, he turned to Miss Ann.

"Would mademoiselle honor me with a dance?"

Nancy's aunt rose rather hesitantly but, oddly enough, she didn't look bad on the floor. There were women as old as she dancing, Johnny saw with a start of surprise.

Nancy cocked her head on one side like a little sparrow.

"He's a gent after all," she said reprovingly.

Johnny didn't answer.

"What have you got against him?" she persisted. "Do you know him?"

"Never met him before."

"What do you know *about* him then?" she said. "You don't want me to think you're just the jealous type, do you?"

Johnny almost laughed.

"Think what you like," he said. "I don't know much
about him, not as much as I want to . . . But I know he
was the last person before you and your aunt who lived in
that museum hotel room of yours."

7

The pier glass in the bedroom, Aunt Ann said, was the kind Mr. Henry James would have called a haunted pool. It was too full of memories this morning to show Nancy whether she had enough powder on her nose. She stepped into the bathroom. There the mirror was at least as modern as the plumbing.

Aunt Ann had gone out. It was her habit to take a morning walk along the quai watching the gulls and the mist rising and saying "bonjour" to old men who rented boats.

But there was the sound of the key grinding the old lock. She'd come back early. Nancy turned her hand mirror idly to be sure her hair was smooth. It happened to catch the mere crack where the door was open. There was the maid, not her aunt, the new maid moving very softly. She was leaning over the table reading the page in the typewriter. Then she leafed through the manuscript beside it. Then she copied down on a piece of paper the names of their books.

Nancy tiptoed and turned the knobs over the basin. Water rushed out noisily and she scrubbed perfectly clean hands. After a moment she went into the bedroom, greeted the maid and showed her two piles of clothing.

"These are for the laundry," she said. "The others to be dry cleaned."

"Pardon, mademoiselle," the woman said. *"Je ne comprends pas l'anglais."*

Nancy told her in French then carefully, smiling into a pair of expressionless eyes.

She collected her coat, purse and vanity case just as usual. It was only when well outside the door that she allowed herself to shiver.

Aunt Ann's thin figure coming along briskly was a welcome sight. Good old reliable New England by the enchanted lake.

"That maid we have now." Nancy tried to speak lightly. "She's gruesome. I wish Lydia were back."

"'One can't get on without a good servant,'* as the marquise would say." Aunt Ann took her arm and strolled calmly toward the station of the funiculaire.

"It's more than that." Nancy described the crack in the door, the furtiveness, the pretense.

"You don't think . . . My vanity as an author! You don't think she might just have been interested, do you?"

"Not when she said she didn't understand English."

"I suppose you're right. We must keep an eye on her." Aunt Ann spoke rather absently; she was unfolding a map she'd taken out of her handbag.

"And keep an eye on everybody else," Nancy said crossly, "especially this Bill Lane we're meeting now."

"Yes, dear, I'm counting on you for that." Aunt Ann was peering at a maze of twisted lines. "He said the Place de la Palud if I can remember the way there."

When they had made the trip uptown and had walked past the square into the narrow streets of old Lausanne Nancy found herself distracted. There was no traffic here. It was odd to hear only the constant blurred shuffle of countless footsteps on the old stones, no ordinary city

---

* Letters of Mme. de Sévigné. To Mme. de Grignan
  Feb. 12, 1676.

noises. It was like in the middle of dance music when all the instruments stop and leave only the drums to carry on. It was exciting. She looked with pleasure at the faces of the Swiss, all going about their business, full of common sense, no one in a desperate hurry, no one paying too much attention to anyone else.

They kept walking steadily upward among more and more people till they reached an open space with a fountain. From there another little gray stone street went up still farther but it was all in ledges like steps and every step was blooming with flowers. Nancy drew in her breath and pressed her hands together. Such flowers! Yellow and white and timid pink hidden in green. Aunt Ann had always had a phrase "the Alpine spring," but who could dream that it would be like this?

Suddenly, in a doorway, a man detached himself from a group and came toward them taking off a nondescript hat.

"Why, it's Bill," Nancy said. "How long have you been there?" She suppressed the word "snooping" but he might have heard it in the tone of voice.

"I've had a good time watching you," said William Lane.

Aunt Ann gave him her hand and supplied the cordiality.

"You look just like a Swiss," Nancy went on. Part of it was the impression of compact muscle, not visible at all, something to be inferred from a special ease of movement, very unostentatious ease. She said, "You're certainly hard to see in a crowd."

"That can be an asset in my job . . . I'm sorry if you insist on men who stand out."

About ten feet from them a knot of people parted to let through an American, hurrying along, no hat on his strange gray hair, a cigarette drooping from the corner of his mouth.

"There you are!"

He strode toward them with the pace of New York and Chicago. The natives were left foaming in his wake, dodging the cigarette which he tossed away.

"It's Captain Millard," Aunt Ann announced in her clear, carrying voice. "How nice to see everybody at the flower market just as one used to . . . Have you met Mr. William Lane?"

Nancy turned away quickly and buried her nose in a bunch of unfamiliar blooms. They had a very faint scent. The old peasant woman behind them began to chant, "Not dear, mademoiselle, not dear at all, not to you."

She heard Aunt Ann saying, "Look, Bill, that's what I want, anemones. Do you have lots of money? If so, buy me the basket, too."

Arm in arm they were moving up the steps to where a sweet-pea colored mass filled a whole stand, red, white, and blue like a very delicate flag.

Johnny Millard said in her ear, "I have a message, baby, from the local J. P. Morgan. Look, do you want these petunias or whatever they are?"

"Those over there, the white ones."

"*Perce-neige,*" the old woman said.

"Do they really pierce the snow?"

She nodded vigorously, counting back the change. Johnny leaned his head down. "He says your aunt is not to go to the Café des Philosophes. It's in a quarter where a respectable woman can't be seen, not any time of day. Besides, it's dangerous. He will attend to it, he says."

"I'll tell her."

"Do more than that. You keep her home. What does she know about joints like that? I believe this banker."

"Oh . . . do you like your job?"

"This part's all right." He pressed her arm, then looked at his watch. "Got to get back, damn it. The guy was in the Foreign Legion. He may still believe in treating 'em rough."

"Well, good-bye now. And thanks, Johnny."

He grinned. "Be seeing you."

He plunged off, going down the market steps like a canoe shooting a rapids.

The crowd swallowed him up. Bill and her aunt were
not visible either. She was surrounded by flowers, incredible ones vaguely suggesting primroses, spring beauties,
crocuses, but all different really. They had a thin pure
scent: you knew they came from high windy places. Oh,
there were daffodils and violets too, but the violets were
double and very pale, a new color. She couldn't resist
smelling them. Just then an accordion struck up, a gay and
yet rather wistful tune. It was full of refrains that seemed
to echo round from peak to peak. Nancy lifted her face
and met the eyes of Bill.

He had appeared from nowhere again but for once she
couldn't be cross. The eyes so obviously approved of her.
He hadn't quite had time to hide the look.

"What is this tune?" Nancy said hastily.

"Le Ranz des Vaches. 'Calling the Cows' to you . . . Pierrot is at his best this time in the morning. Later on when
he's had a lot more drinks he pulls plenty of sour notes."

"I like it."

"So do the Swiss. In the time of Napoleon when a lot
of them were working for him as paid soldiers the officers
never allowed this to be sung in the camps. If it was, there
were always desertions by morning."

A woman with scarlet cheeks and a black apron over
three sweaters had been tugging at Bills arm.

"Oh," he said, trying not very plausibly to act bored.
"Do you want some Parma violets? She claims they match
your eyes."

"I'd love them," Nancy said demurely.

"They have a little more life than the snowdrops that
aviator bought you. What did you do with him, by the way?"

"He had to go. And what did *you* do with Aunt Ann?"

"She's up there," he turned his head, "trying to find out
how to raise those things in Connecticut."

"Shouldn't we go and find her?"

"Not yet. She's quite happy asking questions. Of course,
what you really do to raise anemones is erect a few mountains."

Nancy was indignant. "There *are* mountains in Connecticut."

He waved a hand. "Not as the word is understood here. You have to have Alps. And then you train a couple of glaciers down into the Connecticut River. It's quite simple really, though it makes the swimming cold."

"Bill, I think we *should* find Aunt Ann."

He sighed, "All right . . . There's a mob to get through."

They inched up the street, packed now with people, polite but slow-moving people. When they came abreast of the stand that the red, white and blue flowers had garnished, it was bare. They kept on up until they reached the open place at the top where there were no more flowers.

"We must have missed her," Nancy said. "And yet how *could* we? The street is so narrow."

She looked around with just a little worry beginning to nag her. What had happened? It wasn't like Aunt Ann to leave her in the lurch.

Bill had appeared alone and talked such a lot. He'd detained her. Oh, she'd been silly to think it was because he liked her. He'd done it on purpose. She jerked her elbow out of his hand.

"Come on," he said, rather startled. "We'll ask the person who sold her the flowers."

They went back down in single file, but now even the stand was gone. She felt a breath of nightmare, the icy fear of the trap. The flower sellers had vanished too.

Suddenly, on the right, she heard the accordion. It did sound drunken now, uneven. It was growing fainter as if the player had gone lurching down that dark side street, an alley really. The buildings were so high the pavement could never feel the sun. But, look! That small white thing. Nancy darted in after it and picked up a fresh anemone. She looked ahead; there was another. Her arm was seized by something like an iron band.

Bill said, "Look, Nancy. You can't go down there. It's a bad neighborhood."

"So what? My aunt's been here."

"Your aunt has too much sense to have set foot in this rat run. Any old hag could have dropped some flowers." There was a startling change between the sunny market and this furtive shadow but she said obstinately, "I don't believe you."

She was standing very still and relaxed in his grasp, gazing ahead through slightly narrowed eyes.

"Damn it, my child, this street is full of *maisons closes.*"

She gave a twist that his hand wasn't ready for. She was off down the street like an arrow. Her rubber heels made nothing of the cobblestones; she ran as if she were on a track. Bill pounded behind, stumbling whenever his shoes slipped on a damp stone.

The alley turned a corner. She would only be out of sight a minute, but no, she couldn't go into a house. The doorways even were slimy. Ahead lay a bleak little square. A dingy awning shaded a piece of the sidewalk. Underneath it were four tables with stained marble tops. Against one of the awning rods there leaned a man with an accordion draped around his shoulder. He was counting coins from one dirty hand into another, dropping them now and then and bending over tipsily to pick them up.

Nancy came to a breathless halt. She opened her bag and panted, "Here, take this. The pretty music."

Five francs dropped into his palm. The fingers closed around it unbelievingly.

Bills shoes sounded loud now. Nancy tried to see into the café. A curtain hid the lower half of the windows, but the glass above it held faded gilt letters, partly rubbed out. They said, they really said, Café des Fauconniers. She got behind the table nearest the door.

"You . . . simply . . . can't," said Bill.

He was acting better, she thought scornfully, because of the old drunk. Not so grabby. Even a drunk was a little protection.

"Try to understand," said Bill. "I'd fight for you, but I couldn't win. A place like this always has three or four guys ready to jump anyone they think is a *flic*, a police spy. And they think everyone they don't know is a *flic*."

Nancy hesitated. It sounded reasonable. Then she remembered Bill the talker, so smooth, so well-informed, so pleasant, keeping her while her aunt disappeared.

The accordion man made a pass at his forelock. He shuffled to the door. Where he had been standing on the pavement was a crushed anemone.

That decided her. The door hadn't quite closed and she slid in behind him.

The dim light obscured everything but the bar. It was being wiped off with a rag. There were two or three men at tables, each drinking alone, and they craned their necks at her entrance and stirred.

The bartender looked up and growled, "We don't serve women alone."

She heard the door open and behind her a heavy sigh. "Quite right," said Bill. "Two beers if you please."

Beside the gloom the silence was oppressive. The accordion player had shuffled to the bar. The waiter who brought the beers wasn't the usual anaemic type; he had heavy shoulders and a thick chest. Nancy saw with a sinking heart that the bartender looked like a prizefighter, too.

Still she plucked up her courage. "We are looking for an American lady who lost her way. Have you seen her?"

"No," said the waiter, "I've seen nobody."

Just then they heard a clear rather acid voice, "But I tell you there's a telegram."

Nancy was off her chair in an instant. She burst through the swinging doors at the back of the room.

There sitting calmly with her basket on her lap was Aunt Ann. She was addressing the proprietor and his wife who looked rather grim actually in their little office, like a couple of lumbering animals in a cage. It was a mistake for Aunt Ann to have got in there with them and she knew it, so she was being specially superb.

Because behind the proprietor was a familiar figure. Familiar and yet strange. It was Leedia all right, but the apple cheeks were pale; instead of shining with soap there was a smudge on one of them. She had a little black shawl round her shoulders; a dirty apron hung from her waist and hid her twisting hands.

Aunt Ann was being brisk with, "Come now, my good man and woman," but Nancy could sense that it had worn thin. For one thing, Lydia was on their side of the room, not hers. For another, something in the lowering and yet steady gaze of that apparently stolid pair reminded Nancy of a tiger's head swaying a little as he got ready to strike.

"I tell you," Aunt Ann said. "There's another telegram from this child's mother at our hotel."

The proprietor jerked his head toward Lydia, "Talk to her, dirty one."

"I can't go, mademoiselle," Lydia panted. "I don't want to go." Terror shone out of her round face. "Can't you see that I'm all right here?"

"Why not just come to the hotel," Ann said persuasively, "for the telegram and your suitcase and then come right back?"

The door behind Nancy opened and she heard that sigh, bored, cynical, disgusted, almost a whistle, that meant Bill. Turning she saw the strong-armed waiter come in behind him and saw Bill side-step neatly to be out of his reach. At that she moved also. If there was going to be a match of any kind she was going to be ready to take part.

The proprietor growled at the waiter. He held open the swing door and beckoned. Nancy could see obliquely a corner of the bar. The accordion player was behind it very drunk.

"My friend, my only friend," he slobbered, flinging his arms around the bartender with unconscious strength. *"Trink, trink, brüderlein, trink!"* he howled.

The waiter let the door close, shrugging, and his stupid face met, unprepared, the *patron's* rage. He jumped to the alert and drew in his elbows.

"You'd better leave Americans alone," Bill said weakly. Nancy had never heard anything as milktoast and he looked it too, but three words aimed at her followed in English, "Take the woman."

"Americans," the proprietor snarled. "You have no business here." He stepped from behind his desk. "I'll teach you to stay at home where you belong."

The proprietor's wife started forward. She was heavy but she moved lightly. Lydia gasped.

There was a shrill whistle outside. The waiter pushed the door.

"Chhhhut . . . *les flics!*" he said hoarsely and with almost one motion he grabbed the towel from his arm, dove through the doors and started to wipe off a table.

The bartender had just got free and had his fist ready to hit the drunk. Instead he shook himself and carrying him like a cat a kitten bore him outside as feet tramped in.

Three men entered the back room and you could tell they'd be police in any country.

"What's this? What's all this?" said one.

The proprietor and his wife didn't retreat; they glowered. The police stared at them.

Suddenly Nancy was aware of her aunt. Miss Ann was doing one of her transformations, shedding her stiffness, her age, and becoming an illusion, the essence of the girl who'd carried everything before her, the girl she'd once been.

She said in a delighted voice, *"Bonjour, Monsieur l'Inspecteur Charbonnet."*

She rose with the basket of flowers swinging gaily and held out her hand as if she were meeting him at a tea, as if he were her oldest friend.

The policeman looked skeptical—he was in front of his men—and yet he warmed, he certainly warmed up to it.

"I lost my way," Miss Ann went on, "coming back from the flower market and got into this *very* unattractive place where I *couldn't* be gladder to see you. It was because I saw

Lydia coming in, the little maid who's lost from our hotel. There's another telegram there from her mother." (Oh, no, there isn't, Nancy thought.) "Monsieur Dunois was quite worried because he thought Lydia was with her mother who is ill."

"The girl wanted to work here," the proprietor's wife said. "Why should foreigners come and take away our servants and ruin our business?"

M. Charbonnet gave Lydia one look.

"We'll take you to see that telegram," he said. "Since you're a minor, you can't work anywhere without your parents' consent. I wonder if they know where you are?" He added more kindly, "Perhaps you'd like to get your bundle, and"—with sarcasm—"your pay from madame?"

"No, no," said Lydia, very white. "I'm coming back. I'm happy here." Her voice rose hysterically, "I have nothing to tell you, nothing to tell you!"

"I didn't ask you anything, my child," the inspector said.

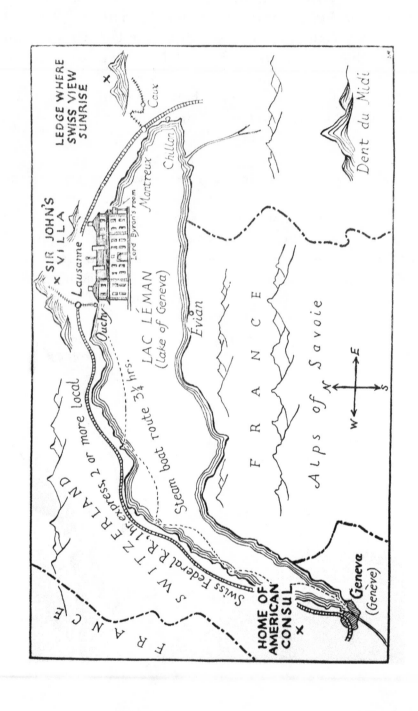

LEDGE WHERE SWISS VIEW SUNRISE

Caux

Dent du Midi

Montreux

Chillon

SIR JOHN'S VILLA

Lausanne

Lord Byron's room

Ouchy

LAC LÉMAN
(Lake of Geneva)

Evian

F R A N C E

Alps of Savoie

E

N

W

S

Steam boat route 3¾ hrs.

Swiss Federal R., lbl. express, 2 or more local

S W I T Z E R L A N D

F R A N C E

HOME OF AMERICAN CONSUL

Geneva
(Genève)

8

Henri Rambert sat in his office smoking a pipeful of English tobacco. It was a kind he'd grown accustomed to a long while ago because its scent pleased an American girl. He was looking out of the window and he was not thinking about banking.

A knock on the door recalled him; he felt like a small boy being lifted back by the collar into the schoolroom.

A policeman entered briskly.

"Ah, it's you, Charbonnet," he said without enthusiasm. "What is new?"

But as he listened his attention focused painfully. So Ann hadn't heeded his warning. She had failed to do what he told her just as she always had. Damn all female Americans! Not women really at all, that one could mold, could teach, but wayward tomboys, not properly conscious of their sex, yes, even at fifty still eluding one, playing with danger, running headlong . . .

He lashed out at Charbonnet. What did he mean by letting strangers get into a dive like that? Wasn't he keeping it under observation?

The policeman, startled, said what was wrong? His men had got there in time.

Rambert jabbed at the air with his pipe stem. "By a hair's breadth! By accident! What if you'd been a few minutes late?"

Charbonnet looked at him curiously. "Do you know these ladies?"

That brought him up short. "Of course not." He must be more careful. He shrugged. "Oh, the older one is a client of the bank . . . What I'm afraid of is an international incident." That would cover it, he thought. "We can't afford another one of those. We can't let the Swiss police become the laughingstock of the world!"

Charbonnet drew himself up. The fellow had a certain dignity.

"Laughingstock, monsieur?"

Rambert leaned over his desk. "Have you forgotten the murder of Vorovski in Lausanne in 1923? I assure you, we businessmen haven't. Neither has the Soviet. He was an official in their eyes, even if not in ours and he was murdered *while being guarded by the Swiss police!*"

"To be sure, to be sure. People have to be more careful about Russia now."

"Some of them thought we should have been more careful then." Rambert rumbled in his throat. "At least they thought a Russian was a human who shouldn't have been killed and then his murderers tried and, though they were proved guilty, let off scot free!"

Charbonnet clapped his hand to his head.

"Of course, of course," he said hurriedly. "Why didn't I think of that? In my youth I knew the list of the jurors, all peasants. They were in fear of their lives. Now it's come back to me. One of the names was Flickinger, the same as this little bonne."

Ramberts pipe had gone out. "Oh," he said. "Curious." He lighted it again, keeping his hand steady. He couldn't bear to think of Ann involved . . . "You mean the Russians kidnaped the Flickinger girl?"

Charbonnet shook his head. "Nobody kidnaped her. It's, worse than that. She went into that pest hole willingly, she, a child brought up in a mountain village as pure and fresh," he waved his hand, "like snow. We can get nothing out of her. She trembles, she won't eat, she begs to go back. When we ask questions, she's ready to faint. Of course, we try to find out who it is has this hold on her, what the hold is. But we find nothing. This is my first light. Perhaps it's the Russians. She'd be more frightened of them than anyone. Perhaps they've said what they'd do to her father if she talks."

"*Voyons,*" said Rambert. "Don't bring in the Russians! Anyone else who knows a little history, a clever spy, could use the same threat. Remember what she found was the body of a man working against the Germans. It's simple, it's logical to think the Germans killed him."

"As you will. But thanks all the same." Inspector Charbonnet was halfway to the door. "You've given me a big idea." He opened it, bowing. "Thank you, monsieur. *Au revoir, monsieur.*"

Since he was backing out he nearly collided with someone waiting to come in.

Rambert heard a loud, "Bless my soul! Can't he look where he's going?"

Sir John Trelawney was fishing for his eyeglass; it had dropped the length of its string. He screwed it in and stared after Charbonnet.

"Seems in a devil of a hurry." He veered round, the bare eye unnaturally vacant and childlike, the wrinkled-up one shrewder, but perhaps it only seemed so because it was partly hidden.

Rambert got up to greet him, pulled out a chair and limped over to close the door. Sir John was a lucrative client like his mother before him. Even during the lean years of the war the Villa Mont Riant had been kept up, the caretakers paid and purchases arranged for, all with sums left with him, Rambert. Sir John's mother, who had bought the place originally, had died there just after Dunkirk. None of the family, of course, had been able to get through. Rambert eventually received a letter of gruff English thanks for his attentions; it had been about two

years on the way. It contained instructions for housing
any of the stranded English that the bank might pick out,
using the villa for the Red Cross and so on.

Sir John said, "Good morning to you, sir." Then with
an air of being very sharp. "Policeman, what? Somebody
been robbing your bank?"

"Not that I know of." Rambert sat down, too. "No, it's
about the murder of my clerk."

"Poor fellow . . . Quite a dog with the women, they say.
Cherchez la femme sort of thing." Sir John shook his head.
"No game for a bank clerk." He leaned back in his chair.
"You mean to tell me they haven't settled it yet?"

Rambert was wondering why Sir John had come. Surely
not just for a bit of gossip. He said, "No. It appears to be
complicated."

"Everything complicated now," Sir John said. "Between
you and me, my dear fellow, Switzerland isn't what it used
to be. Too full of foreigners. I mean there used to be just
the English . . ." He paused, then added hastily, "and the
Swiss, of course."

Rambert smiled. "I'm afraid I'm used to foreigners."

"Not me. Typical Englishman, I fear." Sir John placed
his spread hands on his knees in an earnest, vaguely po-
litical gesture. "Never understand foreigners. The French
now. On our side and all that. So they say even though
they surrendered. Not like the bloody Nazi, at least. But I
don't trust 'em. Never have, never will. There's this man,
Pré Morel." He put a hand on the desk. "Seems all right.
Got his own government behind him. He was always, you
know, close to General de Gaulle."

"I didn't know that," said Rambert.

"You didn't? Yes. I had the fellow to dine. Loosened
up with a spot of port. Not used to port, the French. He
was with de Gaulle in England and Africa. De Gaulle very
unsound then. Suspicious of Churchill. Ridiculous!" (The
Englishman had got the bit in his teeth; Rambert expected
to be dodging flecks of foam.) "Suspicious of Roosevelt,"

he went on. "Ridiculous too. Nearly wrecked the whole show because he thought the Allies wanted permanent air-fields in Africa. Twaddle!" He raised a finger in the air. "Who told it to him, though?"

So this was what he had come to say!

"I was talking with this French fellow," Sir John said, "and I thought, Who told de Gaulle all that? If I'd been close to him then, when he was getting wrong advice, I wouldn't brag about it. Couple of German agents might have been close to him then, too."

He leaned back with an air of triumph. The simplest mental operation seemed a feat to the English, thought Rambert. It exhausted them, even something hoary like raising a hate for the French.

He said, "You make me glad to be a Swiss, monsieur."

The noble lord was plainly disappointed; his bomb hadn't gone off. He was still expectant though he muttered an inquiry about whether a check from London had come through.

Rambert sent to have it looked up, then he relented enough to say, "I'll tell Inspector Charbonnet what you think of de Pré Morel the next time I see him."

Sir John's face lightened.

"One can't help wondering, can one?" he said. "All these new people! There's Miss Thorne now. She was a friend of my sister's, delightful, charming. Everyone's glad to have her here. So much less chance of being bored. But why the devil did she come?"

Rambert remained impassive. He considered giving the barest suggestion of a shrug. But no. It would be more than a lie, sacrilege.

Sir John prattled on. "It's simply that they have so much in America. All that food, comforts that we don't dream of, and the climate's all right too, not like poor damp England that we have to get out of whether we like it or not."

A clerk came in to say the check hadn't arrived.

Sir John hoisted himself with his stick. "My swine of a bank manager!" He grunted. "Wrote me himself but you can't trust 'em . . . Oh, er . . . I beg your pardon, my dear fellow."

Rambert got up smiling—Sir John was always like a vaudeville turn—and walked with him to the door. He remained there humming under his breath *Malbrouck s'en va-t-en guerre* until the young American, laughing rather too loud with the girls behind the desk marked Tourist Information, couldn't help looking round. He retired to his burrow; in a minute Johnny Millard was there, too.

Rambert let him come all the way across the room before he said, "Didn't you get my message to Miss Thorne?"

The flyer looked, very fleetingly, like a private being talked to by a sergeant.

He said, "I'm sorry, sir. While I was giving Nancy the message for her aunt not to go to that place, her aunt was already on the way."

"Why had Miss Thorne been left alone?"

The young man was sweating.

"Bill Lane was with Miss Thorne. I gave Nancy the message and came directly back. It was Bill Lane who left Miss Thorne alone. Nancy reports that I was hardly out of sight when he showed up and kept her back on purpose. She was for joining her aunt but he kept talking and talking."

Rambert murmured, "She never heard from me."

Johnny grinned suddenly. "Just how much good, sir, do you think it would have done? If she's anything like her niece . . ."

The banker smiled. "Is Miss Nancy a pretty girl?"

Johnny whistled.

"I see, I see . . . The new *argot Américain.*" He nodded. "Well, if Miss Nancy is so pretty perhaps Bill Lane had no bad purpose in detaining her. Perhaps he was enjoying her society?"

"I don't doubt that a minute," Johnny said. "But Nancy herself said his actions were queer. She ought to know; she's used to men liking her."

"Ah, used, indeed," Rambert said wryly.

"It wasn't only in the market place," Johnny went on, "that Bill tried to keep Nancy from finding her aunt. When Nancy saw the flowers that were dropped—on purpose, of course—Bill grabbed her so she wouldn't go down that street."

"Again I understand," Rambert said, "if you mean the rue St. Joseph des Champs."

"But in the café?" Johnny said. "No excuse for him there! When they were surrounded by these thugs, Nancy said she felt it would be a toss-up, when the fighting started, which side he'd be on. She never saw anybody who wanted a scrap less."

Rambert didn't answer. He was thinking, these Americans are naive. They expect even now Europe will be a good clean sport like football.

Aloud he said, "Is that all? Miss Thorne herself has no suspicion of anyone?"

"Has she not!" Johnny put a fist on the desk. "She's watching both Bill and de Pré Morel. Told me to tell you about the tart we saw in that tearoom near the Place St. François. The girl was obviously waiting for de Pré Morel, half rose when he came in, and he had started for her table when he saw us and gave her the deadpan."

"He's a Frenchman, after all." Rambert shrugged his shoulders. "That could happen to anybody. That *dancing* is not the Y.M.C.A."

"You ought to know," Johnny said. . . About the other bird, Bill Lane, Miss Thorne made up a sort of test for him."

"A test?" The banker wrinkled his forehead, half in alarm, half pleasure. She didn't fit at all one's idea of a woman, but God, how far she was from dull!

"Yes," said the young American. "It was when Bill Lane went with them to the Post Office. She had a big envelope with a chapter of this book she's writing, all stamped and registered and all, for her publishers. She asked Bill to

put it in the air mail chute and pretended to go off with
Nancy. Anyway their backs were turned. Here's the point.
Miss Ann has a vanity case with a very good mirror. She
let on to be looking into it but had it aimed on Bill. He
put his hand up to the chute but just sort of palmed the
envelope. She saw him slide it into his pocket."

9

Miss Ann was brushing her hair when the knock came at the door. It was Nancy who rustled across the anteroom in her long dress, holding both hands spread out so the nail polish would dry and called, *"Entrez."*

The wooden face of the new maid appeared on top of her figure which looked as if it had been carved from the same block and no joint put in either. "A gentleman is below asking for these ladies," she said.

"What?" Nancy cried. "Already? Is it Baron von Metsch?"

"No, mademoiselle." She neither looked at Nancy nor avoided looking. What training could she have received to produce such a total lack of interest? It was more than the perfect servant's manner; it was weird.

"An American gentleman," the maid said. She held out a square of pasteboard so Nancy could read without spoiling her nails.

"Oh, Mr. Lane." Nancy's voice dropped. "Send him up right away, please. I'll have to get rid of him in time for the train."

She went back and called through the door. "No hurry, Ann. It's just Bill Lane. Its awkward but I'll manage him."

She seated herself on the prim red velvet sofa. There should have been a billowing skirt to go with that sofa and little pointed feet perched helplessly on a hassock. Instead there was a straight, dark dress and dark, stubby evening slippers and a girl whose eyes avoided a certain place on the rug. However, the light came in softly through the young leaves on the plane trees and Nancy thought of all the spring evenings she'd been scolded by her mother for getting a coke too late at the drugstore with little boring boys. Now she was in this romantic room and going to the opera with a man who made every screen actor she'd ever seen look plain.

Bill Lane came in quite briskly but when he saw her he stopped and swallowed. She could see his Adams apple go up and down.

"It's lucky you didn't live a hundred years ago," he said moodily. He laid a rather battered hat on the table, "If you'd been here then Lord B. would have become faithful and where would his poetry have been? Not that I care."

He sat down dejectedly.

Nancy was happy enough to feel kindly toward everyone. She said, "What's the matter, Bill?"

"Just that I hoped to get you and your aunt to go out to dinner. You're all dressed up. I see you're going somewhere else."

"Yes," she announced complacently. "We dined early. We're going to the opera in Geneva with Baron von Metsch."

Bill jumped as if he'd received an electric shock. "No! Not with him. You mustn't! You ought to have more sense."

"I'd like to know why." Nancy's voice had become as frosty as her aunt's. "That's what *he* thinks, that we'll treat him as a leper, but I don't. He was introduced to us in perfectly good company. An Allied party where there wasn't a single fascist except possibly yourself."

Bill groaned. "I knew I'd be in for it sooner or later," he said. "You don't pour out the syrup with a willing hand." He met her eyes squarely. "Listen, child, my stuff is all right. It's realistic. Most American reporters write as if Europe was Sauk Center, U.S.A., and all you have to do is bawl out the Sunday School class and then they'll behave."

She said, "There are lots of *clean* newspapers. If you tried you might get a job with them. Or if not"—she was warming up—"you could dig ditches or anything else honest."

He flung out his hands. "You're as naive as the rest of them," he said.

She shrugged. "And you're sophisticated? Well, so what? It doesn't show. Who cares what your private thoughts are if you keep them private?"

He turned so pale the faint black stubble on his face showed suddenly. She relented a trifle. "Aunt Ann says to wait; you may be going to write a book afterward, exposing all . . . But it won't do much good. Too many reporters write books."

He shook himself. "Count me out then. Let's get back to von Metsch. Can't you see that whatever his politics may be, he's a typical German? That's something no American girl should touch with the end of her finger. If you think for a minute he could consider anyone beside himself . . ."

Nancy stood up. "You call him Rudolph and you pat him on the shoulder and that makes you a hypocrite," she said.

"God help me," Bill sighed. "I always did like a spitfire."

"Well, I like Rudolph," she said. "And I don't believe in being mean to the underdog."

"Oh God," Bill muttered. "I'm leaving town tonight. That's why I wanted to see you. I wanted to be sure you wouldn't go to more places like the Café des Philosophes."

"Oh, have you any little games that you think I'd spoil?"

Bill clenched his fists. "Good-bye," he said. "Remember, you can't always expect the police to turn up in time."

He burst open the door.

The robot maid was coming down the hall followed by Herr von Metsch.

This sight made Nancy's ruffled feathers sink into place. The newcomer was tall and serene and his proud head had a kind of unearthly calm. The slightest smile crossed his face at Bill's quick exit and curt nod but he didn't turn around. He looked at Nancy.

She had stepped back under the window; she knew quite well it made a halo of her hair.

"*Gnädiges fraulein.*" He bent low. "There is no language but our German to greet you in . . ."

The whole interview with Bill dropped like a plummet out of Nancy's mind. Rudolph von Metsch was wearing a cape. She had never before seen a man in full evening dress wearing a cape. It was only a symbol, of course, but she knew. Her travels had been leading up to it and now she knew. This was Life.

The bedroom door swung open and Aunt Ann stood there, bland and restrained in her magnificence, the dark coat buttoned up so tight not a pearl showed, not a diamond.

Aunt Ann, of course, rather took charge. She knew so well what to say always, in the cab, on the train, just enough to make everything easy, never a word more. For the first time Nancy resented this. She felt on such a high plane tonight she could have done it too, and just as well. And there was the delicious, hardly bearable excitement of wondering what Rudolph would say to her when they were alone. They never had been. They'd done it all by looking at each other. Now—she felt in the train—too many people were looking at them.

As they got off on the platform at Genève every face turned to follow them. I suppose it's because we're both blond, Nancy thought. Unconsciously she walked in a different way, quite slow and stately like Rudolph. Her eyes that usually darted around quickly and smiled often became fixed on a far point like his. They were not too fixed, however, to see a little flurry among the passengers. A thin man with white hair detached himself from others.

Aunt Ann said, "Oh, somebody I know. Just wait for me a minute."

So now they were alone. Nancy lifted her face, her eyes half closing like that picture of Rossetti's, that drowned girl in a pool, and Rudolph said, "We belong together, don't we? Everyone sees it, even the passersby."

Her heart went like a bat. There was the most tremendous charge in this. And yet she worried. Did she really belong where he lived, Valhalla or somewhere? And sharply, like a Thorne, she noted that in spite of his absent air he'd really seen the people staring at them.

She looked around, not answering. He didn't expect it.

There would be no trouble getting a taxi. Three drivers were bowing to them at a respectful distance although some other passengers were piled in, several parties to one cab, the ladies holding their skirts awkwardly so they wouldn't be crushed.

Aunt Ann appeared. Rudolph lifted his hand about an inch toward the nearest driver and said, "To the Opera."

Nancy, who'd only seen the Metropolitan, opened her eyes quite wide. This building, in spite of an imposing flight of steps, was only a little theater. Inside, on the black and white squares of the foyer, were scattered small tables. People were sitting there drinking liqueurs and after-dinner coffee. She would have liked to stop. Rudolph suggested it but Ann, for once, was in a dignified form of a hurry. She carried them along, bowing to right and left like Royalty, but never stopping to chat. What was she running away from, her niece wondered, the man with white hair?

When the usher had found their seats, two were in front on the aisle, one in the row behind. Rudolph stepped back but Aunt Ann smiled and tapped him on the arm.

"If you were an American," she said, "you'd be sitting with Nancy. So do. This is for the duenna." She touched the tips of her black glove to the seat behind.

Nancy's bare arm was against Rudolph's sleeve. She would have liked to turn her head to see whether his face was as she remembered it but no, she must stare blindly forward.

Quite soon the lights went out. She hardly saw the familiar costumes on the stage, the clasping and unclasping hands, the darting motions between arias that gave the illusion that a play was happening. She wasn't aware of looking at all because she began to hear *Tristan and Isolde*. Oh yes, it had been sung in New York. She had even sat in a box when it was going on, but this was the first time she'd heard it.

This wasn't just singing, this magic that filled the theater, it was love. She had sat through a performance of that also without knowing what was going on . . . That had been words, poor boy, and imitating others. But now it filled her to the brim, the beautiful, desperate mingling of the male and female voice. The air vibrated like a shell throbbing with the sea. She was carried along in the waves, drowned in them.

Rudolph, she saw, had stopped pretending to look at the stage. His head was turned toward her. Something about him was vague like a sleepwalker; he seemed to be touching her though he wasn't.

The lights came on with the effect of a cold shower. Rudolph said, "Let us go out."

Her aunt made a small gesture of dismissal. Nancy didn't remember until afterward that she looked peculiar. She sat as if she were defying anyone to move her, and defiance was the nearest Aunt Ann could come to looking afraid.

The crowd in the aisle pushed Nancy and Rudolph together. That was the only way she knew other people were there, that and the fact that he towered over them. He found an empty table, seated her and said, "Will you order a brandy for me? I have to speak to the usher . . ."

Nancy felt bereft. Without his presence the charm might be broken, she might sink back into her daily self. She followed with her eyes those haughty shoulders. Why did she have to lit here, the target of too many glances, when she'd rather . . . Good heavens, there was Johnny Millard, propelling by one arm a dazed Diana.

She jumped up. They hadn't seen her, thank the Lord. The very last person she wanted to hear on the subject of Wagner was Johnny. The same for Diana. Dears, of course, but really . . . She found herself pursuing Rudolph with something very like her aunt's determined gait.

He was going toward a bare little room, behind the center aisle, where baskets of flowers were lined up on the floor for the singers. She saw Rudolph tip the head usher who strolled away. Then in the room Rudolph bent over and, drawing from his pocket a thick envelope, he thrust it deep into a mass of red roses. The flowers must have been wired, Nancy saw, because he broke some of them and seemed to be twisting the wire round the envelope.

Before she had time to wish she were somewhere else, before she had time for anything, he turned and saw her.

"Why did you come?" he said. "Why couldn't you have stayed?"

"Oh, I'm sorry," she faltered. "I was lonely. All of a sudden I felt lonely among all those people." She put her hand on the door of the room for support. "And Johnny Millard and Diana Medway were there. I didn't want them to come and sit at the table with us, not here, not in the middle of *Tristan*."

Rudolph stepped over heaps of flowers. He took one of her hands, cradled it for a moment and then tucked it under his arm.

"Of course, of course," he murmured. "I shouldn't have left you. Not when there is so much music that says lovers part . . . And after all—" He looked down at her. "She has a wonderful voice but she's lost her figure. I don't think you'd be jealous of Isolde."

She smiled a little faintly but quite positively. "No."

"Shall we go back and get our brandy?" he said. "And to tell you. It's a long story. It concerns my father."

They walked back, Rudolph keeping her hand close under his arm. When they arrived at the tables people were already streaming into the hall.

"Let's not get brandy," Nancy said. "We might be late. The music is intoxicating enough."

"No doubt of that. But I can't talk inside. I shouldn't want your aunt to know about the flowers . . . You see, my father loved this Dagmar Sondermann."

How very exciting, Nancy thought to herself, and terribly worldly. Catch my father having an affair with an opera singer. He wouldn't dare, the poor old dear.

She said, "Don't worry that I'll tell my aunt. However nice they are, it's always a mistake to talk to older people. I don't do as much of it"—she felt reckless with grammar—"not as much as it looks as if I did."

He simply pressed her hand. They were caught in an aisle full of people who were blocked momentarily by one man going the wrong way. It was the man with white hair, the thin one who limped and who had spoken to Aunt Ann at the station. Had he been down the aisle to see her now?

His dark eyes in their deep sockets veered toward Nancy. He gave a start of recognition, tried to turn away politely but he couldn't. He kept looking back. That damn resemblance, Nancy thought. He's another General Summers. But for some reason Aunt Ann doesn't want us to meet.

Just then the lights went out. Everyone else in the world disappeared except Rudolph; he couldn't because of her hand in his arm. He kept it there, too, after they were seated, after the music began, after it swept them out to sea again.

For a moment Nancy tried to examine Isolde. Rather haggard she was, if you peered at her, but with enough beauty so her voice could save it, make it complete. One couldn't be critical, one couldn't just look. The music stole the senses, all of them. It poured through the theater in such a lovely flood. Its meaning couldn't help but sift through everyone. Nancy wasn't just listening to opera, she was admitting that there could be passion. That it might be like this, hopelessly yearning and supreme and doomed.

Now when the lights went on she couldn't move. Rudolph didn't either. She wasn't seeing him clearly. He might be clothed in a coat of mail and his hair salty with the Cornish sea.

After a few minutes Nancy stole a glance behind. Her aunt's silence was more surprising than theirs. She was such a one for putting a crisp word to everything. Aunt Ann was perfectly still, looking down at the gloved hands in her lap.

The lights went out again and you could almost hear the drawn breath of the audience. The suspense, once the music began, was hardly bearable, though everyone knew, had known since childhood, how the opera came out. You couldn't believe the violence of this feeling would be stilled. You were carried up with the beautiful sound to such a towering height . . . Yet when they died, one lover then the other, that was right too. Such powerful emotion could have no other climax; it was too great for life.

Suddenly there, in front of the curtain, were the singers. They stood in the bright footlights being handed flowers. Isolde, Dagmar Sondermann, got basket after basket. Rudolph's red roses were raised up. Those she took in her arms and kept, bowing repeatedly. Applause crashed through the hall.

Nancy's shoulder was tapped. Turning, she could see by a sort of lip reading that her aunt was trying to say something; there was too much noise to hear. The clapping resolved itself into waves with pauses between. Aunt Ann said in one of them, "My dears, you must excuse me. I will meet you at the train."

She already had her coat on. She slipped into the aisle and lost herself in the slow clots of people moving out.

Nancy must somehow have slid her arms into her jacket and put on her gloves. The first thing she remembered was being out on the sidewalk and Rudolph bending over to say, "We have an hour until the train. Wouldn't you like a little wine and some *poulet froid?* That is, if you won't mind the place? It's not quite *comme il faut* for a young girl. But it's the only place I know where one gets good food at this hour."

This shook off the dream. "I'd love it," she said briskly. "Imagine a whole hour without my aunt. Where in the world can she be? It's probably my only chance in Switzerland to go to a not quite proper place."

She remembered then, rather suddenly, the Café des Fauconniers, but said nothing and once the door opened, the very inconspicuous door to Rudolph's not quite proper place, she saw that this was going to be entirely different. The café had looked poor. This place was all covered with expensive velvet. How they did like dark red! One's feet sank soundlessly into the carpet, enormous folds of drapery hung at windows, more velvet made the seats of chairs. The only light came dimly from high chandeliers and revealed a head waiter in tails, hurrying forward, bowing, murmuring, *"Bonsoir, monsieur le comte, bonsoir, madame."*

Nancy liked the "madame." Rudolph was asking for a private room for supper.

"But certainly, *monsieur le comte,* but certainly."

They were led up a carved stairway into a small red velvet room with its own white damask-table, its own bowing waiter.

Rudolph helped her off with her coat and, when her hand touched his by accident, he raised the hand to his lips. Nancy knew this was against her aunt's rules for young girls, but she'd been kissed dozens of times. Not quite like this, of course, not at all like this because the little dim room echoed with *Tristan and Isolde.*

When Rudolph had got rid of the waiter they both sat with chins cupped in their hands, regarding each other.

"Can you still hear it?" Rudolph said.

"Oh, yes, I can hear it."

The remembered music was torn through by noise from the hall. An American voice was protesting loud enough to be heard from one floor to another, "They came in here, I tell you. I saw them come in the door."

"Good Heavens!" Nancy said. "That's Johnny Millard."

In a flash she had opened the door and was standing above the stairs saying, "Do hush!"

Johnny came bounding up dragging Diana and nearly toppling over the waiter who was toiling up with a heavy tray.

"We just caught sight of you," he panted. "What a race! It was really Diana who made it. Is she fleet!"

Rudolph had risen and was bowing. He was rather formidably silent.

"We wanted something to eat," Johnny offered. "We hadn't the least idea where to go. We figured you knew. And so you do, but the girls mustn't tell their mothers. Do they have bacon and eggs?"

Rudolph spoke to the waiter who took the wine bottle in its napkin and almost ran down the stairs.

"Why get rid of the bottle?" Johnny said.

"It's too light for a man."

"But you were going to drink it," Johnny said.

"No, no. It was for Miss Thorne. The doctor doesn't allow me any alcohol."

Johnny wrinkled his forehead. "I don't get it. Why can't she have her wine just because we came in?"

"That was something only for her. I've ordered another bottle more for your taste, more what Americans enjoy."

"Thank you, old man. You're certainly considerate," Johnny said. "But as it happens, I like to order my own wine." He leaned across the table, his jaw set. "I may not be a member of a fine old culture like yours, and what a fine old culture it has been the last few years! I'm just a plain American but I know my way around. I know this was no place to bring Miss Nancy Thorne."

10

Johnny had been a fool, he knew, to get the Jerry's back up. Damn it, he wasn't used to this smooth stuff. Diana'd helped him all she could—the girl was sharp as a cracker whatever she looked like—but it wasn't enough. Now he was really worried. Von Metsch had indulged in high-class sulks, both in that cathouse where they ate and in the train. The haughty airs had been only for him and Diana. With Nancy the man had made plenty of time, having her all to himself in a front seat. For Nancy's aunt—this was what worried Johnny—had missed the train.

He squeezed Diana's arm as they walked along the Avenue of the Sixteenth of May. Diana looked straight ahead, though the dark wasn't very interesting, as if she'd felt nothing. That was the English of it, he thought; she likes me all right. At her door it occurred to him her mother, who was waiting up, might come down the stairs. He gave her a quick kiss.

Diana gasped.

She said, "I don't like the Count von Metsch either."

Well, I'll be damned, Johnny thought, she knew why I kissed her. Most girls, hell, it was the farthest thing from their minds.

"So long, toots," he said. "You're a good kid. You really are. Be seeing you."

He walked away, almost running as soon as her door closed. Without any hesitation he turned down the Avenue

d'Ouchy to take up his post in front of Nancy's hotel. He
was going to stay there unobtrusively until Miss Ann came
back. He was trying to recall the terrain, to figure out a
really dark place with a view of both the entrance to the
hotel and the balcony, when suddenly he saw them. There
they were, von Metsch and Nancy, walking across the end
of the street—it was well lighted there—walking quite fast
away from the hotel to the little station.

Johnny began to sprint. If he missed the *funiculaire*—
they were plainly going to take it—he'd lose them for good.
Better even to let them see him, ridiculous as he looked
doing a hundred-yard dash in a tux, than to lose them.
They had had time to change; they must have been quick
about it. Both wore short jackets now and Nancy—Lord,
you could tell Miss Ann wasn't back—Nancy was wearing
pants!

Here was the little car just grinding down the hill on
its cog and pinions. He'd have time to slow up, to get his
breath. Also, for once, there was quite a crowd, a few in
evening clothes but most in rough, warm-looking tweed or
leather. Some even carried knapsacks. Quite a number had
those peeled sticks with the crook handle.

He lingered on the far side of the station until nearly
everyone was already on the platform or climbing aboard.
As he went quickly through, that comic character, the old
accordion player, nearly fell in his path. Funny thing was
he fell out of the phone booth. Must have been merely
sitting there to rest his feet; they were wobbly as ever.
He could hardly make the step from the platform to the
train. Johnny gave him a boost, using the man as cover for
himself, and slouched beside him on the back seat. Way
up in front he could catch a glimpse of shining hair, two
heads of it, one smooth, one with a graceful mane to the
shoulders.

Thank God the accordion player didn't tune up. Johnny
didn't want anyone turning around to look back. He was
in the wrong clothes to follow those two, but follow he

would, no matter where they were going. It might be hard on the rented tux. Lucky that he was wearing an old Army raincoat with the insignia off; this was the commonest garment in Europe. He fumbled and found he could button it to conceal his shirt front.

Getting off, he thought, might be a problem, especially if Nancy and von Metsch chose a place where few others were leaving the car. But no, the *funiculaire* stopped by the station, the big one with the through trains, and all the tweed and leather people moved out together. They stood by the tracks, not even bothering to buy tickets, and got on an omnibus train, "Londres—Paris—Rome—Stamboul," into a third-class car that was all in one like a day coach, full of wooden benches. When the conductor came through they all said, "Montreux, Montreux, Montreux" and handed out change. Johnny did too.

He was glad he had carefully left the accordion player. Pierrot was up in front now, near von Metsch and Nancy. A couple of flasks, more like wine bottles really, came from knapsacks and were handed round. The old man took a good pull and drew open his instrument.

Nothing ribald came out, only the slow chorus of "Calling the Cows." A baritone took up the solo part, lifting his voice as if it came from far away.

"Yohba, yohba," he called as if the sound were rippling down an immense valley. Everybody joined in the chorus, heads tipped back and eyes half closed. They were re-creating the mountains with the song. Everybody, that is, except von Metsch and Nancy. The former had refused a turn at the flask quite stiffly, Nancy with an apologetic smile.

Before Johnny could overhear enough, or understand, or make it out, the train stopped at Montreaux. Everyone in their coach got out. They went across the street to where a little *funiculaire* took off, the rails almost straight up like something in a boy's erector set. So they were going up into the mountains. He had thought so from the clothes; they had lost everyone in evening dress long since.

The train was so small it was harder to keep concealed. Johnny took a chance and got into the car behind the one that contained his quarry.

Once they started, he saw it was useless because the lights got so dim. However, when they stopped the first time the lights jerked on again. Nobody got off. Where in hell were they going and why? At least there were a lot of them. He heard the words "sunrise" and "point of view." They all said to the conductor "Caux" so Johnny said "Caux," tucking his telltale legs in their dress pants under the seat and keeping his head down.

Now that he knew about the lights, when they reached Caux he was already at the door and sliding off into the darkness. Nancy and Rudolph were among the first out, too, but he didn't dare follow immediately. He waited until a little group got between. They were all straggling up the same road past a big hotel entirely dark, some starting off briskly with alpenstocks, others waiting to adjust their packs under the dim light of the station platform.

Glancing back, Johnny saw one other figure beside himself not in climbing costume. The outline of an ordinary topcoat and pants and felt hat gave him confidence, but this joker didn't come along. He crossed the platform sideways at top speed and disappeared.

Johnny didn't like it somehow. Nor did he like the dark. Maybe he'd been too cautious and let Nancy get too far ahead. They were out of the sleeping village right away and plunged in a thick, rich smell of pines. You couldn't even see the faint shine of the stars. Somewhere ahead the accordion struck up, a gay tune this time though rather uneven. Pierrot was getting plenty of turns at the flask.

Still the music sent a shock through Johnny. It showed he was too far behind. He doubled his pace, holding his breath to hear the shuffle of other feet so he wouldn't bump into anyone. Finally he got abreast of the accordion just as the pines dropped away, just as they began to breathe the stinging cold of the real heights, the real emptiness.

My God, emptiness, that was it. Where was the girl? That German could have throttled her for all he, Johnny, knew, back under the trees and be halfway down to Montreux by this time.

And then his straining ears heard different music. From far ahead, from way up where the peaks hid a few stars it floated back, that damn opera, that damn Rudolph singing that stuff they'd heard in Geneva.

The Swiss had struck up a drinking song with a rollicking chorus. Johnny hurried forward. He mustn't lose *Tristan,* he could hardly hear it. He mustn't let the yodelers drown it out. The hell with whether anyone saw him. The dawn was coming. So what? Let it come.

Pieces of cloud were unwrapping themselves from mountains. The air had turned all smoky gray and awesome. You looked at a chunk of it and there it was rearing up in front of you like a wall, at another chunk and it was nothing, just nothing. You could look right through it . . . You didn't like to look down because there was no bottom. All you could really see was a few feet of path.

Johnny had always avoided this country in planes; now he was grounded in it. His feet in their thin soles felt the rocks painfully. He was panting. A fresh burst of opera blew back at him. Was it nearer? No. Just the breeze stronger for a moment.

It was that sort of refrain that was repeated over and over. What had Diana called it? The Love Death.

His lungs were bursting. One thing he knew now. There was nothing the matter with those lungs in front of him. Tuberculosis, hell!

He had been bent almost double to go faster so when the path turned a corner (just in time to avoid dumping a man ten or fifteen miles), he was surprised how the visibility had improved.

Through a hole in the mist a long slope was revealed and two tiny figures at the top, hand in hand. No, the man was ahead. He was swinging Nancy up. The two shapes merged. Was one ahead? No, they were side by side, embraced. Perhaps it was some trick of the light. Or Johnny's eyes were funny. He looked off to rest them, then back quickly. The two heads were together; the two bodies made one silhouette. After all, Johnny knew she was nuts about this German. He should have felt relieved she was safe. He didn't. He tried shouting. The wind blew the sound back.

He stumbled up, not looking at the path, his eyes fixed on those two, his chest aching, his feet burning, faster, faster.

But why? They had a right to get romantic. They were just climbing to look at the sunrise—quite a sight, everyone said—probably from that little flat shelf. You could certainly see from up there. On three sides of it there was nothing.

They'd reached it now. Rudolph stretched out his arm, pointing. He should have looked quite natural. It was a thing anybody would do up there, and yet . . . Nancy moved forward. Yes, there across the valley beyond them a finger of gold was touching one peak. But now something happened to the picture. While Nancy stood transfixed, apparently hypnotized by the vast solemn beauty, Rudolph was backing up, was crouching; he was running toward her.

Everything came at once. Nancy threw herself on the ground. An Indian war whoop reached Johnny, a wild bellow. Rudolph tried to stop, checked for an instant, but he couldn't make it. Nancy was no longer in his path. Rudolph's momentum was too great. He went straight on over the edge.

Johnny was scrambling, sobbing, "Don't move! Wait for me! Nancy, Nancy!"

It took forever to reach the ledge. He couldn't see her any longer. He kept shouting. Was she still there? Was she lying flat down? He made too much noise to hear the slight sound of someone descending out of sight of the path, behind rocks, behind stunted bushes, in the slow rolling mist.

He reached the shelf. A head raised itself from the ground very cautiously, very slowly. Nancy's face was dirty; it had been pressed in the dirt. One hand was holding tightly to a root, the fingers of the other were trying to dig into rock.

It was quite still. The light spread softly. Down below you could hear the Swiss yodeling "Calling the Cows."

11

Henri was sitting in a café that morning and he was trying not to feel of his head. He was right opposite the bank; he mustn't give a bad impression. Youth was all very well, "*la primavera, l'amore, la gioventú,*" but he'd forgotten the heads one used to have.

"*Garçon.*" He tapped on his saucer. "A black coffee."

Not that he'd drunk much. It was Ann; it had always been Ann. Years now since he'd spent a night entirely sleepless like last night.

The evening had promised so well! What luck to run into them there at Genève in the station. More luck that his wife's younger brother was with Yvonne and himself. The boy would spot Ann's niece in a second, would be very grateful for an introduction. Yvonne wouldn't mind. It would be so natural. All she would see of Ann would be gray hair and manners perfectly *comme il faut*. Yvonne trusted so much to being *comme il faut*. It would be easy to arrange further meetings.

But from the first it had gone awry. When Ann advanced to greet him he was charmed; too bad that she didn't present him to her party. Then in the entr'acte he'd expected to find them. Surely fate, pure fate had arranged that they should hear *Tristan* together. He naturally couldn't wait to tell her. But she obstinately kept her seat. It took him a long while to locate it. The theater had darkened, the curtain was going up when he left. The niece hadn't come back.

But afterwards, my girl, you can't avoid me afterwards, he thought. Will you want to with the duet throbbing through your mind? Damn your mind anyway. There's a great deal too much of it. Who, *diable,* wants a woman with a mind? I do, I, Henri Rambert.

"*Garçon,* another black coffee."

He'd been in the lobby before her though she left her seat early, and she saw him, of course she did, when that English fool, Sir John Trelawney—may he rot in hell—had blundered out. She took his arm; she smiled at him; she gave him just the look he, Henri, had been waiting for. It was finished then. She was engaged for supper.

One more chance, he thought gloomily, at the station. The last train, the 12:58, arrives at Lausanne at 1:55. She will have to take the train after all. A taxi is enormously expensive. And by now she's been punished. There's not a duller man in Switzerland than that pompous old bore.

There at the station was the niece all right, attended by the German, looking like a vision. His brother-in-law couldn't take his eyes off her. His brother-in-law inquired who she was. His wife did, too.

Could he explain that he knew because the aunt, except for being more brunette, had looked just like her twenty years ago? There'd be too many questions, far too many. Why weren't you in love with her, *mon ami?* I was, *mon amie,* I certainly was.

They said he was absent-minded. They had remarked it all evening.

He'd brushed his hand across his forehead and said. Ah, they had no idea of the difficulty these days about foreign loans. The United Nations, were they going to do anything, one asked oneself? The Marshall plan . . .

His wife said, "But to become impervious to *Tristan,* Henri! It isn't like you. For shame."

He said quite humbly, "I'm ashamed, my dear."

He had never been less impervious to *Tristan*. It was the music that had driven him not to let her out of his sight at all costs. Ann, Ann. His hand shook so he spilled the coffee in the saucer.

And she *had* got out of his sight finally, just as the grave had swallowed Iseult. She had never turned up for the train at all. Just to protect that precious niece, he thought, from himself. Where had she been *enfin?* What had she done while the little one went calmly to sleep in Lord Byron's room?

At that moment his distracted eye caught sight of someone who might tell him—Johnny. He half rose; he beckoned.

And *à apropos* why was Johnny there early, standing in front of the bank before it was open? The porter was just pushing back the ornamental iron grill work, jangling his keys. As the lad came up Henri raised his eyebrows. Johnny's face was colorless except for several gashes where he'd cut himself shaving; there were deep rings around his eyes. The gray hair made it look worse, really shocking.

"Good morning," Henri said. "Something has happened, I see. Where's Miss Thorne?"

"Sleeping, I hope."

"I mean the older Miss Thorne."

"Oh, she's all right. She told me to come to you in a hurry."

"Go on."

"Well, it's a police matter. Miss Thorne wants you to phone the police."

Ah, so she hadn't done quite perfectly without him. He took another look at Johnny and his satisfaction vanished. He threw some change on the table and limped across the street.

Settled behind his desk he got the story out piecemeal, in ragged bits.

"But what made the girl look around in time?" Henri said. "Did she hear you? Did you call?"

"I was hollering all the time," Johnny said. "I was just about crazy. Besides she claims she was braced for something. She was watching out. Didn't trust him."

"But you saw him kiss her. She did not resist."

"That's when she claims she began to worry. Before that she had just enjoyed the climb. It was screwy, that kiss. Didn't feel right." His lip twisted wryly. "I guess Nancy knows how it's supposed to feel."

"Are you sure the man is dead?"

"I looked over the edge. I saw something way down." He shuddered. "I need a drink."

"Not now, my boy . . . So then what did you do? Call the others? Tell them?"

"No, I was worried about Nancy. I thought it would take forever to explain to them. I wanted to get her home. My one idea was to get off that ledge. I took her down a little way and we waited behind a couple of rocks in a sort of side path till the others had passed."

"Charbonnet won't like that. He won't like any of it." The banker reached for the phone and spoke briefly.

In a few moments the inspector was there. Johnny repeated the tale. Henri found that his opinion of police reaction wasn't exaggerated. Charbonnet's trained face showed a struggle to preserve its calm. When Johnny paused the inspector reached for the phone and gave orders to search for the body.

"If they find it, at least one thing is true," he said, "that a man has died. As for the rest—" He shrugged. "Well, figure for yourself. Why should the Count von Metsch try to push a young girl off a rock? He is happy here, compared to the rest of Germany very happy, and he knows it."

"There was a reason," Johnny said. He looked at Henri doubtfully. "I suppose it's all right to lay the cards on the table?"

"I sincerely advise it." M. Charbonnet's voice was pleasant on the surface but it had an edge like a knife.

"Nancy had been to the opera with this guy," Johnny said. "During the intermission they were out in the lobby together. He left her at a table, told her to wait there. I suppose a German girl would have. Nancy got tired of it.

She followed him and saw him put a big envelope into a bouquet of flowers for the prima donna. When he saw he was caught he gave her a cock-and- bull story she believed at the time. But she thought afterward it was quite a coincidence that the singer should have picked up that particular bouquet to carry offstage. There were lots of others."

Charbonnet turned like a shot to Henri. "What is your interest in this? Has money been taken from your bank that you can't account for?"

"Now, now, my friend." Henri lifted his hand. "If it had, you are the first who would have heard about it. My interest you already know. A clerk here, Georges Évanoui, was murdered. The police of Lausanne haven't told me why."

Charbonnet was at the phone again. "Allô, allô, mademoiselle," he said. "Give me Genève. Be quick about it."

"The singer's name was Dagmar Sondermann," Henri supplied.

The inspector's eye raked him.

"I heard the opera too." Henri smiled.

The police of Genève were asked to detain and search not only Frau Sondermann but the whole troupe. He, Charbonnet, would be along to question them.

He banged the receiver down and said, "She's had plenty of time to hide whatever she got *if* the story is true . . . And now *if* Herr von Metsch is dead, perhaps he didn't try to push the young girl over. Perhaps *she* pushed *him.*"

"But I *saw* it!" Johnny shouted.

"Are you an unprejudiced witness?" Charbonnet said drily. "What is to prevent my thinking you pushed him over yourself? The poor man had tuberculosis. He was sick."

"I don't believe that now," Johnny said. "Those two went up that mountain like a bat out of hell. I couldn't catch them. Of course, Nancy has spent her life running up mountains. I know she's good. But she says Rudolph was the only man she'd ever climbed with who could beat her. And he was singing most of the time."

"Singing?" Charbonnet said. He stopped writing in his notebook.

"Yes. Nothing sensible. That damn opera."

"He was singing *Tristan,*" Henri murmured. "How incredible is the German mind. He was singing the *Liebestod,* the Love Death."

Charbonnet merely stared.

"Now I can see it," Henri said.

"So can I." Charbonnet leaned forward. "M. Millard here pushed him over." He said conversationally to Johnny, "You are in love with the girl. She went to the opera with von Metsch, not you. So you were jealous. Tell me." He narrowed his eyes. "Why did you follow them up the mountain?"

"Because of the wine and the bawdy house."

Charbonnet shook his head. "How the Americans amuse themselves!"

"It was your wine and your bawdy house," Johnny said, his voice rising. "And as far as I'm concerned the whole of Europe can go to hell in a basket. Just let them try to get me over here again to fight their damn . . ."

"Here, my boy, take a cigarette," Henri said. "I, too, am an old soldier. One never forgives the people who get one into it. I never did. Tell us about the wine."

Johnny's hand that he put out for the cigarette was shaking. Henri lit it for him. After a drag or two the boy went on with the story.

"But why did you follow them?" Charbonnet said. He too was trying to control himself. "*Voyons,* you had a young girl with you also. It would have been more reasonable to think of her, to take her to a quiet place, respectable, if—as it seems—the parents confide her to you without chaperones. But you thought only of the American girl."

"I didn't trust that German bastard," Johnny said. "I knew he was phony."

"Our Dr. Dollier is famous throughout the world," Charbonnet said. "If he said von Metsch had bad lungs, he had bad lungs. *Voilà.*"

"Then they're a big help climbing mountains."

"You always do an autopsy anyway," Rambert put in. "Do you not? Would it not be routine to examine the lungs when one knows the deceased was under a doctor's care?"

Charbonnet merely shrugged.

"It is just that I remember," Henri said, "when I was a prisoner in Germany in the last war before the last we did everything to pretend illness in order to be exchanged. Some of the men ate tobacco, a cupful just before being examined. They said it made râles in the chest . . ."

"You, yourself, got exchanged very quickly, didn't you?" Charbonnet said.

"I was lucky . . . That was long before your time."

"I just happened to hear about it," Charbonnet said.

"Look here," Johnny said suddenly. "You don't have to believe me about that bottle of wine von Metsch sent out so quickly. Or Nancy either. You can ask Diana Medway. She's an unprejudiced witness."

Charbonnet wrote her address in his book; his forehead wrinkled skeptically.

"Suppose for a moment it is true about the wine," he said, "and your other suspicions. Let us say you went up the mountain to protect Miss Nancy Thorne. Why didn't you join them instead of sneaking up behind?"

"Nancy would have been furious. American girls like to be independent."

The detective shook his head sadly. "I have observed the Count von Metsch. He was very handsome."

"You believe nothing I say." Johnny's voice sounded tired. "But wait till you see Nancy."

"I have seen her. I saw her in the Café des Philosophes where no young girl ought to be. She was there and in the Maison Rouge, you say, in Genève. An habituée of dives *en somme*. Strange taste for a young girl."

"Both times it was an accident," Johnny said hotly. "Here in Lausanne she was just trying to find her aunt."

"Where was this aunt last night?" Charbonnet said. "Why did she let her charge go out on these adventures with an unknown young man? An insane one perhaps?"

"That was the trouble," Johnny said. "The aunt disappeared. Right after the opera. And she missed the train. That was one reason why I kept an eye on Nancy. I'd damn well like to know where her aunt went."

"I can help you," Henri broke in. "I saw her walk off with Sir John Trelawney."

Charbonnet swung round toward him and stared. Henri realized he was knowing too much. He saw it in the screwed-up eyes, heard it in the long pause.

"It's time for me to see these ladies," the detective said finally. "You"—pointing at Johnny—"will go with me.

Henri knew that he should have kept still but he couldn't quite.

"Captain Millard," he said. "When M. Charbonnet is through with you, come back to see me."

Charbonnet motioned Johnny toward the door. "I will come back to see you," he said. "About him, I don't know. But we allow visitors in jail."

Henri didn't much like it but he had no time to reflect. He took a folder from a locked drawer, spread out the papers in it, lit his pipe. This mission of Ann's was delicate no longer. There was no longer leisure for investigation. Too much was coming out into the open too quickly.

His papers contained a list of visitors to safe-deposit boxes the day after Washington Osborne's death, their credentials, their previous business with the bank.

First were six business men, natives of Lausanne, he had known since childhood. Yes, they had foreign sales. What Swiss business had not? Then came the foreigners. They were all known to Ann; that was the trouble.

François de Pré Morel. But he had not just rented a box for this nebulous committee he was working for now. He had owned a box in the Crédit Alpin since 1939. *Halte là*. Don't jump to conclusions. A great many French had done the same. They'd been afraid of the Germans; they'd had not much confidence in the Third Republic. Of course, when the French government called in the gold there'd been a wave of patriotism as well as nervousness. De Pré Morel had visited the vault with his father, who rented it with him, just before, so he said, the younger man expected to be called up. Who could say what American securities or jewels or bank notes they had put in then? Who could say when or how much had been taken out? Or to whom it had been given? Of course only the younger man was in question (his father had died) and François hadn't been in Switzerland during the war. But he'd come often since.

This business of a trade commission was a fine cover. Since de Pré Morel was an old client of the bank there'd been less doubt of him than of new people. But Trelawney's conversation uneasily bobbed up in Henri's mind. He vaguely remembered hearing de Pré Morel, when he was very young, had been a royalist. Then he'd followed de Gaulle. He didn't look like a friend of any republic though he was supposed to be serving one now. To what would he be loyal? France—no matter what her government—or a strong ruling class, and, if the latter, would he sympathize with Nazis? God, what a *salade* was Europe!

Trelawney now—he was next on the list—was in much the same case. His connection with the bank was prewar too, on account of his mother. Lucky for him she'd left a good round sum there. It had been declared, of course, as required by the Bank of England. And the securities also, those that were in his mother's name or his own, Trelawney could never have lived as comfortably as he did on the paltry amount the British let him take out of his own country.

His mother had been a dear old thing with enough good English pride to stand by her in the hard job of dying alone in a strange country. Sir John was a Tory, of course, quite without sympathy for the labor government.

He made no secret of it. He regarded the parceling out of the Empire with horror. Would he go so far as to prefer the enemies of Britain to her working class? Henri didn't think so. The British were apt to be British first and last.

The next was William Lane. It was most unusual for a newspaperman to rent a safe-deposit box. His had been rented just before Washington Osborne's death and was, actually, very near Mr. Osborne's. Not that that would matter when the bank key was necessary besides the individual's key, to open it, and when there was an attendant constantly watching.

The attendant, of course, the day after Washington Osborne's death, had been poor Georges Évanoui. Ah yes, newspapermen rarely had any money no matter how much they made. They only had telegrams. They would go to the cable office and collect and spend it all right away. He made a question mark after the name of William Lane.

Last of all—this would astonish Ann—there was Captain J. Millard. Johnny had rented a box on the day in question. He hadn't mentioned it when he applied for a job in the bank. This was a message one couldn't send Ann by the lad himself. He, Henri, was sure Johnny had connected in his mind the man who took him to his box the day after Washington Osborne's death with the man who was murdered. In other words he knew he'd met Georges Évanoui. Henri was equally sure he hadn't told Ann Thorne. All very pretty to talk about two wars and similar reactions, but it was for another reason Henri had taken Johnny on so quickly. He wanted to have him in the bank under his eye, not on the balcony of Lord Byron's room.

12

The head of Henri Rambert was quite encircled by the smoke of his pipe. He had got down to considering the last day Georges Évanoui was alive.

The man must have discovered something, must have seen something in spite of the careful routine for privacy in the vault. Otherwise why did he say when he was dying, "They took out much money afterward"? No great sums had been withdrawn from accounts, from any kind of accounts. He'd gone into that. The money must have come from a safe-deposit box; Georges must somehow have seen it.

He shuffled the papers about visitors back into their folders and simply wrote a list of names for Ann. One didn't want too much to be found on Johnny; the police might arrest him any moment now. Besides it would be embarrassing to label a list that contained Johnny's own name. If only he'd sent it before! It was the one thing she'd asked of him. Fool that he was to think there was so much time.

His mind returned to Georges again. Had the man merely seen the inside of one of the boxes by accident, a door to a room swinging open or a box being dropped? After all, he was not the regular attendant; he might have been clumsy. Had he become dangerous by accident, or had he been a paid spy, dangerous by design? The latter possibility was the one Henri had finally and uneasily accepted. It should have been Georges' duty to report any suspicion to him, Henri. To be sure, the man's salary was small but his job was steady and respectable. Had he reported to the bank, as he ought, and the bank reported to the police, he would have received thanks, only thanks. Whereas being in the pay of Americans had meant a prospect of real money.

If it was true, as Charbonnet said, that Georges had been in the habit of meeting a *belle blonde* at the Café des Fauconniers, that explained his need for money, especially as she was not an habituée of the quarter. She was a woman nobody knew. The police said she was always putting a scarf up to her face or shrinking back as if she were ashamed to be there.

Henri sighed. He repeated Évanoui's last words, "Monsieur O*sborne* was killed. Not an accident. They took out much money afterward. I don't know how they killed him. Or me either."

No, there could be no mistake, Évanoui was in the pay of the Americans. He already knew something about Osborne's death that he had not told the Swiss police. But he couldn't prove it, "I don't know how they killed him." He already knew that Miss Thorne would be the next agent to succeed Osborne. Only Osborne himself could have told Georges.

After these reflections, Henri said to himself, I should go straight to Charbonnet and tell him all I know, Ann's mission, Évanoui's contact with her. It would have a good effect. It would re-establish me with the police who are beginning to be rude, much too rude to a man in my position. But what would be the result? She might be asked to leave Switzerland. Even if not, I should be thought to know too much about her; they would discover the link between us. At the very least she would be watched so that—he propped his head in his hands—I couldn't see her again. Not often anyway. Oh, life knows better than to ask that of me!

He was not very patient waiting for Johnny and he had to wait a long time. By afternoon, late afternoon, Henri felt bitterly toward the police for keeping him. He snapped the minute Charbonnet opened the door.

"What have you done with my American? Put him in jail?"

"Ah no," said Charbonnet, surprised. "His story was confirmed, parts of it. We found the body of Herr von Metsch. It was examined and there were no lesions in the lungs. Of course, the microscopic examination will take longer."

"Mlle. Medway told exactly the same story about why she and Millard followed the others to the Maison Rouge. She said that von Metsch sent the waiter running away with the wine. Impossible not to believe her. A real *jeune fille.*" He sighed.

"And then they phoned me from Genève that Frau Sondermann and the other singers were already out of the country. They left on an earlier train than they intended, immediately after the performance." He sat down. "We think it best to report this, the affair of von Metsch, for the moment, as an accidental death."

"My American," Henri said. "Where is he?"

"We released him this morning and he went from bar to bar drinking."

"But this is serious!" Henri clenched his fist. "He shouldn't do that."

"No. He has no control. He got into a fight with another foreigner, a Frenchman. Threw a bottle at him. We wanted to put Millard in jail to cool off but no, the Frenchman wouldn't prefer charges. Shut up like a clam. Did the old-fashioned gentleman, type of 1830."

"That could only be one man," Henri said. "M. François de Pré Morel."

Charbonnet's eyebrows rose. "Correct."

Henri got to his feet. "I will go out and get the boy," he said. "If there's a question of espionage—there seems to be—he shouldn't go round spilling all he knows."

"No need to derange yourself, monsieur." Charbonnet leaned back. "The young lady has already thought of it. We were following *her*. First she came here to the bank and inquired for M. Millard. She went to his hotel. Same thing. Then she went back to Ouchy and got her aunt and they made the round of the bars, those two ladies. Can you imagine it?"

Rambert said nothing; unfortunately he could.

"Finally they found their man in the Rossinière and got him out, one on each side, and back to his room. She's pretty enough, that young girl, but too bold, far too bold."

He let his head lean back. "The aunt now, that's another story. In her generation they had more charm. She was very reluctant to follow her niece. You could see she hated going into bars."

Henri had all he could do not to grin broadly. Dear Ann, he thought, how I can trace your handiwork laid out before me in my office! You do not disdain the humble inspector of police, not you. He's too important. Perhaps you also see that he's a good deal of a man. Anyway you have let him have it, the old fascination. One might say at close range with both barrels. How it used to enrage me! But it's very useful.

He said, "So you weren't following Millard. You were following Miss Nancy Thorne. You suspect her?"

Charbonnet shrugged. "Not really. We think she knows more than she's told. When she went out so soon after such an experience, we thought she might lead us to a clue. But no."

"Are you keeping a watch on her?" Henri said casually. "Guarding the hotel?"

"Oh, no." Charbonnet raised his hands. "The aunt is so worried. She will allow no more indiscretions."

Henri's heart leapt inside him, but he frowned, shuffled the papers on his desk.

"You will let me know if I can help you?" he said perfunctorily, in a dismissing voice.

"Oh yes, indeed, monsieur."

Was there a slight smile on the inspector's face as he went out? If so, Henri paid small attention. He was too busy making plans. The fatigue of the morning was gone. He felt twenty. No, he had been insensitive at twenty. Thirty, that was the age. One had lived then.

He would go home early, not that he needed a rest but to please his wife who would think he did. Also to avoid Johnny whose drunken slumber couldn't last too long. Henri would ask for an early dinner, oh, so hesitantly, with that air of the bad little boy Yvonne wouldn't resist. He'd say an old comrade in arms had turned up, a disreputable fellow he couldn't bring to the house. (They were like that, old legionnaires; she'd seen a few). He wanted to play checkers with his friend in a café and perhaps drink a little. No use waiting up; he'd be very late.

It all went perfectly even to the dark corner of a café where he wasn't known. He'd thoughtfully put on an old suit and a dark-colored shirt suitable to the low fellow he was supposed to meet, quite Apache, Yvonne thought.

He didn't mind the waiting, endless quarter hours and half hours chiming out on the cathedral bells. At midnight he added up his stack of saucers, gave change to a yawning waiter and slipped out. The station, the *funiculaire,* were too well lit; he was too well known. He walked down the stairs from the Avenue de la Gare and under the tree shadows of the Avenue d'Ouchy.

He took plenty of time to reconnoiter the hotel, *comme a la guerre,* as in the war, he thought, his pulses pounding. He made a good *sortie,* a good climb to the balcony. His bad leg didn't drag. He was inside, through the curtains, thinking how to wake these ladies without scaring them.

A furious voice whispered, a young voice, "Damn you, Johnny! I told you to stay home." Then it sobbed, "I've told you a million times I didn't want to kiss him!"

An electric torch found Henri, made him blink. There was a gasp.

The same young voice said, horrified, "It's an old man with white hair!"

"Pardon, mademoiselle." He gathered what dignity he could. "It was your aunt I came to see."

Indeed, he was seeing her, though dimly, for she held the torch and a revolver in her other hand.

"Pity these white hairs, Ann," he said. "Don't shoot. After all, I was mortally wounded years ago."

That dry, that acrid voice came to him and it was cold as glacier wine. "This was to be expected. You refuse to grow up. It was the balcony that attracted you. I know you well, Henri. You couldn't resist in spite of the danger it would bring to us."

He drew himself up. He'd spent hours getting ready for this.

"You do me an injustice, my dear. It is as a banker that I come to see you."

There was a giggle from the child's bed, quickly smothered. The torch and the revolver were still pointed implacably.

"Here is the list"—he knew he'd have to impress her—"of those who went to the safe-deposit vaults the day after Osborne's death. I had to bring it to you. Millard didn't show up."

He approached Ann's bed with a firm step and she laid down the revolver, although reluctantly, to take the paper.

"No one drew out any unusual sum," he said, "from an account. Perhaps Évanoui was killed because the Germans knew of his connection with Osborne. If not, it must have been because of something he saw in the vault."

His eyes burned through the gloom. There she was just as always, the lines so beautiful and clean like a hawk or a gull swooping, the skin only a little withered.

She played the torch on the paper, read intently.

"Henri, I'm going to ask you something."

Her voice was changed now. It was just as dry but there was an effervescence in it that he remembered when she was pleased or excited.

"Will you, can you, get witnesses to these identities? Every kind of paper in the world can be faked now, every seal, every signature, every photograph. I must know if these people are what their papers say. Only the evidence of old friends, old acquaintances, is really good. We will pay for you to bring witnesses from their homes."

"That will be difficult," he said doubtfully.

"Get them by air," she said. "We're in a hurry. Don't wait to write; telephone, but not from where the line could be tapped."

"It will be very expensive."

A small voice murmured from across the room, "Now I believe you really *are* a banker."

"Of course, I will do it for you, Ann," he said. "France and England will be easy enough. But America!"

He approached the spot of light, put a long finger on two names.

"These will take longer."

He saw with a poignant pity how her hair was gray. He put out a hand to touch it, still so soft. Then he remembered that execrable child; he snatched it back. He could only smell the faint scent.

"I don't know about these." He pointed again. He sniffed closer. The same perfume, gay, long ago and irretrievable like a Vienna waltz. But he could feel behind him the child pricking her ears.

He said hastily, "It would take too long to bring witnesses from their homes."

"Paris," said Ann. "Try the *Paris Herald*. They will all know Bill Lane. Someone at some time will have interviewed Johnny."

"About Johnny," he said. "He rented a box the day after Osborne was killed. Évanoui was on duty in the vault that day."

"Oh," said Ann. "Oh . . . Why didn't he tell us?"

She folded the paper, put it under her pillow.

"You'd better destroy it," he said, worried now. "And have you noticed the worst thing about that list?"

"I'm not sure."

"Von Metsch isn't there."

He towered over her, straight now, and tense. "Don't you see what it means? Your German was only an underling. He had no safe-deposit box, no account in the bank. He wasn't known there. It's someone else you have to fear and now he is tipped off."

"You mean by Charbonnet? What has he done?"

"Nothing. He was impressed with the fact that von Metsch didn't have tuberculosis, that Millard's testimony, in some ways, was confirmed. He will not make public Miss Nancy's presence"—he bowed toward her—"at the scene of the death. There'll be no mention of it in the papers."

"Thank God," said Ann.

"Don't be deceived, my dear," he said urgently. "That's the main reason why I came. The papers may not know it, but the Nazis will. Plenty of people saw your niece on the train with von Metsch, on the *funiculaire*, too. They will remember. Miss Nancy is now in grave danger."

There was a stunned silence in the room.

"You will take care of her," he murmured. "Don't leave her alone. If I can do anything command me. I must go."

He parted the curtains without even a whisper of the thick cloth. How it comes back to one, he thought. He lifted his bad leg limberly over the iron railing. He listened, holding his breath. Perfect quiet, perfectly dark. The moon wouldn't be up for an hour; he had figured that.

I could have fought in this war too, he thought. They were fools not to take me. As a *sortie* this is as good as when I got the Croix de Guerre.

With the muscles of twenty he put his arms and legs around the post. He slid down gently, straight into the arms of M. Charbonnet.

13

"Let me help you, monsieur," the inspector said with very heavy irony.

He had a firm grip on the banker who was staggering more from astonishment than weakness. M. Charbonnet, his fingers tight as a handcuff on the man's arm, steered him across the road out of earshot of the hotel.

At last, the inspector thought, I have you where I want you.

But M. Rambert was getting his breath back.

"This help—" He nodded toward the others hand. "Surely it's a little excessive? I find it so. You have nothing for which to arrest me, my friend."

"That depends," M. Charbonnet said.

They were walking quietly beside the lake in the dark with nothing near but low bushes, empty benches, boats tied up for the night.

"I was merely going to see a lady," the banker said. "In a romantic way, I admit, unsuitable to my age. But, *voyons,* the police don't stoop to blackmail."

"The rendez-vous," Charbonnet said dryly, "does not impress me as romantic with Miss Nancy there."

"How I agree with you!" the banker sighed.

"You went to exchange news," Charbonnet said, "news that you haven't told me. Just what was it, this news?"

"I warned Miss Thorne her niece would be in danger from the Nazis. I believe in their underground. They'll be sure, to resent the death of von Metsch."

"Was it necessary to climb a balcony in the middle of the night? The police could have told them that."

Charbonnet felt the shoulder he was touching lift in a shrug.

"My interest was personal. I admit it."

Charbonnet's fingers tightened. "The charge against you will be withholding information from the police."

"What do you want to know?" M. Rambert said quickly, too quickly like a fish snapping at the bait without even looking and so caught at once.

Now the inspector could take his time; the hook would hold. He let go the other's arm.

"About M. de Pré Morel," he said, "the police need to know more. When I described the incident in the bar you recognized him at once from my description."

"Yes," said the banker. "He's been a customer of ours for a long time."

"Ah . . ."

That was all he had to say.

M. Rambert said, "Since before the war."

"Checking account or safe-deposit box?"

"The latter. M. François and his father both had keys. The father has since died."

Charbonnet changed even his tone of voice; he would try being friendly.

"The French police have written me," he said. "Too many American thousand-dollar bills have appeared on their black market. They do not seem to have been brought in by tourists; they don't appear where tourists spend their money. Of course, before the war a thing like this could be investigated, but not now."

"And then?" the banker said.

"The French think the bills come from Switzerland. They've traced a few nearly to the border."

"So it's supposed to be our fault again!" Rambert exclaimed. They couldn't be overheard; they were far from any buildings. "We're one little country. We can't operate a secret service for the whole of Europe."

"No, but perhaps we can help. The Sureté says frankly, the Sureté in Paris, that there are financial operations in their country they don't understand. These fascist parties that spring up in France, they have caches of the latest weapons, handsome uniforms, their own newspapers. They are waiting till the Communist threat gets very bad, perhaps till France has civil war if de Gaulle and the Communists really come to that. Then they will say democracy doesn't work. They will seize control, join with the Nazis who are still strong in Germany and," he spread out his hands, "we will have a fascist Europe."

"The Nazi underground," said Rambert cautiously. "It supports all this?"

"So the French believe."

"Colossal," said Rambert. "The money it must take! To be sure, everyone knows the Nazis didn't give up."

"Remark how history has played into their hands," the inspector said. "We are so afraid of Russia; the threat of Russia is so great that we, all the democracies, might even have to support this fascist Europe!" He shook himself. "So I don't like de Pré Morel who journeys back and forth too frequently, or his safe-deposit box, or his Trade Commission, which I don't think even exists."

"But I've had letters," M. Rambert said, "from the French government about the trade commission!"

"That simply proves that there are traitors in that government. You know quite well Russia doesn't permit the Balkans to trade with France!"

"Nevertheless they're trying to exchange a few things they both need, oh very quietly, with no publicity."

"A fine story," Charbonnet nodded. "They had luck telling it to you." He stiffened. "You waste your time telling it to me."

"How can I help you, then?" the banker said.

"With your young fool of an American." Charbonnet grasped his arm. "You find out what he's doing here. I can't. Whenever my men have followed de Pré Morel they've found Millard was following him too."

"This is the first I've heard of it, I give you my word."

They had turned back from the Beau Rivage and were approaching the station of the *ficelle.**

"Then question him and see you get an answer."

"I'll try." The banker hesitated, "And my escapade, it will not be necessary to reveal it?"

"Not unless I suspect you."

"Suspect *me?*" The banker stopped, his head jerking back.

"Why not? The Swiss can be dishonest like anybody else, better than anyone else. They're so practical; they make splendid blackguards."

"But there's no connection!"

"Is there not? Who could have used Évanoui as an accomplice, who could have poisoned him, better than you? As for the bank itself, you must see that you have the best opportunity to falsify records."

"But I can't," M. Rambert sputtered. "We have a system. I beg you to examine . . ."

"Never mind, never mind." Charbonnet waved his hands. "There are just too many threads tying you up to this affair, that's all. You and your bank."

"I can't imagine what." Rambert was fairly choking.

"Well, then, for weeks de Pré Morel lived over there." The policeman tossed his head. "There in Lord Byron's room. Your bank clerk was poisoned and, dying, he went up the stairs in that hotel, up to that very floor. Why? I ask myself. Not—as you pretend you did—for the *beaux*

---

*"String," popular name for the short *funiculaire* between Ouchy and the center of Lausanne.

yeux of the American ladies; he'd never seen them. *I think he didn't know de Pré Morel had moved."*

M. Rambert really choked now. He had to get out his handkerchief. The train was nearly in.

Charbonnet said quickly, "You don't have to sit with a policeman. I'll sit somewhere else. *Au revoir, monsieur."*

From the rear of the car he mused on the man in front, whose sharp profile was tilted back in reverie. M. Rambert had always been a little strange, everyone knew, quite Bohemian in his younger days in Paris. But he'd married finally and settled down. Or had he?

That dark, sleazy shirt looked funny topped by a distinguished head. It was the uniform of the riff-raff of Europe whom this man, of course, had never seen. But wait, he'd been in the Foreign Legion. *Fils de famille* like him had been thrown in with thieves and murderers in World War One, had fought beside them in the trenches. Had the banker amused himself by keeping up the contact?

Rambert's eyes were half closed, his lips moved. He was murmuring to himself. One knew the man really so little! It could be a spies' code, or Verlaine, or the figures of the Swiss National debt. In any case, Charbonnet thought, he could leave the train unobserved. He did.

He slipped gently through the night to join the man he'd left stationed in front of de Pré Morel's new quarters.

Nothing could look more innocent than these. The Frenchman had rented an apartment on the third floor of an old house, reached by an outside staircase lit by a street lamp. The house—it had been thoroughly explored by the police—had no back entrance, no low windows. The servants' entrance and the front door were right near the street. For a man who liked to go on secret errands it must be a handicap. On the other hand, he could take a good look at visitors before admitting them.

Charbonnet didn't disturb the shadows as he joined his man.

SALLY WOOD

His voice was nearly inaudible. "Has the Frenchman come in?"

The agent whispered, "No, monsieur. There's no one come in. Only there's somebody here watching beside myself."

He motioned toward the pocket of an alley.

"The American, Captain Millard?"

"Oh no, monsieur. Him one could always see. This is an operative with experience."

"You're sure M. de Pré Morel went out this evening?"

"As sure as I am that you are standing there."

Charbonnet waited. The silence, the darkness didn't feel right. It was as if something were thrown over his head.

"I don't believe in this," he said slowly. "They want me to, but I don't."

Picking his way like a cat back through the shadows he had used to come by, Charbonnet went on patiently three blocks. Then he returned openly in the middle of the street. He marched up the stairs and rapped on the door with authority.

He was standing so near, when it opened he almost fell through.

M. de Pré Morel, wrapped suavely in a dressing gown, motioned him in.

A shaded lamp was burning over a desk strewn with papers. Curtains of blackout thickness, blinds, were tightly drawn.

"I didn't expect to find you here," Charbonnet rapped out testily. "I was told you'd gone out."

The Frenchman bowed. "Monsieur must have been misinformed."

Charbonnet let that pass. He said, "I came to inquire about that incident in the bar. You were attacked. Why did you not wish the American to be arrested?"

De Pré Morel raised his eyes to the ceiling. "He was drunk and no more than a boy." He added politely, "Won't you sit down?"

Charbonnet sat and thrust his legs out in front of him. "Why did Millard get angry? What led up to it?"

The Frenchman was in his chair, an elbow resting on a pile of letters all with the seal of the Fourth Republic.

"It was nothing." He shrugged. "Just a bar conversation about whether the French did enough, in the war . . . At times, you know, one tires of that. This was one of the times."

"Ch—k." Charbonnet clicked his tongue. "He becomes a public nuisance, that American."

"But look, monsieur." The Frenchman raised his hands, palms up. "In these days if a boy throws only a beer bottle it is nothing. If that is all I have to dodge, equally it is nothing."

"You know a German, von Metsch?" Charbonnet said. "What can you tell me about him?"

"I've met him once or twice." De Pré Morel waved his hand. "Only at large parties. There I avoided him. He's like the other *Bôches*, always whining."

"Where were you in the war, monsieur?" the inspector said quickly.

"Oh, I was captured like the rest of us, but I escaped. Later I joined the *maquis*."

"What *maquis*, where?" Charbonnet said impatiently. "You don't talk about it."

"My father was killed because the Germans knew I was in the *maquis*. After that I formed the habit of not talking."

"But we're neutrals, we're not Germans." The inspector leaned forward. "Where were you in the *maquis?*"

"Most of the time," the words came very slowly, "most of the time I was at Evremont."

Charbonnet rubbed his hands together. "Ah," he said, "And did you know a café proprietor there the Germans did not harm because he was a Swiss, a M. le Noir?"

A flicker crossed that careful face. "I knew M. le Noir, yes."

"Here in Lausanne," Charbonnet said, "have you visited the Café des Fauconniers?"

"I have not had that pleasure, monsieur." The tone was
as near freezing as it could be and remain polite.

"You have missed nothing," the inspector said. "It's not
a good café." He drew in his legs. "Are you acquainted
with a little brunette, Mlle. Aurélie?"

"I know Mlle. Aurélie. Who does not?"

Charbonnet leaned over and fixed him with a penetrat-
ing stare. "I think you know her rather better than most."

The Frenchman raised his shoulders, a man of the
world, imperturbable. "Perhaps, monsieur."

"Le Noir now keeps the Café des Fauconniers. He's
gone back to his real name, Schwartz."

"Tiens."

"Mlle. Aurélie goes there frequently."

"Does she indeed?"

"I thought it might interest you." Charbonnet waited a
moment. "Possibly you know it already?"

The Frenchman rose stiffly as if terminating an audience he had very kindly granted. "I know Mlle. Aurélie.
She is a *brave fille.*"

His little porcelain clock began to chime.

"She has a history. I will not tell it to you." He bowed.
"It grows late . . . Good night, monsieur." He opened his
door.

14

Miss Ann woke early. The sky was still pink over Lac Léman among the whirling gulls. She heard the clank of the milk can and saw the baker's boy strolling out to the street with a large, empty basket. She rang for breakfast.

Only a long habit of discipline had let her sleep at all after Henri's visit. She'd made herself relax, knowing that all her strength would be needed today.

First, memorize the list. It was for those Swiss names she'd kept it. Henri could look them up but she ought to know them. The others one remembered all too well. When she had the names by heart, Miss Ann tiptoed to the bathroom, tore the paper into tiny bits and flushed them down the toilet. She passed through the bedroom again just as quietly, not to wake Nancy, took her silver brush and kept on to the anteroom, closing the door. As the brush slid quite unconsciously on its familiar routine through her hair, the list hung poster size before her mental eyes.

François de Pré Morel. Henri could, in a few days, establish his identity beyond any doubt but that might reveal nothing. What could one do now? The proprietor of this hotel, M. Dunois, would have his address for forwarding mail. She would get it from him.

There was a knock at the door. Ann sprang to open it, thinking of Nancy, asleep. The face of the maid behind the big tray startled her. It remained so motionless while she explained that her niece wasn't ready for breakfast.

"Bien, mademoiselle. C'est tout, mademoiselle?" this woman said like a machine into which you put ten centimes. Her large hand, her strong fingers, closed in some way too capably around the cocoa pot to take it down again to the kitchen.

Miss Ann repressed a shiver as the door swung to, and thought of their first happy breakfasts brought by Lydia. Lydia! But, of course! She would have waited on M. de Pré Morel before they came. She might have seen some little thing. That and not her discovery of the corpse might have been the reason why she was spirited away. Miss Ann poured out her coffee, thinking, I will see Lydia first.

There was another knock at the door, a soft one this time.

It opened to reveal Diana, her arms full of flowers— jonquils they were mostly—and narcissus. She was trying to wear a suitable expression of condolence, but, underneath, her candid face was pink with excitement, lively with curiosity.

"I know it's the most ghastly hour," she said. "I've just come from the market. I was going to leave these, but the maid told me you were up."

She clutched the bouquet helplessly.

"Thank you." Ann held out her hand. "Are you free this morning?"

"Oh, yes. Rather."

"Then you could do me a favor?"

Diana nodded vigorously.

"I want to go out but I don't like to leave Nancy alone. Could you stay until I get back? She's still asleep, poor child."

"I'd love to stay," Diana said.

"It's important," Ann went on. "Strange things are happening around here as you've doubtless gathered. Nancy may be in danger. You'd have to promise not to leave her."

"Wild horses couldn't drag me away," Diana said.

Ann didn't exactly smile; she believed her. Ann dressed hastily and left without mentioning that her goal, after a stop at the office, was the jail.

There quite a bit of the *grande dame* was needed to locate Lydia. She opened her passport, wrote a note to be carried to the girl and spoke slightingly of cheese made in Wisconsin.

Finally she was taken to Lydia in the kitchen of the jailer's wife. Lydia held a baby on her lap and was feeding him goat's milk and farina with a spoon. She was scrubbed, shiny, and starched again and remained only somewhat pale.

"This one is not a prisoner," said the jailer's wife. "But for some reason she prefers to stay. A *drôle* of a taste. I suppose it's the baby. I, for one, have no heart to send her away. She's the best help I've ever had. Excuse me, I'm scrubbing the entry."

She left them. Lydia put the baby back in its high chair, folded her hands on her stomach and said, "What is there for your service, mademoiselle?"

"A few questions, Lydia."

The child hung her head.

Ann went on firmly, "It's about M. de Pré Morel, the man who had Lord Byron's room before we did."

Lydia looked up, startled. "Oh," she said. "The monsieur who coughed."

"Yes."

"I remember him," Lydia said. "M. Dunois worried. So many people come to Switzerland with tuberculosis. They are not allowed in regular hotels. But it was all right. Only a piece of shrapnel in the lungs. Not serious. He had the doctor's letter."

"That's the man. Now can you remember what he did? Who came to see him?"

Lydia blushed. The color made her look healthier, the way she'd been before she began to be afraid.

"M. Dunois didn't like that either," she said. "The hotel is so respectable. The monsieur who coughed was visited by a *fille perdue,* a brunette with a little crescent on her forehead. She was nice to me, always the *bonjour* and from time to time a present. I didn't know how Monsieur Dunois could be so sure she was 'lost.'"

Lydia shook her head.

"And then?" Miss Ann said.

"Alas, he was right. I saw her many times through the small window in the door at the Café des Philosophes." She clapped her hand to her mouth suddenly. "Oh no," she whispered. "I was wrong. Mademoiselle will not repeat it."

"Certainly not," Miss Ann said firmly. "I have nothing to do with the police. I am just trying to look after Nancy. This brunette, who is so definitely 'lost'—you will excuse me, my dear—did she spend the night?"

"Oh, no. It was very discreet. Just now and then a little visit. But there was something else. Some mornings I could see the bed of monsieur had not been slept in. Torn apart, that's all. I did not find it necessary to inform M. Dunois. For one thing I don't know how the monsieur got in and out."

She said quickly, "Did M. de Pré Morel have other visitors?"

"Only the *beau monsieur allemande.*"

"Did he come to the room, too?"

"But no. He came to the café in the afternoon to take his aperitif because they have—mademoiselle knows it—a little orchestra that plays waltzes."

"But M. von Metsch was forbidden alcohol."

Lydia shrugged. "All I know is, I've seen him drinking with M. de Pré Morel."

"Beer, perhaps."

"Ah, then it was strong. I have seen him talking the way gentlemen talk who drink Pernod."

Strange, Miss Ann thought, de Pré Morel despised the German . . . in public. He wouldn't have taken a drink with him.

She said, "Did M. von Metsch also come to the Café des Fauconniers?"

"Never, mademoiselle."

"Thank you," Miss Ann said, rising quickly, forcing a note into Lydia's closed hand. "I won't repeat what you've told me. Even so"—she patted the girl's shoulder—"this is a good place to stay."

Ann was in a fever to get to de Pré Morel. She had neglected him too long and he was, he must be, very near the heart of the matter.

First to the Place St. François, That was how one went anywhere in Lausanne. Then . . . she took the address out of her purse. Seeing the bank loom up in front of her Miss Ann crossed to the other side of the street.

The very thought of Johnny blew like a cold warning on her cheek. He'd got so hopelessly drunk yesterday just when they could have used him, when they needed support. And why did he not tell her that he had a safe-deposit box, that he'd met Georges Évanoui? Could it be possible that she had totally misjudged him? Yes, from the moment he'd climbed up their balcony? Instead of using him like one of the Innocents Abroad, could it turn out that *he* was using *her?*

Miss Ann was so absorbed in her thoughts the rather ordinary looking man had to step in front of her to raise his hat.

"Why, Bill!" she said, trying to make her suddenly drawn breath appear to be pleasure. She couldn't take his hand; the paper with the address was in hers. "How nice to see you," she said over cordially, to make up.

With that he fell into step beside her. Strange that he should be sauntering here, so close to de Pré Morel's. And yet Lausanne was a place where one met everybody all the time. It was constructed that way, full of bottlenecks. She could even hear the unmistakable, inebriated playing of the accordion man quite near.

She saw the picture, in her memory, of Bill stealing the big envelope addressed to her publisher. He must have taken a quick look and sent it on. The acknowledgment of its receipt had arrived that morning. Nothing more. Not the name of the American agent she'd begged for in code. If she only knew whether the papers Bill worked for really *did* have a tie-up with European fascists, such a definite one that it would be natural for one of their reporters— with or without their knowing it—to be a member of the Nazi underground.

Should she waste time putting Bill off the track, or take him with her to visit the Frenchman? If only this impulse of haste, this tumult, were not urging her on!

She suddenly thought she had been wrong to trust Diana. The girl was very taken with Johnny Millard who just as plainly preferred her niece. Would Diana really want to protect a rival? Might she not close her eyes? Or even worse, could she be a tool of Johnny's? They had appeared together very suddenly at the opera after what seemed to be the slightest acquaintance.

Ann thought, I must get back before anything happens to Nancy.

"Bill," Ann said quickly. "We're here. I'm calling on M. de Pré Morel."

She stopped before a flight of steps, marked with a number, that went up the side of an old stone house. The top floor looked like an apartment. There was a brass push button conveniently located down below and brightly polished.

Ann punched it. There was no response. She tried again. Nothing.

"Let's go up and knock," Ann said. "It may be out of order."

Bill said, "In Switzerland these things are never out of order."

He followed her, but slowly.

They stood on de Pré Morel's balcony, or front porch, or whatever it was, knocking. You could see down over the housetops, almost to the lake, and beyond it, mountains.

Ann stopped, her fist in the air.

"Listen," she said. "Do you hear something?"

"No," Bill said.

But she tried the door. It opened.

There was de Pré Morel all right, on the floor, gasping for breath. His face was a funny, blue color. Bill had seen over her shoulder.

"Get a taxi!" he barked. "Stop a car! Anything! We've got to take him to a doctor!" He slid a hand under the man's awful head. "I'll carry him."

Miss Ann ran down the stairs without regard to heels or whether she would stumble. The sight was so unusual a car, coming in second up the hill, slowed down.

She waved, crying, "Sick man! Very sick! Must go to a doctor!"

The driver's eyes, blue and dumbfounded in his stolid face, had left her and were riveted on Bill who was shuffling down, grabbing the rail, a clumsy body dangling from his shoulder, feet bumping behind. One could see back of those blue eyes little wheels clicking like a reliable watch that always told the time. The car stopped at the curb, engine left running; the back door was opened; the driver leapt halfway up the stairs to help Bill.

Miss Ann climbed into the back seat, squeezed in a corner. "Put his head on my lap."

They bundled him in anyhow like an ill-wrapped package.

"Dr. Dollier's Clinic," Bill panted.

The head on her lap wasn't so noisy now. Not that the breathing was better. There were long pauses when he didn't breathe at all. He just lay and turned slowly darker. Then with a dreadful wrench and gurgle he would fight for air.

The car wasn't stopping for traffic or to avoid bumps.

Miss Ann was propping head and shoulders in the best position, waiting, with fierce concentration, for each breath.

They jerked to the curb. The two men hauled out de Pré Morel. She ran ahead of them and opened doors. Through a shocked waiting room she ran and opened the door to a private office.

The two men brought in their burden, laid him on the floor. Dr. Dollier, after one look, went through another door, came back with a colleague. De Pré Morel had stopped breathing finally; the face was black. The new doctor leaned over and took from his pocket a small pen knife.

He slit the unconscious throat. Air sucked in. Then it sucked out as from a punctured tire. It started going and coming in regular rhythm.

The doctor straightened and closed his pen knife.

"You didn't have much time," he said.

15

"I can't understand it," Dr. Dollier was murmuring. "There's never been a case like this before. One of those creosote capsules must have burst in his throat. I didn't believe they *could* break. Unless cut with a knife."

"I'll take him to the theater," the other doctor said, "and put in a tracheotomy tube." He raised his voice, "Call the theater sister," he said. "Tell her to get ready. Also send me a stretcher."

He nodded comfortingly to the three who'd brought the patient. "He will be all right."

They could see already that the Frenchman's face was less black.

Bill took the arm of the man who'd driven them. He was getting his name and address for the proper thanks; they were both asking questions of Dr. Dollier.

Ann backed into the waiting room as if to sit down. Several patients were standing, moving a little closer, peering politely at the figure on the floor.

Using them as a screen she drifted to the door. It was unguarded. In a moment she was out, walking briskly to the *ficelle* which came along quite handily. Very soon she was mounting the stairs to de Pré Morel's apartment.

There she began a systematic search for the brown capsules he took for his cough. First she went through the toilet articles in the dresser. She was just starting for the bathroom when she heard a small sound. Whirling, she saw the outer door was open. There stood Bill. She put her hand on her heart. "You startled me!"

"So did you me. You vanished."

"How did you get here so quickly?"

"Our helpful friend with the car."

"An idea had occurred to me," Miss Ann said rather weakly.

"To me also," he said. The voice was tight. Whether it was sarcasm or some emotion held perfectly in check she couldn't tell. He said, "Shall we look together?"

They moved to the bathroom and there open, on the edge of the wash bowl, lay the box of capsules.

"Don't touch it!" Bill said.

Miss Ann opened her bag, took out a lorgnette. Bill was leaning over—the light was good—his nose almost in the box.

"With a razor blade," he said.

The capsules, at least in the top layer, had tiny marks, like slits part way through.

Miss Ann straightened and said through lips that had been pressed together, "Will you be a witness to our finding them like this?"

"Of course." He paused. "What's the matter? Didn't I carry him to that clinic?"

"Yes, but I can't forget you were so near."

"My dear woman," he said easily, too easily perhaps. "The person who slit these capsules—if they really are slit—did it before I wandered by. He did it while de Pré Morel was surely out of the place. François must have returned before I passed."

"Bill—to be quite frank—you knew what to do so quickly!"

"A Lane always knows what to do!" He was laying it on thick. "Everyone in Lausanne has seen this Frenchman struggling with these pills. And now the thing to do is to call the police."

He marched to the telephone in the living room. While he was there Ann pulled herself together. She had noticed an object of perforated metal on the wall under the window, a radiator of some sort. But she pried at it quickly and the top came off. Inside was a rope ladder, securely fastened to the wall and neatly coiled. She put the lid back and followed Bill. As he hung up the receiver she put out her hand.

"Forgive me, Bill, I've been unfair." She managed a fluttering smile. "I'm in a state of nerves this morning. It's Nancy; of course. Lausanne is turning out to be no place for her."

"Why don't you get her out of here?" Bill said.

"Nowhere for her to go."

"If you're really serious there's always a bit of the U.S. on foreign soil. You could talk to our consul in Geneva. He and Mrs. Harrington would ask her to stay with them at the drop of a hat."

"Oh, I couldn't." There was no way to tell him Charbonnet might object.

"I'd be glad to take her," Bill said.

Ann summoned her most friendly look because she felt so dangerously the opposite:

"That's kind of you," she said. Send the child on a journey with a possible murderer? It was so far from funny she reverted to a forbidding tone. "I couldn't impose on the Harringtons. I don't know them."

"I thought you might know Mrs. Harrington," he said. "She was a Froelinghausen from Philadelphia."

Feet pounded up the stairs and there was Charbonnet to deal with, Charbonnet both sarcastic and suspicious. He kept glancing at Ann, examining her with a curiosity she didn't understand. Surely Henri couldn't have talked to him, couldn't have confided? What reason would there be for that?

Bill made a great deal of not allowing anyone to touch the box that held the capsules. So Ann was sure there'd be no fingerprints. Of course not. A pair of the Frenchman's gloves was lying in his hat by the door.

The inspector didn't keep them long. He already had an idea. He phoned at once for his men to pick up Johnny. That young man yesterday had grabbed an ale bottle from a bar and fired it at de Pré Morel. Here was the suspect. Why be complicated? Besides Charbonnet had been frustrated too long not having been able to arrest Johnny before.

He phoned the clinic and heard the Frenchman had been given a strong sedative and couldn't see even a policeman for twenty-four hours.

"Understood." Charbonnet hung up. "I shall go to the *bureau* to question Millard. You two, I'll see you later."

As she descended to Ouchy on the little *ficelle* Miss Ann's thoughts returned to Nancy with a rush. This attempt to get rid of the Frenchman had been clever. So, in a mad way, had been the German's try at her niece. It was all supposed to look so natural! What accident would happen next? She and Nancy were hopelessly exposed. Even Diana, about whom she had been so trustful, now seemed to be a danger. One kept remembering how she'd looked in Geneva with Johnny, too intimate, far too intimate. Why had Lady Jane let her go there unchaperoned? Perhaps she hadn't. Perhaps she'd known nothing about it.

Their hotel wasn't safe by day with the new maid lurking and it was doubly dangerous by night. She couldn't be sure of waking up in time, not always. And there was no one to help her now that Johnny had proved to be playing at best a double game. If only she could take Bill's advice—without that slippery character knowing it—and get Nancy to the consulate! The next twenty-four hours would be the worst while de Pré Morel got used to breathing through the tube in his throat, while they were waiting to see if he'd have pneumonia. When he could talk—or write—something should break.

By the time she'd walked past the bright quai bordered by the serene lake, her mind was made up. She went across the hotel lobby to the phone booth.

Sun spots from the water were dancing before her eyes. The place was dark anyway compared to high noon outside. No wonder that she didn't see the door of the second phone booth slightly open or the strong fingers that pulled it to.

Miss Ann got Geneva at once. She told Mr. Harrington her niece had had a frightening experience with an insane young man. She'd like to get her out of Lausanne to a place where she'd feel secure till the publicity died down.

"I heard about von Metsch, of course," Mr. Harrington said. "But I didn't know she was with him. How dreadful for her! My wife is in Évian at the moment but we'd both be delighted to have Miss Nancy with us. It was a pleasure to meet her. Such a charming girl! Just the type one hopes will come abroad to give people here the right impression of America."

Lucky he doesn't know, Miss Ann thought grimly, the impression Nancy has given Charbonnet. She expressed thanks. Then she asked, with apparent hesitation, if the consul could meet the next train.

The wire crackled. That was one thing he *couldn't* do. He was so sorry. He had a boring meeting he had to attend that would keep him till four o'clock.

"I, unfortunately, can't go with her," Miss Ann said. "And she's timid about crowds. Or perhaps I'm timid for her. It was a dreadful thing for a young girl to see."

"Why don't you put her on the boat?" Mr. Harrington said. "Very few people on the boat. You'll just have time at your end. I can meet the boat at four fifteen."

"Of course," said Miss Ann. "The very thing." How splendid not to have to call a taxi or appear at the station! The boat dock was in front of the hotel. "Thank, you a thousand times." She hung up.

She hurried off to tell Nancy. There was no way to get rid of Diana; she would have to hear. Their plan, Ann explained, would be to wait till nearly everybody was on the boat. Then to walk out quickly with a light suitcase,

carrying it themselves. Diana—better give the girl a job—
would be left to guard the rear. If she saw anyone they
knew she was to endeavor to steer that person to the terrace of the hotel. There were enough plane trees in front
and enough cedar trees in little tubs so the boat dock was
nearly invisible from the terrace.

Diana's eyes were sparkling at the prospect. Altogether
she looked a different girl, Ann noted, from the calflike
creature, falling over herself with embarrassment, they'd
seen at first.

Not so Nancy. She was tired, moody, and withdrawn.
Partly to cheer her Ann unlocked her dressing case and
drew out the pearl-handled revolver.

"You might slip this in."

Diana's eyes were like saucers.

"Oh, I say!"

"It's only a toy," said Nancy, putting it in her purse. "I
hope it doesn't drop out when I buy my ticket."

But she applied her lipstick with new interest, wiping
it all off twice.

Miss Ann was watching from the window. The stout
craft, with paddle wheels at the side like Mississippi steamboats, was warping into the dock.

"Ready, girls," she said.

Their passage through the lobby scarcely turned ahead.

The little group of other travelers was well up the gangplank, had just disappeared, when Nancy strolled aboard.
Miss Ann couldn't resist one glance at the faces over the
upper rail. There were none she knew. But a man walking
up there . . . something about him rang a bell, something
about that halting, crooked gait . . .

She took herself in hand. This was no time to give way
to fancies. The man was a peasant; he was with a group of
farmers. She turned resolutely back to the hotel. But still
across the road she stopped.

There on the terrace back of a little cedar tree sat Johnny, having coffee with Diana. Quick work. Was it quick

work? The boat gave a reassuring whistle behind her as it chugged off. Miss Ann had to reflect. She'd give them time for their coffee; there were benches by the water.

When she came up Diana turned bright red.

"I'm glad Nancy is sleeping," said Johnny. "Wish I could. But I no more than close my eyes when these so-and-so police get after me again. My landlady gave me a cast-iron alibi for whatever happened this morning; that's the only reason I'm here."

Diana was already on her feet; she stayed on them. "I must go," she said. "I don't know what mother will think. I've been the whole morning getting home from market."

"See you in jail, toots," Johnny said. He fixed Miss Ann with a haggard eye. "What is it all about this time? Charbonnet's been around giving me hell."

Miss Ann sat down.

"Tell me first what you have against de Pré Morel."

"Something that happened in France," Johnny said. "I've been following him if you want to know."

"That is clear now to everyone," she said, sighing, and then, just to be polite, "Did you find out anything?"

"Only," he said, "that there were several meetings between him and this Mr. Osborne that was killed. I never believed that was an accident. Nothing is around here."

"Do you know anything about it?" Ann leaned forward.

"Sorry to say that was my night off. I was drunk."

"Oh." She sank back. "At least you can tell me what your quarrel was in the bar."

"I was carrying quite a load," Johnny said. "I forgot to be careful. I said something like, 'We never knew really which side the French were on in the war and we don't now either.' De Pré Morel didn't like it."

"Tell me every word," Miss Ann said.

"He kept his temper. Said, 'Perhaps you don't know but the Germans do. We killed enough of them.' I stuck my chin out then. I said, 'You aren't particular who you kill. Other French people or Americans are just the same as Germans to you.'"

Miss Ann gave a long sigh.

"The Frenchman stiffened up," Johnny went on. "He said, 'I will ask you to explain that statement.'"

"And did you?" Miss Ann said.

"Oh, no indeed. I was too smart for that, even with liquor in me. I didn't even mention Evremont."

Miss Ann motioned to the waiter who was near to go away. "What *did* you mention?" she said.

"Only that there was an American killed here a short time ago. Supposed to be an auto accident. I told de Pré Morel, 'You're just the boy who could have fixed that accident.'"

"The Frenchman said, in that superior cold way of his, 'If you were in possession of your wits, monsieur, you might have heard that M. Osborne complained of drunken peasants in the road just a few days before he was killed. We who had known him thought he was trying to avoid one of them; that's why he went off.'

"'Possession of my wits'! Get that? I saw red. I said, 'You'd known Osborne, had you? That was bad luck for him. Everybody you know has bad luck . . . Here's some for you.' And I fired the bottle."

Johnny slumped back in his seat. He took a mouthful of his cold coffee.

Miss Ann said thoughtfully, "Was there an inn or tavern on that road where country people drank?"

"I don't know," Johnny said listlessly. "I've never been up there."

Miss Ann sat very straight. "Don't worry about the Frenchman any more," she said. "He's out of it."

She described their finding the man on the floor, his breath almost gone, the wild ride to the hospital.

Johnny stared at her, his eyes fixed.

"So you see," she finished, "he's a victim, not a murderer."

"It sounds good," Johnny shook his head, "but I don't believe it. Where's your proof? Might have been a *real* accident this time. That capsule might have busted by itself."

"You are certainly stubborn," Ann was frowning. "Why?"

"I don't know." He sat motionless.

Ann could have attacked him on many points. She chose only one.

"You have a question to answer yourself." She looked hard at the drooping face. "Why did you rent a safe-deposit box in the Crédit Alpin the day Georges Évanoui was murdered and say nothing about it?"

His eyes, sunken and blue-ringed as they were, did not waver.

He said, "To have somewhere to put a snapshot that I have. It's of this French family that I knew who were all killed by the Gestapo. There's someone else in the photo. It's this de Pré Morel."

16

"Not toward the shore, toward the lake?" the steward said.

Nancy nodded mutely and followed and sank into her deck chair.

How grateful were those miles of empty water! The calm of Lac Léman, she'd noticed before, meant more than no wind. It had a spiritual quality, repose for the soul. Perhaps all the people who had come here in the past to find peace had created it. This water, faintly shining, played over by a faint, fresh breeze, really was peace.

The engines began to hum. The ropes, flung off, slapped on the deck. With a wrench they were headed out into the clear, the clear . . .

She hadn't been able to talk to her aunt, to anyone. The beauty of von Metsch, the physical beauty, was what hurt. It was so mismatched with his ugly emotions. She had slowly, so slowly, that night been able to separate the two. She was quite old enough to know that his feeling for her hadn't been make-believe.

If only she'd been able to talk to someone her own age like Johnny! Johnny could have made Europe seem like a bad dream, but he'd folded up too. He'd left her. He'd slid right away into the solitude of getting drunk.

The clean air smelling of clean water fanned her cheek. How much better lakes are than mountains, Nancy thought, closing her eyes.

When they docked at Morges, at Nyons, she didn't quite wake. She could feel the wood of the boat rub on the wood of the quai, hear the ropes and the gulls. It was all soothing and safe. They were sliding past Coppet, past the terrace of Mme. de Stael, when she sighed deeply. Tristan and Iseult again. She had begun to hear it; better wake up.

Her vacant eyes noticed unconsciously a familiar back. She struggled as if she were throwing off a drug. Who? What? Yes, it must be Sir John Trelawney.

Let me see. Should I worry about him? Can't see why. If anything he ought to be Ann's worry like that banker.

She smiled drowsily when finally he turned round from the rail.

"Don't wake unless you want to," he said. "Lots of time."

"Oh, I'm awake . . . This *is* a restful trip though, isn't it? I'd no idea I was tired."

"You've had a bit of shut-eye certainly. I hung about warding off Johnnies who'd stop and stare. Sleeping Beauty sort of thing. Can't blame them really."

He sat down beside her.

"This week is a round of pleasure for me," he remarked. "Two trips to Genève, both for music. I've been thinking. You'd know more about this than I do."

He searched in his pockets for a letter, found it, unfolded it for her.

Nancy sat up suddenly. "Why, it's a name band! Their records are wonderful. I hope every single dance orchestra in Switzerland goes to hear them! They certainly need to, especially the one at the Rossinière!"

"Oh, is that what it is, 'Swing'?" His monocle dropped out in surprise. "Wish I'd thought of it. I could have invited your aunt . . . and you, too, of course."

"I'm not sure my aunt would have been as interested as I am," she said frankly.

"Oh, I say . . . If you're staying over, why not come and hear them? And have a drink afterward with Mister . . . Mister . . ." He screwed in his monocle.

"Max Royal."

"They asked me to be a sponsor," he said. "Foreign resident, you know. Had to say yes. Principle of the thing."

Nancy frowned a little. "I'm staying with Mr. and Mrs. Harrington," she said. "Of course, I can't make engagements without asking them. But I should think they'd be going."

"If not, come as my guests . . . All of you . . . Delightful."

"Thank you. I'll try to persuade them."

She wasn't hearing Wagner any more; she was thinking, quite rested and refreshed, of a hot trumpet.

"Were almost here," Sir John said. "Let me carry your bag."

They drifted to the gangplank behind most of the others. There was Mr. Harrington, so bland, so confident, a little stout, scanning the faces on the boat. She waved to him. He smiled. She started down the gangplank, empty now.

Sir John had put down her suitcase to fold the coat he was carrying. She felt her arm clutched, yanked backward almost out of its socket. She jerked back with it like lightning to avoid a fall.

There was a shape before her eyes, a jarring crash.

A metal tool box had bit into the wood in front of her.

Sir John shouted; officials came running; passengers backed away. From Sir John issued a stream of profanity that diverted her from the shock she hardly realized yet. Why, the old gentleman had saved her life!

"What are you blankety-blank nincompoops thinking of? Is this any way to run a boat?" He was brandishing his fist at a young sailor. "Leaving metal sliding about! Could have killed both of us. Where is the captain? Damnedest thing I ever heard of. I'm going to get to the bottom of this if I have to . . ."

Mr. Harrington had worked his way to Nancy.

"You were born under a lucky star," he said. "I didn't know Trelawney had it in him. Well, you can trust the

British. One of the fastest things I ever saw. He just happened to glance up." He offered his arm. "I saw the top
deck. Nobody threw that thing. It was just a freak accident."

"What happened?"

"Some careless fool had left a tool box on the canopy
over the deck. When the boat docked it slid down."

He retrieved her suitcase, told the policeman, who'd
arrived by then, where she was staying.

"We'll thank Trelawney," he said, "who richly deserves
it, and then leave." They worked their way through the
crowd. "The dear man will be spouting on for hours," Mr.
Harrington said. "You'll find it pleasanter at home with
Mathilda."

The drive was pleasant certainly. One felt protected
by this city in a valley. As they got farther out the pretty
houses behind trees were hidden frequently by walls that
lined the road. They went through an arched gateway to
the Harringtons.

"Mathilda's bound to be home by now," Mr. Harrington
said. "She'll be glad of your company. This infernal meeting took so much time! My desk is piled with letters I
must answer before dinner . . . Where is madame?" he
asked the neat maid.

"Not arrived yet . . . A telegram for monsieur."

He ripped it open.

"What bad luck!" he said. "Mathilda didn't know, of
course, you were coming. She's staying on at Évian for
dinner. Home by eleven. Couldn't get me on the phone.
We'll have a good time anyway." He chattered on. "Sure
you're over the shock? I hope you don't mind being left an
hour or so?"

He started for the drawing room.

"The cousin of madame," the maid said. "Monsieur, the
cousin of madame is there."

Nancy found herself guided to a room like home, all
chintzy and colonial. But she paid small attention to the

furniture, less to the hearty introduction. She merely stared.

Mr. Harrington looked from face to face.

"You know each other!" he approved. "Then you'll excuse me the more readily. She just escaped an accident, my boy . . . I shall be right across the hall."

He bustled out. The study door closed firmly.

"Bill Lane!" Nancy said. "How did *you* get here?"

"On the boat."

She hadn't noticed before how his mouth snapped shut. A strong mouth.

"You didn't throw a tool box at me, did you?" It came out in spite of her.

"Did he try something? God!" Bill smote his thigh. "I should have stayed instead of hurrying off first so he wouldn't see me . . . I thought he was only a shadow."

"Who was?" She glared.

"Schwartz, the proprietor of the Café des Fauconniers."

Nancy sat down. She felt unable to stand any longer.

"He was not in his regular clothes," Bill said. "He was letting on to be a peasant. The point is, you're being followed, my girl. And not for your health. You've got to be careful."

"That was the idea in coming," she said. "So far it hasn't worked."

"I can only stay a few minutes," Bill said. He kept moving around nervously. "I've got to get out of here, but I had to wise you up. You won't go out of the house, will you?"

She lifted her chin. "I certainly will. I intend to persuade your cousin by marriage to take me to hear Max Royal, perhaps meet him afterward. Sir John Trelawney, who just saved my life, invited us."

"But, child, you can't go to a concert or café or anything like that. Don't you see, in a crowd, it would be too easy to arrange an accident? So far your reflexes have saved you. They won't always. Can't you catch on to the fact the house is watched?"

Nancy went stubbornly to the window to look out. "I don't see anyone but that maid who was here a few minutes ago, leaving. There's a fat woman with her."

Bill looked over her shoulder.

"The cook," he said. His voice changed. "They've disposed of them somehow. A fake phone call or something. And Mathilda . . ." Bill groaned. "They're ready for you, even here. Gardener's out too. They must have known you were coming." He lifted his head sharply. "How did your aunt arrange this trip?"

"She telephoned."

"Where?"

"From the lobby."

"Those booths are not soundproof," he said. "They're a couple of listening boxes. There might be an agent in your hotel."

"Oh, there is! The maid who took Leedia's place. We've known that a long time."

"If they're ready for you here," he said very quietly, "you can't stay. They'll have planned something that will work."

Nancy swallowed. After all, that tool box had been close. She didn't think it was an accident now. "Can't Mr. Harrington ask for police protection?"

"Not without making an incident out of it and, as they say, 'embarrassing his government.' The police of Genève are always being harried by diplomats. We know all right, but what have we got for proof? That tool box didn't impress Cousin Barclay. People rarely believe in danger until they've felt it. Then—you know this, you learned it on the mountain—it's within a hair of being too late."

What did he know about the mountain? cut across her mind. Or about her reflexes? She looked out the window. A more peaceful street had never slept in the spring sun. The danger was right in this room.

"The worst of it is," Bill said, "I haven't got much time. My exit is arriving in a few minutes."

He'd started pacing up and down; far from the window. He ground to a stop.

"I can't leave you here. These are not ordinary spies; these are Gestapo men. They're not employed by any country that has to keep on good terms with the U.S. They'd just as soon invade a diplomat's residence with a machine pistol."

Nancy hoped he couldn't see how she was feeling.

"With all due respect to Cousin Barclay," he said, "his training doesn't fit him for this. I don't think he's quick enough on the trigger."

She managed to say scornfully, "Are you?"

"I could try, little girl."

This scornful tone was good; she kept it up. "What is this 'exit' of yours?"

"I have a friend, a cheesemaker, who lives in the mountains. We look alike. Sometimes when I want to get information I dress in Gaspard's clothes and say a few words of Vaudois. Then people aren't careful; they talk in front of you."

"What kind of people?"

"The underworld, taxi drivers, waiters—"

She remembered the times she'd seen him tired and unshaven. Had he just taken off a smock?

"Gaspard is coming here," he said, "in his farm cart. I'm going out in it."

Bill wasn't pacing now. He was looking intently at the street.

"His wife always comes with him," he sighed. "It's a big responsibility, but maybe you could change outfits with her."

"That's one of the most ridiculous ideas I ever heard of," Nancy said. "Play acting! Fancy dress! This is the twentieth century."

"So it is," Bill said. "Some century. Or haven't you noticed?"

His face looked rather sad; there were deep lines around the mouth and eyes.

"But why"—Nancy was sad too, really, not pretending—"should I believe a word you say?"

"Have you glanced at the man who has come up across
the street and started plastering that wall? That wall
doesn't need plastering."

"I've seen him." She wished she could think clearly.
"Maybe he's a confederate of yours."

"He used to be a waiter in the Maison Rouge, upstairs
in the private rooms."

Nancy shuddered. "How do you know about that?" she
cried. She looked fearfully out of the window.

"Reporters know everything."

Bill pointed. A farm cart was turning into the drive,
a stubby two-wheeled one that could be pulled up mountains. On the seat were a country couple, the man in a
home-made looking suit, shaped to the contours of
his body, and a felt hat with a high, peaked crown. The
woman, Nancy saw with unwilling, pained concentration,
wore a full skirt, a shawl over her shoulders and a cotton
kerchief that covered every bit of hair. On her lap was a
basket of eggs.

Bill dove for the kitchen, Nancy close to him. She
didn't want to stay anywhere alone. He flattened them
both behind the door when he opened it.

When it was closed he shook hands powerfully. He explained at length, simply assuming Nancy would do what
he said. She tried to talk, to ask them questions, but her
schoolroom French didn't get far with their Alpine brand.
They kept saying politely, "What, mademoiselle?"

Bill disappeared and returned with a dress obviously
his cousin's. The face of Gaspard's wife fell. She'd been
eying Nancy's suit which would have fitted her. She took
off her kerchief. Bill said, "Thank God," when he saw dark
braided hair. "You're not too much like Nancy for your
own good."

"Get busy, girls," he said, shooing them into the dining
room.

Nancy found herself in the surprising position of holding out her hand for this woman's clothes. The cheeks of Gaspard's wife, which were red like Leedia's, became even redder; her eyes shone.

"*Excusez, mademoiselle, excusez,*" she kept saying as she adjusted her skirt on Nancy, tied the shawl.

Nancy found her suitcase where it had been forgotten, took out the cosmetics and wiped all her lipstick off.

"I'm disguised now," she said to Gaspard's wife with a feeble try at humor. "Nobody would know me. I don't know myself."

Their two faces looked in the mirror side by side and Nancy rouged her cheeks.

"Encore, encore," said Gaspard's wife, giggling.

Bills voice outside the door said sternly, "Ready?"

Nancy opened her purse, took out her passport, *permits de séjour,* ration card and revolver and slid them into the big pocket of the skirt.

The Swiss girl was staring, pop-eyed.

Nancy hung the long strap of her pocketbook over the other's shoulder. That will make her forget the revolver, she thought, opening the door.

Heavens! she'd taken him for Gaspard for a moment. It was Bill.

He pointed at her hands. She found her scissors, cut the nails to the quick, took off the polish.

The Swiss girl had got unobtrusively in front of the mirror and was leaning forward entranced, with Nancy's lipstick which she had fished out of the pocketbook.

"None of that," Bill ordered. "Nothing to look like Nancy even from a distance. Do you want them to shoot you?"

He turned to Nancy. "Remember, young lady, I didn't get you into this. You got yourself in." He seemed to be making a speech. "I'm going to try to get both you and me out. I may fail. We'd better make it look as well as possible if it comes to that. I've been giving a cock-and-bull story to Barclay. I told him I'm in love with you."

He was marching her with him to the study. "It's the easiest explanation, the quickest. We've got to be quick. Barclay takes an ungodly long time to absorb anything complicated. Remember that Genève is just as hot for you as Lausanne, hotter. Try not to mind."

He rapped on the door and opened it.

Mr. Harrington rose from behind his desk with a wide, welcoming smile.

The plasterer's eyes had never left the house. When he was forced to turn his back to it to go through the motions of working he propped a bit of broken mirror in a chink in the wall.

Those peasants had been there a long time. Could it be that the people in the house suspected? What could they suspect? A telephone out of order was a common thing; if they'd thought otherwise they would have come to look for the cut wire. He himself certainly was too good an agent—he gave a long artistic swipe with the trowel—to raise any doubt.

Ah, here they came, the farmers, stumbling out the back door. The man stopped, half across the yard, and wiped his mouth with the back of his hand. So that's what they'd been doing, drinking. The cook must have left a bottle not locked up. (She'd been called out, of course, in a hurry.) The woman climbed up easier than she'd climbed down; her big basket that had been full of eggs was empty.

The man bit off a large chew of tobacco, hoisted himself to the high seat and chirruped to the horse. They careened out of the driveway, the reins slack, the farmer leaving it all to the horse, his wife swaying beside him with her head down, no more spirit than a rag doll.

Should he go after them? Were they taking a message somewhere? Were they dangerous?

He peered in his bit of mirror and saw the American at the window. What a fine jacket, a good piece of goods. If he had time to get it off the man, after they went in and did their job, he'd like to take it . . . But, of course, the boss . . . He'd better report the peasants to the boss, the *gruppen-fuehrer,* he liked to be called. The agent laid down his trowel, walked nonchalantly out of sight of the house and wheeled his bicycle from among some bushes.

It wasn't hard to catch up with that mountain cart; it was merely ambling. The people seemed asleep they shook so limply when the wheels went over a stone.

He stayed behind. A couple of men were walking toward him and they gave the cart a sharp glance as it passed. One had the barrel chest, the curious rolling gait that frightened those who knew him.

"Herr Schwartz," the plasterer said eagerly. "That cart has just been to the Harringtons. The woman left eggs. I don't know . . . I'm reporting. Should I follow them?"

"For what?" The vast shoulders heaved; Schwartz turned his head.

As they all stared at the cart its driver leaned out and spat, a long stream of tobacco juice accurate as a missile.

"Schweizer Deutsch," said the proprietor of the Café des Fauconniers. "I've seen the man somewhere. It's not a face that strikes me as suspicious. I remember all those . . . We're not even told, of course, how many are working on our side."

The man with the bicycle rubbed one leg against the other to get off the white dust.

"Follow them on the big road," said Herr Schwartz, "for a few moments."

The plasterer pedaled slowly. After they turned into the highway that led to Lausanne he had to keep to the edge of the road to avoid the automobiles, the buses. The little cart was lost among them, too. The farmer's wife shrank back when anything passed. They were certainly not signaling for help, not calling the police.

Then the cart turned left across the stream of traffic, made for a dirt road scarcely bigger than a goat path. On one side of this path was the mountain it clung to, on the other a deep ravine.

The plasterer stopped his bicycle by the roadside and turned it around. He couldn't wait to get back. He was looking forward to the gun play. He patted his holster under the smock; he liked guns. He liked excitement . . . Tina and Gaby and Pernod and a whiff of cocaine.

To think of those poor dolts in that creeping wagon! They would go on forever up that mountain and there wouldn't be any houses and it would get darker and darker.

17

Miss Ann, perched on the rock wall buttressing the road, put one knee over the other and braced her oxfords down against the stone. She had lunched very frugally indeed off a chocolate bar, washed down, so to speak, by an amazing view. She was finishing with a cigarette. Her eyes, though turned in the direction of the downward slope, a heavenly, cropped meadow full of primroses, didn't really see it. She hadn't intended this kind of lunch, not at all.

Her one consolation was that Nancy, whose appetite was far from delicate, wasn't sharing the adventure, wasn't sharing—thank God—any adventures for a while. She opened her purse to be comforted once more by the telegram.

She'd been so worried yesterday afternoon when she tried to telephone Geneva and found the Harringtons' line out of order! All the old doubts had sprung up to torment her. Was it right to expose the child to these dangers no matter what the state of the world, no matter how many young men Nancy's age had died, no matter how much the girl wanted to share their chances? Then the telegram had turned up. She smoothed out its wrinkles.

"Quite happy with Mr. and Mrs. Harrington. Restful trip. Love."

She gave a little pat to the yellow paper. Nancy must have learned the telephone was out of order and sent this to save her aunt anxiety. How the child had grown up! She would not have attributed any real feelings to older people a few months ago, much less been so considerate of them.

Ann's gaze drifted from her lap over the meadow and the lower slopes down to the shimmer of lake enclosed in its majestic ring of mountains. But her eyes were vacant.

She was hearing again what the Frenchman, in the middle of that quarrel in the bar, had told Johnny about Mr. Osborne meeting tipsy peasants. She heard her own question, "Is there an inn or tavern on that road where country people drink?"

Johnny had said he didn't know; he'd never been up there. So she had planned to arrive on those heights over Lausanne in time for lunch and do a little careless questioning.

The trouble was there wasn't any inn, no place to buy either food or drink for miles.

De Pré Morel must have been lying. He must have made up the drunken peasants. That was the most likely, unless Johnny had lied. The alternative was outlandish. Could a murderer have arranged the whole incident so Mr. Osborne would talk about it to make people believe in the disaster that was already planned?

Miss Ann scarcely thought so. She'd seen the hairpin turn where her predecessor must have gone off. There was a brand new piece of fence in one place. She'd been up to his villa, barred and shuttered as it was.

There was only one direction she hadn't explored thoroughly, a side road, lane rather, that went off and crossed a deep ravine. It was too small to be a good location for an inn, too inconspicuous.

Still, one had to be thorough. She slid off the wall, took up her alpenstock reluctantly and started down the little road. Once over the ravine, the road led on and on. You could see for miles down into the valley on one side and up above the tree line on the other. It was perfectly open but you could never see where you were going because always ahead there was a sharp curve. Miss Ann kept expecting to come out on a vast prospect where she could get her bearings. But no. The road played hide-and-seek in the crystal air.

She couldn't decide to turn around; it was too far to go back. She kept hoping to come out on a wide road with signposts or see the welcome track of a *funiculaire*. There should at least be a farmhouse where one could ask the way.

Instead of that the road got choked with bushes. It disappeared in a thicket of young pines. They were in flower; she'd never seen pine trees in flower. She was gazing at the small yellow bells—they fairly trembled with the drone of bees—when her mechanical pace brought her up to a maze of outbuildings. The road led around a garage.

Ann stopped in surprise. Before her stretched the terrace of Sir John Trelawney's villa. More bees were feeding in his flower boxes; below them lay a valley shiny with peace.

Beside the front door, in the startling, pure, celestial light, stood an incongruous figure. It was a ramrod figure, clothed in a black dress, the gray hair piled up like the Queen Mother's. As Ann approached she saw a pince-nez clamped to a Gothic nose and further anchored by a chain that wound up in a tape-measure box pinned to the bosom.

"Good afternoon, Miss Thorne."

A look of wistful eagerness and welcome dawned on the features that had been so grim.

"Good afternoon," murmured Miss Ann. "It is a lovely one, isn't it?"

"Yes, Miss . . . If you will pardon me, I saw you with Sir John when you were here to dinner."

Of course, the housekeeper! An English one.

The eyes behind the pince-nez were traveling over Ann's worn but well-chosen tweeds, her stout shoes, heavy gloves.

At each item new satisfaction crept visibly into that face. One divined the poor woman had had to put up with a great deal in the way of foreigners.

"Lady Trelawney spoke of you," burst from the prim lips. "She used to wish her daughter was in America too . . . So I was ever so glad to see you. It seemed quite like home." The housekeeper shook herself like a crow settling rusty feathers. "Only fancy! A lady that Miss Mary knew!"

"I was very fond of Miss Trelawney," Ann said.

The housekeeper swallowed. She seemed to pull herself together.

"I'm sorry to tell you that Sir John is from home."

"I didn't exactly come to see him." Ann smiled. "As a matter of fact I got lost." She gestured toward the garage. "I was on another part of the mountain and took that road by mistake."

The housekeeper clicked her tongue on her teeth. "It's a dreadful distance . . . I don't suppose, Miss," she said hesitantly, "you would care for tea?"

Quite wrong to be entertained by people's servants . . . Still, the pangs of hunger were keenly gnawing. And those washed-out eyes peered hopefully through their thick panes of glass.

"Wouldn't I just!" Ann said.

A babble of voices rose inside the house, got louder.

"But you have visitors!" Ann said.

"No, Miss, only the Red Cross class. Sir John lets them meet here. Lady Trelawney started it in the war. Would you care to come in?"

"I can't bear to leave this." Ann pointed to the valley. "Thank you—?"

"Mrs. Huddleston, Miss."

Ann sank into a deep chair and gratefully lifted her feet onto a stool.

The front door opened and let out a crowd of chattering girls. They had made some attempt at a uniform; could they be Girl Guides? Like all Swiss children they looked sturdy and cheerful. Ann smiled at them. They smiled back, the instructor also, a serious young woman with a white armband on which was a large red cross.

Hardly had their voices died away in the distance, hardly had Ann begun an inventory of the view when a little maid appeared, staggering under a silver tray—the housekeeper watchfully, importantly behind her.

When the dishes were set out on a table Mrs. Huddleston rearranged them a little, put the most necessary things within Ann's reach. Knowing she wanted to stay, Ann tried to talk with her—even about Mary's days in school. The housekeeper had not been with the family then. She had only been engaged at the time of Lady Trelawney's illness, expressly to take charge of the move to Switzerland. She had become devoted to the two ladies. Sir John had been in India then; he had only been recalled to England by the war. But she had heard of him so constantly that she included him in her loyalty and thought it her duty to stay on—my lady would have wanted it— though she was very homesick.

Much as the housekeeper would have enjoyed a chance to talk longer—Ann offered it plainly—her training was too good. She clung to knowing her place even in preference to this potent lure. Her bony fingers ceased to touch the silver.

Mrs. Huddleston said, "I'll be back, Miss, to see if you need anything."

The tea was superb. Ann knew that somebody's ration points were given for the bread and butter. Summoning all her resolution she only took one slice.

Mrs. Huddleston's angles cut in two the hazy valley.

"You haven't eaten anything," she said, but her eyes beamed approval. "I was wondering, Miss Thorne," she went on, "if you'd be interested to see our Red Cross room? Lady Trelawney had it well equipped. One of the English sisters who was here with her bought hospital furnishings."

"Of course, I'd like to see it!" This was Mrs. Huddleston's chance to converse. It might be Ann's chance, too. She rose at once.

"There are eight beds," the housekeeper said gratefully. "We tried to do our bit during the war even here. There were French orphans with us for a while"—she opened the terrace door—"and some of our own people now and then, stranded, you know."

They had arrived at the room, a sort of half basement with windows high up.

"It's not intended to be slept in," Mrs. Huddleston said. "My lady meant it for a classroom, as they use it now."

The black arm pointed out neat beds lined up, two stretchers, cupboards full of bandages, basins for bath water, a Chase doll, every device a modern hospital classroom could use.

Miss Ann's eyes lingered. It was indeed remarkable to find all this on a mountain side. She said so warmly.

"Now I must leave." She added, "Will you direct me? I don't want to go back the way I came. The big road I walked up—before turning off, you know, on your little one—is dangerous. There's no footpath for pedestrians and with that frightful curve I don't know what one would do if a car should come suddenly round the bend."

"Oh, dear!" the housekeeper said. "That must be the place poor Mr. Osborne was killed. It wasn't a pedestrian; it was a car went off."

"Was that a long time ago?"

"A matter of three weeks." Mrs. Huddleston pursed her bps and nodded. "I remember the date because Sir John was giving an evening party."

"Indeed?" said Ann very casually, very lightly.

"Yes, to the foreign colony. They were all here. Poor Mr. Osborne couldn't come. He phoned that he was detained just a few minutes before the guests arrived." Her head shook till the pince-nez trembled on her nose. "If he had come he might have avoided that dreadful accident."

"I've noticed," Miss Ann said—she had to grind her teeth to make herself go on—"the foreign colony all stick together . . . They don't have much to do with the Swiss."

"Oh, Sir John tried to be kind to the Swiss," Mrs. Huddleston said. "He invited some of them to that very party. I remember the banker, M. Rambert, being there. He had to leave early."

Miss Ann murmured as if from pure convention, "Mme. Rambert is charming."

The housekeeper said, "Oh, she couldn't come. One of the children was ill. That was why he had to leave early."

What a changed world met them as Mrs. Huddleston opened the front door! It was only mid-afternoon but a soaring peak had eclipsed the sun. The bees had gone home; some of the flowers had closed their petals. Instead of happy light Miss Ann would have to walk in deep, clear and oppressive shadow.

The road in front, she was told, led down to the *funiculaire*. She started off briskly enough, her alpenstock ringing on the stones of the terrace.

The view, of course—Ann peered at it—was still magnificent. The other side of the valley kept the sun. The poor little villages at the bottom, though, had lost it and the dark was creeping up and reaching out its fingers like a menace.

The air had changed as quickly as the light. Ann had to walk faster to keep warm. She didn't want to stumble though; she went slower. Footsteps behind her kept on fast. Was it an echo? It must have been; she couldn't hear it now. Ann shivered.

The cold was suddenly piercing. If I'm killed, Ann thought, I mustn't vanish in a mystery like the others. I must tell somebody.

She lengthened her pace, but cautiously so not to sound hurried. At last around a bend appeared the tiny station, empty, of course. It held out no hope, nothing but loneliness. And then as she came up, rather breathless, Ann saw on one of the posts that held up the shelter, a mailbox.

Luckily she had paper in her purse. She scribbled a note addressed to M. Charbonnet. Just as she slid it in the box footsteps approached behind her, light footsteps. Then the train whistled. The steps changed to a blurred shuffle. How wonderful was the Swiss railway system!

Turning around she saw the drooping form of Pierrot, accordion slung over his shoulder.

He raised a fumbling hand to his hat brim.

Ann felt supported by the faint screech of the train grinding down the hillside. She pulled herself together with all the discipline of her past.

"*Bonjour, mon ami,*" she said with truly dazzling friendliness.

Pierrot blinked and swallowed. "*Eh . . . bonjour, madame.*"

He appeared dumbfounded, touched his hat again.

The train with a squeal of rusty brakes drew up. They got in. There was no one else in the carriage. The ticket collector made his way up leisurely and took their money. Pierrot was in the seat directly behind Ann almost the car's width away. He sidled nearer.

"I have something to tell you, madame."

His voice was half whine, half whisper.

Ann leaned sideways, an amused expression fixed as tight to her face as if she were posing for a tiresomely informal photograph. The guard mustn't think the old fellow was annoying her.

"Go ahead," she murmured.

"It was Monsieur von Metsch"—the name hissed through broken teeth—"Monsieur von Metsch, dressed as a woman, who used to meet M. Évanoui at the Café des Fauconniers."

"Was it indeed?" said Ann without inflection.

It was a new idea; could have been true considering the German's looks.

"It was this man dressed as a woman who put the poison in Évanoui's glass."

Ann's smile was going to pieces; she jerked it back.

"Did you see it?" she said.

"Maybe so, maybe not . . . For you I saw it, not for the police."

No, no, this was too easy. She wasn't accepting the accordion player's word. Why had he given her such a fright just now? Had he been following her all afternoon?

Suppose he was a German agent. It would be good policy to fix all blame on a man already dead, load every previous crime on von Metsch.

The accordion bumped along the seat nearer.

"Nobody pays attention to me, madame," its owner said. "I can go anywhere. 'Just old Pierrot,' they say, 'always drunk.'"

"Very convenient," Ann whispered.

"Eh? Well," he nodded. "I'm not so drunk as all that. It was I told the American monsieur to hurry after the young demoiselle."

"You did?"

The battered head leaned over. "It was not good for her to walk in the night with a man who dresses as a woman—who poisons wine."

"It was not, certainly."

But Ann didn't trust him. Johnny had said nothing about being tipped off by this old man to Nancy's danger. Had he been? Again she had to weigh the possibility of Johnny's lying, of his naive manner being cleverly assumed.

Pierrot was breathing on her neck. She wanted to ask about Mr. Osborne's death but she didn't dare. He'd met her too near, he'd followed her . . . Suppose he was on their side and she was missing the only opportunity? Ah, she had it . . .

"Can you tell me about M. de Pré Morel?" she said. The train was crunching to a stop. Ann turned around.

"Who visited him before he was taken ill? I heard you playing. You were in the neighborhood."

He smiled; he put his finger to his lips.

Only then did she see the carriage doors were open. People were scrambling in for the trip back. If she wanted to get out she must get past them. The next few minutes were spent in begging pardons and avoiding feet.

The step down from the carriage was blocked by a man getting in. All she could make out at first was the top of a hat to which she spoke imploringly. The man raised his head; she was looking into Sir John's astonished face.

He backed down to the ground politely, raised his hat.

Before saying a word she sent a searching glance for Pierrot. He had already vanished; he was nowhere. This was a new station to Ann anyway, somewhere above the Place St. François. She could hardly get her bearings.

Sir John was screwing in his monocle. "I say," he said, "isn't Miss Nancy with you?"

"No," said Ann. "She's visiting in Geneva."

"Saw her yesterday," he said. "On the boat." His voice was quite gruff. "She was keen to go to this band concert. Didn't come."

"What concert?" Ann said sharply.

"American band. 'Swing.' Extraordinary. What? Can't call it music. She was most awfly keen though." Sir John shook his head.

"This is the first I've heard of it."

"I telephoned your consul this morning," Sir John said. "She wasn't there. He didn't know where she was."

They were alone on the platform now. The doors of the railway carriage slammed shut. He took a step toward them, then stood still and frowned.

"I was a bit worried because of the accident."

"What accident?" Ann said desperately.

"Oh, on the boat."

He looked with surprise at the departing train. Then he described the accident.

"Harrington saw it from the dock," he said. "He made nothing of it. But I don't like slackness. Talked to the captain. He sent for the fellow who'd been using the tool box"—Sir John snorted—"left it in that idiotic place. Handyman sort of chap; had been tightening up the life-boat." His brow wrinkled. "Man was nowhere to be found."

Sir John shook his head.

"But why?" Ann said. "Why?"

"None of the crew had got off," he went on. "So we hunted. It took us half an hour to find this chap. Lucky we did. Stowed away in a box where they keep extra life preservers. Bump on the head. Out cold."

He looked quite blank and very stern.

"Horrible," said Miss Ann. "I've got to find Nancy." It seemed as if a pitiless hand were clutching her heart. "Come," she said, starting out of the station. "We must hurry."

Once on the street she almost broke into a run.

He panted after her. "Thought the whole thing was curious, myself."

18

The late spring afternoon felt chilly now the sun was low. Johnny turned his coat collar up. He'd chosen the café where you could see the most people and a table, regardless of the draft, far out on the sidewalk with a view down three streets.

He had stepped out of the bank now and then—oh, lots of times—for a quick one. That institution couldn't expect him to be on a regular schedule, not with the day he'd had yesterday. Why yesterday he'd not been in the place except to chat with the police in the morning and look in vain for M. Rambert in the afternoon.

The wind whipped the waiter's apron as he brought Johnny's Pernod.

That liquid sizzled down his throat, cheered him a little.

Johnny was lonesome; he hadn't seen anybody, hadn't caught up with things. He looked searchingly at the passersby. They looked at him even more. When his hat was off, as it always was, the gray hair over what he knew was a young face invariably attracted attention. He had learned not to care, to put on a go-to-hell expression.

He was wearing this now, more defiantly as the Pernod took hold, when his eye lighted on Miss Thorne, rushing along with that old English character part.

This was more like it, somebody to talk to, somebody to chase the devils from his brain. Besides, the aunt might

lead him to Nancy. Or she might go with him where he
wanted to go.

He slapped down his change, gulped the Pernod so not
to waste it, ran across the street.

They stopped when they saw him. He *was* running
rather heavily, felt like a bull charging a toreador; seemed
to make all the blood go to his head.

Sir John grabbed his arm. "Steady on, young feller," he
said.

The Englishman turned to Miss Ann. "Go to the police
if you want to, ma'm." He was keeping on with a conversation just as if Johnny were not there. "But first I should
call up your consul. He may give you more information
than he would me—a stranger, so to speak, though I *have*
met the feller."

Miss Ann was looking queer the way Johnny'd never
seen her; she looked helpless. She wavered before him.

He gathered all his powers.

"Good telephone in there." He waved toward the café.
"Good one. Private."

Miss Ann, without a word, started across the street. They
followed. Johnny's waiter was still wiping off his table.

"A black coffee," Johnny muttered. "Quick."

He sat down with the Englishman; he sipped the coffee
so hot it burned as much as the Pernod. After a few gulps
Johnny leaned over confidentially.

"Where *I* want to go," he said, "is Dr. Dollier's clinic.
The Frenchman should be able to talk now." He clenched
his fist on the cold marble of the table. "Anything that
goes on around here, I believe he's at the bottom of it."

Sir John blinked. "I take it you mean de Pré Morel?
What's the matter with him?"

"Where have you been," Johnny said, "that you don't
know?"

"I've been in Geneva."

Johnny told him tersely.

Miss Ann came back just as Sir John was saying, "How long has he been in the clinic?"

"Since yesterday, about noon."

They jumped up to pull out a chair. She sank down wordlessly.

The Englishman had put in his monocle. It made him look brighter, more able to concentrate.

"Couldn't have been de Pré Morel on the boat then," he said wisely. "He's out of that, anyway." He explained to Johnny, "Somebody on the boat had it in for Miss Nancy, threw a heavy box at her . . . Or, I say, it could have been at me." He looked quite overcome. "But why me?"

Johnny was thinking, not for the first time, this guy cooperates in a dim-witted way. He certainly cooperates. Wonder if he's British Intelligence in disguise? It's a fine disguise. It would be just like them.

Then he saw Miss Thorne's hands. They were partly hidden in her lap under the table; she was pressing and wringing one against the other.

"Mr. Harrington," she said brokenly, "has no idea where Nancy is. He is preposterous enough to tell me not to worry." She trembled suddenly as if with the cold. "I called our hotel. She's not there."

Johnny's hand pressed into the table. "What's keeping us? Let's go to the clinic."

Miss Ann bit her lip. "Didn't Sir John tell you? There's no use going to the clinic. Nancy was attacked in Geneva yesterday afternoon when de Pré Morel was nearly dead right here."

"He didn't do the job himself," Johnny, said. "Of course not." The coffee was clearing everything up. "But we can find out something just the same. Confederates." He had a real inspiration. "De Pré Morel's thick with the Swiss. They could have done it for him."

He'd remembered again that Rambert wasn't in the bank yesterday afternoon.

Miss Ann turned pale. Funny to see her face like a white handkerchief or a piece of paper, all the blood drained away. He was making an impression.

"These Swiss around here," he went on, "they look like Frenchmen. They talk like Frenchmen, but really they've got as much German blood as French. You can't tell where you're at with the Swiss."

"Grain of truth." Sir John raised the eyebrow over his free eye. "In the First World War they didn't trouble to hide it. The Swiss army was known to be pro-German. All their officers were, all their military men."

Miss Ann sat very straight and paid no attention, her hands ceaselessly wringing. She'd always been so decided. Johnny had never known her like this.

"Let's go to the clinic," he said. "Charbonnet's bound to be there. He'll be waiting for de Pré Morel to talk."

"Charbonnet," she repeated, "the inspector." That name had got through to her. "All right, I'll go." She pushed back her chair.

They made a strange little group that trailed down the winding street, Miss Ann keeping ahead. Now she'd decided to go she went like lightning. Sir John would have liked to walk with her—one could see that—but he seemed to feel it his duty to ride herd on Johnny. So they dribbled along single file—Sir John anxiously in between, first dashing ahead to help Miss Thorne cross the street, then looking back over his shoulder at Johnny, finally waiting to help him, much too tactfully, down the stairs.

Johnny put up with it. His head was clear, perfectly clear, lucid, but his feet weren't. The *ficelle* came along; he was boosted in, then at the next stop, out. He shook clear of Sir John, the old fuddy-duddy. He stumbled as fast as he could after Miss Ann.

He and Sir John came panting through the door of the clinic and almost fell against the lady's back. She was standing stock still, rigid.

The breath went out of her, all in one gust, and she fluttered across the waiting room. There she hung, limp, held up in Nancy's strong, round, pretty arms.

What in the hell did Nancy mean, scaring her aunt like this? Not to mention him. Vanishing. Going AWOL. He scowled at that perfect face. Nancy just stood, smiling serenely over the collapsed gray head.

Come to look at her—Johnny was glaring—she had on a mighty peculiar, outfit, a black apron—none too clean— and a skirt a market woman might have worn. A shawl was wrapped around the top of her, and her hair, that rippling hair, was scraped back into a knot so tight she couldn't move her eyebrows. If there wasn't Bill Lane edging up by her. He looked queer, too, but then he always did. He hadn't shaved; his suit might have spent the night on a park bench. And they had one more, sitting all shrunk up in a corner. Three of a kind. The third was the accordion player.

Miss Ann detached herself.

"You frightened us," she breathed. "Where under heaven have you been?"

She adjusted her hat.

"Oh," Nancy said airily. "Oh . . . I've been all right." She looked very complacent like a little, cat that has just swallowed the cream. "I can take care of myself."

Sir John pushed forward.

"Couldn't yesterday."

Nancy's face changed. "I'm sorry." She stepped up remorsefully and put her hand in his. "And I do thank you, Sir John . . . He saved my life, everybody! I haven't even been properly grateful!"

Bill was right by her. He might have thanked the old man, too. But he just looked sulky. He has terrible manners, Johnny thought.

"Nancy." Miss Ann's voice cracked. "Go out and find that doctor." How jittery she was! "Ask him if he can't help us out of our difficulty. We've waited long enough."

Nancy fled, looking rather startled, through the office door. This opened in the wall at a right angle from the entrance and led to doctors' offices. There were arrows pointing, with names—the elevators, you could hear them chugging up and down—a secretary's glassed-in desk, visible for a moment before Nancy closed the door.

They were shut in again together. In spite of a big chandelier in the middle, brightly lighted, the room felt dismal. People had waited here—you knew it—chiefly for disaster. No one except the old drunk in the corner would sit anywhere in the neat circle of chairs.

Miss Ann started to pace back and forth, her heels ringing on the tessellated floor. Behind her the outside door began to open; somebody else was coming in.

He was stooping, as is the habit of tall men in doorways. He paused very modestly, very pleasantly, one foot scraping a little.

"Good evening, ladies and gentlemen," said M. Rambert.

Hah, this was Johnny's chance. Action at last. He eyed the banker like a hawk. At least he felt like a hawk; he squinted trying to sight. Don't fire till you see the whites of their eyes.

He shot out, "Where were you yesterday afternoon?"

The banker's face showed wide and ever wider circles of astonishment like when you throw a stone in water. After a moment it became bland.

"About my usual business," he purred.

Johnny's chin thrust out. "You weren't in the bank when I came to see you."

"That is possible."

"Where were you? Never mind." Johnny veered toward the others. "I can't check it. Tell the police."

"Certainly." Annoyance had crept into that urbane voice. "*If* they ask me."

"And where were you," Johnny moved up closer, "the evening Mr. Osborne was killed?"

"Osborne?" The banker stepped back.

"I can tell you," Sir John broke in heartily. "He was at my house." He looked reprovingly at Johnny. "We all were, all that were in Lausanne at the time . . . except poor Osborne himself."

"M. Rambert," Johnny pressed on. "How long were you there? The police think Osborne was killed about ten."

"Nonsense, young man," Sir John said testily. "The police can't judge the time exactly. Besides"—he slapped Rambert on the shoulder—"M. Rambert was with me all evening."

The banker quirked a corner of his mouth. "Not quite, Sir John. I had to leave early."

A delicate, dry voice cut through their heavy ones.

"Gentlemen," said Miss Ann. "I can save you time. Will you allow me, Johnny, to ask one question?"

They had been gathered in a knot. She motioned them back. They could see Pierrot then, his eyes closed, huddled in the corner.

Her voice like a thin acid very cooling trickled through the tension. "You're not asleep, my friend. You're pretending."

The old man's eyelids quivered.

"Remember?" Ann said. "You were going to tell me. Who visited M. de Pré Morels apartment yesterday before he came home?"

One of Pierrot's eyes opened. It shut quickly. He muttered to himself.

Bill was nearest. He took the old man by one elbow, sat him up. The eyes blinked rapidly, fixed on the floor.

"Whom did you see?" Ann said.

Bill poked him.

Pierrot groaned. "The *milord anglais.*"

"Poppycock!" Trelawney laughed shortly. "The old feller has it in for me because I don't tip him the way the rest of you do for his filthy music." He looked his disgust. "Foreigners!" That was enough.

But they were silent; no one even moved. A weight of distrust, suspicion, even fear anchored each to his place.

Sir John managed to shift his feet. Rumbles came from his throat as he trained his monocle on Pierrot.

"All foreign tunes," he complained. "That's all he knows. Why don't he play, 'Roll Out the Barrel'?"

Miss Ann said softly, "Because it's too English . . . There's nobody in England quite as English as you are, Sir John."

Sir John frowned heavily, trying to understand.

"What do you mean? I'm not in England. I'm in Switzerland. We all are."

He glared round.

Miss Ann shook her head. "You do it beautifully . . . beautifully!"

He ground his heel in the grand manner, started to stalk away.

"Johnny!" she cried. "Stop him!"

Johnny lunged out. Then the floor whacked him right in the face. He could feel it thud unevenly as someone ran. His elbows propped him up in a flock of stars.

"Halt! I've got you covered!"

Rambert had been running but he hadn't made it. He was twisted sidewise now, out of the way of something. Bill was pointing a tiny pearly revolver. It was a toy, lost in his hand.

Behind Johnny a laugh burst out. Sir John turned his back on the revolver, shaking with mirth, and opened the door. Then he stopped. He was looking into the barrel of a large automatic.

"Ah, good man!" he said with relief. He kept perfectly still though.

"M. Charbonnet!" Ann's voice cut like an etching tool. "This is not Sir John Trelawney. This is a Nazi agent impersonating him."

"Nonsense! I don't need to tell you," Sir John snorted. "Jolly glad you've come, inspector. Had enough of these females!"

"What's it about?" Charbonnet kept him covered. "Why not sit down and explain?"

"Because it's too damn silly!" Sir John said robustly. "Drunken beggar says he saw me at de Pré Morel's yesterday." He swung around. "What kind of a witness is he? What is his word compared to a British subject's?"

The door to the offices opened at this point. A nurse put her head in, looked neither to right nor left, said in a bored voice, "Which one is M. Pierre Franchard? The patient has asked for him. He may go up, only he." The roomful hung suspended, motionless, like people in a large, old-fashioned oil painting. Only Pierrot got to his feet, slid like an eel out of the door. They could hear the nurse's steps and his, going across the hall.

Miss Ann broke the silence.

"The real Sir John was killed"—she was addressing M. Charbonnet—"probably in that German prison camp after this man had had a chance to study him. The family papers, and effects, to say nothing of Sir John's sister and his servants, were obliterated by a bomb dropped on Trelawney Great House for that purpose."

There was stunned silence. M. Rambert nodded.

"I'm sure," Miss Ann went on, "if we ask the English we'll find there was something funny about that raid. It had one object, to destroy that house and everyone in it."

Sir John moved then; he exploded.

"Ridiculous!" He turned to M. Charbonnet. "She got it out of the cinema. Don't tell me you're going to believe this?"

"Not everyone," Rambert said smoothly, "who knew Sir John could be destroyed. His cousin Reginald St. Michael and a man who used to be his fag at Eton are flying to Switzerland . . . Then, monsieur"—his white head bent courteously—"if you really are Sir John, you can prove it to them. Meanwhile . . ." He looked up, "I think the inspector might hold you on suspicion."

Johnny was sitting on the floor, trying to grasp ideas that flew around him.

"By God," he shouted suddenly as a light burst, "He and von Metsch, they spoke together in the coatroom at the opera."

"M. Charbonnet!" Ann's bitter voice made them all listen. "He killed Mr. Osborne, I don't quite know how. I think just before that party he gave. The housekeeper said Mr. Osborne phoned him he wasn't coming. The message was perhaps the opposite. It would only take minutes to get by that back road to where Mr. Osborne went off."

Charbonnet said respectfully, "Have you an idea how he did it, mademoiselle?"

"Only the incident of the drunken peasants beforehand which was staged. It wasn't true. The fake Sir John had plenty of agents working for him who could have put on that act. He could have seen that Mr. Osborne talked about it in front of witnesses."

"We can re-open that," Charbonnet said.

"Évanoui told me Osborne had been murdered," Miss Ann said. "Osborne had probably described to him the drunken peasants he nearly ran over. Évanoui would have recollected, perhaps only afterward, that there simply wouldn't be any on that particular road."

Charbonnet's voice rose and broke like an adolescent's. "When did Évanoui tell you this?"

"When he was dying. He said, 'They killed M. Osborne, too. I don't know how.'" She tilted her head. "Sir John has a life-sized doll for the First Aid class in his villa. Could he have dressed it as a farmer, the night of the murder, leaned it somewhere by that road and pulled it down?"

"Tiens!" Charbonnet had recovered. "We were never quite sure if the brakes had been tampered with."

"Everything would be cleaned up now but you could ask the Red Cross class. They would notice if there had been dirt on the doll, a piece chipped off."

"Talk!" Sir John shouted, "beastly, silly talk! You can't prove anything . . . I'll have you up for libel." But in that room he might have been a ghost that you could look through; he just wasn't there.

"Some of his gang might crack"—this was Bill's thoughtful voice—"if M. Charbonnet gets them in time."

"They're already in jail," the inspector said calmly, "everyone from the Maison Rouge and the Café des Fauconniers. They went too far yesterday in Genève; they invaded the home of the American consul."

"Anyone hurt?" said Bill quickly.

"No. A young man in the house got loose and gave the alarm. The police wasted no time."

The door to the offices burst open; Pierrot walked in, a strange Pierrot standing up very straight.

"M. de Pré Morel," he said briskly, "wants me to tell you what he heard in the vault of the bank."

Johnny pulled himself upright, shook his ears to be sure they worked.

"He heard Sir John," the new Pierrot went on, "cursing M. Évanoui for being clumsy. He could hear it all. Évanoui knocked against Sir John so that the box he was carrying fell to the floor, Évanoui bent to help him pick it up and got booted. There must have been a lot of bills spilled out, American ones, Évanoui started cursing back about his *sale argent américain*."

"This is enough," said Rambert, "isn't it? Can we not search his safe-deposit holdings?"

Johnny was now cold sober.

"Who killed my friends?" he said, "my friends in Evremont?"

"Schwartz," Pierrot said.

"Even if we can't get Sir John for murder," the inspector said—he spoke exactly as if the man wasn't there—"we can prove he's a German agent; his usefulness to Martin Bormann* will be gone forever."

---

* Thought to be the head of the German Underground. Martin Bormann succeeded Rudolf Hess as Deputy Fuehrer of the Third Reich. He was tried in absentia at Nuremberg and sentenced to death by hanging when and if found. He has not been found.

Sir John was moving restlessly. Charbonnet kept him covered but was busy listening to the others. His glance kept darting toward them as they spoke.

"M. de Pré Morel," Pierrot said, "has evidence of the contact between Sir John and the two groups of operatives, here and in Geneva."

"*Vive la France!*" said Bill happily.

All eyes turned to him. It was a new note. Could they relax, share this happiness?

But from the end of the room near Charbonnet came muffled noises, a tinkle of glass, an exclamation, a soft thud. Sir John was lying on the floor. Charbonnet crouched with the revolver pointed. Johnny started over, but Rambert was nearer. The banker with two fingers was opening the unconscious lids, peering at the eyes. He sniffed the gasping breath.

"It's real," he said. "It's cyanide."

Sir John was seized with a convulsion.

Charbonnet shoved the revolver in its holster, kneeled and tore open Sir John's coat. He was putting his hand on the heart when the whole figure gave a dreadful shudder, shook it off.

Johnny heard a low cry. There by the inner door stood Nancy.

"What's happening?" she moaned. "Poor Sir John!"

Bill pushed in front of her, cut off the view.

"Don't worry," he said. "He's a spy."

"He saved my life!" Nancy was nearly sobbing.

"Because Mr. Harrington was on the dock," Bill said harshly. "He'd previously ordered the attack."

There was a scrabbling sound on the tiles as Sir John's knees drew up. They all watched, held in gruesome fascination.

All except Rambert. He'd risen to his feet, straightening his bad leg with both hands. He was engaged in staring at Miss Ann who stood watching the writhing, shaking figure with a face carved out of stone.

"What's the matter with you?" said Rambert to her softly. "He was brave after his fashion . . . Have you no feeling? Are you not a woman?"

Miss Ann said, and it might have been stone speaking, "I was fond of Mary Trelawney."

19

Johnny felt rather tired and light headed but he kept walking doggedly. The excitement of the evening would hold
him up for a while. Miss Ann had whispered to him to go
tell the Medways. He supposed he'd always do what that
damn woman wanted, and her niece was just like her.

There were few street lights here on the *Seize Mai*. It
was a temptation to pause between them and lie down
in a nice dark gutter. He didn't feel like standing up to
Lady Jane. The way she looked down her nose at you,
the way Mr. Medway hooked his thumbs in his waistcoat
pockets . . .

Here he was, damn it, climbing up their stairs, ringing
their bell.

The door swung open. Behind it was a little maid and
behind her Diana.

"Hello, toots," he said. The maid was holding out her
hand—"Tell this example of child labor I can't give her my
hat. I don't own one."

At the right of the hall was a fine vista of the drawing
room and it was quite empty.

"What? All alone?" His voice rose cheerfully.

"My parents are dining out," Diana said. "They often
do . . . Won't you come in?"

"Try and stop me. I'll have to spill the news to you
then, sister. The murders are solved . . . Take a good hold
of the chair arm and I'll tell you."

"I don't need to hold onto the chair arm," she said. "How did you do it? I'm sure you were clever."

He told her then quickly so she wouldn't think he was clever.

But she still thought so.

Diana didn't mind about Trelawney once she knew he wasn't English. She pitied the wiping out of the real Trelawneys, that was all.

"Gosh, I'm glad you take it this way," Johnny said.

She gave him a somber smile. "You see we're used to families being killed off."

"I'm not. I ought to be," said Johnny. He remembered suddenly that she probably meant her own family. None of the young generation were left but this thin little girl.

"You're wonderfully loyal." Diana leaned forward. "Think of you coming all this way to find out about your French friends, and discovering these spies, and clearing it all up."

"Hold on a minute, sister," he said. "You must not have heard me. I was on the wrong track all the way through."

"Not in the Maison Rouge in Geneva."

"Oh, that!" he said. "You and I went there together . . . But the person who did the ground work was Bill Lane."

She looked very doubtful. "I don't like Mr. Lane frightfully well."

"That's the part he was playing," Johnny said. "You see he'd been to school here when he was quite young. He learned the lingo. He could pass as a Swiss. He'd been gumshoeing around the Café des Fauconniers and got mighty suspicious. Then those two females, Nancy and her aunt, insisted on going there and he was scared something would happen to them and at the same time he didn't want to show himself up as an American and lose all the confidence that the gang had begun to have in him. That afternoon, he said, added ten years to his age."

"Just what," Diana said, "did he find out?"

"Enough to tip off Charbonnet. The police traced the fake telegram received by Lydia Flickinger to the bartender of the Café des Fauconniers."

"Why did they make Lydia go to that dreadful place?"

"They weren't quite sure Évanoui was dead when she found him. They thought he might have said something. They weren't taking a chance . . . Another thing Bill did"—Johnny warmed to the work—"was to prove that Schwartz was on the top deck of the boat when a tool box fell off and nearly killed Nancy. All Schwartz had to do was lean against one of the guy ropes to the canopy to make the box fall off. That's the man I want to get, Schwartz."

"I thought it was M. de Pré Morel."

"Hell, no. Excuse me, baby. He's French Intelligence. As soon as he's able to talk I'll tell him what I know about the murders in Evremont instead of trailing him like a blasted idiot."

"You're *not* a blasted idiot," Diana said. She blushed.

Johnny realized that she always did at some time in a conversation and he found himself waiting for it.

She said very composedly, "You must be tired." She blushed even more. "Would you like a drink?"

He hesitated. He'd been thinking of rushing back to Nancy but he wasn't sure now he could make it. He felt rather faint.

"To tell you the truth," he said. "I've had as much liquor as was good for me today, or for any other four or five men . . . I can't remember having lunch, though."

She jumped up. "How stupid of me! The cook's out but the *bonne* is making a *fondue* the way they do in her village. It's not bad, really. I'll tell her to set two places."

She came back from the kitchen very dignified. The opening door let out a whiff of bubbling cheese.

"I still don't understand Bill Lane," she said. "Even when he wasn't pretending to be Swiss, even when he was just an American, there was always something very queer about him."

"Not today," Johnny said. "Before, yes . . . I'm sure he didn't believe that line he was putting out, that old fascist bunk, 'Down with the Jews' and so on."

The cheese smelled sharp and good; it made you feel better already.

"Bill used to get so very pale," Diana said. "When he'd come into a room he'd look all right and then he would start talking that way and he'd get as white as a sheet."

"So he did," Johnny said. "I don't believe Bill liked it. He strikes me as a guy that was after something, like myself, only he knew better what he was after and stuck at nothing to get it."

20

Miss Ann was looking out the window at the lake, more breathless, more enchanted than ever under the young moon.

One needed at her age, after that scene in the clinic, a few moments alone. She was glad Nancy, according to the habit of the young, had announced that she wouldn't come back for dinner. To be sure, it was reverting to American freedom but they were going home so soon. What could it matter? This was their last night.

Ann had dined sparsely off a tray brought by M. Dunois himself with a bottle of Neuchatel '37. It was all pushed out now to the anteroom.

She wanted to have the twilight to herself, the Alpine twilight lit not only by the stars but by the white peaks also frosty, also glittering. Inside, it was nearly dark. On the poet's table a dim lamp shone on one open book, a worn copy of the Letters of Mme. de Sévigné.

Ah, he had done it well, Henri! In spite of his first blundering, those attempts to see her, so ill timed, so embarrassing, and the climb up the balcony, ridiculous perhaps, but too much like assault! In the end he had found the perfect gesture. She had to admit it.

The police had been busy a long time with the body in the waiting room. They had all stayed for what seemed years in Dr. Dollier's office, going over everything, having statements taken, reading them, writing their names at the end. Every moment she was conscious of Henri. Either his eyes rested on her carefully, minutely, as if he were storing up details, or, when he looked elsewhere, she felt his presence, only his, exactly as if they were alone in the room. She thought any moment he would come out with an intimate phrase, her first name, that would reveal what could only now do harm. All that was New England in her braced itself for the blow.

It didn't come.

Henri said casually, "I have heard, mademoiselle, that you admire the letters of Mme. de Sévigné."

Had heard indeed! He knew it like his own name.

She said, "You are right, monsieur."

He said, giving the date so low the others couldn't hear. "The letter from Paris, Friday, the twelfth of February, 1672. Read the last paragraph."

"The twelfth of February, 1672," she murmured. "Very well, monsieur."

The police had finished with them then. Dr. Dollier bade them good-bye. Neither Bill nor Johnny, however, wanted to move from Nancy's side. They were talking together, oblivious of the others. Henri looked around, startled.

"It's time for me to meet our English witnesses," he said. "Even though the police will be there, it was I who sent for them. *Au revoir, messieurs, mesdames.*"

He bent and kissed her hand quite formally, correctly. All she could see was the tall back, the uneven gait going out the door.

She had gone quickly too; she'd forgotten, for the moment, to worry about Nancy.

There under the lamp was the letter Henri had told her to read. She didn't need to look again.

> "Good-bye, my very dear, my love. Don't you
> find it's been long, the time we've been apart?
> I'm struck with this grief so deeply I don't

think I could bear it if I didn't love to love
you as much as I do, whatever pain may be
attached to it."

In the old days Henri had been much less devoted to
the marquise than she had. He must have changed. He
must have read the Letters often to have found the right
passage when he needed it.

The old lock of the hall door rattled. A key was inserted.
Ann started up in a hurry and closed her book. There was
no need to put in a marker; she would never lose the place.

Light footsteps flew across the floor. The bedroom door
burst open. Nancy's voice skittered out, young and fresh
and dancing.

"Were you asleep, Aunt Ann? I'm awfully sorry."

"No, dear, I wasn't asleep."

"But it's so dark!"

"Light the lights, then."

They flashed on. Hundreds of glass prisms twinkled,
clusters of fireflies all of crystal, on the side walls, in the
pendant luster. The antique light revived the shabby ele-
gance of the room. It concealed the faded streaks in the
curtains and left only noble folds, hid the mended velvet,
showed the upholstery all in curves for a banned poet.

Nancy paid no attention. Nor did she even glance at
her aunt.

"I must get out of this costume." She was pulling out
drawers. "Much as I love being a Vaudoise." She opened
the closet. "Is there anything left, I wonder, to put on?"

The child looked perfectly presentable. Her hair was
swinging again on her shoulders. The apron had disappeared. The shawl and skirt were only a trifle quaint.

"Don't worry about your clothes," her aunt said wearily.
"Lydia will be here the first thing in the morning."

"Oh, I'm so glad! That's wonderful!"

"It's perfectly safe now." Ann sounded normal. "I told
M. Dunois to get her out of that wretched jail. She is to

help us pack. And I asked the Travel Bureau to wire for any reservations they can get. There's a good chance we can leave tomorrow."

Nancy turned around in the closet, walked out very slowly and sat down.

"I'm not leaving, Aunt Ann," she said.

The blonde mane shone under the chandelier as quiet as the water or the snow. Ah me! thought Ann, now there is this to deal with . . . I have to pull myself together, quickly too.

"My dear," she said. "You've been the greatest help in all this." Every word was deliberate, sincere. "If you hadn't uncovered von Metsch we shouldn't have got along so fast, maybe not at all. Much as I regret your dreadful rashness in going up that mountain with him, risking your life, there's no denying that, for the Nazis, it was the beginning of the end."

Nancy's eyes opened wide. "You know quite well it was just an accident."

"What I know is you're right to be grateful to Johnny." Ann spoke warmly. "We're all grateful to him. It's no small thing to have climbed up after you and saved your life." She paused a moment. "Unfortunately, darling, that doesn't automatically make him a good bet as a husband."

"I never thought it did." Nancy's eyes were still round.

"He attracted me," Ann smiled, "before he did you. He still does attract me—I have a weakness for men like him—but we both know he's unstable. He was far too upset by the war to have got back to anything like balance."

Nancy was lighting a cigarette, eyes on the floor.

Ann thought, this means nothing to her. I shall have to haul out everything. Nothing else will do. I must unlock my heart.

Closing her eyes—it *did* hurt a little—she murmured, "It will take years for Johnny to arrange himself as it took Henri Rambert years."

A small laugh tinkled out.

"You know, Aunt Ann"—the shoulders twitched under the shawl—"I wouldn't call M. Rambert perfectly arranged even yet!"

Her aunt smiled back composedly. "For *him* he's perfectly arranged. *Rangé* as they say here—regular, domestic, bourgeois." She was not, after all, going to reveal the passage in the Letters which, in its fashion, proved it. "You should have known him in his youth," she said. "But I'm glad you didn't. He was a wild man and so charming! I was very fond of him."

The blonde head nodded. "That's the reason you're going home, to get away from M. Rambert."

Her aunt said very low, "There's no parallel, of course, but"—she brought it out painfully—"I've never been sorry, not for a moment, that I didn't marry Henri."

"Our generation," Nancy said with a hint of smugness, "feels differently about marriage."

Ah, one had to be wise now.

"You may be right. I'm a great admirer of your generation. But"—her aunt leaned forward—"I beg you personally to take time. A few weeks or months cant make any difference, and it might avoid so much sadness."

Nancy crossed her shapely knees.

"That's another way we're different from you," she said, watching the smoke from her cigarette. "We don't believe in taking time."

Ann sighed. "All right, Nancy. We won't go home. We'll stay."

Faint lines appeared in the pretty forehead.

"Of course I love to have you here, but as far as going on being a chaperone is concerned . . ." She jumped up. "I don't know how to break it to you, Aunt Ann. I'm already married!"

"What?" Ann cried. "But that's impossible!"

"No it's not, dear. I married Bill in Geneva."

"Bill!"

Ann was hanging on to her chair tightly. She felt as one does in a restaurant when a waiter drops a tray of dishes. They were rolling all over the floor.

"It was what you might call a marriage of convenience," the child said incredibly. "But we've decided to make it stick. What I mean by convenience, the house was surrounded . . ."

She broke off anxiously. "Here's what you need, a cigarette."

She lit it for Ann like a tender nurse with a patient who might not recover.

"Remember? We told you how scary it was, how it got worse and worse, and then Bill came across with this marvelous exit. He simply didn't know how long we'd be together, so before we got into that cart we walked into Mr. Harrington's study and he married us."

"But Mr. Harrington!" It was a gasp. "How could an official of the United States connive . . ."

"He never gave it a thought," Nancy said lightly. "Put it down to love, I suppose. Bill's family has a lot of money and, as a matter of fact, the Harringtons were worried because he hadn't married before. Back in America they were always trying different girls on him." She became solemn. "Bill's frightfully old. That's the one drawback. He's twenty-seven."

She seemed to think her aunt was appalled.

"I've decided to overlook it," she said hastily.

Miss Ann was tapping her cigarette. "Why was it necessary to get married?" she said. "This isn't 1890, after all. I don't discount the danger yesterday, but it seems to me Bill took advantage of it."

"He admits it," Nancy said demurely. "He says a secret agent has to be quick witted."

"Is Bill," her aunt swallowed, "the young man we were sent to meet?"

"Of course . . . Didn't you know?"

There was no answer for a moment. One gull that must have been awakened by a boat gave a loud, raucous cry.

"I wasn't sure." Her aunt said then. "If it's not too much to ask, when did *you* find out?"

"Not until after I married him."

Miss Ann sank back into the dark red plush and the dim carving. She felt old suddenly.

"This perfectly unknown young man," she breathed, "that we were being polite to as a part of our job, a man with the reputation of being anti-semitic, pro-fascist . . ."

"That's the really brave part of it," Nancy said hotly, "for a newspaperman and that's what Bill is. He'll have a hard time living it down."

"How could he say and write the things he did?"

"I'll tell you how and why," cried Nancy. "Bill was one of the first reporters to get into Büchenwald. He never forgets it night or day, and he swore to go after the remaining Nazis. This job turned up and he hated it but he took it. He hated it more after we came. But there was no other way to find out what he did."

"Just what was that?" Ann said, still cool.

"He can tell you better than I. He's waiting to do it."

"Just a moment." Ann waved her hand. "I'm trying to catch up. Nancy, you hardly *know* this man."

"Yes, but I trusted him in a pinch when all my judgment was against it."

"But do you even have a single taste in common?"

"Yes, mountain climbing." The child looked so happy! "Now that Bill's quit being a spy—you see, the mission is accomplished—he'll be a newspaperman again. He's got a contract to write a series of articles on the forming of the Swiss Federation. It was formed—oh, long ago, of course— by Germans. This is to encourage the Germans about their fitness for democracy in their own country. He's cashing in on the fact that the Germans will read what he writes."

"This is breath-taking." Ann hadn't time to smoke; cigarette ash was dropping through her fingers to the floor.

"But what your friends at home will think of Bill . . . your parents . . ."

"He may have to write that book"—Nancy raised her eyebrows—"just the way you said. He planned all along to expose the papers he's been working for."

"It's all so dangerous."

"So are mountains." Her chin lifted. "Ann, I can hardly wait to climb with Bill!"

For the last twenty minutes each time Ann started to recover she had her wind knocked out again. This time it was remembering two days ago when the child said she never in her life would go up another mountain.

Ann merely asked quite faintly. "Is Bill an Alpinist?"

"Of course." Nancy took the cigarette from her aunt and put it out. "I thought Rudolph was good. (Funny how long ago it seems now.) I thought it was unusual to be going up with someone as fast as I am but"—she lifted her shoulders—"Bill is better."

"How do you know that?"

"Why, because he got up ahead of us. He went up the bobsled run, not the path. Knew where it was." Her eyes shone. "Honestly, Bill knows everything about these mountains. The run is straighter than the path and steeper. He could make better time."

"Do you mean Bill was there when Rudolph tried to push you off?"

"Naturally he was." Nancy brimmed over with pity at such ignorance. "Bill was the one who shouted at me. Not Johnny. Pierrot had phoned *Bill.*"

She added kindly, "Poor old Johnny. He was messing around miles below. I could never have heard him." She smiled. "I guess he thought I did. It's asking too much of an echo, but let him think so . . . May I bring Bill up?"

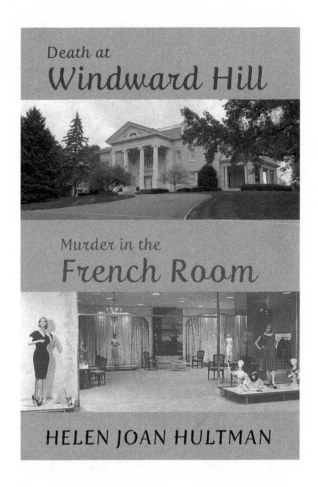

VIRGINIA RATH

DEATH AT
DAYTON'S FOLLY

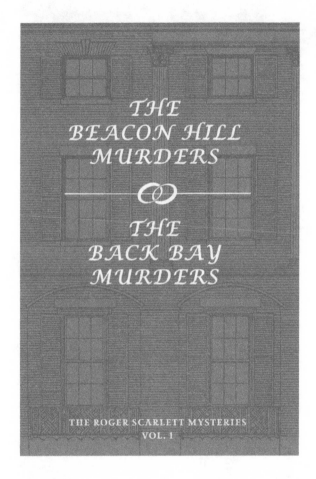

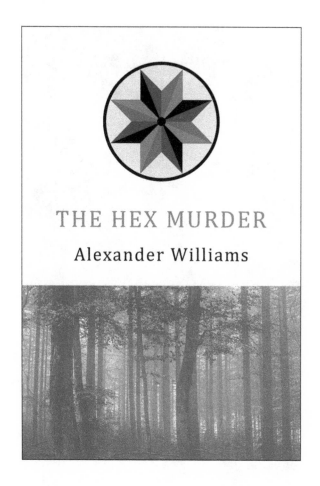

THE HEX MURDER

Alexander Williams

DRESSED
TO KILL

Emma Lou Fetta

ALSO AVAILABLE

THE SERGEANT HARTY MYSTERIES

JOEL Y. DANE

MURDER CUM LAUDE

1

THE CABANA MURDERS

CPSIA information can be obtained
at www.ICGtesting.com
Printed in the USA
LVHW030328250621
691123LV00001B/24